Play the Game

BLUE DEVILS HOCKEY #1

S.J. SYLVIS

Play the Game

Published: SJ Sylvis Books LLC
sjsylvisbooks@gmail.com
Cover Design: Ashes and Vellichor
Editing: Jenn Lockwood Editing
Proofing: Emma Cook | Booktastic Blonde / All Encompassing Books

for my TU girlies <3

USA TODAY BESTSELLING AUTHOR

S.J. SYLVIS

FUCKING HELL.

A narrowed set of eyes sharpens from across the table, and my stomach knots. Air becomes trapped in my lungs, and nothing but profanity wants to spew out of my mouth and into the gaping space between us. It's a known assumption that hockey goalies have a temper, and I'm no exception. However, given the last few weeks, I try my hardest to tone it down so I don't find myself in even deeper shit.

"So?"

I flick my attention to Joseph Curry—my new agent—and his assistant. I blink several times before opening my mouth and allowing my gruff voice to vibrate against their skulls.

"Well," I snap. "I don't have much of a fucking choice, do I?"

Curry's assistant jumps in her seat. I pay her no mind because after the most recent allegations, I have a hard time trusting any female.

"Not really, no." Joseph slides a paper across the table. As soon as I read the offer, I scoff.

It's the only offer, so he's right. I have no choice.

1

The signing bonus is decent, and the salary is more than most people make in a lifetime. It's not too far off from what they offered me at the start of last year, but the Chicago Blue Devils are nowhere near prestigious. They're not as respected as the other teams in the league, and they have a reputation— one that I now fit because I have a record.

In the last month, I've not only found myself in handcuffs, but I now have a whole lot of pent-up aggression and resentment swimming through my veins.

I was let go from the New York Coyotes for my *poor* choices, and to make things worse, half the shit that has come out isn't even true.

Flashes of that night spark as I sit and stare at the contract beneath my fingertips. The memory of the club's music mixes with my pounding heartbeat, and I look down to the tiny scars along my forearm from the sprinkles of glass that whizzed through the air from the commotion I was not only dragged into but blamed for as well.

"Fine," I finally bark, clearing my thoughts with a sharp shake of my head.

My signature is nothing more than a blur as I send the paper flying across the smooth conference table.

I stand abruptly, and although Joseph should be intimidated by my 6'1" frame and angry scowl, he matches my movements and sticks his hand out for me to shake.

My jaw locks as my grip tightens in his, and his meek assistant speaks from behind. "I'll forward you the practice schedule and a list of vacant homes in the area."

She continues to talk and dish out instructions with my back to her. Right before the door slams, I hear her shout, "The Chicago Blue Devils are happy to have you on their team!"

A sarcastic noise leaves me because *of course* they are. I was picked in the first draft right out of college and was one of the first rookies to have a substantial amount of ice time during the season. I'm skilled, and I know it.

But talent means jack shit when your reputation is completely obliterated. My parents continue to remind me that it could have been worse and that the league had the option of banning me altogether, but they chose not to—which is great considering I took the fall for an altercation that had nothing to do with me in the first place.

My sister says I should be thanking my lucky stars that a team still wants me, and all my former teammates from Bexley U, including my sister's fiancé and my best friend, agree—even if they believe my side of the story that the media pretends doesn't exist.

I should just play the game and be thankful I'm still in the pros, but I'm angry and feel cheated.

The only thing I can think to do with those two feelings is put it all out on the ice.

So yeah, the Blue Devils *should* be happy I'm theirs, because I'm going to demolish every fucking team we play this season.

One

SCOTTIE

I CATCH the eye of Kitty—her real name, believe it or not —in the mirror. "How's it looking out there?" I ask.

She rolls her bright-green eyes that are lined in charcoal. "Busy. You better get out there, or Russ is going to come back here and scold you."

Fuck Russ.

A soft breath escapes my painted lips, and there's a pit of disappointment growing deeper with every shift I take at the Cat House.

Don't mistake the name for some sort of sanctuary for kittens.

It's more of a sanctuary for horny men who like to get their rocks off to women on poles who send flirtatious smiles their way. My coworkers deserve Oscars for faking interest at the sight of their semi-hard cocks and nauseating smirks.

Nerves feast away on my exposed skin, and my eyes water when I catch my reflection. I'm in nothing but a skimpy pink bra and matching thong. I'm all for lifting other women up. If their life goal is to be a stripper, then I will root for them day in and day out.

5

For me? It's not a goal or a dream. It's a fucking night-mare. Just like this auburn-colored wig on my head.

The only perk? Fast cash.

"Want a line?" Chastity pours some white powder onto her vanity, and I quickly tear my gaze away.

Kitty scolds her with an exasperated sigh. "You know Cherry doesn't do that type of stuff."

I shove away any memory that tries to surface. If it wouldn't make me look insane, I'd cover my ears with my hands, like I used to do when I was a child. That way, I could tune out the sound of snorting, but instead, I remain poised with my hands down by my sides as I balance on heels that are too high.

The smell of Chastity's perfume cuts through her boozy aroma, and she sniffs a few more times before coming over and draping her arm around my waist. Her metal chastity belt knocks against my hip as she dangles its key in front of my face.

"You know what will give us hefty tips?"

Russ peeks his head into the dressing room—having abso-lutely no respect for our privacy. Then again, we are half-naked on a stage, so I'll cut him some slack. "Other than that enticing chastity belt you're wearing?" he says, interjecting himself into our conversation.

Chastity flips her hair over her shoulder and blushes at the half-assed compliment. "It's a clever little skit to go with my stage name, don't ya think?"

She doesn't wait for Russ to answer. Instead, she turns to me and dangles the little golden key in front of my face again. My eyes follow it like a pendulum as it swings back and forth. "Put this in between your cleavage."

"What?" I stare at her full face of makeup.

Her eyebrow arches, and she smiles deviously. "If you

want more tips, you'll put this in between those bomb-ass tits and let them grab it so they can undo my belt."

Russ claps his hands together. "That's fucking brilliant. There's a whole gang of hockey players out there that will go nuts. They'll be eager to graze those tits."

Hockey players.

"What happened to the no-touch rule?" I ask, clearly panicked.

"Stop pressuring her to do shit she doesn't want to do." Kitty shoves Russ off to the side. She snatches the key from Chastity's hand and puts it in her cleavage instead.

I exhale, and it's obvious to everyone in the room that I'm uncomfortable. My boss crosses his arms and sends me a disapproving glare, but little does he know, I look at myself with disappointment every day, so my feelings aren't hurt in the slightest.

"Chin up, Cherry," he chides, placing his hand on my lower back.

My spine straightens from his touch. *Get your hands off me.*

He gives me a push before whispering in my ear, "You wanted to make fast money, so get out there and work."

After he slides past me, I shake off the filth he left behind and do exactly as he says, because as much as I hate him, he's right.

I need the money, and I need it now.

———

"SHE DOESN'T LOOK like the rest."

I bite my tongue until I taste blood. My hands grip the pole, and I use my core to swing around, putting my backside to the group of athletes.

There are three types of men that come into the Cat

House: the sleazy ones who are married and want to cheat on their wives, the single ones who come alone and have 'pervert' written all over them, and the ones who are out celebrating something. Whether it be a birthday, bachelor party, or a guys' night, they're always tipsy and, most of the time, boisterous.

I catch one of the hockey players, who just so happens to be missing a front tooth, staring directly at my boobs when I twist. He nudges his friend with his elbow and *great,* now they're both staring at me.

"She looks sweet but sexy too."

"She doesn't belong on a pole."

"Where does she belong, then?"

I'd like to know the same.

My ears perk up as I turn again. Another group of guys roars from the other side of the stage, and a little grin falls to my lips when I see some guy unlocking Chastity's chastity belt.

The hockey player with the missing tooth answers his friend, "She looks like she belongs in my bed."

I roll my eyes as they all laugh. I purposefully keep my ass to them because I have to fix my face before I accidentally show them how irritated I am to be on stage dancing in lingerie.

"Where is the new guy tonight?"

"The new guy?" Sarcasm drips from Toothless. "Don't act like you don't know his fucking name. He's the best goalie in the league right now and has been practicing with us for the last month."

Emory Olson.

There's always a hint of nostalgia lingering when I think about hockey. It was one of the only things I had in common with my dad, and it's the one thing I've managed to keep safe from the mishaps in my family. After all these years, I've kept my interest alive and burning because it tricks me into believing he's still here. It's my own little secret.

"Ah, O'Brian? Is that his name?" There's a brush of sarcasm to the man's voice, and I turn to see his face. "Wait. Is it Owen? O'Gregory?"

"Olson," I say, unable to stick to my plan of playing the part of an obtuse stripper with no interest in hockey. It's not the first time I haven't stuck to a plan, so it comes as no surprise.

Toothless's eyebrows shoot to his forehead, and his white teeth—sans the left front—look even whiter under the strobing lights. "Oh! She knows hockey?!"

His entire gaggle of burly men hoot and holler, and I turn on the pole to shield my reddened cheeks. Money is thrown onto the floor beneath me, so at least there's that.

The stoic one in the back of the booth, who appears bored out of his mind, speaks up. "Told you she wasn't like the rest."

"Not often a stripper knows anything about hockey," Toothless says, seemingly more interested than before.

My calf wraps around the pole, and I arch backward with my eyes set on the man who rests his elbows on the table. His mouth opens, and I prepare myself for the insult because I can already tell he's more arrogant than the rest.

"Must be a puck slut."

My eye twitches.

"Don't call her that," another one says. "They prefer to be called puck bunnies."

I nearly choke on anger.

Air gets caught in my chest, which unfortunately shoves my breasts out even farther. I grab onto the pole tighter, like it's my lifeline. I swing my body, pretending their faces are being kicked by my outer leg.

"Olson wouldn't be caught dead here. He's lying low, trying to fix his bad rep."

The men chuckle, and I recall recently hearing some rumors rolling around about his run-in with the police not too long ago. It was all over the news.

"Those allegations are absurd," the stoic one says.

"At least he didn't get her pregnant. You know all about that single-parenting life. Don't you, Volkova?"

Rhodes Volkova.

"Shut the fuck up," he snaps.

"If he got her pregnant, she'd totally take all his money," someone says.

"There is no *her.* That was a rumor. He got dropped from the Coyotes because of the arrest and assault," Volkova corrects his teammates, and I continue to dance as they all talk about their newest teammate.

After many half-assed jokes and quizzes over my knowledge of hockey, the team gets up to leave, and I disappear into the dressing room with a B-cup full of money. Volkova threw me a hundred with a quick roll of his eyes as he dragged one of his drunker teammates out after him.

I stare at Benjamin Franklin and swear he's judging me for the idea that sneaks into my head like a sly little fox. I suck my cherry-flavored lip into my mouth and fold the bill in half, letting the distasteful plan disappear with bigger morals than I was taught to have.

I can't—my phone pings, and my gaze falls to the notification.

A gulp slowly works itself down my throat when I press play on the voicemail. The moment I hear his voice, I clench the hundred in my sweaty hand. *"Hey, Sis."*

I erase the message without even thinking about it.

Fight-or-flight kicks in, and right now, flight wins.

I count the money I made tonight. It's a good chunk, but not good enough.

He's bleeding me dry, and I'm letting him.

But what's a girl to do when the legal fees continue to pile up and gain interest? The outstanding bills are accumulating, and with his constant voicemails becoming more desperate, I don't have a choice.

The hundred that Volkova threw at me like chump change catches my eye again. I shake my head and peel my attention away when I hear Chastity, Rosie, and Kitty pile into the dressing room with their own wads of cash.

"Make out good tonight, sweetie?" Rosie asks, chugging a seltzer that has to be flat by now.

"Rosie." My mouth moves faster than my brain. "Can you cover my shift on Thursday?"

You can't do this, Scottie.

"Sure, if I can find a babysitter. Why? Got a hot date with one of those hockey players you were wooing out there?" She wiggles her eyebrows at me, and my face flames.

"Something like that."

Dread weighs on my shoulders, but the longer I stare at Benjamin, the lighter I feel.

"In that case," she snorts, "I've got you covered."

I smile and count my earnings again. I immediately grab my phone and pull up the Chicago Blue Devils game schedule. I'll deposit the money tomorrow and have a ticket by the end of the night.

Two

EMORY

THE RINK IS home to me, even if I'm practically surrounded by strangers.

The team has welcomed me with open arms—if you consider wary looks and multiple jokes regarding my arrest.

It's the start of the third period, and we're up 2-0. I haven't let a single puck through, and pride swells. I may have disappointed my previous coach and team, probably even my parents too, but right now, I'm proving myself.

That's what this season is about.

I'm here to clean up my destroyed image. I have to keep my head down, perfect my game, build this team up, and *hopefully* get offered an even better deal down the road.

Though, after practicing with these guys for the summer, I've realized that they're pretty fucking good. Their—our—only problem is we're not working together as a team yet.

You've got Malaki, who is one of the fastest skaters in the central division. He's mouthy and jokes too much, but he has skills. Then there's Rhodes, who is more like me than anyone else on the team. We speak the same language, which has been described as 'caveman' by most of the team. Few words are shared between us, but he's the one teammate that I'm the closest with. He's a phenomenal left winger, and his mindset reminds me a lot of Theo Brooks—who is absolutely killing the Eastern Conference, just like he did when we were in college. Rhodes is the captain, and though I've only been a part of the Devils for a short time, I know it's well-deserved. He gets shit done, knowing when to spark anger and when to simmer.

Then there's the devil himself: Kane.

He's a rookie, but his knowledge of the game may give my best friend, Ford, a run for his money. I grew up alongside Ford and didn't think I'd ever meet someone who knew hockey like he did, but Kane is quick-witted and can predict where the puck is going well before the shot is even made.

He's young, though, and testy.

The refs have already had to break up four fights, and he's been in the middle of each of them.

My sights are lasered onto center ice, and I flex my jaw as I wait for the face-off.

Malaki skates over to me, and I can already tell he's got some jab up his sleeve. "Now listen...if someone is manhandling me out there, I expect you to pull an 'Olson.'"

I act unperturbed. "And that is...?"

Malaki chews on the end of his blue mouthguard and can hardly get the words out without smirking. "When you pick someone up and throw them...just like you did at that bar last spring."

My features are unwavering behind my mask, but I want to pick Malaki up and throw him. If I were in practice, I'd do just that.

"Get away from me before I throw *you*."

Malaki starts to skate off with his laughter following him. Before he gets too far, I tell him he better win the face-off, or I really will throw him.

It isn't surprising when he wins it. The puck squeezes out to the left, and a rush of adrenaline pulls my focus. I feel lethal. My mask is positioned correctly, my stick feels light in my grip, and my eyes follow the game. I mentally can't pull away, even if I tried.

Energy flows to my fingertips when the Florida Fins swipe the puck from us and head toward their zone. My heart skips, and an amusing growl leaves my chest when they advance me.

I fucking dare you.

My right hand flies upward, and the crowd roars.

Block.

"Try again," I mutter.

Rhodes sends me a tight nod, and it's as much of a compliment as I'm going to get from him, so I put it away in my pocket for later.

The rest of the game is the same as the beginning. Our defense needs some serious tweaking because by the end of the game, I'm spent. My shoulders ache with tension, and my thighs are shaking from the quick maneuvers I had to use to block the pucks. One out of forty-one shots got through, and I should be elated that we won, but I'm pissy about the one I let slide past.

My team comes over and pats me on the helmet as a way of saying *good game,* and I nod at each and every one of them. Florida has already gone into the locker room with their tails tucked in between their legs. The fans are rowdy and banging on the glass as we head toward the locker room.

"Bro," Kane snickers under his breath when I pop my helmet off and meet his face. "They have handcuffs."

"What?" The word is clipped coming from my mouth.

I scan the crowd and purposefully lock my jaw so it won't hang open at the audacity.

Fans are on their feet with their eyes set on the team, and though some of them are waving blue and white pom-poms and annoying-as-fuck noisemakers, there is a hefty number of them waving handcuffs while shouting, *"Olson! Olson! Olson!"*

Rhodes skates past. "Take it as a compliment," he gruffs before continuing on.

Malaki can hardly keep it together. "Some of the women are wearing fuzzy ones, just for you, man." He joins the crowd with his stick held up high above his head. "Olson, Olson, Olson!"

Jesus fucking Christ. He's egging them on.

"Do you want me fucking to throw you?" I snap. "Because I swear to god I will."

Malaki stops skating right before we enter the opening to the ice. "Why does that girl look so familiar?"

Someone laughs from behind. "You've probably seen her in your dreams."

"Wait, isn't that the stripper? The one who knew all about hockey? We quizzed her the other night."

I can't help but look at Malaki like he's an idiot. "While she was stripping, you quizzed her?"

He nods vigorously. "Yeah, why? Is that weird?"

"Not at all," I answer.

"That's not her. She had red hair." Kane goes through the opening next.

I follow their line of sight, and while I know that only a few seconds have come and gone, it feels like a lifetime.

She is the complete opposite of what I had prepared myself for. All those pornos that Ford and I snuck as teenagers created a very detailed image of what a stripper *should* look like, and it is nothing like the woman in the stands with her glossy lip trapped between her white teeth.

She's soft in all the right places with subtle curves. Her blonde hair lies behind her shoulders, giving way to her medium-sized chest that's mostly covered up by a Blue Devils shirt that has seen better days, and her heart-shaped face is free of heavy makeup like a lot of the women I see.

She's pretty.

Actually, no. She's fucking *beautiful*.

But she's a woman, and as of late, there's barely even a handful of them that I trust, so I keep skating until I make it to the opening. I slide right past Malaki as he attempts to win over her attention, and I purposefully keep my eyes to myself.

———

"I HAVE SOMETHING FOR YOU," Malaki says.

I slam my locker door. "Whatever it is, I don't want it."

A few of my teammates laugh under their breath as they pile out of the locker room with flushed faces and chips on their shoulders.

We've won one game, and they're already acting like kings.

They're getting ahead of themselves.

Before Rhodes skipped out to get his daughter, he caught my attention and shook his head. He read my mind, and it's clear he agrees with me. I'm sure practice will be loads of fun this week while he and Coach bring the young guys down a level to humble them.

Malaki slaps a small piece of paper onto my chest. I slowly drop my head and stare at his hand pressing against my beating heart.

"Dude, take it. Trust me."

I snatch the paper from his grip, and his smile is downright creepy.

"If this is some stupid fucking pretend arrest warrant, I'm shoving you in a locker."

He sobers. "Damn. I wish I would have thought of that. That's a missed opportunity for sure."

I slowly open up the paper with an audience. Most of the

veteran players have left the locker room because they don't give a shit. It's the younger ones that are fully engaged.

When I finally register what's in my hand, a cold sweat breaks out along my neck.

My fingers curl against the gum wrapper, and I growl under my breath.

Absolutely not.

"You gonna go?" Malaki lowers his voice. "It's from that brainy stripper. However, she did say, *'It isn't what you think.'*"

My glare catches him.

"Noted," he says before putting his back to me and heading to his own locker.

It isn't what you think. I'd bet my lucky skates that it is *exactly* what I think.

When I'm in the quiet hall, I open my palm again and reread her note.

Meet me in the west wing bathrooms on level 3.

-Cherry

I sigh and shove the note in my pocket.

But for some reason, instead of heading for my car, I turn and head for the stairs.

Three

SCOTTIE

I PULL my black sheer sleeves down as far as they'll go and trap them to my palms with shaky fingers. It will be a miracle if Emory Olson, one of the best goalies in the division, actually shows up from a stupid handwritten note on a gum wrapper that I found in the bottom of my purse.

You would think someone who has such an elaborate plan to eliminate the problems in their life would come prepared, but no. One gum wrapper and a borrowed pen from a nearby fan, and that's all she wrote, friends.

I walk over to the mirror in the quiet bathroom and puff my rosy cheeks out before letting all the air empty into the space. My blue eyes pool with dread and fear, but I shake the feelings away and fill myself with confidence.

Emory Olson isn't a good guy, if the rumors are true, and considering his previous team dropped him, I'd say a majority of them are. That's why I don't feel bad about this. I am *so* sick of rotten humans getting what they want instead of people like me who try their hardest to do the right thing or make a difference and yet still get shit on.

The jaded woman staring back at me in the mirror nods.

"You can do this, Scottie," I say.

"So Cherry isn't your real name?" His clipped scoff sends a line of fear down my spine. "Who would've thought?"

A scream erupts from my mouth, and my hands fall to the porcelain sink for stability. The very second I see Emory Olson leaning against the tiled wall with his arms crossed over his chest, I immediately forget the objective.

My lips part, and the only thing that comes out is hot air.

I'm not intimidated by men, but I would be a big fat liar if I said Emory Olson didn't unnerve me a little.

Without the rink's glass separating us as a barrier, I'm unsettled. He's much taller and broader than I thought he would be underneath his pads, and there are so many different hues of blue in his eyes that I can't pinpoint the exact shade. When he raises an eyebrow in my direction, his jaw becomes ten times sturdier, and the little bit of scruff along the edge does nothing but accentuate how attractive he really is. Except, the air around him is thick with arrogance, and he looks at me as if I should be kissing the ground he walks on.

"I'm becoming impatient," he says.

I snap out of my stupor, and a rush of defiance zips down my legs to ground me.

My confidence is shaky at best, but I push off the sink and straighten my shoulders. "Do you remember me?"

Emory doesn't hesitate. "No."

Not off to a good start.

I thought for sure that he'd look me over a little more closely and try to rack his brain for a memory that I know doesn't really exist, but he acts completely at ease, and it causes the room to sway.

"Well..." *Shit.* "You should."

My face flushes, and I want to run out of this bathroom like a little damsel in distress because this entire scheme is an act of pure desperation, and I'm failing miserably.

"I should?" Emory asks with a lazy tone. He pushes off the bathroom wall, and you could hear a pin drop with the silence.

Fuck.

I stumble over my words but manage to pull out my phone while Emory erases the space between us. He smells good, like a freshly showered man who wears expensive cologne. He is nothing like the men I grew up around.

He's a few feet away from me when I quickly enlarge the photo and turn the phone around so he can get a good look. He freezes mid-step and looks closer at the image. I quietly swallow and wait for his reaction.

Tight jaw.

Flickering temples.

Narrowing glare that shoots to mine. My hand tightens around the tiny device as I wait.

"That's fake." His voice is low and lethal.

"Is it?" I question.

Of course it is. Photoshop is my most trusted confidant. It's what got me through my adolescent years. I'd spend hours piecing together photos I'd taken of my surroundings to make the real picture seem so much better than it really was.

Emory takes a step closer after he seems to get over his shock. I back up as he continues to prowl toward me until my heels hit the wall. He advances like a villain with his face growing redder by the second.

I swallow and tilt my chin to meet his glare. I have looked into the eyes of very bad men before—corrupted men, ones who've taken advantage of women, evaded the law, and chose drugs over everything else. Yet looking into the eyes of Emory Olson has me losing all ability to speak.

He's intimidating, but there's something enticing about him too. Part of me wants to run, but the other part of me wants to take my soft palm and smooth his stony features.

"What do you want?" He peers down at me so sharply

that I have to angle my head even more to meet his eye. One of his palms presses against the wall beside my head, and I push myself further onto the tile.

Want?

More like need.

"Money," I answer quietly.

Emory laughs. He whispers under his breath, *"Un-fucking-believable."*

His head falls, and I get a whiff of his shampoo. It takes everything in me not to go in for a second sniff. When he abruptly snaps his attention back to mine, the humor has vanished completely. "Money? You want my money?"

I say nothing, but again, it's not a want. It's a need. A desperate need. Otherwise, I wouldn't stoop so low.

"You think you can write me a note on a stupid little gum wrapper..." I follow his movements when he reaches into his pocket and pulls out my note before crumpling it and letting it fall to the floor between us. "And create some photoshopped picture of me taking advantage of you so you can exploit me and force me into giving you money?"

Well, when he puts it like that...

Nope. It sounds just as bad as before.

My stomach fills with dread, and my confidence is quivering. Those morals that I must've been born with—because God knows I didn't get them from my mother—are starting to rear their head and...*what the fuck am I doing?*

"What's your plan, Scottie?" Emory's glare narrows even more, and I can't speak. "If I don't hand over my bank account information, are you going to run to the media with that photo, and then what? Tell them that I took advantage of you? Ruin my life because you're sick of yours?" He scoffs, and I bite the inside of my cheek to keep my lips from trembling. "Is that what you want? To ruin my life and reputation even more? I have never met you, and you want to ruin my life? Fucking typical."

God. What am I doing?

"I—" My mouth opens, but nothing comes out because I'm ashamed. It doesn't matter the reason I need the money. No excuse I can come up with will make this okay.

"I'll work!" I cry. It's a pathetic attempt to rid my guilt and fix the situation, but I try anyway.

"You'll work?"

I nod. "You can pay me for something. Whatever you want. I'm yours."

Emory's forehead furrows. He drops his hand from the wall and crosses his arms. "A stripper offering to do whatever I want? Sounds like a trick."

My jaw slacks, and I gasp. "No! I..." I shake my head. "Not like that. I didn't mean..."

Can someone please come into this bathroom, shove me into a stall, and drown me in toilet water to put me out of my misery? This was a terrible plan built from desperation and fear. I can't even be angry with his judgment.

"You've gotta be a shitty person to specifically hunt me down and threaten to blackmail me for money when you don't even know me."

My cheeks burn. I refuse to look in the mirror, because I know I'll be mortified.

I try to make the situation seem justified. "There are rumors."

"And you believe them? You're mighty brave for being in a bathroom alone with me if you truly believe what the media is saying."

I know the rumors aren't true. It took all of two seconds of looking into his eyes to know they're fabricated truths, if not lies altogether.

"I..." I finally bring myself to look him in the face again, and the disgust painted across his features sends me reeling. "I'm sorry..." I shake my head. "I don't know what I'm doing."

I meet his eyes once more before taking off in a full sprint out of the bathroom. My name echoes from behind, but I keep going because what the hell was I thinking?

Four

EMORY

"NICE DIGS, MAN."

I flip the camera around and flop onto the couch. My sister and Ford share the camera, and I can tell that she's lying on top of him, which still makes my skin itch, partly because I know my best friend is fucking my sister, and partly because I think the majority of relationships are disillusioned and fake.

Don't get me wrong, if anyone deserves true love, it's them. I just think it's very few and far between these days.

"It needs a woman's touch." Taytum drags her gaze from the open space behind me to my face. "Mom didn't do nearly enough when she was there."

"What? It's fine." I look around my new home, thankful I finally found one after months of searching. I act unbothered by the fact that it's nearly empty, but if my mom asked me one more time what I thought about the color sage, I was going to put a for sale sign in the front yard.

"Maybe get some family photos or something. Hang them on the wall? It's kind of...cold." Taytum's mouth forms a straight line, as if she's trying not to hurt my feelings.

29

That was something that started after the shit show last season.

I may have been a bit testy, and it caused everyone to walk on eggshells with me. Truthfully, I prefer her asshole remarks over her trying to spare my feelings, though.

"Cold?" I repeat, glancing at the bare walls. I shrug and bring my attention back to my sister. "I like the cold."

She snorts with a roll of her eyes and climbs off Ford. He watches her walk away in the frame, and I choose to ignore it because if I say something, then it'll just result in him calling me bitter.

"How is her new monitor?" I ask.

I can't question my sister about her diabetes because she gets frustrated, so I ask him instead.

He rubs his hand along his face. "It's good. Takes some getting used to."

I chuckle. "Good thing she has you there to remind her to check her levels, though. Right?"

Taytum shouts from another room. "I don't need reminding!"

Ford and I share a half smile, and he glances up from the screen and winks at my sister. In the midst of the phone call, I start to gather my gear for practice. Ford rambles on about their schedule and pokes some questions here and there about my new teammates.

I give him a roundabout answer, but he can tell something is eating away at me.

"Spill," he says.

"What?"

"What's bothering you? Is it because I'm not on your team?" He sighs dramatically. "Don't worry, *Emory Bemory*. I miss you too."

I snarl. "You're in a completely different state, and you're still on my nerves."

He laughs, and I rest my elbows on the kitchen counter after leaning my phone against the half-opened cereal box.

"Did something else happen?" he asks, becoming serious. "You in the media again?"

"Not yet," I mumble.

"What does that mean?"

I watch Ford move throughout his house, likely to put me out of earshot of my sister. I wait until I hear the door click to let a sigh rush from my tight lungs.

Ever since Cherry—or Scottie, whatever the fuck she wants to be called—showed me a fake photo of me manhandling some girl in lingerie with the same shade of sunshiny hair as hers, I've been on edge. Who does she think she is? Because from our short conversation, I truly can't decide if she's a selfish gold-digger with no respect for others, or if she was acting out of character. Was she dared to corner me in a bathroom and threaten me? It's fucking with my head, and I don't like it.

She was determined but timid. Resilient yet still willing to compromise. All her features were delicate, but there was a thick wall of hardness in her eyes. I haven't been able to stop thinking about her or that fucking photo for days.

"Are you contemplating something or having a stroke?"

I shake my head at Ford's sarcasm. My hands lie flat on the smooth counter, and I fill him in quickly, hoping he can make sense of it.

He blinks a few times before whistling. "Sounds like a missed opportunity."

My fingers press into the stone of my counter. "What?"

"I mean, she'd probably suck some mean dick."

I hear a gasp. "Ford!"

And here I thought he was giving us some privacy with our conversation. I was wrong.

He laughs out loud and shouts over his shoulder at my sister. "I'm kidding, baby!"

"If you make a joke about my sister sucking your dick, I will book a flight right now and choke you."

Ford laughs harder. "You two are so sensitive."

The screen blurs, and my sister's face pops onto it. There are worry lines on her forehead, so it's obvious she's much more concerned than my best friend. "Did she delete the photo?"

I shrug. "She apologized and then ran off."

"She apologized?"

I nod. "Yeah, it was a mindfuck."

Ford pulls the phone back. "You should have struck a deal with her. Pay her to help you fix your shitty image."

Taytum's voice is farther away now. "Stop giving him bad advice! Emory, you need to make sure the photo is deleted and she's not going to do something out of desperation because it seems like she's desperate for money, or maybe she's a puck bunny who likes to use hockey players for monetary gain."

I don't argue with my sister. But something tells me she's wrong.

Ford attempts to defend himself as I head for the door. "Bad advice? Remember when I told Theo to fake date Claire to fend off the puck bunnies in college? Now look at them! Happily in love."

"You're a real matchmaker." Sarcasm. Full sarcasm. "I'll talk to you guys later. I gotta head to practice. Good luck tomorrow," I say to Ford.

Before I hang up the phone, my sister shouts at me to make sure the photo isn't going to pop up somewhere and make things worse for my reputation.

Taytum is right.

That photo popping up is the *last* thing I need.

———

PRACTICE IS JUST as tiring as I knew it would be. Coach and Rhodes snapped at the younger players to get them into action—except for me, because although I'm still considered on the younger end, I'm much humbler than they are, thanks to the growing up I just had to endure. Still, we're all dripping with sweat by the end.

We have an away game in two days. We're undefeated, but it's the start of the season, and an undefeated record doesn't usually happen in the pros. We're bound to lose eventually, and that's not the pessimist inside of me talking. It's just the truth.

Malaki catches up with me as we head for the locker room. "Are you going with us tonight?"

I send him a look. "You think it's best for me to go out and party with everything going on?"

"I think it's best if you bond with the team a little."

The locker room is full of men changing out of their practice gear. We're all tired and sweaty, yet they are hyped up on their plans for the evening to celebrate Kane's birthday. Some of them are trying to convince their captain to go out with them too, but Rhodes has a pretty good excuse—a five-year-old daughter with no mother and a disappearing-nanny problem.

Malaki elbows me. "Come on, man. Just make an appearance."

I wiggle my fingers after my gloves fall to the floor. "When and where?" I ask, fully fucking annoyed, but also, I know that team bonding isn't something to skip out on. It took me a few years in college to understand the importance of it, but hockey is not a one-man type of sport, even if my position on the ice is a little more isolated than the rest.

"Strip club." Kane wiggles his eyebrows.

My chest tightens.

I'm instantly on edge. Last fall, I would have jumped at the opportunity, but now there's a resistance that wasn't there before. The thought of going out with the team wires me in all the wrong ways, yet I find myself agreeing.

If anything, maybe I'll lay eyes on a little blue-eyed devil and leave her a note just like she left me.

Five

SCOTTIE

THE CAT HOUSE IS PACKED.

All the other girls are hyped. I watch in admiration as their outfits become a little more revealing and their makeup a little edgier. They tell me they're just playing a part, but little do they know, me on stage in a red wig is more than enough acting on my behalf.

I'm about to go back on when Chastity saunters up beside me and reaches her hand into the cup of my lacy bra. She gets a cupful and pulls my boobs up a little more.

I gasp, and she winks. Her fake eyelashes are so long they look like furry caterpillars. "Get those tips, babe, or you'll be working here for far longer than you want to be."

The validity of her advice is spot on.

She's right. I need to get my shit together.

What's a little stripping compared to the agony and guilt I'll be forced to live with if I don't do everything I can to help William.

It's not *that* big of a deal.

A haunting voice wisps through my head that I know

belongs to my past, but I quickly brush it away and get to work.

The lights are blue tonight, and it reminds me of the hockey game. All we need is an ice rink with some broody hockey players, and it would be the exact same setup. Even the song is upbeat.

I avoid all the longing stares glued to my bare legs as I walk along the platform to my spot. My hands grab the pole, and as soon as the beat drops in the song, I jump up and wrap my leg around it with a sexy arch of my back.

A few dollars are thrown at my feet, but I ignore them and listen to the song, losing myself in the music instead of focusing on what I'm doing, because the only thing stripping does is remind me of my mother, and I swore I'd never end up like her.

Take a look in the mirror, Scottie.

My heartbeat thumps harder as I spin and move faster. The club is filling up quicker than usual, but that means more tips, and that's what I'm here for.

"You're up, baby girl."

I turn and press my spine against the pole. I peer down at Russ smiling like a perv. He reminds me of a creep that would drive a scary white van full of candy down a street packed with children.

"Over at booth four. You're up." He raises an eyebrow, like he's waiting for me to challenge him.

God, no.

I quickly turn and lock onto booth four. I stare at the pole that's smackdab in the middle of the table. I shake on wobbly legs and pray I don't break an ankle. I peer back down at my boss with a refusal on the tip of my tongue.

"I'll fire you if you refuse," he warns.

I grit my teeth and manage to squeeze out a half insult.

"Will you fire me if I cuss you out in my head the entire walk over there?"

Russ's lip twitches. "No, but I prefer it to be out loud. That's like dirty talk to me."

He reaches forward to help me down, but a little growl escapes. His hands land on my hips regardless, and it takes everything in me not to kick him. I shove his hands off my waist when my heels click on the floor, and I hurriedly make my way to booth four before I have to endure any more moments with Russ's hands on me.

If Chastity were to see that, she'd smack him.

But Chastity and Russ have a weird boss/employee relationship. She can get away with it.

I cannot.

"There she is," a familiar voice muses.

I stop mid-climb onto the little platform. My hands almost slip on the pole, but my spine locks and saves me from falling. Over my shoulder, I see two Blue Devils approach the table with their devilish grins. *Please no.*

My cheeks burn. I turn, letting my palm slide against the metal pole to guide me. When I'm facing the duo, I smile sweetly. "So, this was your doing?"

Their cheeky grins split into full smiles. "Our favorite girl with a wealth of hockey knowledge dancing in front of us?" They get closer, and my heart is in my throat. *Please do not let Emory show up.* "Who else would we want?"

"Well..." My leg curls against the cool metal, and I have to physically stop myself from banging my face off the pole to knock myself unconscious. "Here I am."

"Yes, there you are."

My thick eyelashes wisp together when I hear his voice.

Heat trickles down my body, and my limbs weigh a thousand pounds each.

I turn slightly, pressing against the pole for stability. Our eyes meet, and my lips part. Emory Olson slides into the booth below and peers up at me with his steely jaw set like stone. His tongue slips out of his mouth, and he wets his lips, like he's waiting for me to do something.

I'm frozen.

My hands grip the pole for stability, and my ribcage expands with a lungful of air.

He's angry.

His dark-blue eyes narrow, and the longer I stare at him, the worse I feel. The judgment is crystal clear. If I were to peek into his head for a split second, I'm sure my self-worth would be destroyed.

"Glad you could make it, man." Malaki wraps his arm around his teammate's thick neck and pulls Emory's attention away from me.

I grab onto the distraction like a lifeline and quickly spin around, putting my back to them.

A hesitant smile touches my lips when I meet the flirty looks of the other Blue Devils piling into the booth. If I don't get a ridiculous amount of tips from this, I swear, I'll look into selling feet pics instead.

The next several songs go by quickly, and I try to focus on the beat and the way my body needs to move in order to keep pulling the men's attention, but the only thing I can think about is Emory and the silent insults piling in his head every time I face him.

"So, tell us, Cherry..." Kane, who I learned is a total hothead on the ice, leans back into the red leather of the booth. "Is that your real hair?"

Shit.

He knows.

Like a moth to a flame, my eyes shift to Emory's for a split second. His eyebrow arches, and a hot swallow works down my throat. Something clicks, and I suddenly feel like I need to prove that him sitting there doesn't bother me in the slightest.

I turn back to Kane. "So, tell *me*, Kane... Are you always a hothead on the ice?" I jump up and do a hook spin until landing in front of him. I lean down a little. "You should work on your defense."

The blue lights reflect off Kane's white teeth, and his teammates chuckle under their breath. Some of them throw a few twenties beneath my feet, and I laugh playfully.

Kane sits a little taller. "I think I might need someone to take the edge off before games." My laughter fades. A chill breaks out along my skin when his hand reaches forward. "Do you know anyone that would be up for that?" When his warm fingers wrap around my ankle, my heart stops.

All it takes is a quick trip down memory lane, and I'm spiraling.

Six

MY ARM HAS a mind of its own. It uncrosses, and my hand clamps onto Kane's wrist with swift speed.

"Don't," the word hisses from between my teeth. It comes off as a reprimand, but it's more of a friendly warning—at least that's what I tell myself.

Kane's wrist flexes beneath my grip, and I arch an eyebrow at him. "You don't want to touch someone like her." My heart thumps hard, and I want to reach inside my chest and squeeze the muscle until it relaxes. "Trust me," I add. "Do not touch the women in this place."

I hear Scottie suck in a sharp breath, and I make the mistake of looking up at her. What I expect is a dirty look laced with resentment, but what I get is something that irks me even more.

Fear.

Panic.

Terror.

When she meets my eye, something hitches in my chest, and it irritates me so much that my fingers begin to tighten on Kane's wrist.

"Ah, you're right," he agrees, pulling his arm back.

I force myself to look away from Scottie. I nod at Kane with our silent conversation, and the rest of the show our own personal stripper puts on is a little less risky than before. Scottie's movements are jerky instead of fluid, and it's clear that Kane's flirting did something to her.

I don't care to find out why.

The only thing I care to find out is if she has deleted the photo of us. Then I'll toss her out of my head like a piece of trash.

"Cherry." Malaki leans forward onto the tabletop and taps his fingers against the shiny glass. "What do you like to do for fun?"

"You trying to ask out a stripper?" Hayes smirks over the frosted glass of his beer. He's what we call a bench jockey— only playing in the game if someone gets hurt.

Malaki grins. "Why? Were you planning on asking her out?"

Scottie's soft voice breaks up their conversation. "I can tell you that I don't date hockey players for fun, so you might as well just move past that."

My sarcastic snort has everyone's head swiveling in my direction. Scottie pauses mid-spin.

"You got something to add there, Mr. Grumpy?" Hayes asks.

I shrug and seemingly get more comfortable in my seat. I refuse to look away from the little blue-eyed devil as her tiny scowl deepens. "She does something else to hockey players for fun, and it's definitely not *dating*."

Suddenly, Scottie and I are the only ones in the room. It feels like she's putting on some type of show just for me when she wraps her long leg around the pole and arches her lithe body backward, putting herself *right* in front of me. The ends of her fake red hair touch the tip of my barely touched beer, and her sweet scent makes my nostrils flare. I swallow the tight knot in my throat when I accidentally dip my gaze to her breasts. They're a handful each, and her skin looks silky smooth.

I hate that she's taken my breath away more than once now.

I also hate that I can feel my dick twitch the longer we stare at one another.

She has me by the throat.

But I'm about to have *her* by the throat.

The song ends, and it's time to go, but not before the guys try to get Cherry to give Kane a lap dance for his birthday.

"It goes against the rules of the club." She gives a little shrug of her shoulders. "Sorry, Devils."

Everyone, but me, throws money at her feet, and she happily swipes up the cash with her hand and walks off into the back.

Every patron in the club watches her go, despite there being multiple half-dressed strippers around. Two of the women are putting on some type of show with a chastity belt halfway across the room, but even their audience catches a quick glimpse at Scottie in her tiny white lingerie.

She's a devil disguised as an angel.

I roll my eyes because she is definitely not an angel.

The team piles into cars, and after I make sure no one is driving drunk, I wait a few minutes until the parking lot is nearly empty and head back inside.

I'm calm when I walk into the Cat House for the second time. I give the room a quick sweep and can't find Scottie anywhere, so I casually head toward the back. Knowing I'm not the smallest guy in the room, I lean against the wall and act like I'm waiting for the bathroom until no one pays me any attention, and that's when I start opening random doors.

To most, I'd look like a creep trying to get one-on-one time with a stripper. Maybe even a pervert or stalker. But the moment Scottie lays her eyes on me, she knows exactly why I'm here.

"Care to talk?" I ask, not giving her a chance to refuse.

She's still in her skimpy, white lingerie, but she's removed the wig, and her blonde locks fall gracefully over her shoulders. I do my best to only touch her delicate wrist and nothing else. I pull her behind me and shove us into the empty room next to the bathroom. I turn my back to the black leather couch in the corner and briefly wonder what it would look like if I held a black light up to it.

If I try hard enough, I bet I can smell the stench of body fluids covering it.

Scottie's pulse rams beneath my fingers when she looks from the couch and then back to my face. Something flickers behind her eyes, and it pisses me off. How dare she look at me like I'm the one with bad morals?

A gruff chuckle leaves my mouth.

Her swallow is loud enough to echo throughout the room. My grip loosens, and she immediately pulls her wrist out of my grasp. As soon as she backs up, I advance. She hits the door, and I trap her there with a slight turn to my head.

"You look afraid." I pin her arm above her head. "Worried that your filthy lies are going to come true?"

Scottie's shoulders straighten, and her mighty chin becomes stronger. The effort she's putting into her features to act unbothered is sort of...*admirable*?

I quickly move past the feeling and look at her rising chest. Her soft breasts are rising and falling swiftly, and my eyes travel down past her navel to the curve of her hips.

Why does she have to be so fucking alluring?

She's undeniably beautiful, and I can't stand it.

I hear her mouth open, and I snap to attention.

"What do you want?" she rasps.

Ignoring her question completely, because she isn't in the position to ask one, I take my free hand and place it on her collarbone. A hot swallow works down my throat when I drag my finger down the center of her cleavage, brushing against the frilly lace of her bra.

"I thought the color white was supposed to symbolize innocence." I cup her waist and press her further against the door. There's a tug on my other hand from her trapped wrist, but she's no match to my strength, and she knows it.

"You and I both know that you're not innocent, huh?" She stares at my teasing smirk, and I finally give in to acknowledging her question, because the longer I'm alone with her in this room with my hands on her warm skin, the more I question my own wants.

"I want you to delete the photo of us." I bounce my attention between her eyes and wait for her to give me some sort of sign that she isn't just another untrustworthy woman who wants to ruin my life for the fun of it.

"I did." She says it with a little edge to her voice, and it triggers me.

I lean in closer and ignore the scent of her sweet perfume. Her cute little nose scrunches when I sigh agitatedly. I give her torso a little squeeze, and something wild blooms in her blue eyes. "And you expect me to believe you, Scottie?"

When her free hand grips my wrist, it's a swift punch to my gut. Her palm is so small she can't even wrap her fingers around it, but nonetheless, I feel fucking trapped. Scottie tips her chin with confidence, and I can't stop staring at her glistening red lips. "You have no choice but to believe me..." I get a quick peek of her white teeth when she sucks her bottom lip into her mouth before she frees it with a *pop*. "*Olson.*"

She's fucking with my head, and I don't like it.

With her head still lifted like a defiant little brat, I quickly free her arm and trap her chin with a firm grasp. She tries to

47

pull away from me but fails. I peer down at her, and our mouths are so close I taste her on my tongue. "If I see that photo circling around somewhere, I'll know where it came from." I pause to get my bearings because if I move even a centimeter, my mouth will be on hers. "And you'll regret posting it."

I step away a moment later, and Scottie exhales, like she's been holding her breath the entire time I've had her pinned. She quickly moves out of my way, and I grip the door handle with so much force the wood creaks.

Before I make it through the threshold, I hesitate.

I manage to keep my back to her when a smirk slides onto my face. A single dollar bill crinkles in between my fingers as I pull it out of my pocket and throw it at her feet.

It's demeaning, and I know I've humiliated her.

A hot, angry huff hits my back, and I swear, it follows me all the way to my car.

Seven

SCOTTIE

MID-OCTOBER IN CHICAGO means one thing to me: cooler temperatures are peeking over the tops of the copper-colored trees, and it's time to start saving my pennies for the electric bill come winter.

With William away, I can at least keep the apartment's heat at a bare minimum when I'm not home in order to keep it from constantly running, but with the way the bills are stacking up, his frequent anxious voicemails requiring me to put more money on his books, and the lawyer fees, a little turn of the dial on my thermostat isn't going to do much.

I glance up at the TV and tell myself to turn it off in order to save money on electric, but with the way my life is going lately, it's best to give myself at least one tiny sliver of tranquility, and thanks to my dad, watching hockey calms me more than I'd like to admit—even if I continuously hear the name *Emory Olson* over and over again from the commentators.

"Ugh." I grab the remote and hit the mute button to ignore the constant reminder of the asshole goalie that I picked a fight with.

I mindlessly reach up and run the pad of my finger over

51

my lips, as if I can still feel his breath brush against them. At the exact same time, I watch in awe as he blocks a ninety-mile-an-hour puck heading straight for him. He catches it with ease and tosses it to the ref carelessly as the camera zooms in on his sweaty face. He adjusts his mask, and heat swirls in my stomach when I watch his Adam's apple bob. Emory's gaze lasers onto the rink as he gets in position. There isn't even a twinkle of life in his eye as he prepares for the rest of the game. It's like hockey is second nature for him, and it comes naturally.

My dad would probably call him a *beauty*, meaning he's a damn good hockey player.

But I unfortunately now know Emory outside of the net, and his broody personality could use some serious work.

In his defense, he has every right to hate me, but I ignore that little mishap like the entire thing didn't even happen.

I unmute the TV and begin to gather some of William's old coats that I'll have to replace eventually anyway. His recent voicemail replays in my head, and my stomach knots. It's hard to remember what he sounded like before he was sentenced. Now when I think of his voice, all I hear is distress, fear, and the clanking sounds of a prison in the background.

The legal fees are continuously gaining interest, and although the lawyer says he believes that my brother was wrongfully convicted, he won't petition for an appeal until I pay past dues, so my worries are stacking up right along with the bills.

Piling the coats on one another, I start to shove them into a bag and focus on the sounds of skates over ice, the roaring crowd, and the commentator's excitement as the game ends with the Devils' goalie—*who must not be named*—having a near shut-out for the second time this week.

My attention snags when the sounds of the game disappear and new voices hit my ear. It's the postgame broadcast, and of course, their first topic is Emory.

"The Devils are lucky to have Emory Olson on their roster this year."

"Despite his record and new allegations, he's still playing like nothing ever happened. It looks like he's trying to prove himself in the league, and I've gotta say, it's working."

"New allegations?"

"Oh no. Jerry hasn't heard."

I slowly turn to see a group of knowledgeable men in their pricey suits sitting at their table with papers in front of them and a screen showing the Devils' score in the background. They all chuckle, and the one who seems to know the tea has a look of unease on his face. My finger presses on the volume, and the screen cuts to an image of a social media post that seemingly looks fake.

"Apparently, this woman said that, last night, Emory lured her to his house and that he took advantage of her. The police were involved, but there were no specifics given."

"Well, considering he isn't sporting handcuffs, it must have been another allegation that had no real substance."

"I think he'd still play good hockey if he were in handcuffs."

Each man laughs again as I drop to the couch in my living room beside a mound of worn coats. I cover my mouth with my shaky hand. I'm not one to let a threat linger, so I grab the pile of coats along with my keys and rush out the door.

There is no way I'm letting Emory Olson think *I* was the one who started this rumor, because that is exactly what it looks like.

———

THE PARKING LOT is pretty empty when I make it to the arena. My in-desperate-need-of-an-oil-change car rattles when I turn off the ignition. Cool air swirls around me like some sort of warning. I spot Emory's car right away: an expensive Audi that's completely black. *Seems fitting.* After he trapped me in a private room at the Cat House the other night, I peeked out the back door and watched him leave. He zoomed off in his expensive car, and I cursed him the entire time.

My heart skips a beat every few seconds with each step in his car's direction. I've been threatened many times in my life, so I don't understand why I'm so nervous when it comes to Emory. A guy like him, surrounded by wealth and an ego bigger than the entire state, can't do much to a girl like me. It's not like he'll make friends with the scumbags of this city who already have my name in their little black book with a big ol' circle around it.

I hesitate when I reach his car. There's an ache in the center of my breastbone. I wouldn't be surprised if my heart beat right out of my chest and landed at his feet. On my tiptoes, I peek through his tinted windows to see if he happens to be inside, but I know he isn't when I hear a crunch of gravel behind me.

I spin with my hands up as a shield from an instinct buried deep in my memories. A strangled noise fills the empty space between us, and Emory's eyebrows furrow at my reaction. His confusion doesn't last long when a gruff chuckle breaks through the shock of me standing beside his car.

"Here to rob me?" he sneers, walking right past me like I don't even exist.

I let the jab go and swallow my pride. "It wasn't me." Spinning on the loose asphalt beneath my shoes, I watch Emory open his car door to throw his bag inside. My guard falls when I get a whiff of his freshly showered scent.

Wow.

Emory Olson is all man. He's an animal on the ice but

resembles a Calvin Klein model off of it. His suit fits him in all the right places, hugging his biceps and thighs perfectly. He's left the front of his white button-down open, just enough to where I can see his tanned skin. My mouth runs dry.

His good looks are intimidating, especially when he looks at me with a tinge of anger.

Why do I find him even more attractive like this?

It should be worrisome that there's a small part of me that likes to irritate him.

A shaky breath clamors from my mouth when I snap back into reality.

"I didn't create that fake profile and say those things." I cross my arms over my jacket. "It wasn't me."

My voice carries at the end of my sentence as I attempt to defend myself, and I start flinging out more excuses, telling him that I was at work all night and how I didn't have time to mock up any more photos of us.

Emory's eyebrow hitches, and a single strand of his damp hair falls to his forehead. "Can you take a breath before you pass out?"

I immediately do what he says and pull a gulpful of cool air into my mouth. The moment it hits my lungs, I go in for another round of excuses. I'm panicking. The threats and worries are piling up, and all of a sudden, I'm suffocating.

"I swear, it wasn't me! I deleted the photo of us, and I let the entire thing go. I just came here to let you know that I didn't start any more rum—"

Emory steps forward, and his hands wrap around my waist.

My back hits the side of his car, and suddenly, I forget my own name.

Eight

"BREATHE," I demand.

I'm peering down at her pale face and forcing a calm into her to the best of my ability. Scottie is absolutely unhinged, and I sort of feel bad for her. The thick ends of her eyelashes brush against one another when she locks onto me with her big blue eyes. A quick whip of something hot slashes at the back of my neck, so I remove my hands from her waist and take a step away.

A surge of her warm, sweet breath hits me in the face when she exhales, and it takes everything in me not to sniff the air like some fucking pervert. *Get a fucking grip.*

"I know it wasn't you." I roll my eyes.

I'm irritated. I don't like that she has me all twisted up inside, and pairing that with the crazy chick from last night is a recipe for a bad fucking mood. I was one missed puck away from snapping my stick in half during the game.

Scottie peers up at me with innocent doe-like eyes, and it's a contradiction in itself. "You believe me?" she asks with a timidness to her voice that I've yet to hear.

My forehead furrows. "Unless you can shapeshift into a

57

bleach-blonde woman with fake tits and a need for a psychiatrist, then yeah, I believe you."

I stand with my arm on my open door and stare at Scottie. She's wearing loose jeans with holes in the knees and a thick jacket that needs to be zipped if she plans to stay warm. There isn't an ounce of makeup covering her smooth skin, and it's a shame how deceptive she can be, because she's beautiful. How can someone who appears so innocent with the prettiest, flawlessly placed features be so deceitful?

After a few seconds of silence between us, I sigh and explain further. "She showed up at my house, so yeah, I know it wasn't you. I had the police escort her off my property." I pause when our eyes catch. "Unless you hired her to do your dirty work for you?"

Scottie looks offended, and I have to keep myself from smirking because, at the end of the day, it really isn't something to joke about. Frustration still runs through my veins, and although Scottie is nothing like the woman at my house, the truth still stands: she tried to blackmail me. And that gives me a pretty good reason to put her on my blacklist with the rest of the women I come into contact with.

I slowly start to climb inside my car to distance myself from her because, knowing my luck, a journalist with a craving for drama will pop out of the bushes and snap our picture to spin some story about me dating a stripper.

If only Scottie was Miss America or something, then I'd jump at the opportunity to clear up my image like Ford suggested so it would stop the rumors that are damaging my reputation even more.

Before I slam my door, Scottie moves to block it. Her eyes are wide with concern. "You should get an alarm if she knows where you live."

My eyes narrow. Does she really expect me to take advice

from her? When I say nothing, she continues to ramble with more *stellar* advice.

"I'd get one with a camera so you can see who is at your door. She may have given your address out or posted it on social media." She shrugs and tucks a loose piece of light-colored hair behind her ear, like she's embarrassed.

My chest does something strange, and that doesn't fly with me, so I huff with irritation. "I sure hope she didn't give *you* my address." Scottie's forehead creases. I lean out of my car so she can hear the tightness in my voice. "Who knows what a woman like you would do if you knew where I resided."

Her jaw falls open, but she clamps her lips together as soon as I shut the door. My car comes to life, and I rev it once while looking at her through the window. Her eye roll is so appealing that I want to press on the gas again, but before I can manage, she turns and stomps in the direction of her own car.

I should drive away and hope that's the last time I come into contact with her, but something keeps me inside my Audi with it idling. Every few seconds, I glance into my rearview mirror to get a glimpse of where she's going.

Before I can stop myself, I shift into reverse and back out slowly after she speeds off. I follow her taillights like a full-fledged stalker because there's something *so* fucking enticing about her. Scottie is bold, but there is something below the surface that contradicts it.

I want to know why she was so desperate for money that she conned me into meeting her in an empty bathroom only to apologize seconds later. Or why she came all the way over here on a chilly night, well after the sun had set, to clear her name and offer me advice on a security system.

And where the fuck is she going now?

My foot plays with the brake as I trail her sad little car that is one pothole away from losing a tire. I keep enough distance so she doesn't realize I'm several cars behind her, but the farther we go downtown, the more my Audi stands out like a sore thumb.

My agent warned me that this part of Chicago was not for the fainthearted and reiterated I should avoid it at all costs. The road is becoming darker with broken streetlights, and the sidewalks are overgrown with weeds popping up through the many cracks. The houses are run-down to the point of demolishment, most with broken windows and plastic wrap flying with the gusts of wind.

Sweat covers my palms as I grip the steering wheel and park off to the side, refusing to go any farther. I squint when Scottie seemingly has the same thought and parks several cars ahead of me.

I watch her get out of her car while holding something in her arms.

A blanket?

A tent?

Fuck, is she homeless?

I sit up a little taller in my seat and almost get out of my car to follow her, but she stops right in front of a group of people standing mindlessly in the middle of the road. It's right out of a movie: a steel trash can with a small fire inside burns brightly, and what appears to be several homeless people huddle around it to catch some warmth.

Their faces light up when they see Scottie, like she's the little moon on their dark night. My jaw slacks with confusion when I see her handing out...*coats*?...to each one of them. She even helps some of them as they struggle to pull the warm jackets over their bony bodies.

Jesus.

What is it with this woman?

The cool night air wraps around my tense shoulders when I climb out of my car and step onto the sidewalk. I lean against the side of the hood, checking my back a few times to make sure no one is sneaking up on me, and continue to watch Scottie hand out coats to the homeless. Some are lying on the cold sidewalk, and my heart catches when she takes the fabric and drapes it over their sleeping bodies.

I duck down when she spins and heads for her car, but I slowly stand back up when I see her pause mid-step. She looks over her shoulder, and I follow her line of sight with a weird sense of protection backing my moves.

To my surprise, it's a severely malnourished woman. Her arms are exposed, and they resemble toothpicks. She smiles when Scottie turns all the way around, and even from the distance separating us, I count several missing teeth.

Scottie's steps are hesitant as she moves closer. My fist clenches when she jolts backward after the woman tries to reach for her, but deep down, I know Scottie is a lot more resilient than I originally gave her credit for. The woman's hands lower, and she nods in Scottie's direction.

What happens next confuses the hell out of me.

Scottie's shoulders are exposed first and then her bare arms. She shimmies out of her jacket and holds it out for the woman to take.

As soon as the woman has it, my little culprit rushes back to her car.

She's long gone before I'm even inside mine.

The entire ride back to my house, I can't help but come up with all kinds of different scenarios about Scottie—all of which make me want to find out more.

Nine

SCOTTIE

"HOW ARE YOU DOING?"

I make a face at myself in the mirror with the amount of blush I have on my cheeks and try rubbing to blend it a little more. My brother takes too long to answer my question, and heat starts to make its way down my barely-clothed body.

"*William.*" There's an authoritative tic to my voice that I acquired the moment I practically adopted him.

"I'm..."

I lower my hand, forgetting all about my too-pink cheeks. "Hey, talk to me."

"I need more money," he blurts.

My lips part, and I want to be angry and resentful, but how can I? To say my brother is naive is putting it lightly. He doesn't understand social cues like others, and the only person to blame for that is my mother. I may not have noticed the alcohol she consumed while pregnant because I was too young to do so, but over the years, I've researched enough to know who's responsible.

The only problem with suspecting William has Fetal Alcohol Spectrum Disorder is that it is highly complicated to diagnose,

63

especially if you are without health insurance. To make matters worse, the only advocate William has is *me*. I still remember the moment I met with my high school principal and guidance counselor during conferences. They were expecting a parent to show, not William's barely older sister who was still a student herself.

FASD requires multiple assessments. It's a complex disease, and now that William is a legal adult and currently in prison, the chances of anyone listening to my pleas for help are long gone until I can at least get him out.

Something has to change. Otherwise, William will continue to walk down the wrong path, and I'll be in debt for the rest of my life, spending every day trying to protect him from people who use and abuse him. Spoiler alert: the men inside that prison will use anyone they can, and unfortunately, William is the weakest link.

"What do you mean you need more money?" I ask, holding my finger up to Kitty.

She comes over to blend in my blush a little more and adjusts my pink bra strap.

"Give me one sec," I whisper.

"I'll cover for you." Kitty disappears, and I know it's to distract Russ before he comes hunting me down to get on stage.

"My friend Ike needs money," William says.

Anger surfaces. "Well, tell your *friend* to get his own money."

"But I owe him."

It doesn't take a genius to understand that owing someone in prison isn't a good thing. Just like it doesn't take a genius to recognize that these friends of William are manipulating him and—oh, that's right—*using* him, which is ironically the same thing that landed him in prison.

I pinch the bridge of my nose. "What do you mean you

owe him? Just because someone tells you that you owe them, doesn't mean that you actually do."

"He protected me."

My heart sinks. *I should be the one protecting him.*

When I say nothing, William clears his throat, and I swear, he still sounds like that little eight-year-old boy who came home naked because a boy at school manipulated him into taking the clothes right off his back. "Someone was messing with me, and Ike stepped in. Scottie, I'm...I'm afraid. I don't like it here."

I drop my head and shut my eyes. I give myself approximately three seconds to get my shit together, and then I pop back up and level my voice. "I know you don't. I'm doing everything I can to get you out, but with having to pay the lawyer fees, keep a roof over my head, feed myself, and put money on your books, it's... I can't keep up."

"Cherry!" I jump. *Shit.* "Listen, I gotta go. I'll see what I have leftover to put on your books. Check back tomorrow. I love you. Remember what I've taught you about people, okay?"

"Scottie, wait."

I nibble on my lower lip and rush over to the side door. Russ is going to come get me any second now.

"If anyone comes by—"

"Cherry. Get out there! What are you doing?" Russ comes around the bend in the hallway, red-faced and sweaty.

I end the call quickly, not because I'm afraid of my boss but more so because I can't lose my job.

Not now, anyway.

"Sorry," I mutter.

He curses under his breath and mumbles something about me being lucky that I'm hot. My stomach churns, and I wonder what Russ would do if I threw up on his shoes. Actually, he'd probably still bark at me to get on stage and then force me to clean up my own vomit after my shift.

I pull back the curtain, level my shoulders, and quickly morph into *Cherry the Stripper* instead of *Scottie the Desperate*.

––––––

ONE HOUR LEFT until my shift is over and done with. Russ always puts me on the first shift and saves the veterans for the late hours, knowing they're the ones willing to go above and beyond. To do what? I'm not exactly sure. But considering it's behind the doors labeled *private*, I have a pretty good idea.

"Hey, babe?" I turn and meet Chastity's furrowed brow across the short distance between poles.

"Yeah?" I breathe out.

"Some guy is asking about you."

I quickly look around the Cat House, weaving in and out of the strobe lights that give me a headache, and half expect to see one of the hockey players, even though they had a game.

"Where?"

Chastity's bottom lip juts forward. "Hmm, I don't know where he went. He was staring at you for a long time, though. I'm surprised you didn't notice him."

Of course I didn't notice. I go fully internal each time I'm on the stage.

Surprisingly, the next hour flies by, and although Chastity and I have been watching for the mystery man, we both come up empty-handed. I climb off the stage with a bra full of cash and practically skip to my car after changing. I secretly check the stats of the hockey game on my phone and smile to myself when I see that the Devils won again. Not wanting to use too much of my data, I quickly power down my phone and slip it into my bag.

The parking lot is dark and eerie because Russ is too lazy to replace the lightbulbs out back, and he's too cheap to hire any security to escort us to our cars. Some would say that Russ doesn't care about his employees, and as I walk to my car in the pitch black without an ounce of protection, I'd say they are right.

"Cheap ass," I mumble under my breath.

Usually, I have one of the other girls with me, and I occasionally give them a ride home, but tonight it's just me.

I open my bag to grab my keys but stop as soon as I hear the crunching of gravel. I glance down, and I'm on the flat asphalt without even a pebble nearby.

"Is someone there?"

Seriously, Scottie?

Suddenly, I'm the star of a horror film. Now who isn't reading social cues correctly?

I firmly grip my keys and slip the pointiest one through my first and second finger while making a fist. I quickly revisit the hazy lesson my father taught me when I was young on how to punch correctly, and though I've had to latch onto the memory a few times throughout my life, it isn't a skill I naturally possess.

I can pretend, though.

Spinning with the wind, I hold my hand to my chest and look at my surroundings. Shutter, the stray cat that won't disappear because I continue to feed it, scurries into the alley in fear, and it causes the hair along my neck to stand.

"Scottie Monroe?"

The voice comes from the left, and I turn a little too fast and lose my footing. Two hands catch me by my upper arms, and when we come face-to-face, a chill races to the soles of my feet. His eyes flash with something dangerous, and the first thing I notice is the tattoo peeking up from the collar of his long-sleeve shirt.

"Get your hands off me," I demand, proud that I sound confident. All those years of fending off mom's boyfriends are paying off. Thankfully, it wasn't all for nothing.

The man chuckles, and it sounds like he has a throat full of loose gravel. "Relax, princess."

I growl and fling his hands off me. He goes willingly, but in between choppy laughs, he manages to let me know why he's at my place of employment. "I'm here to make sure you got the message to pay."

My first thought is my mom. But she's too far off to even recall she has a daughter half the time, so that leaves one person. I think back to the phone call from William, and there's a sadness lingering that I can't get rid of.

"Let me guess." I feel defeated. "You know Ike?"

He snaps his finger at me. "You betcha."

"Tomorrow." I swallow my pride. "I'll add money onto William's books tomorrow."

Gravel crunches, and I shove my fist with my key pointing out like a weapon into the gaping space between us. "Don't come closer."

My vision blurs, and my heart skyrockets. Heat pools in my lower stomach, but I'm cold at the same time. The guy's hands go up in defense, but when I look back at his face, I realize he isn't looking at me. He's looking past my shoulder.

I sigh in relief.

It's about freaking time Russ starts being a decent boss.

My hand lowers, and I peer behind my shoulder. Except, I don't come face-to-face with my slimy boss who apparently still doesn't care about me or the rest of the girls walking to their cars at night.

It's Emory Olson.

And for the first time since meeting him, he isn't looking at me with that familiar tinge of vengeance. He's looking at the stranger instead.

Ten

EMORY

DOES Scottie really think she can hurt someone with her keys in her fist like that? Part of me wanted to stay back in the shadows a little longer to see her take a swing, but my body reacted without my brain's approval.

The whites of her eyes grow large when I continue to erase the distance between us. Her soft lips part with confusion, and I hope she has some sort of intelligence behind that pretty face, because if she doesn't play along, then I may just find myself in the same position I was in before moving out to Chicago.

The fuck you will.

I grip the thought like a lifeline because I owe this deceiving little cheat nothing, even if she does hand out coats to the homeless after dark. One good deed does not forego the rest.

My arm slides around her waist, and although she's as tense as the pole with the broken light three feet behind us, she doesn't push me away or try to key me instead of the stranger. "Is there a problem here?" I ask, staring at the man across from Scottie.

71

"You her bodyguard or something?" he jokes, slipping his hands into his pockets.

My heart pounds, and if Kane doesn't come out of those front doors soon, I'm going to beat the living shit out of him —new teammate or not. Honestly, Coach would probably thank me after because Kane has been a real shit lately. He plays good hockey, but he's a little fucked up in the head— hence why I had to crawl out of my bed right after falling asleep to come get his drunk ass. He called me because he knew I'd come, being the newbie and all.

To have the energy to go to a strip club and drink copious amounts of alcohol after a close game like the one we just had is almost unheard of. But then again, the fans have labeled Kane as an animal, and he's all about proving them right.

"Bodyguard?" I repeat, pulling Scottie in a little closer. My large hand covers her shaking fist, and I slowly push it down. Even through the shadows, I see the fire burning bright in her blue eyes, but I was right: she does have a brain, because she lets me take full control of the situation. I turn back to the man and watch him assess my stature before looking me in the face again.

I raise an eyebrow, and I know he's thinking very carefully on what to say to me next.

Scottie clears her throat which pulls his gaze back to her. "Tomorrow," she says.

What's tomorrow? Is she meeting up with him tomorrow? Who is this scumbag? Her boyfriend?

My jaw clicks. I came over here because I apparently didn't learn my lesson the first time I stepped into an argument or altercation that had nothing to do with me, but now that I'm over here, I'm reminded very quickly why I should drop Scottie's weaponed hand and walk away.

When I begin to loosen my grip, the man begins to back away. "Tomorrow," he repeats, looking from Scottie to me.

My chest loosens as soon as he disappears into the thick night, and I finally drop her hand. She turns just as quickly, and her sparkly, makeup-coated eyes narrow on me, as if *I'm* the problem.

"What are you doing here?" she snaps.

A sarcastic chuckle tumbles out of my mouth. "Apparently, protecting you."

Her irritated glare does nothing but cause my lip to twitch.

"Excuse me?" Scottie's arms cross, hiding some of her tattered Chicago Blue Devils sweatshirt. The team's old logo is worn and faded, and if I were a better man, I'd take my jacket off and give it to her because I watched her give her jacket away to a homeless woman the other night, but that feels like some sort of truce, and I wouldn't want her to get the wrong idea.

If I give her an inch, she'll probably try to take a mile, and I'm not really in the giving mood.

Not with her.

"I didn't need your help!" She flips her sandy locks behind her shoulder with attitude.

I click my tongue. "Mmm, yeah you did." I tip my chin at the set of keys still in her hand. "Were you going to...key him?"

Her cheeks ripen with heat. "That's none of your business."

Suddenly, I'm met with her backside as she starts to head for the back lot. Her hips sway for a few steps before she rethinks walking in the same direction as the mystery guy. She turns, and our eyes meet. "Why are you here?"

"That's none of *your* business," I repeat.

Her shoulders slowly drop, like her guard is falling. I should turn and head inside for Kane and leave her to her own weapons for whatever lurks in the dark, but my mouth opens instead, and it tells her right away that I'm curious.

"Was that your boyfriend?"

Scottie seems shocked.

I raise an eyebrow. "And don't say none of your business."

She crosses her arms again, and if it wasn't obvious before —when she was prepared to punch a man—that she's feisty, the stance she's giving me now makes it clear. Her hip pops with sass, and the confidence in her tone is *so* enticing that I crave to knock her down a few levels.

"But it really isn't your business," she says.

I grip the back of my neck and give it a squeeze. "Yeah, but you tried to blackmail me, so I think you kind of owe me..." Her eyes narrow. "Don't you agree?"

Silence is shared between us, and the more we stare at one another, the more I feel like we have each other in a chokehold. I have to force myself not to look away and allow my eyes to travel over her soft features and perfect body, because that'd give her the wrong idea, and I can't let that happen.

Scottie is the first to break. Her arms drop by her sides in defeat. "No," she whispers. "He's not my boyfriend."

Just then, there's a commotion behind me, and out comes Kane—flying like a fucking bird in the dead of night. He lands with a thud on top of the gravel. I pinch the bridge of my nose and curse under my breath.

Graduating from college and entering the pros, you'd think this behavior would stop. I was a partygoer and often found a new girl every weekend while attending Bexley U, but I grew up.

Unfortunately, Kane hasn't.

I bark at the bouncer. "Watch it!" If he injures Kane, we're going to have an even harder time with our schedule.

"Tell him to keep his hands to himself, and I will."

Irritation skims the surface, and with Scottie's light footsteps behind me as I walk over to Kane, I can't help the next thing pushing past my scowl. "Don't act all protective over the girls now when you can't even walk some of them to their car in the dead of night." I inch my chin to Scottie, knowing she's behind me, and busy myself with helping Kane to his feet.

He's groaning and moaning, complaining of sore muscles, which is likely from the game and not from the WWE wannabe who just threw him to the hard ground.

"Let's go, you fucking idiot," I mutter, putting an arm around his torso.

I ignore Scottie and the wannabe bouncer having a hushed conversation. I'm sure she's telling him that she's fine and she doesn't need someone to walk her to her car at night after her shift, but I disagree.

I'm breathing heavily by the time I get Kane into the passenger seat of my car, and when I turn around, there she is, standing with her arms crossed over her chest and a knowing look on her pretty little face.

"So that's why you're here."

I grip the top of the door and allow my anger with Kane to fuel my tone. "Did you think I was here for you or something?"

Scottie's eyes narrow for a split second. "Of course not."

I sarcastically laugh under my breath. "Was that a look of disappointment on your face I just saw?"

She gasps, and I have to force myself not to grin. "What? No!"

I shrug. "It's a good thing I came. Otherwise, you'd probably be arrested for keying a man or..."

The rest of my sentence disappears with the gust of wind because, whoever that man was, she felt the need to protect herself. There's an urgent need to press her further, but I refuse to act interested because *I'm not.*

Scottie and I both give our attention to Kane because he pokes his head out of the car, and his drunken gaze lands on her. "Emory. Is this your...girlfriend? Introduce me. She's hot."

"For fuck's sake," I mumble.

It's like Ford and I never went to opposite sides of the United States. I'm somehow still dealing with an idiot.

"Just...shut up," I stress, pushing on his chest to make him sit back in his seat.

His hand lands on my wrist, and I flex it beneath his half grip. "Wait. Is she your *wife*? You're married, aren't you? I wish I had a wife. Wait, why are there so many rumors about you and other women, then? That doesn't make sense. Are you cheating on her?"

A rush of something hot flies through my body. Irritation? Embarrassment? Anger? Over my shoulder, I glance at Scottie, and when our gazes crash, I quickly shut the door on Kane and round the front of my car.

Right before I escape to the driver's seat, I hear her soft voice, free of any anger or attitude. "Thank you."

The change in my center console rattles when I slam my door. I grind my teeth together.

Kane slurs under his breath. "She seems sweet. I like her. Don't cheat on her."

It takes everything in me not to punch him square in the jaw.

It takes everything in me not to punch myself square in the jaw too, because instead of peeling out of the parking lot and leaving Scottie be, I squint through the darkness and watch her walk all the way to her shitty car to make sure she gets there safe.

Eleven

SCOTTIE

FOUR CUPS OF COFFEE, a cold shower, and one biscotti later and I'm still exhausted from my nighttime adventure with a scowling goalie who irks me in every way. My hands shake too much to apply the lipstick, so I hand it to Hunter with a sigh.

"Nervous tonight?"

"Nouh," I try to answer with my mouth forming an O as she smears lipstick on my lips. When she's finished, I talk normally. "I'm tired, so I drank too much caffeine."

"You should try speed, girl," Hunter says.

Kitty pops in to defend me, like usual. "She doesn't do that stuff, and we all know it. Stop trying to pressure her."

Hunter rolls her eyes. "It was just a suggestion. Chill."

"It was a shitty one," Chastity mumbles from a few mirrors down.

Despite the stigma that strippers have, they aren't as bad as everyone makes them out to be. We all have our own story and reasons for ending up at the Cat House. Most women hate us —or the idea of us—and the men look at us like we're their next meal, but it pays the bills.

Kind of.

My bank account is a little less now that I was forced to put more money on William's books because of my visitor last night.

Chills cover my arms.

I rub at the tiny bumps on my skin and get ready for my shift, trying my best to ignore the pit in my stomach. Fear brews beneath my nerves, and it stays there for the next two hours as I move seductively, getting showered with dollar bills.

My rent is due soon, I'm living on ramen noodles, the water coming from my kitchen sink tastes funky, and I got another notice from the law firm.

"I'm fine," I quietly mutter to myself. My hands fall to the pole, and I do a back hook spin while watching Chastity disappear with a man with gelled hair and a suit that could pay my rent for the year into one of the private rooms. Envy makes itself known. If I were willing to do that, I'd make so much more money.

But I'd never.

"You *are* fine," a man mumbles.

Our eyes meet, and I can already tell that he's slimy.

I purposefully stay on the left side of the pole in case he gets any wild ideas and tries to touch me.

He grumbles when I don't reply. "What? No thank you?"

I smirk, and I know it comes off as flirty, but on the inside, I picture myself levitating over the bar and kicking him right in the mouth with my heel.

My long hair touches the floor of the platform when I tip my hips to the ceiling for an inside leg hang. Once I feel the pole dig into the side of my torso, I wrap my inside leg and slide my hand against the metal to spin slowly to the other side of the pole. Fire zips through me when I feel a tug on my fake auburn hair, and I nearly slip when I realize it's the man.

"There's a no-touch rule," I remind him, feeling the blood rush to my head.

He pulls tighter, burying his fingers under my hair. "None of the other girls tell me not to touch them."

This asshole.

Panic surfaces, and I fearfully search the Cat House for Chastity. She'll break this guy's arm if she needs to. Harry, my favorite bouncer, is at the door with his back to me, and *shit, just let go.*

Profanity threatens to slice through my pursed lips, and there's an instinct promising to show itself if he doesn't let go of me within the next few seconds, which will likely lead to me getting fired, and then I'll really be shit out of luck.

I open my mouth to try and convince him to let go of me, but before I can mutter a single word, he does so on his own. I breathe out a sigh of relief and am tempted to take his shot glass and down the liquor in it before slamming it on his head, but instead, I play nice and smile sweetly. "Thank you."

He leans back in his seat and crosses his arms over his obvious beer belly. "Now you owe me."

Emory pops into my head with the recent memory of those exact words coming from his mouth. Although I'm not proud of it, and I wouldn't admit it aloud, I keep thinking of him while I take commands from a patron that needs to be thrown out for even thinking that I owe him. Picturing Emory is much better than the alternative.

"Show me your best moves, baby."

The song changes, and I know it's my cue to climb down and take my break. I slide past him, but when his hand reaches out and slips around my waist, I stop breathing. "Want to go to a private room?"

My refusal cuts through my panic before I have room to think. "No."

"No?"

If I wasn't pissed off and trying to remain calm, I'd laugh at the audacity of this man.

"She can't go to a private room with you."

I jerk with a spin, causing the man's callused hands to rub against my bare skin. Blinking through my shock doesn't help my confusion even in the slightest. Emory stands no more than three feet in front of me with a tense jaw and a gaze lasered on the hand against my waist.

"Why can't she?" the man asks, gripping me a little tighter.

I move past Emory's death glare and try to catch the eye of Harry, but with Emory's height and broad shoulders, I can't see anything, even with heels on.

"Because..." Emory steps forward, and my heart races. "I already booked her for the night."

"What?!" I blurt.

There's a pinch on my skin from the man squeezing me tighter, and I wince. Emory's eyebrow arches, and I swear his jaw becomes as sharp as a knife. "Let go of her."

Violence edges within his tone, and the only thing that races through my head is the sports commentators' voices and how they constantly bring up Emory's arrest for assault that led him here, to my hometown.

I'm seconds from stepping on this man's toe with my heel, but he proves that he's smarter than he looks, because he lets go at the last second. I stumble forward, landing with a thud against Emory's hard chest. He snaps his hands to my forearms, gripping them roughly. Yet, for some reason, they feel safe.

I glance over my shoulder, and the man scoffs, as if he's waiting for me to refuse going into the private room with Emory.

Which, I do.

But not because I'm trading him out for the perv behind me.

I turn toward Emory. He's wearing a hat, likely because people are beginning to recognize him, but I can still see the challenge in his blue eyes. "I'm not going into a private room with you," I say quietly.

His lips twitch. "Yes, you are."

"I am *not* that type of woman, despite where I work." Anger heats my skin, and by the looks of it, Emory enjoys seeing me all riled up.

The breath leaves my lungs when his hands drag down my forearms and land on my hips. He pulls me in closer, and the entire Cat House disappears.

My heart races with his touch, and when he leans in closer to whisper in my ear, I black out. "You either go in that room with me, or I leave you with him, Rogue."

I have to force myself to speak. "Rogue?"

A warm gust of his breath hits the side of my face with his deep chuckle. "Yes, *Rogue.* You're my little swindler, Scottie, and don't forget that you owe me."

"And you think I'm going to pay you back with sex?!" I try to keep my voice down, but I'm near hysterics.

People are starting to stare at our embrace, and if I wasn't so stubborn, I'd just follow him in that stupid room and refuse there, but I'm headstrong, and that's something that will never change.

Emory tenses. "What? No. *Jesus.* Will you just trust me and accept that I'm trying to help you?"

"I don't trust anyone."

"Neither do I," he snaps back. "Especially you. But you don't have a choice. Your options are limited."

I peek over my shoulder once more, and it only takes me half a second to succumb to Emory. "Fine," I hiss.

Emory snorts. "That wasn't so hard now, was it?"

I roll my eyes and his flare. The muscles along his jaw

flicker before a swallow moves down his throat. "Now take my hand and lead me to one of the rooms."

I do as he says but mumble under my breath. "You're so bossy."

"I'm not bossy. I just know what I want."

A totally uncalled swarm of butterflies fills my stomach as I enter a completely make-believe world of utter bullshit where a guy like Emory Olson would *ever* want a girl like me—one with enough baggage to weigh us both down to the point that we couldn't even move a pinky toe.

Get a grip, Scottie.

Emory obviously wants something from me, and he's already made it clear that it isn't to force me into prostitution.

I quickly shake my head at Chastity when she gives me a strange look as I drag Emory to a private room. As soon as we're inside, I drop his hand, and he shuts the door, locking it behind us.

It's the same room we found ourselves in the first time he cornered me at my place of employment. I guess that's our thing. I cornered him at the hockey arena, and he's cornering me at the strip club. What a pair.

I gulp as soon as he turns toward me. His ego takes up the entire room, and I want to beg for some space to breathe, but he doesn't even give me an inch.

"Cameras," I blurt.

He flips his hat backward and shows off each one of his stony features. "What?"

I flick my chin to the corner of the room. "There are cameras in here, so if you try anything, I'll have proof."

Emory drops his head and laughs under his breath. "You're all about proof, aren't you, Rogue?"

The insult stings because I'm not proud of what I did—or attempted to do—but it's warranted, so I say nothing.

Emory slowly stalks toward me, and I stay completely still.

If I were locked in this room with anyone else, I'd panic. I hardly know Emory, and there is some hesitation lingering, but he doesn't stir up unwanted memories of being in a locked room with a stranger. I don't feel safe, but I don't feel threatened either.

"Are the cameras for your protection or for your boss to get off on his girls seducing other men?" Emory asks, standing no more than a foot away from me.

I can't help but laugh. Emory's eyebrows hitch.

"I can assure you it's the latter. Russ doesn't care about our protection."

The grinding of Emory's jaw echoes throughout the near silent room. His eyes slice to the chair in the center of the room. "Then I guess we better give the asshole a show."

He must see the protest on my face, because before I can refuse, he steps in close, grips my chin, and tilts my face to his. "You were desperate enough to destroy my career for money, so don't tell me you're not desperate enough to give me a lap dance to quiet your boss so I can tell you exactly why I'm here."

My voice breaks with obvious desperation. "Why are you here?"

Emory smirks, and I hate that it's so hot. I stand back and watch him stride over to the chair. When he takes a seat, somehow looking hotter than any man at the Cat House, in his backward hat, casual black hoodie, and jeans, he chuckles. "Dance and I'll tell you."

Twelve

EMORY

I'M COOL, calm, and collected.

My heart is beating out of my chest, but that's only because I want to strangle Scottie's boss because what kind of man puts cameras in the private rooms to watch the strippers with their clients? All I can picture is a sweaty man with his dick in his hand, beating off while watching a ton of monitors in his stuffy office.

The racing of my heart has nothing to do with Scottie standing in front of me only wearing two very revealing pieces of fabric. One for her round, perky breasts and the other hardly covering her perfect ass. I'll admit that she's hiding more of herself than some of the women in this establishment, but that's probably why every man's eyes are drawn to her instead of the others.

At least she leaves something to the imagination.

Not much, but there's a dark part of me that begs to see her nipples hidden by the lacey material.

I brush the thought off and get back on track.

"Dance, little Rogue. Or else your boss is going to be disappointed." I lean back in the chair a little more and spread my legs, appearing relaxed and completely unbothered by her standing there half naked. My thighs are tight from practice, and my neck has a knot in it bigger than the one that formed in my core when I made the decision to come back here to propose an absolutely insane idea.

When Ford says an idea is crazy, you know it's damn near close to being certifiable.

But desperate times call for desperate measures.

All of a sudden, the lights dim, and Scottie lets out a shaky sigh. Music starts to play from somewhere, and I'm back to picturing her boss sitting at his desk with his hand in his pants. He's clearly ready for a show if he's controlling the lights and music.

Scottie slowly strides over the floor, and to my surprise, she keeps her eyes pinned to mine. They flare with something wildly inviting, and it's like, all of a sudden, she's flipped a switch. Her hands land on my shoulders, and she straddles my legs. Her hips start to sway back and forth, and it takes every ounce of my willpower not to grip her tightly around the waist and succumb to the sensuality that she's putting off.

Fuck her for being so goddamn alluring.

I don't look away because what kind of man would I be if I refused a challenge? Scottie dancing on top of me is like my own personal trial into heaven. If I fall for the temptation, I'll go straight to hell.

My lazy gaze falls to her breasts spilling out from her dark bra, and I have the sudden urge to rip that fake hair off her head to see her blonde locks. *Shit.* I force myself to picture her boss at his desk with his hand in his pants so I can keep my dick under control. I silently remind myself of how backstabbing this little sexy thing can be and get on with the real reason I'm here.

"Tell me why you need money." It's not a question, and I expect an answer.

"Are you going to tell me why you're here?" she refutes, swaying with the music. The low lights paint her in seductive shadows, accentuating the dips and valleys of her curves, and I can't stop staring.

I grind my teeth together. "As soon as you tell me why you need money."

Scottie stops moving for a second, and my heart skips a beat. "That wasn't the deal."

I lean farther back into my seat, and it accidentally brings her in closer.

Oops.

My hands land on her hips out of reaction. I peer up at her and force the words out. "Turn around."

She wants to refuse. There's a streak of defiance in her that I want to stroke in the worst way, but instead of telling me no, she follows my command, and I really fucking hate that it turns me on.

I tip my head backward after one quick glimpse of her ass. The panties are cut in the right spot, and the curve of her cheeks makes my hands tingle.

"Do you need money because of that guy last night?"

Scottie pauses for a quick second before swaying with the music again.

I reach up and give her red wig a little tug, and she sends me a death glare over her shoulder. I smirk. "You've seen me play hockey... I refuse to lose. So answer my question."

Scottie's ribs expand with a heavy breath right before she takes off her wig and drops it to the floor. She sends her blonde waves tumbling down her back with a tip of her head. My stomach tenses when she erases the space between us and sits on my semi-hard dick, rubbing herself over me.

I should tell her to stop.

I should just take her by the hand and walk us both out of this establishment because there's no way she'll pick working as a stripper after I present her my deal, but damn, I don't want her to stop.

I'm having too much fun with this little game I'm playing, and it's been way too long since I've had my dick in a woman. My hand gets the job done, but it's hard to remember that with her like this.

"I need money for a lot of reasons," she finally answers. "Now tell me what you want and why you're forcing me to give you a lap dance."

I snort. "I'm not forcing you to do anything. My hands aren't even on you."

In fact, they're behind my head as I relax into the chair and let her do her thing. It feels a little degrading to make her dance instead of just laying out my plans before both of us head out the front door, but I can't let her off *that* easy.

Not after she tried to force me into giving her money.

Scottie spins with the change of the song and peers at me through thick eyelashes surrounding her pretty blue eyes. Her lip disappears behind her teeth, and I want to smear the red lipstick off her lips in the worst way, because as sexy as she is like this, I liked her better with hardly any makeup on and wearing a faded Blue Devils sweatshirt.

I tip my chin and stare right into her eyes. My hands slowly come out from behind my head, and I rest them on her waist. Hers land on my shoulders and eventually move to my nape where she grabs the short ends of my hair.

My fingers dig into her bare belly as the words leave my mouth. "Marry me."

Scottie freezes. Her eyebrows furrow, and there's a faint popping sound from her lip slipping out from behind her teeth.

It only takes a few seconds for her entire body to stiffen. The pretty blue color of her eyes hardens to ice, and she snarls. "Are you kidding? Is this some type of payback?"

Her warm breath fans against my face with her angry scoff. I grip her harder and pull her in close. "Sit," I demand.

"No."

Why is that word so enticing coming from her mouth? Her defiance is a temptation like no other.

I force her into my lap, and I'm prepared for her to either scream or slap me, but I rush the words out before she can do anything. "I'm not kidding. Just hear me out, Scottie. You at least owe me that."

I watch her delicate shoulders loosen, and she scoots forward over my dick, erasing most of the space between us. Her fingers dig into my hair again, and she pulls harder. "Fine. But I will bite you if you're just fucking with me, Olson."

A chuckle flies out of my mouth. "Keep moving over me, or your ex-boss isn't going to get off to our little show."

"*Ex*-boss?" she asks, grinding over me a little faster.

My attention falls to the emptiness between us, and there's a part of me that wonders if she's as turned on as I am. I won't admit it out loud, because there is a deep-rooted part of me that hates her, but apparently, there's a very fine line between hate and lust.

I make my way back to her face and keep a hold of her stare. "If you're going to be my wife, you will not be working here."

"Who said I'm going to be your wife?" she scoffs lightly, pulling on the ends of my hair again.

My fingers retaliate, and I squeeze her hips. "Your desperation. You need money. I need a wife. So, I'm here to make a deal."

Scottie leans down and moves to the side of my neck, still putting on her little show. Her mouth moves to my ear. "Why do you need a wife?"

"To stop all the bullshit rumors," I answer, staring directly at the doorknob, praying her boss will walk in here so I'm forced to stop this little cat-and-mouse game we're playing. "I need someone to help fix my reputation. If I have a wife, and some elaborate backstory of our life and relationship, then it'll stop all the gossip and the never-fucking-ending women making rumors up to get money out of me."

Scottie pulls back immediately because I've obviously struck a chord. I meant to, hoping it'll remind her of the entire reason we're in this situation to begin with.

"You think a stripper from the Cat House marrying you is the end-all, be-all?" Her confusion is valid.

I shake my head. "I think a woman who gives out coats to the homeless late at night who fell in love with a hotheaded guy like me and waited until I finished college and reached my dreams is."

Of course I've already worked out half of our backstory.

If I want this to work, I have to be prepared to see it through.

Surprise flickers across her features. "How do you know—"

I cut her off. "It's not important. Yes or no, Scottie?"

I've gotta admit, this is probably the most romantic way anyone has ever asked a woman to marry them. A forced lap dance in a strip club, with a prenup, NDA, and a contract waiting to be signed in my car.

What can I say?

I'm a romantic at heart.

Thirteen

SCOTTIE

MY STOMACH FALLS.

Marry me.

I've dreamt of those two words for as long as I can remember. When I used to play make-believe as a child, I'd almost always end up acting out my favorite scene. The one where my Barbie—with the half-chewed hand from its previous owner's pet—would marry Ken, and they'd live happily ever after. But that was all make-believe, and whatever this plan is that Emory has conjured up in his head is just that: make-believe.

I climb off Emory's lap quickly, almost falling over in my stupid heels. I'm full of unease, and my cheeks are hot with humiliation.

"Get out," I demand, wishing my tone was full of fury instead of embarrassment. My arms cross as soon as Emory's nostrils flare. "I get it," I say. "You're still angry about what I did. But my life is *not* a joke, so stop fucking with me and get out."

Here comes the fury.

My voice rises, and my heart thumps with frustration. It's not even directed toward him. I'm angry that I had to put money on William's books that I was putting away for lawyer fees. I'm angry that I'm still feeling sick over seeing my mother the other night. I'm angry that I was pelted in the face this morning with water from the leak in my ceiling. And to make things worse...I'm fucking hungry.

Emory's eyes dip down my body lazily before he comes back up and reaches my fiery gaze. Something unreadable flashes across his face, and the only thing it does is make my stomach flop. "This isn't a joke, and I'm not fucking with you."

I huff. "You want me to be your *wife*?" The word falls from my mouth like it's poison. I can hardly say it. "Are you crazy?"

He smirks. "All goalies are crazy."

It's true. They get a bad rep, and Emory's just keeps getting worse. But *still*.

"You obviously have no problem making things up..." He shrugs. "And it's clearly not difficult to photoshop pictures."

It isn't easy for most, but for someone who has taught herself photography and read every book the library offered, it is.

Emory slowly stands up, and my arms fall to my sides.

"What's in it for me?" I ask, hating that I'm actually considering it. *Am I the crazy one?* I can't randomly marry a pro hockey player and go along with this entire made-up story about us.

Can I?

Emory's wearing a cheeky grin, but the only thing I can focus on is the blue color of his eyes. Either he's a very good liar or he's actually as crazy as I am.

"Money."

The word floats out of his mouth effortlessly, and I feel the stress melt from my body. I'd be a fool not to take him up on his offer—if it were real.

"And you expect me to believe you?" I look around the room for a camera, other than the one Russ is probably staring at with anger because I'm no longer dry humping Emory. "I don't trust you."

Emory's snicker echoes around the room. "And you think I trust you?"

Ouch.

I narrow my eyes to hide my hurt. "Yet you want to marry me?"

His nod is more of a quick jab. "Contract is in the car."

Oh, God. He *is* serious.

My eyes bounce back and forth between his sharp blue ones. I'm balancing over the edge of insanity and actually considering this.

Emory takes a step toward me, and as soon as his hand wraps around my waist, goosebumps fly to my skin. Fire flushes through my veins. If I say yes, it'll be like making a deal with the devil.

He peers at me with his steely gaze. "What'll it be, Rogue?"

I gulp but can't look away.

"You either leave with me or you can stay here and strip. It's not life or death..." I blink slowly. "But it seems like it is for you."

Just then, the door flies open. Emory's grip tightens around my waist, but I still manage to spin and meet the face of a sweaty Russ. He looks from me to Emory before landing back on me with a scowl.

"What are you doing?" he snaps.

My lips draw back in a snarl from his tone. This would be the perfect time to knee him right in the balls, except if this whole thing with Emory doesn't work, I'll have to come crawling back to him for a job because there aren't many other jobs—that are legal ones—that pay the way stripping does.

"What does it look like?" I cross my arms because Russ has looked at my spilling boobs three times in the last ten seconds.

"It looks like you aren't pleasing a client." Russ's pupils dilate with anger.

I feel Emory's hand tighten against me when his warm breath caresses the side of my neck. "What'll it be, Scottie? Yes or no?"

I quickly weigh my options. Stay here and slave away while fending off slimy men with no respect for me, or go with Emory and put up with his overbearing ego and annoying smirk.

My stomach drops to the floor, and my independence goes next.

I turn my head, and our lips are a breath away. "Yes."

Emory's smile sends something exciting into my chest. He removes his hold on me and grabs my hand, pulling me past Russ.

"Whoa, wait. You can't just take her!" Russ grips Emory's bicep, and it stops him in his tracks.

Ever so slowly, Emory turns and glares at my now ex-boss. The air turns cold, and Russ grows pale.

"You don't own her." Russ looks at me over his shoulder before Emory chuckles and finishes his sentence. "I do."

My spine straightens, and if Emory's grip on my hand wasn't like a padlock, I'd rip it away and tell them both that neither of them own me.

Next thing I know, I'm being rushed down the dark hallway with Russ disappearing from behind. When we round the corner, I attempt to whip my hand out of Emory's, but he pushes me up against the wall before I get a chance. My wrist is pinned above my head, and his palm cups me around the waist to keep me still.

"You got something to say, Rogue?"

I quietly hiss. "You do *not* own me, Olson."

His smirk pisses me off, and I'm suddenly rethinking my future. "You're kinda cute when you're angry."

My chest expands with frustration. Before I can say anything else, Emory lets go of my waist and places his hand on my cheek. His fingers get lost in my hair, and when his thumb gently traces my lips, I completely forget that I just agreed to be this egotistical, irritating man's fake wife.

"Let's get one thing clear, baby." Fiery butterflies swarm my stomach. Emory presses his thumb against my mouth with force and wipes off my cherry-red lipstick. "If you're going to take my last name, you will no longer be working for that man. Got it?" My head falls forward with a tug of my hair, and I wish I could snap back with some type of refusal or insult, but he has me in his clutches.

After a few seconds, he finally lets go of me, and I gasp for air. I didn't realize I was holding my breath until my vision begins to straighten. His jaw sets as he waits for my compliance, which I refuse to give.

"Tomorrow. One o'clock. At the arena. And bring a pen."

I blink twice, and he's already halfway down the hallway, walking toward the back door, leaving me standing there with smeared lipstick and spinning thoughts.

Scottie Olson.

I guess it has a ring to it.

Fourteen

EMORY

"CAN I talk to you for a few, man?"

Rhodes wipes the sweat off his forehead with the back of his hand and glances around the emptying locker room before giving me a subtle flick of his chin. I take that as his version of *yes*, so I wait a little longer, and when most of my teammates are gone, I turn and face my captain, who is impatiently leaning against the lockers with his arms crossed.

He raises his eyebrows at me.

"Do you think this team has potential?"

Rhodes narrows his gaze. He's trying to figure me out, likely wondering where this conversation is headed, but nonetheless, he takes the bait. "Two months ago? No. But now?" He shrugs. "Maybe."

I nod and rub the back of my sore shoulders before really getting down to the nitty-gritty. "I want to help bring this team's reputation back up."

Rhodes chuckles. "I think you brought it down another level when you were signed."

True.

"I think I have a plan to help my reputation, which will hopefully lead to helping the team's reputation."

Rhodes sighs. "I can't wait to hear this."

The only person who is aware of my proposal to Scottie is Ford, which in turn means Ford and Taytum, who is probably having a goddamn fit over the idea. That or they've come up with some bet to see how long it lasts until it blows up in my face. Rhodes is the captain of the team. If I have his approval, I know he'll help get the team in check if they happen to recognize her. Scottie is a bit of a mystery. I couldn't find her on social media, but that doesn't mean no one will recognize her, with or without the red hair and stripper pole.

"I'm getting married."

Rhodes blinks. I give it a few more seconds, and nope, that's the only response I get.

"I'm getting married to help my reputation and to hopefully stop the rumors. The random women spewing lies about me has to end. They're showing up at my house, and the media is running with every fucking lie, painting me to be some crazed monster with a bad temper who mishandles women. Our team is full of misfits," I say. "And after getting to know the guys and learning their skills on the ice, it's completely fucked. We can be good. We don't have to be the joke of the pros. Because believe it or not, we are."

I pause and wait to see if Rhodes has anything to add. The only thing he does is blink again, but I swear I can see his wheels turning.

"I need your help, though," I add.

Rhodes pushes off the lockers and squares his shoulders. "Let me ask you something."

I nod.

"Are you truly trying to rebuild this team's rep, or are you only worried about yourself and where you're going to go after your contract ends?"

"Both," I answer truthfully. "But who knows, maybe I'll stay here if we can get our shit together."

I feel like a child, like I'm asking for his permission. My chest fills with hope and desperation while I wait for him to grunt something out. He's either going to confirm that I'm absolutely fucking crazy, or he's going to jump on the crazy train with me.

"Why are you asking me?" he finally asks, taking a seat on the bench.

I sigh. "Because you're the captain. These guys worship you."

"But what does it have to do with you getting married?" Rhodes shakes his head. "I didn't even know you had a girlfriend."

Here we go. "That's the thing. I don't."

Silence fills the locker room. Everyone is gone, but with our two personalities in the same room, it's jam-packed with tension.

"Well, then..." He shakes his head. "Yeah. I don't get it."

"It's a contract marriage."

I snap to attention when Rhodes laughs. It's a deep sort of rumble, but he throws his head back and continues to cackle. I glare, and he shakes his head. "That's a terrible idea. You're even crazier than I thought."

"I pay her, and she'll act like my wife. She'll come to the games and sit with the other wives, post all that ridiculous relationship bullshit on my socials, be by my side for a few events..." I shrug because, truly, what could go wrong?

"It'll at least silence the media and their constant fixation on my personal life. Fixing my reputation is one step closer to fixing this team's reputation." When our eyes catch, I add more to help my case. "Think about it. No one takes this team seriously, but imagine when we continue to dominate, and they realize they were wrong about us.

Players are going to want to be on this team instead of being forced onto it."

Rhodes thinks for a few moments, and I check the time. It's almost one, and I have a feeling that my new fiancée is punctual. Not that I mind making her wait a little. It's good to let her sweat some.

"This is going to end badly," he says.

I cock a brow. "Does that mean you're on board?"

Rhodes stands and grabs his bag. When he starts to walk past me, he pauses, and his subtle nod is the only answer I need. "Tell me what you need me to do, but when it ends up like I know it will, don't come running to me for help."

My lip lifts. "You should have more faith in your goalie."

He gives me a once-over. "What do you need me to do?"

"Just make sure the rest of the team goes along with it if they recognize her."

Rhodes rolls his eyes, and I'm pretty sure he mumbles something under his breath before walking out of the locker room.

I grab my shit and head in the same direction because there's a contract that needs signing.

———

I WAS RIGHT.

Scottie is waiting for me with a cute little scowl on her face. There's a chill in the air that whips at the ends of her hair, sending the long strands flying behind her, giving way to her tense shoulders.

"Glad you could make it," I say, approaching my car.

Scottie pushes off my driver's side door, and I have to keep myself from smirking at the sound of her girly growl. "You're late."

"And yet, you still waited," I retort. "Just drives my point further."

Scottie steps away when I reach around her to open my car. She smells like honey and something sweet. I don't like it.

"What point?" she asks.

I grip my door, half inside the driver's seat. "That you're just as desperate as I thought."

A gasp escapes her mouth.

I keep my cocky grin to myself and flick my chin to the passenger side. "Get in."

She mumbles something about me opening the car door for her, and I chuckle. If this were a date, I'd be a gentleman and do exactly that. But as of right now, the contract isn't signed, and there isn't a single person around to witness anything. I have approximately twenty minutes until I have to act like her husband.

When we're both enclosed inside my car, I feel like I'm being suffocated by her sweet scent. It fucks with my head for a few seconds before she clears her throat, and I regain consciousness.

Right. *Contract.*

"I have to say..." I get comfortable in my seat, spreading my legs out some while giving her the side-eye. "I'm not surprised to see you showed up."

Scottie stares at me, looking so tiny in the passenger seat. At first, she seems angry, maybe even a little offended. But I can see right through her stony glare. There's a softness there. Something sad...and fragile.

It messes with my head just like the smell of her perfume lingering around the interior of my car does.

Quickly, I reach forward and grab the papers I had drawn up by my lawyer. Scottie shifts in her seat and eyes them like they're an invitation to hell, and to her, it very well may be.

We hardly know each other.

She's a stripper with a need for money, and I'm a pro hockey player with a hefty bank account and a desperation for a better reputation.

The top of the contract has the words *Marriage of Convenience* in bold. A thick swallow works itself down my throat before I drop the papers into her lap.

I hope she's ready to play the game.

Fifteen

Marriage of Convenience Contract Agreement between two parties for all intents and purposes of a legally binding marriage.

This agreement made on the <u>14th</u> day of <u>October</u> in the year <u>2024</u> to end in exactly one year from the signature date. Between _____ hereafter called the "Groom" and _____ hereafter called the "Bride."

The Groom and Bride enter into this agreement to provide for circumstances relating to their marriage; and both have read and agreed to the following conditions by way of initialing each item or part.

1. Bride agrees to no longer be employed at the establishment titled <u>Cat House</u>.

2. Bride agrees to move into Groom's house residing at <u>76 Hart St, Chicago, IL</u> until the end of contract date.

109

*3. Bride and Groom both agree to engage in
    physical touch and act with affection when
    in public.*

*4. Bride and Groom both agree not to engage in
    physical touch with anyone other than each
    other, so long as it is not in a sexual
    manner.*

*5. Bride agrees to take over the Groom's social
    media accounts and post appropriate
    content weekly regarding their relationship
    so long as it is in a positive manner.*

*6. Bride is able to have free rein in the home
    and do as she wishes unless an outing is
    required and/or a game, so long as it does
    not violate clause #4.*

*7. Groom agrees to pay Bride $2,500 on the first
    of every month for personal use.*

*8. Groom agrees to cover the cost of living for
    both parties including but not limited to
    mortgage, water, electricity, groceries, and
    any other household bills.*

*9. Groom agrees to pay Bride $100,000 at the
    end of contract in addition to the monthly
    stipend amount.*

———————— ————————
Scottie Monroe Emory Olson

I REREAD the contract several times and try to ignore the constant shifting from my future husband sitting beside me.

Emory leans over his center console and points to number one. "That also applies to any other strip club. I figured it was implied, but..." He shrugs. "I can have the lawyer add it in there if you wish."

I turn and glare. "That won't be necessary."

The contract crinkles in my hand as I take in the rest of the stipulations of our marriage. I tossed and turned all night long, dodging the little water droplets that kept dripping on my forehead from the leak in my ceiling. I realize that I'm crazy. I'm practically marrying a stranger for money, and that feels awfully close to prostitution.

Yet, here I am, in his car, with a pen in my shaking hand.

I point to number three. My heart beats wildly, and I completely ignore the little voice in the back of my head that wants me to believe I'm excited over the thought of him touching me. That surely cannot be the reason I'm feeling jittery all of a sudden.

"And when we're not in public?" I ask.

His eyebrows draw together. "Are you asking me if I expect you to put out for me when we're behind closed doors?"

My lips part, and nothing comes out of my mouth.

He smooths his forehead and shows me that cocky grin of his. "Or are you *asking* me to touch you behind closed doors?"

"What?" I exclaim. "N–no." I stumble over my words, and the pen slips out of my sweaty fingers. I should take it as a sign and climb out of his car, refusing to sign the contract, but when I make a decision, I stick with it. My dad always taught me to make a choice and commit to it. I never go back on my word. Ever.

Emory chuckles, and it instantly annoys me. He stretches his muscular legs again and stares out the windshield. I peek at the scruff along his jawline before he turns and our gazes crash. "I won't be touching you unless you ask me to. The rumors you hear aren't true. That's the entire reason I need a wife and for the media to believe that I'm in a committed relationship."

I relax a second later and exhale. Emory squints, and I can tell he's trying to figure me out.

Good luck, though. I can't even figure myself out.

"Everything looks fine," I finally say.

Emory nods curtly and leans over the console into my space. I drop my attention to his mouth and freeze. *Is he going to kiss me?!*

At the last second, he reaches down and scoops up the pen that's by my feet. I clench my thighs together and pray he doesn't touch me, because I'm clearly out of sorts. I quickly snatch the pen out of his hand, scribble my initials at each indicated spot before sloppily signing the bottom, and thrust the paper back into his lap.

He hands me two more pieces of paper: an NDA and a prenup.

I sign them both willingly because not only am I embarrassed that I'm marrying a man for money, but I don't want a single thing from him after it's all said and done.

I'm a simple girl.

All I want is for my brother to be taken care of and to be comfortable enough in my finances that I can finally work on building a photography portfolio instead of constantly trying to make ends meet.

I'm just *so* fucking tired.

"Well, that should do it," Emory announces, gathering the papers and tucking them away.

I nod and put my hand on the door to escape. "When do I move in?"

"Now. We have an appointment at City Hall in a few hours."

I pause with one foot on the pavement.

"I'll follow you to your place and help you gather your things."

Panic sets in. "Um, no. I can handle it."

Emory looks from me and then to my car and then back to me. "Do you live in a cardboard box? Because that's all that's going to fit in that tiny rust bucket."

My cheeks flame. "I can handle my belongings. Just give me the address to your house."

Emory holds out his hand. "Unlock your phone and give it to me."

God, he's bossy.

I place my phone in his hand and watch his face flood with confusion. "How the hell do you even see anything on this screen?"

"It's just a few cracks."

Emory shows me my phone, as if he's emphasizing how insane I am. "Just a few cracks?" He doesn't wait for me to answer. Instead, he shakes his head in disbelief and, I assume, types his number into my contacts before handing it back over.

"There. Now you have my number and address."

As soon as I reach for the phone, Emory's fingers close on mine and trap them. I jerk my gaze to his.

"That's privileged information. Don't share it with anyone."

I can't help the laugh that rushes from my mouth. His fingers tighten, and sparks crawl up my arm. "You're not the pope, Olson."

His eyebrow crooks with a challenge. "Well, I wouldn't want my information falling into the wrong hands and have another stripper show up out of nowhere, exploiting me for money again."

Ugh. I snatch my phone from his tight grip, and he drops

his hand into his lap. His smirk drives me absolutely crazy, to the point that I practically dive out of his car. Before I escape, he leans over and peers up at me with a cheeky grin and teasing ocean-blue eyes. "See you at home, wifey."

I catch a quick glimpse of his hot wink before slamming the door, and it's the only thing I think of the entire drive to my apartment.

Sixteen

EMORY

WHAT AN AMATEUR.

It seems my little Rogue isn't as crafty as I thought.

Of course I put her location services on and shared it with myself before she climbed—rather aggressively—out of my car and escaped into hers.

Little Miss Independent has made four trips to her boxcar from her apartment, and each time, she tries to rearrange her belongings to make them fit. It isn't working, and we'll be late for our appointment at this rate.

I sigh with annoyance and open my door, letting the breezy Chicago wind rush into my car. As soon as my foot hits the cracked pavement, I feel eyes on me.

This is the type of neighborhood that my agent warned me about.

Dilapidated buildings. A few homeless loitering around. Children without shoes running down the street, chasing a ball that desperately needs to be blown up. Vehicles that are somehow in worse condition than Scottie's parked along the side of the road. It's not as bad as the homeless camp I followed Scottie to the other day, but it's a close second.

As soon as I enter the apartment complex, a stench of mildew hits me in the face. It's Grandma Lottie's basement all over again. When Taytum and I were younger, I'd convince her to play hide and seek down there. Except, I'd never come and find her.

Ford was always the one that went back for her.

I jog up the stairs, knowing Scottie has to be on one of the upper floors with how red-faced and sweaty she is each time she heads for her car. A few stray cockroaches scurry away, avoiding my large feet. I stand at the top of the stairwell on the second floor. I listen intently for someone huffing and puffing, but I hear a few curse words instead.

"*God dammit.*"

I stuff a chuckle down my throat and roll my lips.

"*I need to exercise more.*"

As if swinging around on a pole isn't exercise?

"*Ow. Shit!*"

Before I can stop myself, I turn toward Scottie's adorable cursing. I head for the echo of something crashing and find her on the dirty floor, holding her ankle in a tight grip. Her eyes widen, and she quickly tries to scramble to her feet.

"Wh—what are you doing here?" she stutters, trying to brush her sweaty hair away from her face.

I roll my eyes and head straight for her.

She's kind of a mess, and I can't decide if I feel bad for her or if I'm amused by her.

Maybe a bit of both.

Instead of answering her, I bend down and scoop her into my arms. Naturally, she protests and slaps my chest. Ignoring her again, I carry her through the open apartment door, and it takes everything in me not to let my jaw fall.

This is where she lives?

Fuck, no wonder she needs money.

There are cracks in the walls, mismatched kitchen chairs at

a small table, one measly tattered couch, and don't even get me started on the "bed."

I stop in my tracks when I see a random pot on her mattress.

"You do know that's not a stove, right?"

She huffs. "Put me down."

I set her on the kitchen counter. It's not big, but neither is she, so she fits just fine.

"Let me see it," I demand.

Scottie's soft lips purse, and to no surprise, she keeps her legs dangling and refuses to show me her ankle. "What are you doing here?"

"I thought it was obvious." I gesture to her chaotic state. "You clearly need help moving into my house, and what kind of husband would I be if I didn't show up?"

Scottie shrugs. "I don't know. Maybe the fake one that you are…"

A deep laugh leaves me. "There's nothing fake about it. Papers are signed."

That seems to shut her up. She breaks our eye contact and looks off to the side, as if she's rethinking our scheme. I take it as an opportunity to slip her shoe off and look at her injured ankle.

Blue-painted toes stare back at me. I ignore the softness of her leg as I grip her by the calf and examine the red spot forming on the outside of her ankle. "Do you have ice?" I look around while still keeping her leg in my hand. I eye the small refrigerator.

"I'm fine." Scottie tries to pull her leg away, but I tighten my fingers and stop her. The kitchen is such a small space that I can reach over and open the freezer while keeping her trapped.

It's completely empty.

No ice.

119

No frozen pizzas.

Nothing.

I glance at her out of the corner of my eye. She's looking in the complete other direction. Her plump bottom lip is trapped between her teeth as she nibbles on the flesh like it's her only source of food.

With a bad feeling in my gut, I shut the freezer and open the fridge.

Jesus.

There's one near-empty package of cheese slices, some off-brand hazelnut coffee creamer, a few oranges, and...a half-eaten biscotti? It's worse than a poor college student trying to save money.

This is just...sad.

I slowly shut the refrigerator and quickly run my gaze down her slim frame. It's clear to me that she doesn't eat out much—not to mention, she obviously doesn't have the finances for it. My curiosity piques even further, but I stuff the little tidbit of information in the back of my mind and get on with it.

"Well," I sigh, "I guess we can ice it at my place after we get married." Which I guess is her place too.

Scottie catches my eye, and it only takes looking into her baby blues for a split second to know she has a wealth of fuckery trapped somewhere behind them. I suddenly want to know everything there is to know about her. Where is her family? Why does she live in a shithole? How did a girl like her end up working at the Cat House?

Slowly, I drop her leg and let it dangle beside the other one. My heart thumps harder than it should when I take a step closer. My hands suddenly have a mind of their own as they creep up her legs and move to land on her hips.

Her sweet gasp catches me by surprise, and I clench my teeth. It's hard to focus, and I *never* have a hard time focusing.

A hot swallow works down my throat when I lift her up and slowly place her feet on the floor. My hands linger for a second too long, and I hate that she notices.

I step away quickly and run my hand through my hair.

"What else do you need?" My question is gruff, and it confuses her.

I stare at the furrowed lines along her forehead and follow her line of sight. "Just my photography stuff."

"Photography stuff? You're a photographer?"

She laughs sarcastically, and for some reason, it bothers me.

"Not officially." Suddenly, she looks embarrassed. Pink tints the apples of her cheeks before she half-limps over to a black camera lying on top of her makeshift bedside table that I'm pretty sure is just an old cardboard box turned upside down.

I wait and watch as she scoops it up and places it in a case. There are a few other odds and ends that she grabs, and then she sighs. She glances at me over her shoulder. The setting sun shines through the one window in her little apartment, and the glow casts her in the softest light, making her look less like the woman who tried to blackmail me and more like someone who is seemingly...innocent.

She hobbles down to her knees. There's a rustling of papers before she stands back up and is holding a thick pile of photos in her hands.

"Okay, I'm ready."

I raise an eyebrow and stalk over to her. She moves out of the way when I bend down to grab the pitiful—yet innovative —bedside table and flip it right side up. I open the flaps and dump the cockroach onto the floor, watching it run and hide.

"There."

Scottie slowly drops the photos and some envelopes into the box, and although I know I shouldn't, I take a look.

The photographs are mostly old and faded. One catches my attention, and I can't seem to stop staring at it. It's a man wearing a Chicago Blue Devils T-shirt, and I think it's the same one she wore to the game she came to. It's not nearly as worn in the photo as it is now, though. He's standing in the stands of the arena, and a little girl is on his shoulders with blonde pigtails and a huge smile.

I think it's Scottie and her dad.

Feeling like I've intruded on something I shouldn't, and shockingly feeling a little bad about it, I shut the cardboard box.

When I look back at my new wife, I'm not surprised to see that she's nervously nibbling on her lip. I try to fall back into my usual unapproachable, aloof self and ignore it. Scottie and her nervous habit of nibbling on her lip will not thaw my cold exterior.

"Well, let's go. We're gonna have to stop at City Hall before we go home," I announce.

Wanting to harden the soft spot I start to feel for her, I decide to take a dig at her place.

"Do you want to take your pet?"

Confusion crosses her face. "What pet?"

I gesture to the corner of the room where the cockroach ran to. "Your cockroach?"

Her eyes burn with anger, and I smirk the entire time I follow her as she limps out of the shithole apartment.

Seventeen

SCOTTIE

SHIT.

I stop and curse my sore ankle when I notice the dour look on my landlord's face in my attempt to sneak out of the complex after Emory.

"What do you think you're doing, girl?"

Nothing in my life comes easy.

Of course Gerald would be here, of all days, to question me moving out.

At least Emory is outside, putting a few of my boxes into his car so I can drive to his place without cardboard blocking my view.

Or is it *our* place?

Gerald clears his raspy throat behind the plexiglass separating his office from the entryway, and I square my shoulders. "I'm moving out. My letter of termination is upstairs on the table." I place the keys on the counter with a loud clunk.

"You can't do that. You're violating your lease agreement."

I instantly have a headache. If I wasn't trying to build my credit up so I can be a responsible adult one day and get a loan, I'd leave Gerald high and dry.

I mean, if I was willing to blackmail a random pro hockey player for money, who's to say I wouldn't skip out on paying this creep rent? But nonetheless...

"I will pay the remainder of my lease agreement as soon as I can."

"As soon as you can? Does that mean you'll be late on your dues again? Because I'm telling you, girl...I will turn you into collect—"

I interrupt him before Emory comes back and inserts himself into something I want him nowhere near. "I'll pay on time."

"You better, Ms. Monroe! Or you'll regret it."

Asshole.

I shoot him a glare before turning around and running straight into Emory's hard chest. I wince as his hands fall to my upper arms. When I peer at him from my much shorter frame, he's glaring at my ex-landlord. My face turns fifty shades of red. *Please tell me he didn't hear that conversation.*

"It's Mrs. Olson," Emory corrects him, as calm as ever. His fingers tighten against my biceps, and my heart does a weird flip. "I don't want to hear you threaten my wife again."

Wife.

A gush of something warm rushes from his fingers wrapped around my arms all the way to my toes.

I'm at a loss for words.

It's a marriage of convenience. A fraud.

We're bound by a stupid contract, and there isn't an ounce of love between us, yet I'm tricked into letting myself believe that his devotion is real.

It's a swift kick right to my stomach because, God, how I crave to have *one* person on my side. For once.

"I don't see a ring on that girl's finger."

Emory's entire body tenses, and I panic.

I push on his chest, and he immediately gives me his attention. Anger swirls in his eyes, and instead of being an ocean-blue color, they're arctic.

Memories begin to surface, and chills run to my arms. The number of times I've had to step in between a heated argument, stop someone from fighting—usually someone trying to hurt William—and block a blow so my mother wouldn't get her lights knocked out is obsolete. Each time I'm reminded of the violence, my stomach clenches.

"Let's go," I whisper.

Emory furrows his forehead and glares at Gerald over the top of my head, then grunts. Thankfully, he turns around, and we head out the door, welcomed by the crisp scent of autumn.

After a few painfully awkward seconds, Emory finally asks the question I don't want to answer. "How much do you owe?"

I know the number off the top of my head, and on the drive over, I worked out my finances for the next year as Emory Olson's wife, figuring it all out.

"I've got it under control," I say.

We stare at each other for a few long seconds before he accepts my answer and starts in the direction of his car. "Follow me to City Hall."

I can't help but roll my eyes.

He is so bossy.

"Did you just roll your eyes?"

I cross my arms and do it again, emphasizing that he isn't the only one who can be insolent.

I'll admit, Emory makes me a little nervous. He can be intimidating, and arrogance practically bleeds from his pores. But in the same breath, he intrigues me, and there's a wild part of me that wants to push his buttons like he does mine.

His deep chuckle makes my lips twitch, and I hope he doesn't notice. He shakes his sandy hair before climbing into his car and revving it loudly before I even make it to mine.

I turn my car on and rev it too. Embarrassing as it is, my car makes a loud popping noise each time I turn it on, and gray smoke puffs from the exhaust. I peek in my rearview, and Emory is slack-jawed. He shakes his head a second later and pulls away.

I want to be defiant and refuse to follow him.

But I have to.

Because I've signed the contract, and as of this evening, we will officially be married in the state of Illinois.

———

"WELL, that does it, you two lovebirds. You gonna kiss your bride?"

Rhodes snorts, and his daughter claps from on top of his shoulders. My face burns, and I'm sweating. This is not how I imagined my wedding would go, but it seems fitting because my life is such a fucking joke.

"Shut up," Emory barks, snatching the phone from the wooden podium.

Apparently, his friend, Ford, is an officiant, and it's surprisingly legal to have someone "marry" you through a video chat. I didn't protest because the less people present, the better.

Rhodes, who is aware of our contract, and Chastity, who graciously agreed to be here at the very last second—and was forced to sign an NDA by Emory—are our witnesses. As of right now... I guess I am considered a married woman.

"Are you sure this is what you want?" Chastity whispers after pulling me out of the video frame as Emory begs his sister to help *sell* our marriage to his parents.

I'm certain Taytum thinks poorly of me.

I just married her brother for money. For all she knows, I'm just another gold-digging woman.

In an attempt to practice my lies, I nod. "Yes. Of course this is what I want. Plus, it's a little too late to change my mind."

Chastity arches an eyebrow. She's dressed down today, and you would never know that she's one of the top strippers at the Cat House. "Out of all the girls at work, you are the very last one I'd ever assume would be in this position."

I grab her warm hands and give them a squeeze. "And out of all the girls, I knew you'd be the only one to understand."

"I mean, if I had some hunky pro hockey player ask me to get married out of convenience, I'd jump right on his dick."

I snort and try to hide my laugh.

Rhodes curses under his breath and walks away with his five-year-old daughter.

"But you? Miss Independent? I'm just...surprised."

My voice drops. "I need the money."

"That badly?"

The last voicemail I got from William echoes throughout my head, and I nod. "He's willing to pay me monthly, and I'll get a hefty amount after our contract is up." It'll be more than enough to reopen William's case. "Plus, I hated those men looking at me."

Chastity smiles deviously. "And I love it."

I laugh, and it catches Emory's attention. Our gazes snag, and my stomach fills with unease. *Did I seriously just marry him?*

I shake off the worries.

There is no room for regret or doubt in my life.

"Well, should we take a picture so you can post it on social media?" Emory stands with his hands on his hips, waiting for my response.

After a glimpse of the room we're tucked away in, I laugh.

A quick marriage at City Hall with a stripper, a scowling hockey player, and a five-year-old as our witnesses is preposterous. Emory wants me to paint us out to be happily-in-love newlyweds on his socials, and he thinks *this* setting is going to cut it with the media?

"What's so funny?" he asks, deadpan expression and all.

Rhodes snorts again and puts his wiggly daughter on the floor. She bounces over to Emory, messy braids swinging behind her shoulders, and gazes up at his tall frame. "She needs a ring, dummy."

Emory's lip curls. "She does?"

She takes her small hand and slaps her forehead. "You may be good at hockey, but I don't think you're very smart."

"Ellie," Rhodes attempts to reprimand his daughter, but a laugh bursts out of my mouth at the same time Rhodes shakes his head in disbelief. Emory's eyes flick to mine sharply, and I cover my lips to try to hide my amusement.

Emory sighs, and I swear I feel his warm breath all the way across the room. I watch him bend down to get on Ellie's level, and although his voice softens, I still hear him.

"Wanna go with me to pick out the ring?"

She nods so vigorously little pieces of hair fall out of her messy, woven braids. "Daddy! Can I?! Can I go pick out a pretty ring?"

Rhodes grips the back of his neck and squeezes it.

"I can keep you company while they go," Chastity muses, half-joking.

"You're coming with me," I say to her, saving Rhodes from the aneurysm he's about to have.

Emory's jaw tightens. "And you're going where?"

I cross my arms and raise an eyebrow at my new husband and his insolent tone.

"To get a dress."

His eyebrows furrow. "We're already married. Why do you need a dress?"

"For our wedding photos."

His jaw slacks, and I sigh. I gesture to the room and land on the peeling wallpaper that's straight out of the 1960s. "If you want me to sell our marriage to the media, we're going to need something more than a quick city hall elopement in a room that reeks of must."

Emory scowls, but in the end, he murmurs the word *fine*.

I wave goodbye to Ellie, and she gives me a thumbs-up before mouthing, "I'll pick out a big ring!"

I giggle softly. Emory catches me smiling, and something races across his face that I can't decipher even if I tried.

When they're all gone, I look over at Chastity. "You ready?"

"Where are we going to get a dress?"

I grab my keys off the table. "The thrift store, obviously."

Eighteen

EMORY

THE RING on my finger is heavy.

A little black box sits on the counter, and it's fucking with me. I keep staring at it, like it's going to disappear.

I know the media is going to lose its shit when the first photo of Scottie and me surfaces—that is...if she ever comes home.

My neck cracks with a snap when I hear the rumbling of an exhaust in the distance. My nerves settle right away. I check the time on my phone, ignoring the texts from my agent and parents, demonstrating their confusion and worry over my recent marriage, and make my way over to the window. I stare out of it like an unhinged stalker, watching Scottie parallel park on the street.

"At least she can do that," I mumble.

She stares at my house, and even from this distance, I see that she's gnawing on her bottom lip again. I've been married to her for less than twenty-four hours, and I already know her nervous tics.

When she exits the car, I walk over to the front door and beat her to it.

She jumps with her clenched fist mid-air for a knock.

"You know...you don't have to knock, considering this is your home for the next year."

A year.

I'll be living with her for an entire year.

Sharing a bed.

Shit.

Rhodes's warnings are beginning to ring true. I didn't think this through.

"Oh, well, I didn't feel right just...walking in." Scottie's blonde hair falls behind her shoulders as she tips her head to look up at the house. She blinks a few times in awe, and I wish I could hear what's going through her mind. After seeing where she was living, this probably seems excessive.

Chicago homes aren't what I'm used to. There's practically no yard, and I could spit and hit my neighbor's porch. Mine is one of the more expensive homes in the market and larger than the rest along the street. It reaches for the clouds and sits well above the dogwood tree out front that my realtor raved about—like I care about its bloom cycle.

"I'll have a key made for you." Which is another thing I didn't think through. "Let's get the rest of your stuff before someone sees you standing here looking all awkward."

Scottie pops her hip. "I'm not standing here awkwardly."

"You're looking at my house like it's a castle." In an attempt to wound her, because I hate that my pulse grows faster when she's near, I say something I know will insult her. "But to you, it probably is."

Her pupils flare, and I bask in the sudden rush of adrenaline.

"You're a dick." Her attempt at a comeback makes me laugh.

Her hips sway with a fiery attitude as she heads for her car, but I catch up to her quickly, pulling her back at the last second before she dies at my feet. The horn of the Mercedes blares as it flies past, and Scottie's fingers dig into my forearm as we are just barely missed. Her breathing is ragged and uneven, so I keep my arms around her waist, tucking her to my chest. "Insulting your new husband isn't very nice. Especially after he just saved your life."

Her dainty chin tips, and she peers up at me. "Well..." She pauses. "You insulted me first."

I can't help but laugh again at her immaturity. I remove my hand from her waist, eager to put space between us. I start across the street for her car. Over my shoulder, I call out to her and say, "Make sure you look both ways this time."

My mouth twitches when I hear her mumbling something under her breath. Her car door creaks loudly, causing a flock of birds to fly away. I shake my head at the audacity of her crappy car, sort of feeling sorry for her, and go to grab her boxes.

Before my hands even skim the cardboard, Scottie darts in front of me and pushes me out of the way. "I've got it."

I grunt when her ass brushes against my dick. I step backward and look down at her perfect round peach in the tight jeans she's been wearing all day. My groin tingles, and it's then that I realize I'm going to have to constantly remind myself that this woman tried to blackmail me and ruin my career.

"Fine."

I step back and rest my forearm on the top of her passenger door. I watch with amusement as she stacks several boxes on top of one another, making it so she can't even see. It's almost painful to stand there and do nothing. After witnessing a few of her wobbly steps, I realize that I don't care if she doesn't want me to take her boxes. I'm taking them regardless, because so far, in the last few hours, she's fallen onto her ankle and has almost gotten hit by a car.

I grab the three boxes out of her hands and ignore her angry little huff.

"Quit acting like a brat," I say over my shoulder.

Scottie squeezes her eyes shut before turning and grabbing one more thing out of her car. I almost poke at her again, but as soon as we're both inside my house and the door shuts, I'm suddenly aware of the situation we've found ourselves in.

My expansive open floor plan suddenly feels smaller.

The air is tight, and we're both tense.

Our steps echo as Scottie follows me to the stairs like a little duckling.

When I open the door to our bedroom, she steps in hesitantly and glances around quickly.

My bedroom is larger than her entire apartment, but I keep my mouth shut and observe her as she takes in the room.

"You can take the left side."

Scottie spins like the wind. The dress bag crinkles in her arm, and her eyes widen. "Wait, what?"

I nod to the left side of the bed, placing her boxes on the floor. "I sleep on the right, so you can have the left."

Her brows snap together. "I'm not sleeping in bed with you."

I'm beginning to think she just likes to argue with me.

"Well, have fun sleeping on the couch, then. I don't have a guest room."

In what seems to be complete disbelief, her jaw slacks, and her long eyelashes flutter against one another. "How do you not have a guest room?! This house is huge."

"It's not that big," I say. "And let me correct myself. I have other rooms, but they're unfurnished, so it's either you sleep in bed with me, on the couch downstairs, or the floor. You pick."

I have a fully furnished guest room, courtesy of my

mother, but I act like I don't just to spite my new wife and the horror on her face at the thought of sleeping beside me.

She rolls her pretty blue eyes, and it does something to me.

With irritation, I turn to leave her to unpack alone. Before I get too far, I stop in the doorway and grip the top of the frame to settle myself. My back faces her, and my fingers dig into the wood. "Ring is on the counter."

My muscles tense when I hear her sarcastic huff of breath.

"How romantic," she mumbles.

As I head downstairs, I silently hope with each step that I've made the right decision in marrying a poor stripper, with what seems to be a big heart and a sarcastic tongue, to fix my reputation when it's all said and done.

Nineteen

SCOTTIE

THE COFFEE IS TOO BITTER, and I wish I had a biscotti to go with it, but there is no better way to wake up than with a pot of coffee brewing and some quick stretches to soothe my sore muscles from sleeping on the couch.

It's a comfortable couch, much softer than my thrift store couch with the torn seams. I've slept in worse places, but I was crammed on my side all night, and apparently didn't move an inch, which caused a kink to fester in my neck.

I glance around my new home, feeling more like an intruder than anything.

It's only been one night, but I woke up with the same heavy feeling in my stomach, silently tossing around my new name.

Scottie Olson.

The little black box on the shiny, marble counter continues to pull my attention, and I swear it keeps getting closer. I glance at the winding stairs, trying to hear if my new husband is awake, and then move back to the box.

Is it moving closer, or am I crazy?

139

With shaky hands, I place my coffee cup down on the counter and slowly reach for the box.

The velvet is soft against my fingertips as I brush the edges, feeling for the crease.

My knees are weak, and I start to sweat.

Just holding something this important...and expensive... makes me feel like a criminal. The smallest seed of guilt plants itself into my chest, but I dig it up a moment later when I think of William behind bars for something he didn't do. *Never lose focus.* It's something my dad used to say, and if I try hard enough, I can hear his voice encouraging me.

This is for William and what's left of our family. Besides, it's not like I'm just some freeloader. I already have a full schedule planned, with dates and all, for posting on Emory's social media, announcing our marriage and relationship going forward.

Sucking in a quick breath, I open the box and freeze.

I gape at the big, solitaire diamond and each tiny cluster that sits perfectly aligned on the thin gold band. My lips part at the breathtaking beauty of the ring. It's simple and delicate, but with the size, it surely makes a statement.

I cannot wear this.

I spin and put my back to the living room. It feels like the furniture is watching my reaction, and I don't like the way it's making me feel.

The box snaps shut, and I run my fingers along the velvet again, only to open it up and stare again.

Wearing something this valuable feels wrong, given the way I grew up. Not to mention my debt and how much money I have to come up with to open William's case again... It's unethical.

"You should have seen the ring Ellie tried to get me to buy."

I slam the box shut and turn quickly, slipping on the tiled

floor. My back rams into the sharp edge of the counter, but I hide the bite of pain.

Emory's lip twitches, but for once, he doesn't insult me.

He walks farther into the kitchen, wearing dark-gray sweatpants and a black hoodie. He grabs my cup of coffee off the counter and drinks it in one gulp. My jaw slacks when he lifts the back of his hand and wipes the excess liquid from his mouth. "Thanks for the coffee."

My lips slam shut, and my brow furrows.

Rude.

Emory rounds the counter and grabs a container out of the fridge then pops it into the microwave. I watch his every move and find myself wondering how someone so large can get around so gracefully. He makes the kitchen seem smaller, but I have an inkling that it has more to do with his ego than his body stature.

Without looking up from what he's doing, he asks, "How was the couch?"

"Great," I lie.

It takes everything in me to stand straight and not massage the knot in my neck.

Emory nods and stares at me in between heaping bites of eggs. My heart beats faster the longer he looks at me, and I hate that I can't read his mind. The house feels tight, like the windows are going to shatter at any second, so I finally look away and break our intense stare-off.

"I..." I clear my throat. "I have a schedule for posting on social media about our wedding and future marriage."

"Oh, do you?" he muses.

I know he's smirking, just from the way his words sound. Heat crawls up my back when I slide my phone across the counter.

He catches it at the last second. "It's no wonder your phone is cracked."

"Someone else cracked my phone." I slam my mouth shut at the audacity of my brain allowing that to come out.

He scrutinizes me. "Who cracked your phone?"

I shrug, attempting to hide my lie. "It just fell at work one night."

What a pitiful excuse, and if Emory is as smart as he seems, he'll see right through it.

He pairs his airy chuckle with a shake of his head, and I know I'm correct. He doesn't press, though.

I shift on my bare feet, waiting for him to finish looking at the schedule, hoping he's okay with it. A part of me feels like he's my boss. It's a mutual agreement. Our "marriage" is a convenience for both of us, but I can't help the deeply rooted part inside of me that is constantly trying to please other people.

I learned from my high school counselor, when she urged me to come into her office after hearing of my home life, that childhood neglect will fester into traits like pleasing people, low self-worth, and mistrust in almost every relationship going forward.

Unfortunately, she was right.

Emory finally clicks my phone screen off. "Looks good to me."

A relieved sigh falls from my mouth. "Good. We will take our wedding photos today."

There's a slight rush of excitement at the thought. I haven't taken photos in so long that my fingers itch to even hold my camera for a few seconds, getting lost in the moment. It may be a fake marriage, but I'm going to capture every feigned moment and make it believable.

Emory snaps me out of my thoughts. "I have practice."

Right. Pro hockey player...as if I could forget.

"We will do it after, then. Do you have a suit?" I shake my

head. Of course he does. He wears them to all the games...not that I've noticed.

After placing his container in the trash, Emory rounds the kitchen counter and nods to the stairs. "They're in the closet. Have your pick." He pauses next to me, and I turn slowly. With a lazy look in his eye, he scans me from head to toe, and I'm suddenly self-conscious.

I refuse to let him see that he makes me uncomfortable, though, just like I refuse to go down a path of self-consciousness because I'm so used to not being good enough.

When he reaches my eye again, he winks. "See you after practice, wife."

My stomach flips, and my cheeks burn.

I say nothing because I'm in shock from the way his wink sent a line of fire straight down my spine.

I'm clearly impressionable when it comes to Emory's blue eyes and flirty smirk. I could easily find myself in a world of disappointment by letting myself believe there is something more than just a contract marriage between the two of us. There is no room for heartbreak in my life, though.

The door opens, and I watch Emory head out of the house, hockey bag in tow.

Right before he disappears, he leans back and catches me staring. "Oh, and don't even think about pawning that ring for money."

I gape at him, and his chuckle follows him the rest of the way out the door.

Never mind.

I am not impressionable when it comes to my new husband.

Not at all.

Twenty

EMORY

THE TEAM WAS CONFUSED when I showed up to practice with a ring on my finger.

Most of them kept their suspicions to themselves, only giving me the side-eye, but after Malaki wouldn't stop poking around, Rhodes eventually pulled him aside and made him shut his mouth.

After all, he was the one who handed me her gum wrapper note that first night and recognized her right away, even when Kane argued about her hair color. Before I left to head home, I ushered him to my car and slipped him an NDA. He signed it willingly but not before pretending to be wounded that I didn't trust him.

He said something about wanting the same thing as I did —a better reputation for the team—and reiterated that we're all here to do a job.

Apparently, at the moment, mine is playing dress-up with my new wife to pose in front of her camera for our fake wedding photos.

I sigh when I open the front door, hoisting my hockey bag higher onto my shoulder. The house smells...sweet. There's a soft floral scent wafting throughout the open space, and sure, it's a nice smell to come home to after a long day on the ice, but it irks me in the same breath, because I know it's *her*.

"You're late."

I crane my neck to the living room and almost lose my footing.

My knees buckle, and I'm punched in the gut with her appearance.

What the fuck did I get myself into?

There stands my new wife, bound by a feigned contract, wearing a wedding dress that accentuates every delectable curve of her body and highlights how tragically beautiful she truly is. With bright-blue eyes and high cheekbones that shimmer under the natural light of the room, I'm sort of at a loss for words.

It surprises me. I blink a few times before I finally speak. "Wh–what?" I grip my bag tighter and snap myself out of the trance she's put me under.

"You're late," she repeats.

It's hard to ignore the attitude in her tone, and my eye twitches.

"You've been my wife for twenty-four hours, and you're already getting angry when I'm not home on time?" I grunt and turn my back to her, hating that seeing her in a wedding dress has me all twisted.

The silk of her dress makes a noise that catches my attention as her feet slap against the hardwood floor. *No shoes?* I refuse to look at her cute feet.

"I need natural light for our photos!" There's an urgency in her tone that pulls me back around. Her hand falls to my forearm, and she slips my bag off my shoulder, letting it fall with a thud to the floor.

My brow furrows as I look at her small palm gripping my arm.

"Let's go!"

"Go where?" I let her pull me through the house over to the stairs because I'm simply confused.

She turns back and peeks over her delicate shoulder. The dress shows off some skin, and I hate that it's so soft looking. I also hate that I remember how she felt in my lap that night I proposed to her...the word *propose* ostensible in every sense.

"To get dressed!" She lets go of me, and a piece of her pinned-back blonde hair falls into her face. "Go!"

The moment I step in front of her, she pushes me from behind.

"You're bossy," I call over my shoulder.

I catch her with her hip popped out and her arms crossed over her slightly plunged breasts. "Well...takes one to know one."

With a quiet chuckle, I turn and jog up the stairs.

"And shave your face!" she shouts from down below.

I roll my eyes and head straight for the bathroom to grab my razor, per my *wife's* request.

———

"ALRIGHT. WHERE DO YOU WANT ME?" I seem irritated and impatient, but I have to admit, it's kind of amusing to watch Scottie observe the space and test her camera, only to step away with a furrowed brow and pursed lips.

She shushes me without even looking in my direction. There's a little line in between her eyebrows, and when she sucks her lip into her mouth and pins it with her bright-white teeth, I can't help but stare.

"This isn't going to work!" She huffs and taps her chin with her fingers.

I ignore her little fit and run my eyes down her slender

frame. She's small but still has noticeable curves, and the wedding dress looks like it was made for her.

In the midst of Scottie gathering her camera and tripod thing, I blurt out a question that's been bugging me. "Where did you get that dress?"

What if she's been married before?

I think back to the man that was handling her like a ragdoll at the Cat House. My ears burn, and I ask the next question before she can answer the first.

"Have you been married before?"

Scottie stops what she's doing and immediately looks at me. It takes her all of three seconds to burst out in laughter. Something moves in my chest, and my ears cool. I keep my lips flat, but hearing her laugh makes my cheeks twitch.

I feel myself wanting to smile, which is annoying.

"What's so funny?" I ask, following after her as she drags the tripod up the stairs. "And where are we going?"

I grab the equipment from her, and surprisingly, she lets me carry it. It's probably due to her being in a tight wedding dress that likely doesn't allow much movement, but for the first time since meeting her, she isn't drowning me with her independence.

"We're going to your bedroom."

My lip turns up in the corner. "Wow, already? I thought you'd at least hold out for our one-week anniversary."

Scottie stops right in front of me, and next thing I know, I take an elbow to the ribs.

"Ow, fuck. I was kidding." I rub the spot she hit and continue to follow her to my room.

"It wasn't funny," she says, as deadpan as ever.

"But asking you if you've been previously married is?"

Scottie tries to take the tripod from my hands, but I pull it back. I cock an eyebrow, and she sighs.

"No," she answers. "I've never been married. I don't have

time to date, let alone find a man willing to marry a poor stripper with enough childhood trauma to weigh down a semi."

Scottie slams her lips together and quickly averts her gaze. I get the feeling she didn't mean to say the second part of that sentence. Before I can comment on it, she snatches the tripod out of my hand, and I watch in silence as she sets it up again and tests the lighting.

"Okay, it's ready. We don't have long before the lighting disappears, so come on." My bride wafts her hand at me, and out of spite, I move extra slow. Her hands fall to her hips when she pouts, and I stare at the finger that should be wearing a ring.

"So did you pawn the ring or..."

Fire burns in her pretty blue eyes. She scoffs and stomps off in her bare feet, only to return a few seconds later with the ring dangling off her pinky. She messes with the camera again and then rushes over to the spot near the window.

"Come stand right here." She gestures beside her.

I stride across my carpeted floor and adjust the navy suit that was lying on the bed when I got out of the shower. I stand inches away and look down at her all dolled up.

She's gorgeous. All glowy and shit. If this weren't a fake marriage, I'd tell her so, but I don't owe her compliments. I owe her a paycheck.

That's all.

"I want you to put the ring on my finger slowly and look down at me the entire time you're doing it."

My shoulders tense. "Alright."

Scottie places her warm hand in mine, and I hold it gently.

"Okay, go," she whispers, taking a step closer.

My heart rams behind my ribs, and it's the only thing I hear in between the shutters of the camera taking numerous photos of me slowly slipping the diamond ring on her slender finger.

A rough swallow works its way down my throat.

This feels...intimate.

Scottie rushes off and checks the camera. Her face lights up with excitement, and then she comes back over to me, sending her soft scent in my direction.

"Now I want you to stand behind me and wrap your hands around my waist."

Ah, shit.

I'm uneasy, and my shoulders lock when she puts herself to my front and backs up so we're flush.

"Like this?" I ask, voice husky.

"Yeah." She's breathless. Her ribcage expands in my grip, and a fire sparks to life in my lower stomach.

It's been months since I've taken a woman to bed, and my body is making that very clear at the moment. My jaw locks when Scottie grabs my ring finger and starts to wiggle the ring past my knuckle. "Do the same to my finger, and act like you're putting my ring on again. We're going to do it at the same time and take a series of photos."

I swallow and do as she says.

The camera clicks, and at the exact same time, like we're synced, we slowly push the rings onto each other's fingers.

My pulse is flying. I look down at her neck and see the little thump beneath her smooth skin, matching the speed of mine.

We're too close, and there isn't a flicker of angry tension between us at the moment.

There are no teasing remarks threatening to come from my mouth, and the air of attitude she usually carries is long gone.

I'm not sure I like this.

Scottie's pinned-back hair rubs against the front of my suit, and our eyes catch.

"Are we done?" The hope in my tone is obvious.

Scottie's lip is trapped beneath her teeth, and she shakes her head.

"Now I need you to act like you're going to kiss me, because two photos of us placing rings on each other's fingers isn't going to be enough if we want the world to believe that this is a real marriage."

My jaw clicks.

With her in my arms, looking up at me with her sparkling blue eyes, it feels awfully fucking real.

Twenty-One

SCOTTIE

I CAN'T CATCH my breath.

My legs feel weak, and I know I've made the right decision not to wear shoes under my thrifted wedding dress, because I would have broken my ankle by now.

Emory makes me nervous but not in the way that I'm used to. Instead of a knot in my stomach, I'm jittery with anxious thoughts and excitement, which is conflicting.

The suit he's wearing was obviously tailored to fit his body and his body alone. The sleeves hug his large biceps, and the crisp white collar hits right below the roll of his Adam's apple each time he forces a slow swallow down.

"You want me to act like I'm kissing you?"

My heart races with the rasp in his tone. His perfect peach-colored lips have me in some type of fog, and I can't look away from them.

A single, quick nod is the only response I give my new husband.

Emory's hand falls to my waist, and the only thing separating his palm and my skin is the silk of my wedding dress. I gulp when his eyes bounce back and forth between mine.

"Why not an actual kiss?" he asks, pulling me in closer.

A rushed breath flies from my lips when I gasp.

Emory's jaw flickers on the side, and I'm at a loss for words. He leans in closer, and our noses are almost touching.

I angle my chin, and he slowly grins. "Too afraid you'll like my mouth on yours, Rogue?"

The first click of the camera echoes around the tense room, and my heart jumps. Emory's fingers dig into my back, and I stare at his mouth before trailing up his smooth face and locking eyes with him again.

I thought I knew what bedroom eyes were after looking into the faces of men while I danced on a pole. But I was wrong. Emory looks at me like he wants to devour me and take his time doing it too.

He angles his face, and I mimic him. Our noses rub against each other, and I can almost taste him on my tongue. My body slams into his when he pulls me in closer, and his other hand creeps up each of my curves until it brushes against my neck. He cups my cheek, and our lips brush so gently that I wonder if I imagined it, but after another click of the camera, Emory breaks me out of my daze.

"Are we done?" he asks, voice straining.

"Wh–what?"

"Are we done with the photos?" he repeats.

I blink several times before his hand slowly caresses my face, landing right at my mouth. Heat spreads when his thumb faintly rubs against my bottom lip. "You should take a breath, Scottie."

At the exact time I inhale, my ringtone goes off. I jump away and almost trip, trying to get to my phone. Boulders of dread fall to my shoulders, and the weightlessness I felt when I was in his arms flees.

I tense when I squint past the cracks on my screen and see

the number. "I, uh...have to take this." I'm flustered, and Emory knows it.

"Not sure how you could even see who's calling, but I'm assuming that means we're done with our photo shoot." Emory turns and heads for his master bath, and I scramble out of the bedroom door as quickly as I can.

After listening to the automated voice from the prison and saying, "I accept," William's voice hits my ear.

"Scottie?"

"I'm here." I lean against the wall beside the door and chew on my lip. "How are you doing?"

There's too much noise in the background of the call to figure out which is what, but the longer William is in that place, the more I worry about his well-being in the long run.

I glance back at the bedroom door.

William is easily influenced, but maybe I am too, because for a second there, I believed that Emory actually wanted to kiss me as badly as I wanted him to.

Though, I'll deny it until the day I die.

I clench my eyes and wait for William to answer me.

"Everything is...okay."

I'm not convinced.

"What's wrong? Did something happen?"

A shout echoes before he answers. "No. I just don't know anything anymore. I'm confused."

Here we go.

"Tell me what happened," I coax, softening my tone.

He sighs but says nothing.

"William." I'm frustrated and worried at the same time. Part of me is angry with my mom for leaving me to deal with the repercussions of her behavior and the other part is angry with fate for taking my father away, because he was the only stable thing in my life. It's been a long time since I've felt sorry for myself, but I'm just so...fed up.

I look at my wedding dress and have the urge to laugh.

What am I doing?

I'm playing dress-up with a pro hockey player and acting like some housewife for money so I can afford to appeal my brother's prison sentence, only to have to figure out how to prepare him to succeed in society with a disability that isn't even documented? It's just absurd.

"One of the guys asked me to do them a favor, and I did."

Favors in prison. Now *that's* absurd.

"But?"

"But I think I've made some people angry."

I pinch the bridge of my nose. "William, how many times have I told you that your behavior and choices have consequences? You're in the position you're in now because of those choices. You can't let people talk you into doing things."

I'm in *my* position because of those choices too.

"I know, but..." There's more commotion in the background, and William sounds scared. "I've gotta go. They're cutting my time short."

I panic. "I love y—"

The phone call ends, and I feel sick.

I cradle my stomach and drop the phone to the floor. It bounces off the soft carpet, and I shut my eyes. Stress hinders me from moving, so I just stay right there, pinned against the wall with my thoughts spiraling.

I'm not sure how much time has passed, but when my breathing feels controlled, and my stomach stops turning, I open my eyes and search for my phone on the floor.

I freeze when I see a pair of men's bare feet in my peripheral vision.

How does someone that works their body to the brink of collapsing daily have such nice feet?

I turn and peer at Emory. He's leaning against the doorframe with one shoulder, and my phone is in his hand.

It's painful to look at him.

Embarrassment stains my cheeks, but I dig down to the smallest amount of self-worth that I have and act as if nothing happened.

He watches me with rapt attention as I stand up taller. I cross my arms over the silky, low-cut dress before holding my hand out. "Can I have my phone, please?"

His eyes show a challenge. "No."

"No?" I question, attempting to pop my hip out.

It didn't work because of my dress, but the attempt was there.

His attention falls to my waist before he creeps his way back to my face.

"Turn."

"Excuse me?"

Emory stalks toward me with my phone still in his tight grip. His free hand drops to my hip, and he spins me around. "I said turn."

I can't breathe, and I have no idea why I'm letting him boss me around. If it were any other man, I'd stomp on his foot and curse him out, but with Emory, it's different.

The sound of my zipper echoes throughout the long, empty hallway, and my dress loosens around my shoulders. A shiver sweeps through my bloodstream when I feel the faint touch of his knuckles graze my spine. "Go change and meet me in the kitchen."

I open my mouth with a refusal ready to go, but Emory is already halfway down the hall and heading for the stairs when I turn around, half-holding my dress.

"Are you going to give me my phone back?!" I shout, heading for my bag that's still unpacked in his bedroom.

Emory ignores me, which is nothing new.

HER SOFT FOOTSTEPS catch my attention, but I am fully aware of her every move, even when she isn't heading in my direction.

It's only been a couple of days since she's been my wife and living in my house, yet I already feel her taking up space that isn't necessarily reserved for her.

Not just in my home but my head too.

"Can I please have my phone?" Scottie's arms cross over her worn Blue Devils shirt that's two sizes too big. I drop my gaze to her bare legs, and she's lucky that I get a glimpse of the tight black shorts she's wearing underneath. Otherwise, I'd turn her right around and send her upstairs to demand she put some pants on.

The last thing I need is my fake wife walking around the house without pants.

I spin Scottie's half-broken phone on top of the counter and smirk. "Maybe if you ask me nicely."

Her eye roll excites me.

My new daily goal is to irritate her and watch her blue eyes fill with annoyance.

159

"Olson, give me my phone." Scottie stomps her bare foot against the tiled floors, and I snicker.

I kind of like it when she calls me by my last name.

"Okay." I sigh.

Scottie's eyebrows furrow with my non-combative response. Her attention falls to the phone I've placed in the center of the island. "That is *not* my phone."

"It is now." Her old phone is in my hand, and if I wanted to push her to the brink of violence, I'd snap it in half. I limit myself, though. I do need her help, after all.

"What do you mean?" She reaches toward the device.

I notice that the wedding ring is no longer on her finger, but I don't say anything. If she only wants to wear the three-karat ring that I let Rhodes's daughter choose when we're putting on a show, then so be it.

"My wife can't have a phone with a cracked screen like that. So I got you a new one."

Scottie's faint gasp fills the space between us, but I don't acknowledge it.

I rap my knuckle against the counter. "I also switched you to my plan, but you have the same number. I just transferred everything over after forging your name on the release form and explaining that you were my wife. All your photos and contacts are on there too."

Her little jaw slacks in disbelief, but a moment later, she snaps it shut and sends me a glare.

A week ago, it would have pissed me off.

But now, it just amuses me.

"I do not need a new phone!" The device slides against the smooth counter, and I catch it with a quick reflex. *Note to self: get her a LifeProof case.*

My mouth twitches, and I send it flying back to her. It's like we're playing shuffleboard, and she has to know that I never lose at anything. "Yes, you do."

Angry lines burrow into Scottie's forehead, and her cute mouth puckers with anger. "I can't afford a new phone, Emory." Her cheeks flush.

I blink through the confusion. "Wait, what?"

"If you're taking this out of my pay, I don't want it. I can't afford a new phone. I have other things I need to pay off."

So she needs money because she's in a lot of debt?

Scottie shoves the phone back over to me. I trap it beneath my fingers. The counter that separates us is acting like more of a barrier. Anger and embarrassment flow from her body, and I'm in a spiral of fuckery and curiosity.

Grabbing the phone in a tight grip, I round the corner and invade her space. She doesn't move an inch. The only thing she does is peek at me from the corner of her eye.

"I'm not taking this out of your pay," I say, voice low.

Her shoulders fall, and her head goes next. If I had to guess, she's trying to hide her shame from me.

A tight breath gets lodged in my throat when I reach for her wrist. I turn her hand so her palm is facing me, and I drop the new phone into it before curling her fingers around the device and shoving it into her chest. Her bottom lip gets trapped between her teeth, and it takes just about every ounce of restraint for me not to free it from the nervous habit.

I dip my head. My mouth is right beside her ear. "It's non-negotiable."

She turns, and our lips are so close I can feel her warm breath mingle with mine. I raise an eyebrow, ready for her to become combative with me.

"I don't remember seeing it in the contract." She raises the same eyebrow.

"If I'm paying for it, what does it matter?" I lean away from her because the longer I breathe her in, the higher I feel. "Not to mention, the contract says I'm responsible for paying the bills."

161

"It's my bill. Not yours."

I snort. "You're on my plan now, baby. So, it *is* my bill."

Something flashes across her face, and she takes a step away, but not before she looks at my mouth for a quick second. She snaps her baby blues back to me and sighs. "Fine. Whatever."

Feeling victorious from winning, I head for the fridge to prepare one of my ready-to-eat dinners, that I have been living off since college, with a pep in my step. The meals are full of protein, and although they're pricey, it beats trying to cook for myself on the schedule that I'm on during the season.

Shit.

With my back turned to Scottie, I realize that I have nothing for her to eat unless she wants to eat one of these, which is highly unlikely.

I continue preparing the meal and pop it into the microwave. She's moved to the couch in the living room, and she looks so tiny in between the large cushions. A laptop that looks like it's been through the wringer is perched on her criss-crossed legs, and there are small, black-rimmed glasses perched on the end of her nose as she stares intently at the screen.

The glow of the computer paints her cheekbones with a bluish light, and it's really disturbing that I feel a twist in my lower stomach the longer I look at her.

She's pretty.

Especially when she isn't putting up a front, acting all tough and independent.

When the microwave goes off, Scottie doesn't even move. All of her concentration is on her computer.

The entire time I eat my food, I watch her.

She either has no idea, or she's *that* focused on whatever she's doing on her computer.

Maybe she's in college? That'd be a reason to need money.

I clear my throat when I'm finished with my dinner and stand to go upstairs.

Long gone are the days where I'd go out with the guys, get shitfaced, end up in some girl's bed, and stay up until the wee hours of the night. Now, it's an early bedtime and morning workouts before the sun rises.

I go back and forth over whether or not to leave Scottie to fend for herself. She'll find something to eat if she's hungry, right? She has her blanket and pillow perched on the end of the couch, all nice and tidy-like.

She's fine.

Like a stealthy creep, I walk behind the couch and head for the stairs—but not before I glance at the computer screen.

I almost fall when I catch a glimpse of the photos she's editing. My feet refuse to go forward. Instead of moving, I stand there and watch as she zooms in on my hand on her face with our mouths almost touching. She blurs the background of my bedroom so all the focus is on us, and I have to admit, the photo looks damn good.

We look...*real.*

"Wow."

Scottie jumps and slams the computer shut, like she's watching porn instead of editing our wedding photos. "God, make a noise next time!"

"I'm not sure you'd hear it if I did." I chuckle. "That was some pretty intense concentration. I made a meal and ate it, all while watching you, and you didn't notice."

Her eyes grow large. "You were watching me?"

"Does that bother you?" I know very well that it does.

She turns away from me. "No."

I snort. "You suck at lying."

Her faint growl reaches my ear, and I smile behind her back.

"Anyway…" I begin to back away, leaving her to her devices. "I'm going to hit the sack."

Scottie's shoulders loosen, and she begins to open her laptop again.

"Are you going to eat dinner?" I ask, backing farther away from her.

"Dinner?" she repeats, looking at the time. "Oh, uh… yeah."

Is she lying?

"What are you going to eat?" I lean against the stairs, waiting to see what she'll come up with.

She shrugs with her back to me. "I'll find something."

"Well, there isn't much. You should probably grab some stuff you like at the store because all I have are prepped meals and protein shakes."

She laughs lightly. "Trust me, I'm used to throwing things together to make a meal. It's fine."

My brows furrow with her response. I don't like the feeling it gives me when I think about her not eating or just *throwing things together* to make a meal.

With a heavy sigh, I turn and force myself up the stairs.

I'm halfway up them when I hear her say, "Goodnight." I pause for a second but shake my head and go right to my room in an attempt to get her off my mind, because come tomorrow, I know our photo will be posted all over social media, and the gossip will spread like wildfire.

Ready or not, here comes Mr. and Mrs. Olson.

Twenty-Three

SCOTTIE

MY NEW PHONE IS NICE.

Too nice.

I pretended to be asleep when Emory woke up this morning and messed around in the kitchen, likely making one of his "meals" that smelled inedible. But whatever, I'm not going to put on an apron and pretend I'm some dutiful wife and make him home-cooked meals. That isn't in the contract, and I'm not going to act like this is something it isn't.

I blow a big breath out, and my loose hair flies back. I clench my eyes when I hit "post" and inhale all the air in the living room. Emory walked into the arena for practice as the Chicago Blue Devils' hotheaded goalie with a bad reputation and rumors surrounding him, but he's going to walk out with new rumors that just so happen to be true—like being married to little ol' me.

The photos turned out beautifully. I spent hours editing them and staring at the pure bliss of what I captured, knowing very well that photos don't always show the true picture. That's the one thing I love about photography. It can be so subjective. The photos I have of my dad are all of him smiling, but it doesn't show the pain and suffering he was enduring. I prefer to remember him as the smiling man, watching a hockey game with me perched on his shoulders, instead of the frail man he became that later led to his death.

The vibrating of my phone pulls my attention, and I'm shocked to see how many comments have accumulated on the photo of Emory and me in such a short time. One after another, they continue to pile in. Women are disappointed that Emory is married, some stating that it can't be true. There are questions about his *mystery girl,* and our story, and even some congratulations thrown in there too.

I kept it nice and simple. One single photo of his hand wrapped around my cheek while he held my face steady. His wedding ring is the center of the photo, and you can see a slight angle of mine.

Dizziness sweeps through me the longer I stare at the screen. Opinions and rumors flood the comment section, and I quickly shut the screen off, standing from the couch to head into the kitchen. My stomach growls, and I know I told Emory that I'd find something to eat last night, but I was too focused on editing to scrounge around in the kitchen. My eyes fall to the black credit card on the counter with a handwritten note.

For food. Don't eat my meals.

I snort. One thing is for certain: Emory Olson is not a romantic.

Or maybe he is with a woman he's actually in love with.

Either way, I grab the credit card with a pit in my stomach, hating that I'm using his money to buy groceries. I had no issue attempting blackmail, yet my hand shakes with his credit card. I feel like a thief, but this is what I signed up for, so I swallow my pride, grab my new phone, and head for the door.

———

THE BAG of cat food crinkles in my hand as I climb out of my car and search the parking lot. I leave my phone in the center console, knowing that William won't be calling this time of the evening, and walk toward the dumpster. The usual crowd is at the Cat House, and it's nice to be here without having the stress of working the stage for once. Being married to Emory and sharing a house with him isn't for the faint of heart, but it's ten times better than stripping and pretending like the men that watch my every move are a boost to my confidence instead of an attack on it.

"Shutter?" I creep behind the building and shake the bag of food. "I know you think I've forgotten about you, but I haven't."

I haven't been here for several days, and if Shutter is still around, he'll be hungry. Russ kept asking who was feeding the stray cat, and we all denied it, though the girls knew it was me. I may be married to a pro hockey player now, but that doesn't mean I'm too good to feed the homeless. That includes home-less cats too.

I've avoided the house since I dropped off the small amount of groceries I got from the store, leaving Emory's credit card in the spot he left it. God forbid he thinks I ran off with it. He'd probably call the police.

And fine, I'll admit it to myself...I'm being a chicken.

We both know our marriage is a sham, but with it out in the world, even if only on social media for the time being, it feels different.

I don't want to face him.

Avoidance is key.

169

I sigh and crinkle the bag again. The music from inside the club thumps through the cracks of the back door as I pour some cat food onto the rocks and hope that Shutter will come out later when things are quiet and less scary.

The gravel crunches with the weight of tires, and I stare into the parking lot, wondering which man will show up tonight. It's a fancy car, sleek and polished with dark-tinted windows that blend in with the evening sky. Their lights flick off, and when my eyes adjust, I press against the brick wall to hide.

I'd never forget his face.

You'd think these very wealthy, attractive men would be able to find a woman for the night instead of coming to the Cat House to watch strippers, but apparently Mr. Handsy gets off on touching us inappropriately and getting angry when we don't play along.

Hence why my phone was cracked before Emory replaced it.

I stay pressed to the side of the building until he's out of sight. Part of me wants to go inside to warn the girls, but after a hush works itself through the lobby, they'll know who showed up.

I glance back at the entrance once more before making a beeline to my car. When I turn the corner, I put on the brakes. The loose asphalt is slippery beneath my shoes, and I skid backward, letting go of the cat food in the process. Little pebbles of fish-shaped Meow Mix pelt my skin as I land with a thud on the hard ground.

"Why is my life a joke?" I groan.

"For fuck's sake." Emory stands over me with his hands on his hips and a dark hoodie pulled up over his head like he's trying to be incognito. "I'm going to start calling you Clumsy instead of Rogue."

I sit up quickly, even though my back aches. "Clumsy?" I exclaim. "You scared me! What did you expect?"

He gets down to my level. "I didn't expect you to be here, that's for sure. Don't you remember signing the contract that said you are no longer employed here, Mrs. Olson?"

My name comes from his lips with distaste, and I'm offended right away.

"Of course I remember." I bypass his outstretched hand and climb to my feet all on my own.

His head drops with a chuckle. When he stands and towers over me, he places his hands on his hips, and I'm pretty sure he's about to berate me.

"I'm not working," I explain, putting a little extra emphasis in my tone. "Obviously," I mumble under my breath.

"Then what are you doing here?"

I mimic his stance and put my hands on my hips too. "What are *you* doing here?"

Emory's eye twitches, and heavy silence passes between us. At this point, I'm not sure if our little arrangement is going to work out, because it's clear that we're both irritated with one another, and bickering occurs within every conversation we have.

"You weren't at home," he states. "And you weren't answering your phone." I open my mouth to explain, but he cuts me off. "I knew you'd be here." He shakes his head with disappointment, and I'm instantly defensive.

I stomp my foot, and he looks amused.

"Nowhere in that contract does it state that I can't come here. All it says is that I can't work here." Before he argues with me, I step forward and glare up at his half smile. "And just because we're playing make-believe and considered husband and wife to the world now, doesn't mean I have to give you an itinerary on how I spend my time. You don't have a game tonight, so as far as I'm concerned, my whereabouts are irrelevant."

"You're my wife. Your whereabouts are absolutely relevant." He pauses, and I swear he enjoys our little tiff. "Which is exactly why I shared your location with myself before giving you that new phone."

I gape at him. *How dare he?*

A line of profanity threatens to explode from my mouth, but then I see his lips twitch, and I glare harder.

"Are you laughing at me?" Heat coats my skin, and I want to stomp on his annoyingly large foot.

His smile takes me by surprise. The bright-white color of his teeth stands out in the dark, and I have every intention of scoffing, but then he begins to laugh, and I'm at a loss for words.

"I'm sorry, but—" He chuckles again. "You're standing here in a strip club parking lot, yelling at me and acting so self-righteous, but the only thing I can focus on is what looks to be..." Emory's hand stretches toward my hair, and instead of moving, I stay completely still. He grabs something and inspects it. "Cat food? In your hair."

I zero in on the tiny piece of Meow Mix in between Emory's fingers and feel the urge to laugh too.

I don't, though.

Because there's no way we're going to be on the same page.

"Don't tell me..." Emory clicks his tongue. "You're a crazy cat lady, aren't you?"

My scowl begs to flip into a smile. I look away and down the alley that Shutter likes to frequent. I blink to steady my vision and can't help the relief that spreads along my face from his little shadow.

"God, you are, aren't you?"

I snap at Emory. "Shh!"

He throws his hands out in front of himself in disbelief but shuts up.

Shutter stops dead in his tracks and eyes Emory like he's a predator, but when he shifts his yellow eyes back to me, he lets out a tiny meow.

"Hey, you." My resolve falls, and I forget all about my sparring match with my archnemesis. I walk toward Shutter as he slowly creeps around the side of the building. When I get close enough, he meows one more time and falls to his back, waiting for me to rub his belly.

My fingers sweep over his black fur, and I lower my voice. "You thought I forgot about you, didn't you?"

He gives me a little love bite before popping to all fours. He scurries on quiet paws to the food I left behind and starts to gobble it up like he hasn't eaten in days.

I sigh wistfully and watch him eat a few more bites before turning around to head back to my car.

Emory is leaning against my door, and I'm half-afraid a piece of rust will fall to the ground when he pushes off of it. "We're not taking that cat back to my place."

I roll my eyes. "As if I'd ever suggest that."

I shove my key into the lock the old school way and open my door to head back to *his place.* Emory grips my door tightly when I try to pull it closed. I peer up at him to wait for his next demand.

"I don't want you to come back here."

Seriously?

"I'm feeding a stray cat, Emory. I'm not putting on a skimpy bra and panties to strip like before."

"The cat will find food somewhere else."

The nerve.

"You're not seriously trying to tell me that I can't come back to feed a stray cat, are you?"

Emory gives me a look like he's angry but offended at the same time.

"You're not used to a woman talking back to you, are you?"

His laugh is loud, and I can't tell if it's sarcastic or not. "Actually, I am. My sister talks back to me all the time, but it doesn't usually stop me from getting what I want."

I take that as a challenge.

A devious smile slides onto my face. "Well, consider me your first, because I'm coming back to feed Shutter whether you like it or not."

"Shutter?" His head falls in disbelief. "Of course you named him."

"See you at *your place*." I taunt, pulling on my door with all my might.

My car pops with a loud noise when I turn it on, and Emory scoots backward like it's a gunshot.

To his benefit, it resembles the sound.

I speed off in the direction of his house but not before I catch him looking at Shutter and all the spilled cat food I just wasted.

Twenty-Four

EMORY

NEXT ON MY list of things to do for my wife was to get her a new car because I'm truly terrified of the one she drives around in. But somehow, instead of purchasing a new vehicle for Scottie, I got her a fucking pet instead.

I park behind her 1999 Honda and know she's already inside the house. She's probably pretending to be asleep, like this morning when she was obviously avoiding me. The meowing starts up again, and I turn to stare at my new companion.

"If you do that all night, I'll take you back to the dumpster."

He meows again, but I prefer that over the hissing he was doing when I tried to get him into my car. I ended up scooping up the cat food that Scottie very graciously spilled all over the parking lot and lured the nuisance into the backseat.

"Don't bite me," I warn, reaching for him. He backs his skinny frame into the passenger door in fear, so instead of grabbing him, I open my door and step out onto the sidewalk to wait for him to glide out.

I casually step up the porch stairs and stand near the door

with his laser-focused gaze glued to my every move. I walk halfway inside and stand there, wondering if he'll follow me.

I'm not a cat person.

I'm not even a dog person.

Truthfully, I don't think I'm a people person either.

I never even had a pet growing up because we were too busy. We spent all of our days at the rink, practicing and traveling to weekend-long tournaments, only to come home on Sunday to do it all over again the next week.

I smell Scottie the second I step into the entryway. Her scuffed-up white Converse are sitting beside the door, right next to my hockey bag, and I listen intently for any movement. A black furball rushes into the house before I can shut the door. He sniffs Scottie's shoes before letting out a high-pitched meow.

Next thing I know, Scottie slides into the foyer on fuzzy socks that have cherries all over them, an oversized T-shirt, and tiny shorts. Her hair is in a bun on the top of her head, and the smile she wears is enough to make me do a double take.

When she sees me staring at her mouth, she quickly fixes her face and snaps back into the defiant brat she is when it comes to me.

"You're that concerned about me going to the strip club that you kidnapped Shutter?"

"Kidnapped? Don't you mean adopted?" I shut the door behind me with my foot. Shutter scurries away, darting behind Scottie's bare legs, only to glare at me from afar. "I told you"— I drop my keys right beside hers on the small table by the door —"I always get my way."

Scottie's sarcastic laugh is barely audible. She bends down and scoops Shutter into her arms, and I'm a little perturbed that he doesn't hiss at her like he did to me.

"Did Mr. Cocky scare you?" She rubs her nose along his

face. I can hear his purring from across the room. "Did you get him a litter box?"

I'm quick to answer. "No."

I didn't even think of that.

I open the door behind me. "He's an outside cat."

Scottie glances down at the black cat in her arms and begins to talk to him like he's a human. "Did you hear that, Shutter? He called you an outside cat. The audacity."

"I'm serious, Scottie," I say. "Outside. Now."

She rolls her eyes, but for once, they're actually soft and playful. I may even go as far as to say there's a spark of happiness in them.

All over a dumpster cat.

"Fine," she drags out the word as she passes by me. Her elbow skims my chest with Shutter cradled in her arms. She places him on the porch and looks down at him. "One second."

I stand back and watch her rush down the hallway. I hear her clanking around in the kitchen, and my eyebrows rise as she comes back with two bowls. One is empty, and the other has water in it. She places them down in front of Shutter, who's waiting patiently on the porch, and gives him a pet in between the ears. Then she turns and walks back through the door with a tiny smile on her face.

The air around her shifts. It's like this cat took away her hard exterior and replaced it with a version of her that I've yet to see.

After I give Shutter one more scathing look, I shut the door and head for wherever Scottie ran off to. She sits on the couch with her blanket and the mug Ford got me for Christmas that reads, *I banged your sister,* acting as if I don't exist. She stares at the blank wall, like it's better to look at or something.

"Are you purposefully acting like I don't exist?"

She turns to me. "Hmm?"

My lips flatten, and I sigh. I cut right to the chase. "I have a game tomorrow."

Steam floats in front of her face from the mug. "I'm well aware." Her lips fall to the rim, and she gently sucks whatever liquid is inside.

Is she fucking with me?

I sigh loudly. "I expect you to be there." My gaze falls to her naked finger. "With your ring on."

She peeks at me from atop the rim and gives me a subtle nod.

"You have a box seat, next to the other wives."

That gets her attention. Scottie's shoulders tense, and she places the mug on the coffee table. "What? Why? I can't just sit in the stands and enjoy the game?"

I leave her for a second and head to my bag. "You're Mrs. Olson now," I call over my shoulder. "That means you sit with the rest of the wives."

There's an argument waiting to be had, but instead of putting up a fight, Scottie leans back into the couch cushions and gives me a sharp nod. "You're right."

My extra jersey flies through the living room and lands on her lap. Her fingers graze the blue material slowly. "That's what you'll wear instead of that worn shirt you love so much."

Scottie's finger trails the letters of my last name with her lip trapped in between her teeth.

"Do you remember our backstory?" I ask.

Her gulp echoes around the room before she pins me with a determined look. "Yes."

I shift uncomfortably. "I was...busy in college."

Her eyebrows knit together. "Busy?"

Why do I feel guilty all of a sudden?

I flex my jaw and cut right to the chase. "I fucked a lot of women."

Her mouth flies open. "Oh."

This is uncomfortable. "We can just chalk it up to me trying to...get over you?"

She nods, and her face softens. "Yeah, okay. I'll do what I need to do to make us believable."

I turn and head for the stairs to get away from her. I thought I enjoyed irritating her the most, but there's something highly addicting about her obeying me with those pretty, doe-like eyes.

———

HERE GOES NOTHING.

Blood flies to my fingertips and the icy rink air cools my already sweaty skin. In reality, the crowd is loud and rowdy, but when I'm standing in front of the goal, I hear nothing but my own heartbeat.

I'm laser-focused.

As always.

Until I happen to look up at the jumbo screen in the middle of the arena and see Scottie's face in the center. At that exact moment, the sounds of the arena come swooping in, and I grip my stick tighter.

The announcer's voice echoes throughout my helmet, and my pulse races. It's absurd how my life is such a concern in the hockey world. Fans quiet down to hear, because apparently my love life is more exciting than the game we're about to play.

My agent says that being the talk of the hockey community is a good thing, and my recent marriage and exposure to my private life will make me more desirable to other teams because it'll bring in more revenue, but it's still irritating.

Never mind my stats.

Let's chat about the ring on my finger and my pretty wife

in the stands, wearing my number on her back. I won't tell her, but she wears my jersey well.

The only good thing that's coming out of this is that the media is talking about the photo of Scottie and me almost kissing on social media instead of the recent allegations placed against me that can't possibly be true because I'm *married*.

I shake my head and give the okay to my teammates, who start flinging pucks at me from left and right. With each block, I start to focus a little more and stop thinking about what Scottie is talking about while she sits with the other wives.

I'm not worried about her fitting in or playing the part.

I've seen her turn it on and off before. She's climbed on top of a stage in sky-high heels and a red wig. It only took spending a few minutes with her to know that the Cherry persona was just a ploy.

Just like her Mrs. Olson persona.

When the game is about to start and the warm-up music dies down, I allow myself one quick glance at her in the box off to the left of the rink. Our eyes catch, and the smile she throws me is so believable I almost find myself falling for it too.

I send her a quick wink, just in case other people are watching us, and then get in the zone.

My new wife is watching.

I might as well play a damn good game.

Twenty-Five

SCOTTIE

"SO, tell us! How did you and Emory meet? We had no idea he was even in a relationship until that photo popped up."

Angela, the one with bright-red hair and cute freckles leans into the conversation. "The group chat was blowing up."

Hattie nods, and her freshly blown-out hair moves with her. "It's true. When there's a new girl on the block, we have to converse." She laughs, and I'm not sure if it's a good or bad thing that they had an entire group chat about me.

"Well..." I tuck my hair behind my ear nervously.

Her hand falls to my arm. "Don't worry! It was nothing bad! We just wanted to invite you to hang out with us. We tend to stick together. I know it doesn't seem like it, but it's kind of hard to be one of the wives, especially when kids are involved."

We both look over to the squawking baby refusing to sleep in the back corner of the box. There's a couple of the wives over there, trying to help the mom who looks beyond tired yet still as pretty as ever.

They all seem nice so far. Welcoming, even.

Which is a change from any other time I've ever found

myself in the middle of a group of women. I didn't fit in with the popular girls in high school. No one wanted to be friends with the poor girl who was more into the school's hockey game versus the way the boys stretched on the ice.

I glance out the glass to see if the game has started, because the one thing I don't have to fake tonight is my love for the sport. "When Emory and I reconnected, we decided to keep our relationship private. But after the media continued to run with any rumor that popped up, we decided it was time to settle the score and put an end to it." I smile softly. "We weren't together when he was in college, but we got back in touch shortly after he graduated."

I hate that I'm lying right through my teeth, but it's so easy to do when I know my future depends on it.

"I did my own thing and kind of watched from afar, letting him achieve his goals, but when he reached back out, it was like no time had passed."

Angela swoons. "That's...honestly...that's so selfless."

I laugh and convince myself to believe the story falling graciously from my mouth so I don't trip up in the future. I turn my attention to the ice, and the rest of the wives do too—all except the one with the baby. She's more concerned over rocking her daughter, who has discarded her blue bow onto the floor.

My heart beats with a passion I've only ever felt when watching hockey or holding a camera. I eye my bag, craving to pull it out to take some pictures, but for my first game as Emory's wife, I decide to keep it hidden and use my phone instead. I'm not sure if Emory got me a phone with an amazing camera on purpose, but it takes pretty good photos. I've already been on the jumbo screen once. I don't want to be on it again with my camera, bringing even more attention to myself than before.

When everyone is distracted, I place my left hand on the

glass and use my phone camera to focus on the rink. My hand is off-center and blurred just slightly but not too much that you can't see the massive ring on my finger. I catch a shot of Emory guzzling water through his helmet and remind myself to post the photo after the game.

I'm just out here doing my job while the other wives are oblivious.

By the time the third period starts, my voice is raspy, and I've found myself in a rhythm with everyone. I wasn't expecting it, but they're just as much into the game as I am. It's the first time I've ever watched a game with someone other than my father, and I'm actually having an okay time.

Anytime we score a goal, Angela and I give each other double high-fives and smile onto the ice while the scoring player does his celly. Emory has only let one puck slide by, and it was Hattie who pointed out that the camera was zoomed in on my face, showing me on the jumbo screen. I was mid-conversation with Angela and one of the players' fiancée, persuading them that it was okay. I dove into the statistics and everything, unable to hide my true knowledge of the game.

They nodded, and their eager looks only prompted me further.

Throughout the rest of the game, we talked about all things hockey, and by the time the game ended, I was closer with them than I'd ever been with any other woman my age.

"Oh my god. I feel like I've learned so much from you." Georgia tips the rest of her beer in her mouth. She's engaged to one of the rookie players and is as sweet as can be.

"And you were the only one who was able to get Nola to stop crying," Vivian says, looking at me like I have some motherly touch.

I don't. However, I can't not smile at the innocent face wrapped in a Blue Devils baby blanket, sleeping peacefully in her arms.

"You don't have kids, right?"

William's face pops into my mind for a split second. He isn't my child, but there were a lot of times that I felt like he was.

I shake my head.

"Do you and Emory want kids?" The question from Vivian is purely innocent, but I panic.

My face warms. I quickly put my attention back to the arena. The players are already off the ice, but for some reason, I want to make eye contact with Emory, as if he can give me an answer from just a look.

"Vivian!" Angela scolds. "They just got married! Give them a second before expecting babies."

"Sorry. I just wish there were a few other little ones running around."

"Rhodes has a daughter, right?" I ask, trying to take the attention off me and Emory.

They nod but share a strange look with one another. "She only comes to some of the games. He can't keep a nanny to save his life, so she's probably at home with some random teenage babysitter."

"You ladies ready?" Georgia skips toward the box suite door.

"Ready?" I ask.

Angela pulls me with her after I quickly grab my bag. "Occasionally, after the games, we head to an exclusive club downtown to hang out with the guys. Surely Emory told you that?" She turns to look at Hattie. "Didn't Corbin pass along the word to Emory?"

She thinks for a moment before shrugging. "I think, but text your hubby and let him know you'll be with us. He can't say no if we kidnapped his wife."

There's that word again: wife.

I pull open my phone, and to no surprise, Emory's

number is programmed in there as *Husband*. I type a quick text and threaten his life for not telling me about our *after-plans.*

Twenty-Six

EMORY

MY PHONE BUZZES while I'm mid-change, and I expect it to be my parents for their positive after-game message or, as of late, their dismay over my marriage. But instead, it's Scottie and I already know what's coming before I read the text

> Really? No warning at all?

I knew she'd be frustrated with me, but in my defense, Corbin pulled me aside seconds before the game and filled me in on what they do after the games and warned me that his wife would likely talk Scottie into going.

> I didn't have time to tell you. I was a little busy, in case you didn't notice.

I pull my shirt on and shake out my damp hair. Corbin throws me a nod and tells me he'll see me there. This isn't the norm for after a game, but since Coach Jacobs gave us the day off tomorrow and we have a one-day break, this is apparently a *thing*. The team is pretty focused on hockey—we all live and breathe the sport, just like with any other pro hockey player I've known. It's our livelihood. But even veteran hockey players have said there has to be a balance in the world of work and play. I'm not sure I really believe that, but it's apparent that my new wife was persuaded by Corbin's wife, so off I go to play another fucking game.

> How could I not notice? Your ego took up the entire arena.

I silently laugh at Scottie's insult. Even through the phone, she has a bite to her tone.

> And you screaming my name did the same.

Of course I saw her cheering from her box seat. The entire arena did because she was on the jumbo screen more times than I was. I smirk at my text, and something hot moves against my skin. I watch her little bubble pop up, like she's typing. When a message doesn't come through, I take the initiative to drive her mad even further.

> Nothing to say back to that? I wonder where your mind went when you read that text.

I highly doubt she had the same dirty thought I did, but I can't help myself. I am already picturing her scrunched-up nose.

> My mind is full of other things. Like how I'm going to kill you when I see you.

I'm heading to my car when I pull open my phone to text her back.

> I love it when you talk dirty to me.

> I wasn't expecting to play husband and wife in front of people so soon. I needed a warning. Or perhaps some practice.

My car starts up, and although I'm tired after the game, there's something brewing in my stomach that is awfully close to excitement. Over the last several months, I haven't felt the itch of a thrill except for when Scottie entered my life, which is worrying.

> How hard can it be? Just treat me like your last boyfriend. Act like you're in love with me.

> Though you probably don't have to act.

When Scottie texts back, my car plays it over the speaker:

> That would be a great idea, except I've never had a boyfriend! And I'm most definitely not in love with you.

I slam on the brakes, and the seatbelt almost chokes me. "What? Never had a boyfriend?"

My car repeats what I said aloud, and I panic. I reach forward and try to hit "don't send," but a second later, I hear: *"Message sent."*

I grip the steering wheel tightly. Not only is Scottie unprepared, but now, so am I.

———

"THERE HE IS, FOLKS." Applause breaks out when I walk into the club downtown that I've never even heard of. I send the guys a glare. I'm not one to want attention, and I'm really not one to brag to my team. I only brag to Scottie because I know it irritates her.

"A beer for our number one goalie?" Matthew comes over and presses a full cup of ale into my chest. I grip it and begin to search through the strobing lights for Scottie.

This is mostly exclusive to the couples on the team, and in order to keep up the charade of my freshly new marriage, it's something that Scottie and I needed to attend. I'm used to hanging with my teammates from the Coyotes, but that got me in trouble, which in turn has led me to this moment right here.

A few sips of beer and a lengthy conversation about the game later, I finally ask the question I've wanted the answer to since stepping foot in the club.

"So, where exactly is my wife?"

That word is becoming a staple in my vocabulary.

Corbin nods to the stairs. "They're comparing our dick lengths on the dance floor."

Dylan chuckles. "There's no need. Everyone knows who has the biggest dick in the room."

Just then, Malaki, who isn't even in a relationship, sits down next to us, like he's been waiting for the perfect moment to make himself known. "Obviously, we all know it's me."

Of course he'd show up, even though no one invited him.

"The only single guy in the club?" I crack. "That checks out."

The guys laugh, but Malaki scoffs. "I'm not ready to settle down. That has nothing to do with my dick size. My focus is hockey. Not..." He looks down and bounces his disgusted face to all of our ringed fingers.

"Commitment, someone to come home to every day, support...love?" Dylan asks.

Malaki snaps his fingers. "Exactly. No thanks. I only have room for one obsession in my life, and it's hockey."

It's then that I realize I am going to have to pull my shit together, because so far, my new wife and I have done nothing but take a few fake photos together, share some angry texts, and piss each other off. My obsession is hockey too, but now I'm going to have to make it seem like it's *her*.

Corbin rests his back against the bar. "You just haven't found the right girl, and how could you? Your idea of going out is visiting the strip club every chance you get."

My jaw aches, and I stare directly at Malaki.

Don't.

His lazy gaze skims by, latching onto me for a split second. But then he shrugs. "Nothing wrong with a girl who can dance."

"Speaking of..." Matthew gestures to the dance floor, and after a few seconds of searching, I find her.

An upbeat song is pouring through the speakers. The women are dancing together like they're the only ones in the club. I have a strong feeling that every man in here, single or not, is staring at them. I'm in too much of a trance to notice, though. Scottie is in the middle of the floor, spinning Matthew's fiancée around in a circle with my last name glued to her back. They're both laughing, and God, my wife is beautiful.

With her wavy blonde hair flowing around her flushed face, she's having the time of her life, weaving in and out of the strobing lights. I have never seen her look the way she does right now, and I'm captivated.

Is she tipsy?

For the first time since meeting her, she doesn't seem uptight or too focused to even crack a smile. Instead of stress flowing off her shoulders like it's her entire personality, she's airy. Like a fucking ray of sunshine in the middle of a dark club.

Her laugh catches my attention again, and a gush of warmth flies to my fingertips.

"She's done for now," Corbin muses. "They've fully accepted your girl into their circle."

I say nothing.

Instead, I relax in the barstool and keep my gaze pinned to Scottie who has yet to notice me. Or maybe she has, and she's just avoiding looking in my direction to spite me.

I wonder what she'd do if I went up behind her and wrapped my hands around her waist and took over the role of being her dance partner? She'd have no choice but to play along then, because now, we have a live audience.

Before I can torment her, Hattie, Corbin's wife, drags her by the hand, and they head to the bartender carrying a round of drinks on his tray. I scrutinize her every move, choosing to ignore the men nearby that can't stop looking at her ass in those tight jeans.

There's no need to get jealous.

I know on paper she's mine, but in reality, she isn't.

Hattie's bottom lip pops out when Scottie refuses a shot, which provokes my curiosity. Maybe she knows her limits, or maybe she doesn't drink.

I'm beginning to realize that I don't know my wife very well at all.

The guys are mid-conversation about the game, and I take the opportunity to open my phone to text Scottie.

> You don't drink?

> Depends on what kind of wife you want me to be.

Without looking at her, I fire off another text.

196

Not the sloppy drunk kind.

Well, in that case...

I swear the air in the club grows hotter. Like a puppet, I feel a tug on my attention and find her staring at me from across the club. She doesn't take her wild blue eyes from me when she reaches for the shot glass in Hattie's hand and tips it back in one gulp.

My eyebrow cocks, and my breath hitches.

A deep growl vibrates within my chest as I type another text.

You're asking for trouble.

Her eye roll pushes me over the edge.

I can blame it on my sudden exhaustion from the game I just played or the touch of jealousy I recognize when I watch the male bartender eye her for a little too long. Or maybe it's the fact that I've found myself in another club with my team-mates, just like before, when I inserted myself into someone else's bullshit and found myself in the back of a police car.

Get over here and act like my wife, Rogue.

Or else the bartender is going to drop every last glass balancing on his tray when I happen to walk over there and calmly tell him to keep his eyes to himself.

Instead of acting like a caveman, I take another sip of beer and try to relax. I have a good head on my shoulders. I'm one to learn from my mistakes, so I move my attention to Scottie again instead of the bartender who is egging me on just by existing.

Her back is to me when I feel another text come in.

> I'm not sure I like the way you're bossing me around.

I can't help but chuckle. I'm not sure I have ever had a woman talk to me the way Scottie does. She looks so sweet with her sunshiny appearance. Her light hair and eyes are appealing and soft in ways that draw everyone in a little closer, but that mouth is going to drive me absolutely crazy.

> I'm not sure I like the way you're drawing attention from every male in this bar with my last name on your back.

Without giving myself a reason to back out, I stand abruptly and keep my sights directly on her. I may have even gotten up mid-conversation with my teammates, but I can't seem to care.

Scottie laughs at something Georgia says. She places her hands on her shoulders to brace herself. When Georgia makes eye contact with me, I know she's warning her that I'm about to swoop in.

Scottie straightens quickly on the dance floor, but without allowing her to turn or run away, I slip my hands to her waist and steady her.

"Don't run," I whisper down into her ear. "You're my wife, and we're in public. Remember?"

She turns her head slightly and angles her flushed face to meet mine. I raise an eyebrow and whisper in her ear, "There are eyes in here, so it's time to act like my wife."

Too many eyes if you ask me.

"Have you ever heard of asking nicely?" She says it with a sweetness in her tone, but I know her well enough to recognize the sarcasm.

"I thought I was being nice when I didn't turn you into the authorities for trying to blackmail me. I thought I was being nice when I saved you from that classy strip club you were working at too."

Scottie's bony elbow hits me in the ribs. My stomach tightens from the hit, and now I'm irritated.

The music shifts to a different song, and either it's in my head, or it's on the provocative side. "I think I'm the one who's doing the saving, Olson."

There she goes again, using my last name.

"Again. You're asking for trouble, Rogue."

"What are you gonna do? Withhold my pay?" She's acting bold, so I pull her in closer. I take my nose and drag it up her neck, resting right beside her ear. I feel her body go eerily still against mine. I can't pay attention to who's around us because I'm too invested in our war. What was supposed to be a normal celebration of after-game drinks with the team and other wives is turning into yet another quarrel. Scottie makes things complicated, always wanting to argue or defy me, yet I can't keep myself from craving our interactions or provoking her further.

"I have my ways of punishing you that have nothing to do with violating the contract," I rasp.

Scottie's fingers press into my wrist, and I hope she can't feel my pulse thrumming against my skin with every dirty thought that's swarming my head.

She tempts me further when she says, "Like what?"

The thoughts that race through my head are filthy, and it's a shame because I know it's not where her mind is, especially if she was telling the truth about never having a boyfriend.

To the media, I'm a man who is obsessed with hockey and focused on the game more than most in the league, even with my tainted reputation. But after all that is said and done, I'm still a man. One who has sworn off women since a few tarnished the rest with their rumors and scheming ways—the woman pressed against me included. I'm a man who hasn't slept with anyone in what feels like forever, and unfortunately, it's fucking with my head.

Scottie can't be trusted, even if, on paper, it looks like she can. It doesn't matter that we're both wearing rings on our left hands, telling the world and everyone in this club that we are husband and wife.

What we have is an arrangement. There are liabilities at stake, and I refuse to let her teasing words and perfect body that I can't stop picturing naked sway me into falling into a trap that could ruin my reputation further.

So instead of listing ways I'd *like* to punish her, I go with something else. "Keep acting like you're not being paid to act like my wife, and you'll find out."

I thought it was the easy route. A warning that she'd heed because we both know I'm not forcing her to act like my wife. I'm *paying* her.

But I was wrong.

Scottie turns all the way around, and the look that flashes across her face stirs up my natural need to win. The only problem is that my idea of winning, at the current moment, is kissing her just to prove a point.

Twenty-Seven

SCOTTIE

"CHALLENGE ACCEPTED."

It comes off as me flirting, and it's because of the alcohol I've had.

I don't drink.

It brings up too many unwanted memories and triggers something that I want no part of. But leave it to Emory to irritate me to the point that I go against my own defenses.

He smiles, and it's a nice change from the stoic, broody glare I always get.

His hands move a little lower, and his dangerously hot expression shifts. "That's the way you want to play?" He sounds excited, and I gulp.

Shit.

I've bitten off more than I can chew, but there's no going back now. In fact, I'd rather chew my own arm off than let anyone, especially Emory Olson, see any sort of weakness I carry.

"Yep," I answer, letting the *P* pop from my mouth. I push closer to him, and my stomach flips. "I may be your wife, but that doesn't mean you get to boss me around or insult me every chance you get."

He laughs.

My nostrils flare with anger, and the alcohol in my system burns brighter. "And the threats stop now too."

Emory closes the gap between us. Our bodies press together tightly, and it probably seems like we're just newlyweds, unable to keep our hands to ourselves, but little do they know, we're sparring. "You're tempting me, Rogue."

"Tempting you to do what?" I act unfazed by his strained voice, but heat sweeps down my back.

His hands tighten against my waist, and my heart skips a beat. I can't remember the last time I was touched by a man my age who wasn't throwing twenties at my feet while tracing every curve of my body with their slimy eyes.

I can easily feel myself slipping into a fantasy with Emory that simply does not exist.

It all started with the box seats. I was forced to pretend like I don't have a load of debt, a convict brother who needs my help, a dead father who left me with abandonment issues, and a mother who hardly recognizes me and would rather live with a needle in her arm than try and come back to reality.

"You're tempting me to prove a point."

His answer snaps me out of my thoughts. "What point?"

"That you're mine."

I open my mouth to argue, because it's my default, but he takes control so quickly I don't have time to think.

Emory drags his hand across my hip and pins me against him by gripping my chin with enough force to get my full attention. "I'm going to kiss you."

My eyes widen.

"Prepare yourself because, remember, everyone in this club thinks I've fucked you, Scottie. So act appropriately."

"Emor—"

Every single thought disappears.

Him.

That's all I feel.

His mouth falls to mine, and at first, I think it's a shock to both of us. There's an electricity buzzing between our bodies, and the tension is so tight my chest constricts. His fingers grip my face tighter as his other hand slowly skims over my curves like he's touched me a million times before. Just when I think he's done and he slowly lets up on my mouth, he goes back in for more.

I'm at his mercy.

The warmth of his mouth on mine flows through my limbs freely, and I find myself opening up for him. He kisses me again and again, sweeping his devilish tongue back and forth. He presses his lips harder into mine, like someone is trying to pull us apart, and the smallest little bit of fear slips through at the thought.

When a little noise escapes me—without my permission— it snaps him out of whatever spell we're both under. He pulls back, and although he doesn't show it on his face, I feel it in his grip.

He's just as shocked as I am, even if he was the one in charge.

And I guess that's what he was trying to tell me this entire time. I'm his, whether I'm being paid or not, and he's just proved it to anyone who's watching.

After glancing around the club briefly, I'm pretty sure everyone was watching.

Malaki wiggles his eyebrows, and I'm sweating from the attention.

Emory clears his throat, and I watch him fight through some type of thought. Our eyes meet and, with a grumbly voice, he says, "Since I've proven my point, I think it's time to go."

His warm palm falls into mine, and we say a brief goodbye to his teammates and the wives. As soon as we're outside, the cool air coats my heated skin, and I inhale deeply. I feel drunk, and it has nothing to do with the tiny shot I had.

I reach inside my purse for my keys but stumble forward when Emory pulls the bag from my shoulder. "You're riding with me."

A little high from the kiss, I'm slow to be combative. I follow after him for a split second before snapping out of it and stopping abruptly in the middle of the sidewalk.

It doesn't take long for Emory to realize I'm not moving. He turns slightly, looking at my mouth once before moving to my eyes. "Scottie, I'm tired. Let's go."

"What about my car?" I ask.

He gawks at me. "What about it?"

I look around at my surroundings. It's well past business hours, but the city is still very much alive. Replacing sleek vehicles and business men biking to work are Ubers and gangs of drunken college students mixed in with the homeless who are trying to score a buck.

"Someone might break into it or...steal it."

It might seem silly to be attached to a shitty car like the one I own, but the hunk of metal is a part of me. I saved up for it, and as of late, it's one of the only things that I consider mine.

I'm proud of it.

Emory's laughter pisses me off. I cross my arms over the jersey he made me wear. I'm seconds from ripping it off just to irritate him.

"Oh, you're serious?"

"Yes," I snap. "You might be new to Chicago, but I'm not. Downtown is..."

I glance around once more to prove my point but stiffen immediately when I recognize a familiar face.

A chill whips through me.

My thoughts spin out of control, and I suck in a soft gasp. A tremble racks my bones, and I hardly hear Emory when he says, "If someone steals your car, I'll buy you a new one."

A hollowness carves into my stomach the longer I stare at her.

I try to avoid the places I know she frequents, because these interactions stay with me much longer than I want. Seeing my mother in the state she's in drives a knife in so deeply I'm left feeling sick over it for days.

Look away, Scottie.

"Come on, Scottie. Don't make this any har—"

I hurry forward and almost run into Emory's chest. He studies me with confusion when I frantically nod. "Okay. Let's go."

I lean into him for silent support, and although he has no idea why, he allows it. The little line of worry smooths after he shakes his head, ignoring my insane behavior.

When we reach his car, I don't fight with him over opening my door, which is probably just something he's doing because so many people are out and about—most of them having gone to the game themselves. I turn once more to glance at the group of homeless loitering outside of the small convenience store on the corner because I can't help myself.

Seeing her in this state is what destroyed my youth years ago, and it's only gotten worse since. There's a pressing ache in the center of my chest, pulling on the walls I've built over the years.

I drag my attention away and dig my nails into the leather of Emory's passenger seat. My jaw hurts from the pressure, and my ears ring until Emory's large hand lands on my arm. I jump and make eye contact with him. The lights on his dashboard move against the side of his face, and his furrowed expression tricks me into thinking he's worried. His attention shifts past me, and he gazes out the window in the direction that I was staring off into.

He says nothing.

Instead, he leans in close and grabs the seatbelt from beside me. He pulls it taut against my body before shifting his car into gear and speeding off toward his house.

I wait until my heartbeat settles and I regain the ability to speak again before I glance over at him and say, "You're not buying me a new car."

He scoffs. "You're impossible."

I shrug and settle back into the seat. "You married me."

THE SCENT of cleaning supplies mixed with bacon creeps underneath my closed door, and I lie in my bed, trying to figure out what the hell Scottie is up to downstairs. The sun has yet to rise, and that means it's just too fucking early.

After tossing and turning three more times, my curiosity gets the best of me. I fling the covers over my sore muscles and pull on some sweatpants. I forgo the shirt because it's my house, whether Scottie is living here or not, and honestly, I feel like I need to level the playing field a little bit.

The kiss.

The fucking kiss that was born from a rivalry and the need to establish my dominance. Last night, we found ourselves in some twisted competition over who has the most power, and after I felt her open up for me to deepen the kiss, I'm not sure I have any power when it comes to her.

I'm irritated by it. It left me wanting more, which was not the plan.

I descend the stairs one by one, counting on the little bit of light from the early morning sun to guide my way. The smell of breakfast gets stronger with each step I take toward the kitchen, and my mouth waters. It smells damn good.

When my feet touch the floor, I stare at the glossy streaks of wood beneath me. I scan the living room, wondering if my mom made a surprise trip, because the last time my house was this clean, it was because of her.

Scottie's bed, also known as my couch, is untouched.

Her pillow and blanket are still folded nicely at the end of the cushion, and it looks like she may have even vacuumed them at some point.

My brow furrows. I run my hand through my messy hair and walk farther into the living room, landing at the large opening in the kitchen.

There's a quick hitch in my breath when I spot her standing there with her back to me. She's leaning up on her tiptoes, reaching for the plates that are just out of reach. Part of me wants to stand back and see what she plans to do, but I find myself moving forward. I round the island and silently creep up behind her. Her ass, in those tiny little sleep shorts, grazes against the front of my sweatpants. I clench my abs and reach beside her, grabbing onto the plates that she's desperate for.

Scottie's shriek slices through the sizzling of bacon, and it takes everything in me to stay impassive. There will not be a reaction coming from me over how I'm just now noticing the perfect shape of her lips. And those smooth legs peeking out from her sleep shorts? Couldn't care less. Pristine, perky breasts edging the top of her little tank? Nothing to see there.

"Need a hand?" I grunt, scattering every last desire I have from our close proximity.

Scottie's eyelashes flutter several times before she swallows. The longer we stare at each other with nothing but the sizzling bacon in the background, the more I lose my hold on my irritation from her waking me up with the smell of a freshly cleaned house and breakfast cooking on the stove.

"Ow, shit!" Scottie jumps back, ramming her ass into my dick again.

My stomach drops, but I quickly move her aside and grab the greasy pan from the stovetop and turn the gas off, eliminating the large flame. When I turn back to look at my little arsonist, she's inspecting her arm. Little red dots appear on her skin.

"Are you trying to burn the house down?" I ask, grabbing the dish towel.

I wet it with cool water and lightly press it against Scottie's arm, ignoring the tug of her independence. My grip tightens on her bicep as I keep the rag pressed onto her slightly burnt skin.

"No," she finally answers, looking away. It's as if she can't stand the fact that I'm taking care of her arm. "I was just..."

"Making me breakfast?" I raise an eyebrow before removing the rag and inspecting her arm.

She huffs. "Who said this was for you?"

I briefly eye the stack of pancakes off to the side. "Unless you plan to eat your entire body weight in pancakes, I'd say there's plenty for us to share."

After seeing that her arm is fine, I let it go and watch her busy herself with pulling the bacon off the pan. With her back to me, she throws a ridiculous statement over her shoulder. "I was making breakfast for Shutter and myself. Not you."

I snort while grabbing a plate. With three slabs of bacon and five pancakes stacked on top of one another, I drag a stool out and take a seat. In between each bite of food, I survey the kitchen and the rest of the house.

The math isn't mathing, and I'm damn good at math.

"Did you sleep?" I shove another bite of food in my mouth while observing her very closely.

Despite the dark bags underneath her eyes and messy bun on the top of her head, she still resembles a little ray of sunshine—but now with lack of sleep.

Scottie pauses with the carton of oat milk in her hand. *Is she lactose intolerant?* Her gaze briefly dips to my bare torso before she mumbles, "Umm..." She shrugs and quickly turns toward the fridge to continue putting away all the ingredients she used.

"You didn't, did you?" I push again, not letting her get out of answering me. "You cleaned my entire house." I pause, waiting for some type of reaction from her, but I get nothing. "And you made me breakfast?"

She spins, and I refuse to give her another chance to deny it, because there's no way she made this for a damn cat.

"Why?" I ask.

"I didn't do it for you."

I stand with my empty plate and walk over to the sink. She doesn't stay next to me. Instead, she rounds the island and sits in the same seat I was just in. "No. I mean, why didn't you sleep?"

Her mouth opens, and I can't keep myself from staring at it when I hear her soft voice. "I don't know. I just...couldn't sleep."

Forcing myself to look away, I sigh. "Maybe if you stop being stubborn and sleep in the actual bed, you'd be able to sleep."

She laughs, and it takes me by surprise. Mid-wash, hands sudsy with soap, I crane my neck to watch the giggle float out of her mouth. "Trust me, it has nothing to do with a bed."

I arch an eyebrow, expecting more of a response than that.

"Oh, wait. I forgot...you don't trust me." Her lips flatten before she takes another bite of food, wrapping her lips around the fork. My mouth waters, and I'm blaming it on the taste of pancakes lingering on my tongue. "I can sleep practically anywhere," she adds. "I slept on the floor for years before I got a bed."

I stand there, washing the same dish for far too long, repeating her words in my head.

"What do you mean?" I finally ask.

Scottie seems so unaware of how outlandish her response is. She just shrugs and repeats herself.

"You slept on the floor?"

She nods slowly this time. A pinkish tint creeps onto her cheeks, and I kind of hate that I feel sorry for her. I'd usually choose this time to poke at her so I can watch her nose scrunch with annoyance, but I can't bring myself to do it. Instead, I finish cleaning my plate and the rest of the kitchen when she slips outside onto the porch, knowing she's done plenty over the last several hours while I was asleep.

After Scottie comes back inside, having had a full conversation with the damn stoop cat that hisses at me every single time I leave the house, she places her hands on her hips and gives me a look. I'm not sure if Shutter had a pep talk with her, but the pink tinge of embarrassment on her cheeks has left the party, and my sassy wife is back in action. "Are you ready to take me to get my car?"

I narrow my gaze. "You think it's safe to drive when you've been up for twenty-four hours?"

Her angry huff sends something exciting into my bloodstream. I dip my eyes down to her mouth again before I berate myself and pull my attention back to her jutted lip.

"I'm fine," she argues with a little stomp of her foot. "Plus, I just made you breakfast."

"Oh, so it was a bribe?"

She shrugs casually and leans her hip against the island. "It can be."

I laugh under my breath at her ability to seem so sweet one second but clever the next. I swear, she's tempting me.

Tempting me to do what? I have no idea. But my new wife is stirring something up inside of me that I have never felt in my life.

We stare at each other from across the island. The entire time we're at an impasse, I don't allow myself to look at her mouth. My jaw tightens when I place my hands face down on the counter. I try to press into the stone to give me some sort of stability so I don't become complacent to the way she's looking at me.

"Let's make a deal."

Fuck, what?

"We already have a deal," she counters. "I play the role of your wife, and you pay me, remember?"

"Right. Except, I know nothing about you, and you know everything about me."

Scottie eyes me suspiciously, but she doesn't put up a fight yet, so I keep going.

"I'll take you to get your car—"

"And you won't buy me a new one," she interrupts me.

For fuck's sake.

I reword my statement. "I'll take you to get your car...and I won't buy you a new one...as long as you start answering questions."

Scottie's face is made of stone, but her eyes tell a completely different story. The fear inside of them, over me asking her some questions, is all the more reason to ask them.

"What'll it be?"

"I can just call an Uber to get my car."

Ever so slowly, I glance at her purse sitting on the end of the counter. Knowing her better than she thinks, I race her to it, which isn't hard to do because three of my steps are five of hers. At the last second, I lift her keys up in the air and watch with amusement as she tries to reach them by jumping.

I lean down to her level. "Too slow, baby."

She pouts, and her warm, angry, pancake-scented breath hits me in the face.

God damn, that smells sweet.

"You're a dick."

I slip her keys into my pocket and throw her words from the night before right back at her. "You married me."

"Don't remind me," she mumbles, following me toward the door.

When we make it outside, something hits me in the back. I turn and catch my balled-up hoodie before it hits the ground.

"Put a shirt on!" Scottie zooms past me after petting Shutter between the ears. "And you get one question a day, so choose wisely."

I smile to myself and follow after her, knowing I've won.

Twenty-Nine

SCOTTIE

> Did you sleep last night?

I NUZZLE SHUTTER'S head with my chin as he snuggles in closer. His purring is almost louder than my phone's text tone. Rubbing my hand down his silky black fur, I type a quick text to Emory while smiling to myself.

> Is that your question for the day?

He texts back within seconds, which is surprising because he's about to climb on the ice for a game. I already have it ready to go on my phone because, for the life of me, I can't find a TV in his house. What man doesn't own a TV? I'm afraid to snoop around, fearful there are cameras somewhere, so I have the app downloaded and will watch it that way.

> No.

I wait because I know he'll fire his real question off in a matter of seconds. He stuck true to his word and has only asked me one question per day since dropping me off at my car and following closely behind until we got back to his house, which was when he asked a question that made my cheeks burn with humiliation. He didn't believe me that I'd never had a boyfriend and assumed I was lying. I had to explain to him that, although I have dated before, I've never been in the type of relationship where chocolates, movie dates, and early morning cuddles were involved. The only time I see those things in my future is if I plan for them in order to keep our show of a happy marriage believable.

Shutter lets out a loud sigh when Emory texts again, clearly agitated that my phone is interrupting his slumber.

> This is my question, and answer quickly because I'm about to head out for warm-ups.

> Are you letting the demon inside the house while I'm away?

My body stills. I search around the room for cameras with a pounding heart. I bounce my attention to every corner of the living room while I lie on the couch with a rigid spine.

Shit, how does he know?

> I'll know if you're lying.

Being my typical snarky self with my new husband, I quietly snap a photo of Shutter on my chest and send it to him.

I send another text and roll my lips together while I wait for his response. It's been a very long time since I've texted back and forth with anyone that wasn't related to work or William. I almost don't know what to do with the jitters I feel in my stomach, eagerly waiting for a message.

Instead of a text coming through, a call comes.

I panic with my finger hovering over the answer button.

The defiance I have when it comes to Emory lingers, but I answer the phone anyway because my curiosity gets the best of me.

"Hello?" I answer quietly.

Emory's face appears because he switches it to a video call at the last second. I smooth my features so I don't give anything away, but imagine my shock when I see the background of a locker room behind his seemingly stern face.

"Really?" he says, sending me a look. "Get that psycho thing out of m—" He pauses, and something flickers across his face. "Our house."

Our house.

As much as I want to poke him further, I don't, because not only is he about to go play a game against one of the best teams in the league right now, but I'm his wife. The snarkiness has to stay behind closed doors, and the flirtiness has to emerge.

"Our house is warmer," I say, nuzzling Shutter again.

"He's a cat. He'll be fine. Put him back outside."

Emory's eye twitches when I smile deviously. His head tilts, throwing his sandy hair over his forehead. His good looks annoy me so much that I can't help but play with fire. "Make me."

I squint and try to tell him something with my eyes. Everyone has some misconception about goalies being stupid and a little bit crazy, but in my educated opinion, goalies are the complete opposite. They're always on guard, observing the ice and knowing which direction the puck will go well before it even does. They know when to engage and when to sit back and watch, which is exactly why Emory catches on to my flirty tone right away.

His lip lifts into a dangerous grin that digs right into my

chest. My heart beats harder, and Shutter stretches on top of me, probably sensing what I won't admit.

"You temptin' me?" Emory asks, voice full of mirth.

I shrug shyly, and my cotton jacket falls a little off my shoulder, showing off my bare skin. Emory glances at it briefly before moving back to my face.

"Sounds like a challenge," someone calls from the locker room.

Emory grunts, which sort of sounds like a laugh.

"The real challenge is getting your grumpy goalie to soften a little for this sweet little kitty." I kiss Shutter on the head. "Maybe after you win the game?" I say, playing my part a little *too* well.

A flash of uncertainty crosses Emory's face, and I smile at him with a little slip of my breath. Kane's face takes over the camera screen, and I quickly move my jacket back up to cover my skin. "You rootin' us on, Wifey?"

"Wifey?" I hear the distaste in Emory's voice and almost roll my eyes.

Stellar acting skills.

"She isn't your wife," Emory snarls, obviously trying to cover up his tracks.

Kane ignores my broody goalie. "You watching us?"

I nod. Of course I'm watching them. I watched them well before I ever met Emory. "I'm counting on you guys to win, but the Bears are tough. They're predicted to win." I become serious. "Their offensive line is rock solid, so make sure you watch out for number eleven."

Kane cranes his neck and looks at Emory with confusion. "Where did you find her? I want one."

Emory snatches the phone out of his hand, and his expression is completely unreadable. He blinks a few times before Coach Jacobs' voice booms throughout the locker room. "Let's go, Devils. Get the fuck on the ice."

I snort at his choice of language.

I move the camera down so Emory can see Shutter on my chest. "Shutter says good luck."

He scoffs and does a quick scan of the locker room before looking highly uncomfortable.

Is he nervous for the game?

Wait, why do I even care?

"I'll call you after the game," he says hesitantly.

"Okay..." My eyebrows crowd, and I know he notices my confusion.

"I..."

Why does he look like he's in pain? And again, why do I care?

"I love you."

My mouth opens. The thoughts that come with hearing those three little words send me into a frenzy. I'm confused when I feel the tinge of anger. That's probably something a therapist should dive into, but that costs money, so I'll put that little feeling in the back of my head and hide from it.

I snap out of it when Emory clears his throat. My skin is hot to the touch, but I force the proper response out. "I love you too."

We stare at one another for a second too long before he hangs up.

I breathe heavily for a few seconds while holding the phone in the exact same spot, and that's when the exhaustion hits me. I know I can't force myself to stay awake tonight, because my body is protesting, but when my phone buzzes, I'm suddenly wide awake again.

TV is in my room.

Oh.

223

> But that cat better not be caught dead in my bed, Rogue.

I slowly stand with Shutter in my arms and head for the stairs. Another text pops up.

> Stop right where you are and put him outside.

My feet freeze dead center on the first stair. I turn slowly and shift my attention around the living room again. Emory is either highly attentive and knows me much better than I think, or he's being a complete stalker and watching me.

Although, can he really be considered a stalker if it's his house?

> Are you watching me?

> You're the one who told me to get cameras, remember?

That's right. I did. But that was before I thought he'd be watching me!

> Don't do anything you wouldn't want me to know about while you're in my bed.

Heat trickles down my spine at the thought.

> You're so cocky that you think I'd actually be turned on from just being in your bed? 😶

> I don't think, sweetheart. I know.

His response irritates me so much that I *might* do something in his bed just to spite him.

Thirty

EMORY

"WELL, your little hockey groupie was right. Number eleven tore us to pieces."

I turn around and glare at Kane. "Hockey *groupie*?"

"I'm sorry. I mean your *wife*." He rolls his eyes, and my ears burn.

I can't blame him for being angry and not choosing his words wisely, because that's how we all get when we lose, but if he ever calls Scottie a groupie again, I might snap his hockey stick in two and shove it down his throat. Kane is a punk with a temper, and if I wasn't trying to fix my reputation, I wouldn't let this one slide.

All it takes is one look from me to know he's overstepped, especially in front of the rest of the team. He turns his back, and we all silently undress, waiting for Coach Jacobs to come into the locker room and roar about how disappointed he is in the sloppy plays that were executed. That's what makes being a goalie so difficult. My teammates practically play a completely different game than I do.

I'm in between the pipes, blocking shots with every ounce of determination I have while they fuck up on the ice over and over again, allowing thirty pucks to fly at my face. I can't do a thing about it either, other than weave and block until they get their shit together.

It's always easy to blame the one letting shots get through, and my ego isn't *that* big—except according to Scottie—to think I've never fucked up a game from not doing my best at blocking, but everyone in this locker room knows that this loss had nothing to do with me and everything to do with their miscommunication.

I'm prepared for a fight to break out with the tension filling up the locker room. Rhodes and I make eye contact. We're both ready to step in if necessary, but I'm hoping that everyone can keep their shit together so we can climb onto the bus and head to the plane before it gets too late.

There's nowhere like home, even if I'm sharing it with a little blonde-haired devil.

My bed is calling my name, and I better not find fucking cat hair in it.

When Coach finally makes his presence known, he just stands in the middle of the locker room, puts his hands on his hips, and shakes his head—which is honestly worse. I don't know if he was expecting some backtalk or choice words between his players like in the past, but the team stays silent. Most of them bounce their steely gazes to Rhodes and then to me. When neither of us say or do anything, they take that as their cue to stay silent too.

Nothing is said until we get onto the plane.

As captain, Rhodes feels obligated to say a few gruff words that hover between anger and encouragement, but that's it.

My guess is there will be a shit-ton of drills run tomorrow during practice and maybe some tweaks of the lines.

When we land in Chicago and I turn my phone back on, I realize I forgot to call Scottie after the game. I'd said I'd call her afterward, because I knew the team was listening to my conversation, but she's the first thing I think about when the plane's wheels hit the runway.

I reread our texts, and strangely enough, they pull me away from the anger lingering over our loss. After Coach barks at us to be at practice tomorrow, I climb into my car and pull open the camera app.

It wasn't until I was away and thinking about her that I thought to look at the camera.

Did it border on unethical?

Sure did.

Was it a stalker-ish thing to do?

Fuck yeah.

But she kind of asked for it when she came to one of my games, waited until I was alone, and cornered me in the bathroom. *That's* stalker-ish.

The security company recommended I put cameras in every room of the house, in case of theft, but the real reason I agreed was because of the crazed women showing up on my doorstep. I wouldn't put it past one of them to get in my bed naked.

When I look at the cameras, though, no one is in my house except the person that's supposed to be there.

My fingers tighten the longer I stare at her sleeping on my bed. She's wearing the same thing I saw her in earlier: tiny shorts and a thin jacket that's barely covering her shoulder. She's curled into a tiny ball on the opposite side of where I sleep, with her blonde hair exposing the slope of her neck.

There's a pinch in my groin, and I exit out of the camera app with too much force. I throw my phone off to the side and shift my car into drive.

I was the one who insisted she sleep in the bed with me, but that was before I knew what kissing her felt like. Now, I'm not sure I'll get any sleep with her beside me, whether she's awake or not.

———

"SERIOUSLY?"

A hiss slides out of Shutter when I step onto the porch. He arches his back at me, and his green glowing eyes are more of a glare than anything.

I'm happy to see that Scottie actually followed my command for once and put him back outside, but did she somehow inform him that I'm the one responsible for his living arrangements on the porch instead of inside my house?

You'd think he'd like me, since I'm the one who rescued him, but that's clearly not the case.

When I get inside and shut the door, flipping Shutter off in the process, I notice that the couch is still empty. The house is as pristine as it was when Scottie stayed up all night to clean, and the blanket and pillow she uses hasn't moved an inch since I've been away. I'd hoped she'd be in her rightful spot in the living room by the time I got home so I didn't have to deal with waking her up.

A noise from upstairs pulls my attention. After dropping my bag near the door, I kick off my shoes and head for my room. The closer I get, the more I recognize the familiar voices of some of the most well-spoken sports commentators on TV.

They're recapping the game from earlier, but I can't pay attention because of the sleeping woman on top of my bed. Unable to stop myself, I move closer to the edge of the mattress and trace the delicate curve of her bare shoulder with a lazy gaze.

Despite how tired I am, my dick still makes himself known.

Fuck. This is getting weird.

I turn around in frustration.

I feel like the biggest fucking pervert in the world for

standing in the middle of my bedroom with a semi, just from looking at a woman in my bed.

Especially *her*.

My teeth grind so hard my jaw throbs.

I glance at the TV in disbelief. As if I needed the reminder, a photo from my social media is on the center of the screen behind Charles Cannon and Mike Hale.

Scottie must have taken it the day she made breakfast, unbeknownst to me.

The focus of the photo is her holding a coffee mug with her biscotti nearby, but in the background, slightly blurred, there I am, without a shirt on, eating the pancakes and bacon she made.

Mike makes a joke that my new wife must be my good luck charm because of how well I performed during the game, despite the failed efforts of my teammates. They mention the upcoming Hockey Fights Cancer charity event, and a zip of excitement flows throughout me because she'll have to go with me.

My excitement has nothing to do with wanting her to be my real wife or anything. It's just that she's entertaining to be around. She doesn't put up with my shit, and her clever comebacks keep me on my toes.

If anything, I'm less bored with her around.

After giving her one more quick look, I decide that after I get ready for bed, I'll wake her up.

I eye the shower, silently thanking myself for rinsing off in the locker room, because I might accidentally spend too much time washing my dick with the thought of my fake wife in the next room showing off her soft skin without having any idea what it does to me.

After pulling some sweatpants on and forgoing a shirt, I open the bathroom door and immediately land on her unmoving frame.

I stand over her for a second and reach out to shake her awake, but instead of actually doing so, I grab the remote instead and turn the TV off. Next goes the light, and I decide that if she doesn't wake up when I get into bed, then that's her problem.

Though, the longer I lie beside her, listening to her soft breathing surrounded by her feminine scent, the more I'm realizing that it's my problem.

Thirty-One
SCOTTIE

WHY CAN'T I wake up?

I try to pull myself away from what's unfolding in front of me, but no matter how hard I try to move, I don't.

Wake up, Scottie.

"Mom, please don't do it." I don't recognize my own voice. My stomach hurts, and when I cradle it, it looks like a child's arm. It's a memory, and I know how this will end, but I'm afraid to see it.

Wake up, Scottie.

A tremble moves through my body, and I gasp.

I shove the covers from my legs and flip off the bed, landing with a thud on the carpeted floor.

"What the fuck?"

I run.

I have no idea where I'm running to, or what I'm running from, but I'm gone.

Turning to the right, I bolt to the closest door. I fling it open, and it's pitch black, which only heightens my fear.

Wrong fucking door!

I turn and run again but bounce off something hard.

Hands grip me, and I scream.

"Scottie, calm the fuck down!"

I shake, and my skin is sticky. When the lights flick on, I squint to avoid the harsh glow. My eyes flutter as quickly as I tremble, and the hands on my biceps squeeze, pulling my attention to the gruff voice telling me to calm down.

Two eyes, the color of an ocean storm, lock with mine, and I find myself trying to pull away because I'm suddenly realizing how insane I must seem.

God, how embarrassing.

"Let go of me," I plead.

Emory, in his sleepy state, which is annoyingly more attractive than one would think, shakes his head. "No. You're shaking, for fuck's sake." His voice lowers at the end, and a thick swallow is my only response.

My eyes water, and I turn away. I'm mortified and completely drenched with sweat. I weakly pull on my arms again, but Emory doesn't let up. Instead, he drags me over to the shower and holds onto me with one hand while reaching inside and turning the water on.

It doesn't take long for the water to grow warm. Emory and I are surrounded by steam, and I can hardly stand. My chest is full of anxiety, and my breaths are shallow, but he doesn't comment on it. His tired gaze drags down my arms when he moves his fingers to the zipper of my jacket. He unzips it, and the warm air coats the chills on my skin, revealing a tiny, cropped tank that only comes to my belly button. When the jacket falls to the floor, he glances at the rest of me briefly before turning his attention away. I stare at his sharp jaw, suddenly forgetting why we're even in the bathroom to begin with.

"I'm going to step out while you take a shower and calm down."

I can't even manage a nod.

The entire time I shower, I push away the small snippets of the dream I knew would come for me after seeing my mother the other night and focus on the warm water pelting against my skin.

When I'm finished showering, I smell more like a man than I ever have before. I slip into the nearest towel and eye my sweaty clothes on the floor. There's a shirt hanging off the doorknob, and I have no idea if it's clean, but it's either I walk out into Emory's room in nothing but a towel, or I walk out in his shirt that has a zero chance of slipping from my shaky grip.

After pulling his shirt over my head, I realize it's more of a dress on me, which is perfect because even my underwear is damp with sweat, and I'd have to be really desperate to pull those back on.

I run my fingers through my wet hair and finally get the courage to open the door.

I have a hopeful thought that maybe he had fallen back asleep, but as soon as I see the glow from his bedside table, I freeze.

Emory snaps to attention, catching me off guard. His strong brow furrows, and I have no idea what's going on in his head. His chiseled stomach is on display, and each one of his abs flickers when he tenses. When I tug my gaze back to its rightful spot—*his face*—he's staring at something different: my legs.

I've never felt more self-conscious in my life. I'm infuriated with myself. I never let people see my vulnerabilities. Just because Emory is my husband doesn't mean he's privy to my deepest, darkest fears. My weaknesses are better left buried, just like my worries.

Emory eventually drags his attention to meet my face, and instead of giving him the time to ask the questions I know he wants the answers to, I head right for the bedroom door.

Before I make it there, his tall frame comes into view, and he slides right in front of me. "Get in the bed, Scottie."

For a second, and I mean a *very* quick second, I feel a tug in between my legs. It stuns me so much that when Emory's hands fall to my hips and he starts to push me backward, I let him.

The backs of my thighs hit the mattress, and he forces me to sit. He's so close that all I'd have to do is spread my legs slightly and he'd be able to step right in. Then he'd realize that I have zero panties on and—*God, why do I want to tempt him?*

I shyly peer up at him because he's still standing in the same spot, a mere foot from me. My mouth parts for a soft breath to escape, and the only thing I can think of is the way he kissed me the other night.

My body craves a distraction that my subconscious is shaking her head at, knowing my coping skills are completely unhealthy.

"You're sleeping in here." His callused hand falls to my chin, and he tips my face even more. My breathing is erratic at best, and I couldn't argue with him if I tried.

I nod once, and he has a wicked look in his eye.

I look at his mouth and trace the outline of his lips, remembering how soul-stopping it was to feel them claim me the other night. It was the ultimate first kiss of first kisses, and to think that it was fake...

Imagine if it were real...

Imagine if he actually felt something for me other than distrust or sympathy...

I wonder what it would feel like to be wanted by someone as unwavering as Emory Olson. He's so sure of himself—even more so on the ice. When he uses a tone that borders on possessiveness with me, I find myself loving every single inflection in his voice.

After I nod, I expect Emory to walk to his side of the bed

and leave me to lie on my own, but when he squats down to get on my level, my heart falls to the bottom of my stomach. His warm hands graze my calves to swing my legs over the bed, but he stops at the last second. His fingers dig into my skin, and when I see the look of shock on his face, I know he knows.

His eyes snap to mine, and I almost choke. Too afraid of rejection from the man I have to spend another 358 days with —not that I'm counting—I blurt out an apology.

"I'm sorry!" I try to squeeze my legs together, but he doesn't let me, so I continue to ramble. "I'm sorry I fell asleep in your bed. I didn't mean to. I finished watching the game, and the next thing I know, I'm having one of my nightmares, and running into your chest, and—"

Suddenly, I'm pulled forward to the point that my butt is barely on the side of the bed. "Stop it." Emory is quiet, but his tone is still demanding. "You're my wife. You're supposed to be in my bed."

"I'm your fake wife," I remind him. "Which means it's not your responsibility to deal with me and my trauma."

"Just like it's not my responsibility to deal with you wearing my shirt with nothing underneath it?"

The room is on fire.

My face is on fire.

And in between my legs is on fire.

"Right," I whisper. "Exactly."

A shaky breath clamors from my mouth, and I hate that Emory's hands are still on me. It's difficult to keep our stare-off intact because the more I look at him, the more attractive he becomes.

Blue eyes that darken with something enticing, a husky voice that is both possessive and greedy, and a mouth that I know is talented... He's making it hard for me to think straight.

The sleepy state he was in a short time ago looks more like

he's high on the thought of touching me, and that has to be me tricking myself into thinking something that's untrue to make myself feel better about the thoughts I'm having.

"It's after midnight," he states. "So I'm cashing in my question for tomorrow right now."

I mentally prepare myself because I know he's going to ask about my nightmare. "Okay," I whisper.

"Do you want me to make it my responsibility?" Emory loosens his grip on my calves and slowly drags his hands over my legs until they rest on my bare thighs.

"Wh–what?"

"Do you want me to touch you, Scottie?" There's hope in his blue eyes, and I want to give in to him so badly it hurts.

Goosebumps fly over my flesh like fireworks, and he notices. I suck in a breath when he skims his fingers against my skin, moving to the inside of my legs. He pushes them open wider, and I let him.

"Yes or no?"

He's looking directly in between my legs, and I know I need to say no. This is not part of our arrangement. When no one is around, we're not supposed to...*touch*.

"This isn't in the contract." I can hardly say the words.

There isn't a speck of humor on his face. Only determination, lust, and something so dangerous I can't help but want to stroke it. "I wrote the thing. I know what's on it. I asked if you want me to touch you."

I open my mouth, but my eyes flutter closed when his finger traces the inside of my leg, seemingly getting closer to my sweet spot.

"If you don't want me to touch you, tell me now. Otherwise, I won't be able to stop." His hand freezes, and I almost pout. "I'm a man, and you're in my bed, wearing my shirt without any panties on, looking at me with those blue eyes full of want."

Thoughts of what this will mean make my heart beat harder and faster. I'm on the edge of a cliff, and I have no idea if I should jump. I always know what I want, but sometimes what I want isn't what I need.

Heat pulses in between my legs, and I have a feeling he can feel it.

He swallows loudly, and I watch the muscles in his jaw flicker back and forth.

Do I want him to touch me?

God, yes.

But what I want and need are two very different things.

I've learned that the hard way.

Thirty-Two

WHAT THE FUCK am I doing?

This is all her fault.

One second, I'm flipping out of my bed in the dead of night and taking care of the woman I call my wife while she's seemingly in the middle of some type of panic attack, and the next, I'm kneeling on the floor in between her legs, silently begging her to let me touch her.

This is a terrible fucking idea.

I know it down to my core.

But...

But her pussy is picture perfect. I've never seen a prettier one.

And her skin? It's soft in all the right places and smoother than the ice after a Zamboni machine.

"I do want you to touch me..." Her voice is addicting, and if I'm being honest, I feel that way even when she's sassing me. "But..."

But?

She has a 'but'?

"I can't let you because this will never work if we start

crossing lines, and I need this marriage to work more than you know."

For a second, desperation fills my every thought. I'm coming up with excuses and even considering telling her that I'll pay her more, which stops me right in my tracks.

She's not a fucking prostitute. What the hell am I doing?

Her shaky sigh pulls me away long enough to where I can force out an agreement. "You're right."

I stand quickly and turn my back to her. After tucking my dick into the waistband of my sweats, I walk over to the light and flip it off.

We're blanketed in darkness, which is a relief. I'm not in the right state of mind to continue looking at her sitting on the edge of my bed in nothing but a T-shirt. I've always thought she was attractive and alluring in the most agonizing way, but it's the way she just gazed up at me that pulled on every last restraint I thought I had honed.

She didn't resemble the woman that attempted to blackmail me or the tough, independent one who loves to mouth off to me. The more time I spend observing her, the more I realize my perception may be slightly incorrect.

I've witnessed sides of her that she doesn't know about, but after seeing her hidden desire and learning how tempting she is, I realize that I need to get my shit together and focus more on my goal and less on my dick.

As soon as I land on the bed, Scottie moves to stand. Thankful for my height and long arms, I grab onto the fabric of her shirt and drag her back.

"I won't touch you. But you're sleeping in here tonight."

"That's not necessary," she says quietly. "I'll be fine downstairs."

A sarcastic noise leaves me. "I didn't ask."

She matches the noise, but I cut her off before she can say

anything else. "Get in the bed and go to sleep, or I'll just follow you downstairs and sleep on the couch beside you."

Don't fucking tempt me, Scottie.

"There isn't room on the couch for both of us."

"Exactly." My response is a warning, and it's one I know she'll heed.

Her sigh is loud on purpose, and I can feel her eyes roll from across the bed. After a few minutes of her moving all around, I finally turn toward her and see a mound in front of me.

"What are you doing?"

Her shadow appears from the top of some sort of barrier. "Building a pillow wall."

Amusement flies to my lips, and I'm thankful she can't see my face through the dark.

"Wow, you trust yourself so little beside me that you have to create a barrier?"

"This isn't for me. It's for you." Her laugh is snarky as hell, and I know we're past the hot-and-heavy moment between us.

Without being able to control myself, I take my arm and shove every last pillow off the bed and onto the floor.

She gasps.

I smirk. "We'll see who's the first to break, then, huh?"

"It won't be me!"

I roll over and put my back to her. "I guess we'll see."

The bed barely moves when she flips over too, facing opposite of me. "Yes, we will!"

I wait until the tension settles and silence takes over to say, "Night, wifey."

All I get in response is a loud, exasperated sigh.

———

WATER COOLS MY SKIN, and I shake the droplets away. The fans are antsy with the score of two to two, and we're nearing the last few minutes of the game. Practice was brutal, but it always feels good to be back in our home rink with the majority of the guys showing up with a level head after being in their own beds.

My head is the furthest thing from level with Scottie being around, especially after the other night, but I'm focused enough on hockey that it doesn't affect my skill on the ice. It'll be a cold day in hell if I ever let a woman distract me to the point that my game is off.

I slip my gaze to the box seats for a second, and there she is with Corbin's wife, pressed against the glass with their attention on the ice and nowhere else. They're talking, but I have no clue what about. I do a double take because Scottie's hair is pulled up into a ponytail, and she's wearing some bow like a cheerleader. After looking at the other wives, I see that they're all wearing the same one.

I chuckle under my breath.

Scottie sure has played her part well, already becoming best friends with the other wives in the league.

Maybe I can use that to my advantage when I drop the bomb on her that she has to go to the charity event with me that will be fully packed with the media watching our every move as husband and wife.

The whistle blows, and I snap out of it. I move to pull my attention away but not before her gaze finds mine. She gives me a slight nod with a tilt of her lips, and knowing how much knowledge she has of hockey, I know she's not faking the hope in her eye that we'll win.

It's kind of cute that she's rooting us on so hard.

The puck slips out to the left, and the Knights get the first touch, sending it soaring to their center. I bend at the legs and stand in my rightful spot with my attention fully on the little black biscuit.

Scottie pops into my head at the last second.

All I can picture is her with that damn biscotti, dipping it into her morning coffee and licking her lips afterward.

Fuck, get out of my head.

I give my head a harsh shake, and a rush of adrenaline flies to my fingertips when red and yellow jerseys blur in front of me. To the fans, the game is fast. The players rush back and forth over the rink like a stampede, but to me, everything is in slow motion. I already have the sense that they're going to score, because things are getting messy and sloppy, but I'll be damned if we lose again.

My teammates have cleaned up their act compared to our last game, and now it's my job to support them and shove the puck down the other team's throat.

"Fuck off," I grunt, doing a half split and whipping my arm out to the right. The puck slams into my glove, and I smile to myself, trapping it against the ice.

The crowd loses their shit, and Malaki flies toward me with a cheeky smile. "That's our boy."

I give him a look because I'm not a boy, but nonetheless, I give the puck up and get back into my position. There are two more attempts on a score from the Knights, and each time, I freeze the puck in an attempt to give my team a chance to slip it off to Rhodes.

Coach gives me the signal at the end of the third period when I glance at the clock and see that we're tied. We've practiced the drill multiple times, and I know they're going to call me to the bench at the last second so we can up our chances of scoring with another man on the ice.

As soon as we have position, I skate as quickly as I can and flip over the side of the wall. Kane's blades hit the ice, and he owns his nickname of being an animal. He's aggressive, and although Rhodes can't stand his attitude, he knows he's good, so they work together and send a puck soaring into the net.

I stand on my skates, and as soon as I see it hit the top left corner, my mouth curves into a slight smile. "Now that's teamwork."

Coach claps me on the shoulder, and for the first time ever, Rhodes slides over to the rest of the team and hits me on the chest with his fist. He's trying to hide how pleased he is from everyone else, but for me, looking at Rhodes is like looking into a mirror.

"Is that a smile I see?"

He pounds his gloved hand on my chest again but clenches his jaw to act unfazed by the changes we're already seeing in the team.

Between the two of us, we're going to build this team up to the top, and we'll no longer be the laughingstock in the pros.

I tear my helmet off and grin. Rhodes grumbles under his breath and heads for the locker room after the ice has cleared. I stop at the last second when I see that he's staring into the stands.

Scottie is smiling brightly with her rosy cheeks and bright-blue eyes. Behind her is Rhodes's daughter, perched behind her in a piggy-back ride. The bow she was wearing is now in Ellie's hair, and she looks happy.

Like she can feel me staring, Scottie's eyes are drawn to mine. She gives me a strange look and then turns back and smiles at Ellie.

Rhodes curses under his breath after saluting to Ellie, who does the same to him. "I swear to God, that nanny better be in the box with my daughter."

I'm almost positive she isn't, because I think I just had a silent conversation with my wife...which means we're more like husband and wife than I thought.

Thirty-Three

SCOTTIE

"LET'S GO GET YOUR DADDY," I say to Ellie, fixing the bow in her hair. Her eyes lit up the second she saw all the wives wearing one. Nola even had one, although the bow was bigger than her face, and her ponytail had maybe three strands of hair in it.

After Ellie's nanny went to the bathroom and never came back, I sat her down in between my legs and braided her hair before clipping the bow onto the end.

I say goodbye to the wives, who are all looking at Ellie with a touch of empathy in their eyes. She's quiet while we walk to the lower level of the arena, passing all the rowdy fans who are walking in the other direction to get back to their cars. Little girls her age aren't supposed to feel the weight of abandonment like she's feeling at the moment.

I'm not sure what happened to her mother, and I know Rhodes is doing the best he can, but there's a sorrow that I recognize in Ellie. She carries it well from what I have witnessed, but it's a sadness that I know all too well.

It's one of those sorrows that are invisible to the naked eye, but if you've been through it, you can see it right away.

"Daddy has to talk to the reporters today," Ellie says quietly, dragging me toward the locker rooms. I'm thankful she knows the way, because I sure don't.

"Oh?"

She nods, pulling me to keep up with her. "I always like to watch him because he gets nervous."

I laugh under my breath. I think she's getting *nervous* mixed up with agitated.

My phone vibrates in my back pocket while I allow a five-year-old to lead me down a dark hallway. The security guard took one look at Ellie and let us through, which is nice to know they're not letting random women back here.

Random women? I brush off the flare of jealousy, because it's totally uncalled for.

> Rhodes is worried. Ellie with you?

> Yes, we're on our way to you…I think? I'm letting Ellie lead the way, and although she's a determined little thing, I have no idea where we are.

> Rhodes says she knows the way.

I send him a thumbs-up emoji, and before I know it, Ellie and I are standing behind a cluster of reporters with microphones, headsets, and cameras. I pull her back a little so she isn't in the limelight, but when she spots her dad, she desperately reaches up on her tiptoes to see better.

My heart warms.

God, she's just like me.

Rhodes is her whole world, like my dad was mine.

I pray she doesn't lose him.

Losing one parent was hard enough, and even if my mother is still physically alive, she hasn't been my mom for a very long time. Losing two parents was just plain cruel.

Swinging Ellie onto my back again, her tiny hands rest on my shoulders, and we watch Rhodes answer questions about the game without an ounce of emotion on his face.

"See?" Ellie whispers her popcorn breath into my ear. "I told you he was nervous."

I roll my lips together to hide my amusement.

"Your dad doesn't get nervous," Emory adds, making me jump. Ellie's hands tighten along my shoulders as she starts to argue with Emory. She puts him in his place, and I find it hilarious.

He raises his eyebrows after she finishes her argument. When she goes back to watching her dad, Emory snags my eye. I catch sight of his grin even if he tries to hide it.

"Good game." I keep my voice smooth, sounding bored. I can't be *too* nice to him. He might get the wrong idea and think I'll end up in his bed with no panties on again.

My stomach flips. Every single time I've caught Emory staring at me since I ended up in his bed, heat rushes to all the quiet parts of my body, and my mind fills with the most inappropriate thoughts.

It's a sickness, and the only cure so far is avoiding him, so back to the couch I went even though he was openly displeased.

"Did you just compliment me?"

Ellie keeps her attention on her father but inserts herself. "She did, and also, most people say thank you when someone compliments them. My dad said it's rude not to say thank you."

A laugh bubbles out of my throat, and when Emory's white teeth appear behind his lips, I think everyone feels the shift in the universe, because all of a sudden, the cameras swing to him.

He quickly steps in front of me and Ellie, shielding her from the cameras.

Rhodes slips out from behind the chaos, and I do the same. I place Ellie on the ground between the two of us, and with Emory being in the spotlight, she's hidden.

"Hey, *printessa*," he whispers down to his daughter in Russian.

"Did you have a nervous belly, Daddy?"

He grunts. "Something like that."

He's angry, and when he looks at me, I give him a look that hopefully tells him that I understand.

"Did she give any excuse?" he asks.

He's referring to the nanny, I assume. "Bathroom."

Ellie pipes up. "I think she fell in."

I laugh out loud, while Rhodes curses under his breath before squeezing the back of his neck with his large hand. "Thank you for watching her."

I place my palm on his arm, even though I can tell he isn't the touchy type. There is something about him and his daughter that I resonate with, and I think he knows there isn't anything underlying when I give it a squeeze. "I will watch her anytime. Just have Emory get a hold of me, okay?"

"Here's your bow." Ellie tries to pull the bow out of her braid, tugging on her hair.

I stop her. "That's yours, silly."

She smiles brightly. Her dad scoops her up and takes off down the hall, peppering her with kisses to make her giggle.

When I turn back to Emory with a soft smile on my lips, I see several cameras pointed in my direction. My smile falls immediately, and Emory's eyes are wide with an apology, like he's trying to warn me.

Oh no.

"Well, there she is...Mrs. Olson!"

Shit. Shit. Shit.

I may have signed a contract to be Emory's wife, but

nowhere in that contract did it say there would be cameras and sports reporters shoving a microphone in my face.

With my gaze pinned to Emory's, I bite the inside of my cheek and slowly walk to his side.

I am *not* wife material in real life. Photos, I can deal with. Actual footage? Kill me now.

"We can't help but notice your dedication to this team, Mrs. Olson. We've been hearing you yell louder than Coach Jacobs."

A breath of air whooshes from my lungs with a fake laugh. I shrug and peer at Emory briefly before looking back at the reporter. "I grew up watching hockey, so it's a given that I'd be such a fan."

"Such a fan of watching your husband, I assume?" The female reporter wiggles her eyebrows and laughs annoyingly.

With a closed-lipped smile, I nod. Emory inserts himself, and I'm not sure if he does it to save me or to save *us,* but I'm thankful either way. "She grew up watching me. I think she may be sick of me by now."

That's right. I almost forgot that Emory and I have a history that goes beyond me trapping him in a bathroom and trying to exploit him.

The reporter laughs again. "I highly doubt that. Chicago is becoming obsessed with their newest Blue Devil goalie." She turns to me again, and I want to die. I lean into Emory, and he catches me around the waist, steadying me. "I think they're becoming obsessed with the two of you, actually. Not only are they invested in the game but they're invested in your new marriage and the team's loudest cheerleader."

Thank God I gave the Blue Devils bow to Ellie. Otherwise, they might give me pom-poms and make me perform in between periods.

"Well"—Emory shifts awkwardly—"we thought it was

time to stop the rumors so everyone can focus on the game instead of my personal life."

"They're definitely still invested in your personal life," the reporter argues. "Especially after seeing how adorable your wife is. Not to mention, supportive."

There's a part of me that wants to laugh because if only the press knew that I keep their star goalie up at night because he continues to check on me—something he thinks I don't know about. If I wasn't so stubborn and slept in the bed with him, he wouldn't have to do that, but I don't trust myself one bit, and I'm already embarrassed enough that he had to witness me that unstable state to begin with.

"That's her," Emory says cheerfully, which is a clear indication that he's lying through his teeth. He wraps his arm around me tighter, making a show for the camera. "My wife is supportive beyond belief. She keeps the house tidy, makes me breakfast on my off days, rubs my sore muscles after a killer practice, runs me a hot bath, irons my suits..."

The reporter's cheeks match mine.

Hoping the camera doesn't see, I take my elbow and dig it into Emory's stomach. He rumbles out a quiet chuckle without so much as a twitch of his mouth. If he thinks I'm going to do any of those things, he's out of his ever-loving mind.

"I have to ask one question before I let you two go." She gestures to the camera. "We asked the public to send in questions for their favorite players, and you won by a landslide." I want to scoff because that'll be *great* for his already enormous ego. "One of the most asked questions was if you have nicknames for each other."

Without giving Emory a chance to throw me to the wolves as some type of sick joke, I pipe up right away. "Oh yes, Emory has a nickname for me. Don't you?" I turn and smile at him. He calls me Rogue daily, so this will be easy-peasy.

His eye twitches, and I have the sudden urge to push back his still sweaty hair from his face to see him better.

"Uh, yeah." He leans into the microphone and says, "Biscotti."

Biscotti?!

My face blanches. I hope the camera is focused on Emory instead of me.

That's what he came up with? A cookie? What happened to Rogue?

"Biscotti?" the reporter repeats, clearly amused.

"Yep." Emory pulls me in close and reaches up to squeeze my cheeks like I'm a child. "She's my little Scottie Biscotti." At the last second, he turns to the camera. "But next time, ask me something about hockey." He winks before taking my hand to lead me away, knowing very well that I'm simmering.

Thirty-Four

EMORY

"SCOTTIE *BISCOTTI*?!"

Her jaw drops, and I wish I had a biscotti so I could stuff it in her mouth. I turn my back when I have another thought of sticking something else in her mouth and busy myself with filling my bag with all my gear. The locker room has completely cleared out, which I'm thankful for, considering Scottie stomped her way through the door and followed me to my locker without giving two shits if any of my teammates were in here.

"What? I could have said *Cherry*." I shrug sheepishly. "And you like biscotti, don't you?"

Just then, my phone starts to vibrate in my locker, ricocheting off the metal. I grab it and almost hit the decline button. I'd bet my left testicle that Ford is only calling to give me shit for what I just pulled on TV, but with my sister's diabetes diagnosis, I always answer his call.

As soon as I hit the green button, all I hear is laughter.

For fuck's sake.

"Sco–scottie..." More laughter. "Scottie Bisc—I can't even say it."

"Do you need something, or are you just calling to be a dick?" I snap.

"Scottie Biscotti—I...*I can't* stop laughing. I have never seen you look more panicked than you did at that moment."

I growl and peek at Scottie, who's standing in the middle of the locker room with her arms crossed over her perky chest with obvious annoyance. Her perfectly arched eyebrows rise as if she's saying, *"See?!"*

"You referred to your wife as a cookie, which is hilarious for so many reasons."

Ford is on my last fucking nerve.

"THANK YOU!" Scottie shouts. "Even he knows how ridiculous it is."

Nope. Nada. I will not have her on good terms with Ford, because despite there still being many months left of our marriage, she is not going to grow close to the people I care about the most.

She cannot insert herself into any more of my life than she already has.

I turn toward her. "You threw me under the bus! So that's what you get, Biscotti."

"I thought you were going to say Rogue!"

There's a loud noise from the phone, and I look down to see my sister's face. Taytum's lips are rolled together, and the very second I hear Ford's hyena-like cackle in the background, Taytum bursts with laughter.

"I have to come visit so I can see you act like a loving husband in real life." There's a twinkle of amusement in my sister's eye, and I'm about to hang up. "I'd pay money to see it firsthand. Watching it on camera isn't enough." She's busting at the seams.

My jaw clenches. "You act like I don't have an affectionate bone in my body."

"Emory," she argues, becoming serious. "Tell me a time

when you've been affectionate. I need at least one time where you've been caring or lovey-dovey. Just one. Because what I remember from college is you banging a new girl each weekend."

"I've had a girlfriend before," I grumble, glancing at Scottie again, who's still standing with her arms crossed. It was my junior year of high school, and it lasted all of three weeks, but still.

Taytum laughs. "My question still stands."

My sister is right.

I'm not the type of guy who wants to dote on a woman and act beyond the normal scope of attraction, but I hate that she's right, so I mumble under my breath. "Fuck off."

Scottie snorts sarcastically, and I shoot her a glare.

"I'm hanging up," I say to my sister.

"Wait!" she shouts. There's a devious look on her face that I've seen time and time again. "Let me talk to Biscotti. I want to meet her."

"No—"

All of a sudden, my phone disappears out of my hand, and my *wife* is walking off with it, talking to my sister and brother-in-law as if she's a part of the family.

Like everyone else, they seem infatuated with Scottie right away, and I'm agitated.

"Give me that." I snatch the phone as I quickly follow her and hit end on the call.

Scottie narrows her pretty eyes with a huff of breath. I ignore her and continue busying myself with my gear. There's a part of me that wants to get back at her for throwing me under the bus in front of the reporter and for acting all friendly with my sister.

Anytime I slip a little and find myself in awe of her or swept away by the smile on her face, I get angry afterward, and the only way I know how to beat it is to level the playing field.

SJ. SYLVIS

So, with a devil on my shoulder, I turn around and start to strip.

Her brows snap together. "What are you doing?"

I shrug. "Changing."

"In front of me?" Her voice grows squeakier, and I bask in the control I've gained.

"You're my wife..." My lip curves. "Of course."

Scottie gawks at our surroundings. She seems surprised that she's in the locker room, like she followed me in here with one thing on her mind, and that was reprimanding me for the nickname.

After the surprise vanishes from her face, she seemingly falls back into fighter mode. Her arms cross, and she pulls her shoulders back. My smirk deepens, waiting for her next move.

I love messing with her.

"You can drop the act. No one is in here."

She's so tempting when she's angry. The way her nose scrunches and how her chin becomes mighty. I find myself moving closer to her to erase the space between us. I tell myself it's to make her independence waiver a little, but I know better.

This isn't for her.

It's for me.

I want to touch her even if I keep denying it.

In fact, the more I deny it, the worse it gets.

"And what if I told you there was someone in here?" I tease, keeping my voice as level as possible. There's a slight husk to it that I hope she can't hear, because it'll blow my cover. I'm used to taking what I want, and although she's technically mine, I shouldn't go there.

"There isn't," she counters.

I move closer and feel the hesitation coming off of her in waves. Before she can have a second thought, I wrap my arm around her lower back and pull her in close.

I'm shirtless and thankful that I kept my lower half covered, because I'm about to sport something I can't hide.

As if I can summon an angel, I hear something from the hallway. I know we're about to be interrupted by someone, and I take that as my cue to push this a little further.

My heart skyrockets when I skim my hand up her body and grip the side of her face. Excitement rushes through my body when she doesn't pull away.

"What are you doing?" she whispers.

I feel her relax in my grip, and my stomach dips. Her eyelids droop lazily as I stroke her cheek with the pad of my thumb.

Does she like my hands on her?

"Being your husband," I say nonchalantly. The teasing tone I had is gone, and now, I'm sucked in.

The way she peers at me through fluttering eyelashes punches me in the chest. I want to kiss her so badly and for all the wrong reasons.

Out of my peripheral vision, I see the door opening, so I act swiftly.

I kiss her hard, and it's just as blinding as the first time.

I can't breathe, and my heart fucking stops.

My tongue strokes against hers, and I know I'm not imagining it when she mimics the movement. The grip I have on her waist tightens, and I bring our bodies flush.

I should stop, but I can't.

I deepen the kiss and open my eyes to watch. When my teeth sink into her plump bottom lip, her eyes flutter apart, and I can no longer deny the urge I have to make her mine. When I finally let up on her mouth, we both turn to look at our audience.

It's the cleaning personnel.

I silently thank them for stepping in and giving me a

reason to kiss my fake wife, because *fuck,* it felt so damn good, and I can't find it in myself to regret it.

"Sorry about that," I say to them, not sorry at all. "I thought we were alone."

The man holding a mop nods, and the women all blush.

Scottie steps away immediately but not before her eyes drop down to see my hard length.

Looks like I can't hide my attraction after all.

Her cheeks turn a cute shade of pink, and she quickly spins. "I'll see you at home."

She rushes past the cleaning personnel and sends them an apology before disappearing altogether.

While I finish getting dressed and fill my bag with my gear, I grin to myself.

You can run, Scottie, but you can't hide.

I look down at my boner.

Apparently, neither can he.

———

THE HOUSE IS dark when I get home. I suppress a laugh while I jog up the front steps, ignoring Shutter and his angry glower in my direction.

I make no attempt at being quiet when I enter through the front door, knowing very fucking well that she isn't actually asleep. My phone goes off for the fiftieth time since leaving the arena—apparently it isn't only Ford who found my interview funny.

It's all over social media.

Even my former teammates from college are sending me texts.

Ford started a group chat with Theo and Aasher, and they continue to create memes of my interview that I know will show up on the internet.

I'm used to being in the spotlight, but this is the first time it's for a reason other than my jail time or a rendezvous that never happened, so I'm not mad about it.

That was the entire point of this whole thing anyway. Having Scottie by my side was to silence the negative things in the media, and so far, it's working.

"I know you aren't asleep."

I chuckle under my breath when the lump on the couch makes no movement.

It's probably a good thing she's pretending to be asleep and avoiding me.

I'm not sure I trust myself at this particular moment, so instead of poking her any further, I go upstairs to my room. I leave the door cracked, which is something I started doing after she had that crazy nightmare, just in case something happens while she's downstairs on her *bed*.

I meant to tell her about the spare bed, but I've still yet to actually do it.

I like to think it's because I'm stubborn, but after looking down at my still semi-hard dick, I know that's not the reason. *I want her in my bed.*

I step into the shower and try my hardest to ignore the feeling of her tongue moving against mine while in the locker room. I shove away the mental image of her peeking at me through her long lashes, showing off lustful eyes that are too captivating not to notice.

I lean my head against the shower wall. Both of my hands press into the hard stone while I try to clear my head.

Stop thinking about her.

I pretend I'm back in the game, blocking pucks. I go over the plays and visualize my teammates as they fly over the ice, but then pops in Scottie, yelling my name in the stands with my jersey on, and I'm suddenly gripping my dick.

Fuck. Go away.

Moving my hand up and down, I picture her face and the perfect glimpse of her pussy from the other night.

I can't deny that she's irresistible.

It's the kissing.

It's fucking everything up.

And the tiny shorts she wears, or the long T-shirts that make it look like she has nothing on underneath them.

How easy it would be for me to pull the hem up slightly and touch her in between her legs.

My cock is rock solid, and the more I think about her, the faster my hand moves.

If only she were on her knees in front of me and I could tug on those sun-colored strands of hair.

"Damn it," I curse under my breath with water droplets falling off the edge of my nose.

My eyes open, and I turn away from the grip I have on my cock. I try to pull myself together and think of someone other than the one woman who can hardly look me in the eye without scowling.

But that's going to be awfully fucking hard to do considering she's staring at me through slightly fogged-up glass.

Thirty-Five

SCOTTIE

LOOK AWAY.

I need to look away.

Scottie, look away!

Oh my god, I can't.

Words no longer exist, and my stomach dips with need. I try to steady myself against the vanity, pushing into it farther and farther until it cuts into my back. The minty toothpaste that was perched on the bristles of my toothbrush has fallen to the floor, and I'm suspended in time.

It was supposed to be a super-quick in and out thing.

Emory left his touch on me after the locker room, and it rattled me.

Looking back to just a minute ago, I thought my plan of acting nonchalant and walking into the bathroom for toothpaste, knowing he was showering, was a clever way of retaliation.

He wanted to act like we were husband and wife by stripping in front of me in the locker room? As if it was the norm for us? Then *fine*. I'll do the same and charge into the bathroom while he is showering to show him that his bare chest and bedroom eyes don't affect me one bit.

What a colossal mistake that was.

The second he turns and spots me, I drop my toothbrush.

It takes a nosedive to the floor, but neither one of us moves to look at it.

Water drips from his tight jaw to the shower floor, and every one of his muscles is locked. The longer we stare at one another, the more the glass door fogs.

I clench my legs together, and my pulse picks up speed.

Emory Olson is beyond attractive.

He knows it.

I know it.

And my body knows it.

My lips tingle with the thought of his mouth on mine, and every time he touches me, whether it's for show or not, I find myself having to ignore the twisting in my stomach that lingers for far too long.

"Enjoying the show?" His voice is deep and husky.

What would it feel like to have his rough whisper skim my skin?

I haven't been touched in so long.

Honestly, I'm not sure I've ever been touched in the way I know Emory Olson touches someone.

There's a possessiveness to his grip that could trick any woman into thinking he'd do anything to keep her.

And I crave it.

I crave it so much that my legs shake.

I can see his flickering muscles even though I refuse to look at what his hand is doing. He bounces his eyes back and forth between mine, waiting for my answer.

"I just needed toothpaste." Warmth coats me from my head all the way down to my toes. My voice comes out like a soft flutter, and when my teeth unknowingly sink into my lower lip, Emory's eyes light up.

I turn away, leaving my toothbrush hostage. I take one step but stop when his voice floats around the steamy bathroom.

"Don't go now," he grunts. "It's just getting good."

Oh, my god.

Go, Scottie.

He's tempting you on purpose!

My feet are glued to the floor, and I pretend I can't hear my subconscious's pleas through Emory's throaty noises.

This is so bad.

I'm not going to be able to look him in the eye come tomorrow morning.

But I swear I feel his grip on me tighten.

I turn around hesitantly, and he immediately gets ten times more attractive while stroking himself.

He slowly raises his eyebrow at me, as if he's surprised. I raise my chin, and it's too late to leave now. If I run, he'll know how much of an effect he has on me.

If he touches me, he'll know too.

"Want to know what I'm thinking about, Scottie?" he asks breathlessly.

I'm afraid to know.

I'm suffocated by the hot tension between us every time we're together, but it's hard to know if he feels that way too. For all I know, Emory is getting off on tricking me into thinking he finds me attractive. He *does* love to irritate me.

My breathing turns from slightly erratic to sharp and fast. I reach behind me and grip the edge of the vanity to steady myself after he swipes his forearm against the foggy glass. There's a throb in between my legs that pounds with each beat of my heart. Sweat prickles my neck, and I know Emory has noticed how captivated I am.

"You do want to know, don't you? I can tell by the look in your eye."

Typically, I'd argue with him. I'd tell him he doesn't know anything about me, but he's right.

I want to know if he's still thinking about the other night like I am.

"Yes," I rasp, throwing him off course.

There's a glint of surprise there that I don't see often, and his hand starts to move faster. I take a peek and suck up all the moisture in the air. Emory's hand is large, but it doesn't make him look small by any means.

"You."

His answer pulls my attention, and my breasts grow heavy. He looks at my chest, and I hate that I'm not wearing a bra, because when his jaw slacks, I don't have to look down to see my nipples poking through the cotton of my T-shirt.

"Fuck," he groans. His sultry gaze travels back to my face. "You like knowing I'm picturing you, don't you?"

I swallow and try to push myself to leave the bathroom.

"I'm picturing my wife on her knees, sucking me off until I can't take it anymore."

His wife.

Why do I love the sound of that?

It's like he can uncover the secrets trapped inside my head.

He knows how to push my buttons and what'll take me over the edge.

"You can fool everyone else with that sweet smile and pretty blush on your cheeks, but I know you better than you think."

I'm panting, and although he's talking, I can't stop looking at his tight grip and fast strokes.

"Tell me what you like, Scottie. I want to know if I'm right."

He is.

He is *so* right.

I answer, unable to pull myself back to reality. "Wife," I say. "I like it when you call me your wife."

Did I really just admit that? My cheeks are warm, and I want to take back what I just said, but then he makes a sexy noise, and I buckle at the knees.

"Me too," he groans, struggling to speak. "I like referring to you as my wife because that means no one else gets you."

I fall back against the vanity, hoping it'll keep me upright.

"Don't worry. Your secrets are safe with me."

His head flies backward, and the muffled noise he makes is the hottest sound I have ever heard.

Holy shit.

The look he gives me after he finishes could stop my heart if I let it.

"Your turn...*wife*."

THE STEAM from the shower continues to fog the glass door, and I wipe at it again, eager to see what Scottie will do.

The euphoria hasn't worn off yet. I'm still hard as a rock from staring at her through the billowing steam.

She starts to shake her head with lust-filled, hazy eyes, and I open the shower door, unable to restrain myself. I'm not thinking about tomorrow, or next week, or the next several months that I have to spend touching her in public and sharing a home with her. The only thing I'm thinking about is how fucking hot she'll look when she comes.

"I thought you liked playing games," I say, grabbing a towel off the hook.

She follows my every move as I wrap it around my waist and erase the space between us. I notice the white of her knuckles as she holds onto the vanity for dear life, and if I had to guess, she's relying on it to keep her steady.

Without caring if she protests, I grip her around the waist and lift her off her feet. I set her on the edge of the bathroom counter and pull her oversized T-shirt up so I can see more of her smooth legs.

Irresistible.

When we're this close, she has me by the throat, and she has no fucking idea.

It's easy to keep my distance when we're apart.

But when we're together? It's hard to focus.

"What are you doing?" she whispers, peering at me through her soft eyes.

I curse under my breath when I take my hands and run them up the insides of her calves, slowly skimming her soft skin all the way to her knees. Without removing my eyes from hers, I push her legs open and move closer.

"I said, it's your turn."

She shakes her head. "I... I shouldn't." Through her denial, she arches her back and lengthens her neck, like she's egging me on or something.

If I look closely enough, I bet I could see her tiny pulse beating through her skin as quickly as mine is.

My hands move to the outside of her thighs, and I drag them up until I feel the hem of her panties. I slip my fingers underneath the silk, and she sucks in a choppy breath. "Where's my confident wife at?" I tease. "The one who loves to drive me crazy and always wants to have the upper hand?"

There's a tiny crease in between her eyebrows, and I'm confident that I have what it takes to make her succumb.

"Hmm?" I push, tugging on her panties.

I keep my attention glued to hers when she lifts up slightly, allowing me to pull her panties down until they're in a pool at my feet, right beside her toothbrush.

"I just don't think you touching me is a good idea," she admits, staring up at me with eyes that are full of hidden desires. I want to act each and every one of them out until the end of our marriage.

A raspy chuckle leaves me. "That's why you're going to touch yourself."

The divot between her eyebrows grows deeper. "In front of you? I—"

Words disappear on the tip of her tongue when I grab her wrist and hold it hostage. She clenches her fist, and I burn all over when I push it between her legs. Her knuckles skim the inside of her thigh, and I watch in awe as goosebumps break out along her skin.

She likes this so much more than she's willing to admit. I love her defiance. It keeps me on the edge of my seat.

"Like I said," I repeat, "your secrets are safe with me. Who's going to know that you came into my bathroom late at night and watched me fuck my hand at the thought of you on your knees and then got yourself off on top of my bathroom counter?"

Scottie's cheeks turn an adorable shade of pink, and I love pushing her buttons so fucking much.

"You don't even have to tell me what you're thinking about when you finger yourself." I shrug confidently. "I already know it's me."

There's a wicked look in her eye, and I push her hand up higher to meet the warmth I feel brush against my skin.

God damn.

It would only take one little shift to the right, and I'd know just how wet she is. My curiosity grows when I feel her wrist move a little in my grip, and it takes everything in me not to lift her shirt higher so I can see what she's doing.

"Don't be shy." My voice is low and throaty. "I'm your husband, remember? There's nothing wrong with you touching yourself."

Without being able to take it, I release her wrist and cover some of her hand with mine. I realize this is what it must be like to be blind, but I have to admit, not knowing what she's doing to herself and only feeling her hand move has me mesmerized. My heels press into the floor as I steady myself. A shaky breath falls from the little space between her lips, and I have the urge to plunge my tongue inside her mouth so I can taste the desire.

Her finger moves in circles, and the faster it gets, the harder I grow. I grip her thigh with my free hand and shove her legs further apart. Without being able to keep a hold on my restraint, I look down, and my vision blurs.

She has the prettiest pussy I have ever seen.

Her finger swipes against her clit, and she makes a noise that I'd love to have on replay.

When I push on her finger with mine, her eyes open, and she latches right onto me.

Our gazes crash, and she can hardly keep hers steady as I press further, making her finger disappear inside.

God.

I'm going to have to fuck my hand again.

I press her palm against her clit and move her finger in and out of her, knowing the slower it goes, the wetter she'll become.

"That's it," I whisper. "Look how well we work together when we're on the same team."

Her breaths become choppier, and my heart stops when she starts to move her hips.

Fuck.

Pulling my attention from in between her legs, I focus on her face full of pleasure.

Soft in all the right places with a tinge of pink on the apples of her cheeks.

When her white teeth sink into her bottom lip, I let her take over. My hand remains steady on hers, but she knows what feels good, and I'm just here to enjoy the show.

A wicked little noise leaves her, and she throws her head backward. I know an orgasm when I see one. My other hand clutches onto her delicate neck, and when she whimpers, I choke.

I'll never be able to look at her the same.

I'm not sure I'll be able to keep my hands to myself either.

After Scottie finishes riding her high, I pull her fingers out from in between her legs and hold them up in between us. "Good game," I say, winking at her.

My mouth waters with the thought of how she tastes, but instead of licking her clean, I wipe her fingers on my towel and take a step away, leaving her looking ravished, relaxed, and somewhat irritated at the same time.

Fuck, what did I just do?

I bend down and swipe up her panties and toothbrush.

The thumping of my heart is so loud I can hardly hear her quick breaths when I lean over her. She doesn't move, and I'm not sure if she's trying to keep up with her charade of acting unbothered by me or if she really is unperturbed.

What started as a quick rinse off from the game turned into orgasms for both of us, and I'm reeling. I'm trying my hardest to pretend I'm not affected in the slightest, whereas she seems completely *fine.*

After rinsing off her toothbrush and applying more toothpaste onto it, I lean out of her space. I dangle her panties off my pinky and hand her the toothbrush. A flash of uncertainty crosses her features before she snatches the pair of panties and jumps down to slip them on. Without batting an eyelash, she turns and starts to brush her teeth in *my* sink, and I swear she's sticking her ass out on purpose.

I'm beginning to think that Scottie may just beat me at my own game.

Thirty-Seven

SCOTTIE

THE AROMA of freshly brewed coffee pulls me from the most restful night of sleep I've had since moving into Emory's. My nostrils flare as I breathe in the scent again, and when my eyelashes flutter open, I'm surprised to see the living room bathed in sunlight.

"Someone is sleepy this morning."

I sit up quickly, causing the blanket to fall to my lap. My heart leaps out my chest and lands on the floor with a thud, right beside Emory's annoyingly attractive bare feet. He's standing over me like a creep, and when I crane my neck to see him sipping on coffee, I'm hit with the memory of last night.

Oh, God.

It's no wonder I slept so well.

Embarrassment flies to my cheeks, and in an attempt to hide it, I fling the blanket off my legs and stand. As stubborn as he is, Emory actually takes a step backward and moves out of my way. I stalk to the kitchen on the hunt for coffee because I'm suddenly feeling *very* peeved.

What was I thinking?

Last night was an out-of-body experience. All I can picture

is Emory standing over me with his hand in between my legs, coaxing me to touch myself.

It's like I'm just handing him ammunition to use against me whenever he sees fit.

I have yet to forget his trust issues when it comes to women, just like I have yet to forget his threats before agreeing to become his wife.

Just as I'm about to snap some remark at him about forgetting last night ever happened, I stop in the middle of the kitchen.

Sitting on the middle of the counter is my favorite I-fucked-your-sister mug with steam drifting over top of the rim. Beside it is a white bag with the logo *Chicago Bakes* stamped on the front.

Did he...?

I pull the warm mug toward me. It's the exact shade of tan that I like, and I have no idea how he managed to pour the right amount of oat milk in it. The white bag crinkles when I hesitantly open it and look inside. My mouth waters when notes of vanilla and almond drift toward my face.

I'm at a loss for words.

My peeved mood disappears as I waver between confusion and satisfaction.

For the life of me, I can't remember the last time someone did something nice for me without there being strings attached.

Aside from William making me PopTarts every morning, despite me telling him I didn't like them, I can't recall a single event when someone made me something to eat or, better yet, poured me a cup of coffee.

My eyes gloss over, and I almost drop my cup.

With a shaky hand, I place the mug back on the counter and smash my lips together until I hear Emory clear his throat.

"Eat up, Scottie Biscotti."

Instead of being angry at the stupid nickname he gave me on national television, the smallest smile falls to my lips.

"You have plans." He sounds too cheerful.

There goes my smile.

I pull the mug back to my chest, letting the warmth seep through my thin cotton shirt. When I slowly turn, I catch Emory's quick glance at my bare legs sticking out from beneath the hem. Butterflies take over my stomach, and I curse every last one.

I clear my throat, just like he did. When he drags his gaze back to my face, he tips his mug backward and chugs the rest of his coffee.

"Plans?" I'm instantly apprehensive. I *swear* if he mentions last night or something about cleaning his bathroom sink, I am going to throw the biscotti at his head.

"You need a dress."

I pause. "Excuse me?"

"I forgot to mention the charity event you're expected to be at."

My eyebrows rise. "You mean the charity event that *you're* expected to be at. You're the star hockey player. I'm just—"

"My wife."

The look of rugged possessiveness that takes over his face is completely uncalled for. What else is uncalled for is the thrill that I feel when I hear him call me his wife in that tone. Is he doing that because I admitted that I liked it?

I hold up the biscotti in my hand and point it at him. "Is this why you got me a biscotti? Are you trying to bribe me into going to a charity event with you?"

Emory's deep chuckle makes its way in between my legs, and I silently curse. "It's kinda cute that you think you have a choice."

My nose scrunches even though I know he's technically

right. These are the types of things I agreed to do when I signed the contract and became his wife.

Emory strides into the kitchen, and I refuse to move out of his way when he gets close. His coffee mug clinks against the counter, and when he raises his eyebrows, I know he's expecting me to argue.

I open my mouth to do just that, but Emory quickly grips the biscotti in my hand, and it catches me off guard. He shoves it inside my mouth and whispers in my ear, "And no. That's not why I got you a biscotti." I'm still shocked when he turns and heads for the stairs. He calls over his shoulder before climbing the steps, "I got you a biscotti because I know you love them."

I want to be annoyed with him.

But with the taste of sweet almonds on my tongue, a good night's rest, and a sated body, I can't find it in me to snap out an insult.

Instead, I quietly eat my biscotti and sip on my coffee with a genuine smile on my lips that I promise to make sure he doesn't see.

———

AFTER RESEARCHING dress shops in the area and texting the group chat that Hattie started and figuring out what the other wives are planning on wearing to the event, I'm ready to go. Emory shouted throughout the house that he was leaving for practice, which is something he's never done before, so I don't waste my energy on perfecting my scowl while walking toward the foyer.

My first stop will be my old apartment complex to pay the remainder of my lease. I haven't touched my account since I bought my $25 wedding dress from the thrift store, but with the first payment sitting in there from Emory and it being the first of the month, I need to make a visit to Gerald.

The last thing I need is for my old landlord to turn me in to collections. He's probably sitting outside on a lawn chair, waiting for me to pull up so he can torment me and take my money for a shitty apartment that houses cockroaches.

I stare at the little table by the door that *should* have my keys on it, but instead, there's a note with Emory's keys resting on top.

With dread, I grab the torn notebook paper and read the note.

> Scottie Biscotti-
>
> I took your car to practice because I'm getting it serviced.
>
> I'm tired of people ducking when you turn it on.
>
> P.S. Make sure to buy a red dress. I like you in red...it reminds me of your alter ego, Cherry.

Emory's keys dig into my palm as I huff with irritation. I open the door and look at Shutter.

"People do not duck when I turn my car on," I mutter, rubbing my hand along his soft fur.

He meows, and I think he may be arguing with me.

"They don't," I say, knowing how insane I am for arguing with a cat.

After finally figuring out how to start Emory's car, I'm surprised at the power I feel vibrating through my fingers from the engine.

Oh, this is nice. Too nice for me to drive.

I settle back into his seat and ignore the crisp scent of his cologne as I put the car into drive.

After a few rough touches of the brake, I smile to myself and weave in and out of traffic, going much faster than my car can manage.

I'm on the highway when Emory's name flashes on the screen. I answer it with a flick of my finger.

"Yes?" I say, much more bubbly than normal.

"Stop speeding in my car, Biscotti."

With a roll of my eyes, I push on the gas harder. "I'm not."

"You are going eighty-two. Slow down."

How the–

"I have the app." Judging from his tone, I'd say he's annoyed. "It tells me everything about my car, including its current speed."

Of course he does.

"You're the one who left your keys." I slowly back off the gas but probably not enough for his liking.

"I'm well aware. Stop speeding."

A sarcastic noise leaves me. "I don't like the way you're bossing me around."

He sighs loudly. "And I don't like the way you're constantly on my mind. You're distracting me at practice, so stop it."

The car jerks. *On his mind?*

In a panic, I move to hang up, but I see that he's already ended the call.

I turn up the music to drown out my pounding heartbeat and think of all the ways Emory irritates me instead of all the small gestures that most would call sweet.

Don't lose focus, Scottie.

I grip the steering wheel and continue reprimanding myself.

We may be legally married, but the actual marriage is

make-believe. Emory and I are nothing but a fictitious fairy tale, and I can't forget that.

After pulling up to the apartment complex, I'm almost embarrassed to climb out of Emory's car.

How silly it must look to my old neighbors and landlord to see me in something as expensive as this when not even a couple months ago, I was snuggling up on my couch with ramen noodles and throwing shoes at the cockroaches who liked to play hide and seek.

Thankfully, Gerald isn't sitting outside in his lawn chair, but as soon as he sees me enter the building, he hobbles to his feet behind the yellowing plexiglass window.

"What are you doing here?" he snaps.

His upper lip is in a sort of snarl as he looks me up and down with disgust.

"Paying my rent, like I said I would."

The wrinkles along his face deepen with his confusion, and my heart falls.

"You turned me in to collections, didn't you? I told you I would pay, Gerald!" I cross my arms, and my shoulders tense. "I ignored all the problems of this stupid apartment complex that are completely against code and still offered to pay the rest of my lease, and you turn me in to collections?" I shut my eyes and try to breathe through the frustration.

"I didn't turn you in to collections. Pay up," he grunts.

I open my eyes slowly and can see right through his smooth features and calm voice. Two seconds ago, he was looking at me like I'd slapped him, and now he's looking at me like a puppy wanting a treat.

"Quit lyin', you stupid fool," a voice from behind me says.

I turn and see my old neighbor, the only one who offered a kind smile every once in a while. She's too old to be working, but she's still supporting her children and grandchildren, always giving them what's left over from her checks.

Betty holds onto the railing with one hand, and the other is pointing at Gerald. "You know that man came and paid off what she owed. Stop tryin' to get more money out of her."

My heart physically moves inside my chest.

I look all around the grimy building, trying to make sense of what I just heard.

Gerald calls Betty an old hag, and she gives him the finger before turning to go up the stairs. I dash after her, almost tripping on the laces of my Converse.

"Wait, what do you mean?" I step in line with Betty and take her bag to carry it. She stops for a second and rubs her sore shoulder before continuing up to the third floor.

"That one man. The tall one I saw helping you move your things out."

The tall one? I laugh. That's not usually the word most people use to describe Emory, but she isn't wrong. He is tall.

Utterly gorgeous too.

Insanely athletic.

Has an irresistible confidence about him.

Not to mention his world-stopping kissing abilities.

Oh my god. Shut up.

"His name is Emory," I say.

She nods, stopping to take a breather. "He came and paid all your dues a while ago. Shortly after you moved out."

My lips part. The tiniest smile falls to her wrinkled lips, and she pulls her bag out of my hand but not before giving mine a quick squeeze. "If he didn't tell you, that means he's one of the good ones. He didn't do it for any reason other than to take a burden off you."

Betty starts to walk up the stairs again as I try to wrap my head around the fact that Emory came here without my knowledge and paid the remainder of my lease.

"Betty!" I jog up the rest of the stairs after her and pull out some of the money that I was going to put toward my lease. "Here."

Her eyes fall to the cash in my hand, and she starts to shake her head, but I slip it inside her bag anyway. "I like to pay it forward."

I should save it and put it toward the legal fees, but sometimes, you have to take care of people who never expect it.

Thirty-Eight

EMORY

I'M the last to enter the locker room, always waiting for the rest of the team to pile in first. I pull my helmet off as sweat slides down my face and onto the floor. The guys are quiet when I enter, which immediately sets me off-balance.

I find Rhodes standing off to the side, half undressed with a smirk on his face.

I'm on edge.

None of the guys said a single thing about my biscotti nickname from the other night, which is odd. I've been waiting for one of them to let me have it like Ford did, but it's like they didn't even catch the interview.

"What?" I finally snap.

Malaki snorts before I see his shoulders shake. I narrow my gaze and stomp off to my locker—which is exactly when I realize why the entire team is acting like a bunch of idiots.

And there it is.

"Really?" I snap.

There, on the bench, right in front of my locker, is a silver platter with a mound of fucking individually wrapped biscotti on top. I stare at the cookies, and Scottie enters my head for the fifteenth time since I left her this morning.

"You guys think you're hilarious, don't you?" I turn, giving each and every one of them the finger. A rumble of laughter works its way through the locker room like an avalanche. Even the coaches pop out of their office and laugh too.

Usually, I'd be perturbed that I was the team's current target, but with the constant bickering and personal competitions they seem to have on the ice working against one another, this is veering on camaraderie. Sure, they're bonding over making fun of me, but they're connecting nonetheless, and that's a step in the right direction.

"To our benefit, it wasn't our idea." Corbin pulls on a shirt, but as soon as it's over his head, I see his crooked grin.

Malaki laughs. "But damn, it was a good one. I've watched the interview three hundred times since it aired."

I give him a look. "You need a girlfriend to fill your time."

"If only I could find my own Scottie Biscotti."

"Does she taste like a biscotti too?"

Okay, that one isn't funny. I snap my attention to Kane, and he throws his hands out with innocence, but I still recognize his cocky smile. "I'm kidding!"

I curse under my breath and unwrap a biscotti, taking a bite. Scottie's mouth tastes better, but I choose not to acknowledge the thought. "Alright," I say in between bites. "Who is the culprit? Whose idea was it?"

"Well, you see, I got a call." Malaki chuckles.

I know right away.

I pick up my phone and dial Ford.

He picks up after one ring. "Hey, bro."

"You're not fucking funny."

He makes a noise before bursting out in loud laughter. "The laughs I get outweigh all the times you've told me that exact line, so I disagree." My teammates chuckle from behind, but I ignore them and start to undress while Ford continues to talk on speaker phone. "And it was your sister's idea."

"No surprise," I mumble. "She's been with you for too long."

Ford takes no notice of the comment and starts to talk about his upcoming game. The entire time he's talking, there's a pesky thought in the back of my head that has blue eyes and a bratty mouth. I have a sudden need to know where she is.

"Wait, before you go..."

I stare at my phone and wait for Ford to say something stupid.

"What?" I'm impatient.

"Your parents are on their way to your house. K, later."

The call ends, and I stare at it for far too long.

Wait, what?

I call him back, but he declines it because he's an asshole.

Fuck.

I knew it would get to my mom sooner or later that she hasn't met Scottie. I'm a damn fool for thinking I could go an entire year without having her meet my family, but I was willing to try.

I ignore my teammates as they all snatch a cookie from the platter on the bench, and I text Scottie after looking up her location.

> Did you find a dress?

No. I hate them all. I'm not going.

I bet she looks good in every single one.

I pull up her location again and furrow my brow.

> What store?

….a boutique.

I zoom in on the map, and my shoulders drop.

Scottie, that's a thrift store.

It's a boutique to some.

Why does she make me want to smile?

Meet me here.

I send her the address to a dress shop the internet says is the most popular one in downtown Chicago. I know she'll protest, so I type another quick text.

I have a biscotti with me.

Stop trying to bribe me.

After taking a picture of the leftover biscotti that my team ravished, I send it to her. She texts back right away.

I'll be there in twenty.

I grin and put my phone away. Before I get dressed, I head for the showers with a little bit of adrenaline backing my moves.

I should be frustrated that Scottie and I are going to have to act all lovey-dovey in front of my parents who are attempting to surprise me, but instead, I'm eager.

Which is totally fucked.

———

THE BELL CHIMES when I walk into the store. I shut it quickly, annoyed that I have an audience outside. I am blaming it on Scottie's car and the rumbling of the exhaust that still rings throughout the busy streets despite it being at the mechanic shop all morning.

"Welcome to Bodice and—" My welcome committee trips when she sees me.

Well, that's embarrassing.

Before I can help her, she snaps to a standing position with rosy-red cheeks. "Sorry, I...wasn't expecting a man." Her eyes fall to my left finger, and she shakes out of her stupor. "Are you here to buy your wife a dress or...?"

I stay relaxed when I hear a familiar voice. Her sass is at an all-time high, and I can't help but grin. Not to mention, was she hiding from me?

"No, he isn't." Scottie is so mouthy, and it's addicting.

I ignore my wife and step toward the rack of dresses. "Yes, I'm looking for a red dress. Something that would pair well with a woman who has a streak of defiance in her."

Scottie huffs, and I smirk at the sound.

I hear her ask the young dress seller for a moment alone, and when the girl scurries off, I finally turn and give Scottie my attention.

Her arms are crossed with those perfectly sized breasts pushed out. She blows a strand of blonde hair out of her face and pops a hip, propping her worn Converse off the floor. "This store is way too expensive."

I answer with a question of my own. "Were you hiding from me?" She's standing awfully close to a dress rack, and I'm beginning to think she ducked down below when she saw me enter the building.

"No, you just didn't notice me standing here."

A quick laugh leaves me. "Impossible."

Something flashes across her face before she storms over to

295

me and grabs my arm. I stare down at her small hand before leveling her with a look.

"Let's go," she urges. Her eyebrows rise to her forehead, and I have the urge to smooth out her worry lines again. "I'm not paying six hundred dollars for a dress I'll wear once."

Over the last several weeks, I've gotten used to Scottie's frugal ways. I wasn't born into a family that had endless amounts of money, and I know first-hand what it means to struggle. In fact, just a couple of years ago, my parents almost sold our home to be able to afford Taytum's insulin pump.

It's obvious from Scottie's living arrangements and the fact that she was willing to exploit me that she has some serious hardships when it comes to finances. But for some reason, I find myself *wanting* to buy her a dress from this high-end dress shop that she seems uncomfortable in.

Two weeks ago, I wouldn't have given a shit where she got a dress, just as long as she got one. Now, my wallet is doing a backflip in my pocket to spend every last dime on her.

Not that she would be impressed by that.

Scottie isn't that type of woman.

She isn't charmed by money—not in the way one would want to charm her, at least.

If I had to guess, she's more captivated by small gestures, like a fresh biscotti waiting for her in the morning.

My chest grows tight at the thought because, fuck, was I trying to impress her?

"Come on." Scottie's hand grips me harder, but instead of letting her drag me toward the exit, I walk in the opposite direction. A few women shopping for dresses give us the side-eye, and it makes me want to pull Scottie in even further.

Her irritated puff of air hits me from behind as I pull her toward a rack with long dresses. Ford and I tagged along with Taytum whenever she went prom dress shopping, so I unfortunately know what I'm doing in a dress shop.

I start to grab a few dresses—all red, just to piss her off. I don't have to look at her to know what size, because I have every one of her curves memorized.

"Here." I hold out three different dresses and blink at her, waiting for some sassy remark. Except, she doesn't react like I expect.

Her arms fall to her sides, and she stands there, looking at the dresses like I'm offering her an organ instead.

"Scottie," I groan. "They're just dresses. You let me put a ring on your finger, but you can't accept a dress?"

"It's not that!" Her voice rises, and her little jaw clenches.

My fingers dig into the fabric of the dresses with the urge to reach out and move the hair out of her face so I can see her better. Last night really did me in. I'm feeling things that are making it really fucking hard to keep my hands to myself.

And not for the perverted reasons like I'd expect.

I just...want to touch her.

"Then what is it?" I ask, softening my tone. She may think I'm trying to shield my voice to keep our conversation private because the retail worker has popped out a couple of times already, but I know that's not why.

Scottie stares at her scuffed shoes while she nibbles on her bottom lip. "Why did you pay my lease?"

My forehead furrows. "How do you know about that?"

She finally meets my face, and my stomach tightens with the shiny gloss covering her baby blues. "You think I'm going to let you pay"—she reaches forward and looks at the price of the first dress and scoffs—"eight hundred dollars for a dress when you paid off the rest of my lease off?"

"I paid much more than that for the ring on your finger," I counter.

She rolls her eyes. "That's different!" She looks around at the growing number of shoppers before coming in close and whispering, "I'm giving that back."

The hell she is.

The room shifts with the shocking thought.

I clear my head and grab her hand, dragging her toward the fitting room.

"Emory!" she whines.

I pull back the curtain and take one look at her face before coming to the realization that I can't trust she'll actually try any of the dresses on. When she steps in front of me with another annoyed sigh, I follow her in. The curtain rings drag against the rod slowly, and when Scottie turns around, she jumps.

"What are you doing in here?!"

She's appalled, and I fucking love it.

"Turn around," I order.

The tone of my voice brims with possession, and with the little flicker of fire in her eye, I think she kind of likes it.

Scottie's mouth parts. "Are you serious?" she asks. "What are you going to do? Strip me down to my bra and panties and put the dress on me?"

I grin and take a step toward her. "That's exactly what I'm going to do."

Thirty-Nine

SCOTTIE

I FEEL LIKE A CHILD, which is fitting because I'm acting like one too.

"Turn around, Biscotti."

The sound of my foot stomping on the dressing room floor causes Emory's lip to hitch. I dart my gaze behind his large frame, and he takes a step forward.

"There's no way out, so just turn around and get this over with."

He's right.

I'd have to dart around him and run like the wind if I truly wanted to evade trying on one of these high-end, costly dresses, so I give up and spin around. I catch his eye in the mirror and roll mine at the triumphant look on his face. He reaches forward, but I rip my shirt off before he has a chance to do it.

"I don't need your help."

I zero in on his face. His blue eyes are wilder than normal. "Funny, you did last night," he mutters.

My entire body floods with heat. I turn around in nothing but my jeans and bra. "We are *not* talking about last night."

Emory leans against the wall and crosses his arms. He is so hot I have to look away. I've purposefully kept the image of him in the shower out of my head, but with him sharing the small space with me, it's all I can think about.

"Good, because I don't think words could describe last night."

Oh god.

I bite the inside of my cheek and unbutton my jeans, pretending that his sultry gaze following my every move doesn't make a difference.

Last night was a short blip in time where I momentarily lost my footing. The fact that he got me a biscotti, took my car to get serviced, and secretly paid the remainder of my lease is nice and all, but it doesn't change anything.

"Try that one first." Emory nods to the bright-red dress, so I make sure to grab a different one.

I hear his deep chuckle when I toss the hanger on the floor, just to make a point. When I glance at him through the mirror while stepping into the silky dress, my stomach flips. His kissable lips are slightly parted as he stares at me from behind. My heart skips, which is never a good sign. I quickly try to pull the dress up past my hips, but by the end of trying to get it on, I'm a shaky, scrambling mess.

Emory stays glued to the wall, watching me, and I know I look like a disaster. I'm chaos, while he stands there, completely relaxed in harmony.

I reach behind myself and attempt to pull the zipper up and pray to God I can do it on my own, but after I almost snap my elbow, Emory pushes off the wall and slides up behind me. His presence is heavy. The smell of his cologne fills the small dressing room, and I suddenly feel like I'm in a daze.

Focus, Scottie.

Our eyes snag in the mirror. The energy buzzing between us is undeniable. My body is seconds from betraying me, even with my pragmatic ability to deny that anything is happening between us. I have a sudden need to back up against him just to feel his body heat mingle with mine, but I don't.

I stay completely still and try to smooth my features so he doesn't know that ever since he kissed me in that club, weeks ago, I haven't quite been the same.

His finger brushes against my spine as he pulls the zipper higher, and I stop breathing. Why do his touches suddenly feel seductive?

Last night was a mistake.

That much is clear by the fact that I can't breathe properly with him behind me.

The sound of my bra unclasping catches my ear, and I snap to attention.

"You can't wear a bra with this."

He's right, but a warning would have been nice.

Maybe then I could tell my nipples to stop rearing their pebbled heads, giving me away.

One strap falls down to my elbow, then goes the other. A chill moves down my spine, and I know Emory notices. Surprisingly, he says nothing. He stares down at my bra after I discard it to the floor, then his lazy gaze moves to the mirror.

In an attempt to hide my betraying breasts, I place my hands there to hold the dress up.

It's a beautiful dress, and the feel of silk against my bare skin tells me it's worth the eight-hundred-dollar price tag. The color looks good too, even if Emory was trying to irritate me by pulling all the red dresses off the racks.

Though it isn't a low-cut dress, it's still sexy. It's classy with a tight bodice full of pretty lace that shows some of my skin underneath. It flows gracefully around my hips and to the floor. When Emory's hands fall to my waist, the movement pulls some of the fabric out of the way. We both stare at the slit in the front that gives a clear visual of my leg.

It's hard to see myself in something like this.

I didn't go to prom. I've never had the opportunity to wear a dress besides the moment I put one on for our wedding photos, and this one makes me feel...desirable.

"Well?" he asks.

I look everywhere but the mirror.

Emory steps backward, and the second he removes his hands, I want them back.

Clearing my throat, I shrug. "It's fine."

"It's fine?" he repeats.

Still keeping my stare pinned to the hanger laying on the floor, I nod.

I feel him move close to me, and I can't keep myself from meeting his face in the mirror.

His light eyes darken like a storm, and his heavy brow line deepens. "It's more than fine."

In an attempt to look away, I drop my chin, but he's there to catch it.

His fingers squeeze it gently, and his whisper brushes against my ear. "Hasn't anyone ever told you how irresistible you are?"

I stare into his eyes and refuse to acknowledge the heat simmering underneath my skin from his touch.

"What can I say to get you to see what I see when I look at you?"

I swallow my pride. If he's being sincere, then I guess I will too. I lower my shackles, and a quiet, sad laugh leaves me. "I'm pretty sure that every time you look at me, you're reminded of how we met. You probably see nothing but desperation and selfishness."

"I wish that's what I saw," he admits.

His rough, callused fingers drag down my neck and over my collarbone until he lands at my waist. I tremble in his grip, and I curse my body for giving me away. It craves the contact between us, and he knows it.

Suddenly feeling like I need to gain some type of control, I take the initiative and ask my own question, instead of only allowing him to ask them. "What do you see, then?"

"I see a ring on your finger."

I glance down at the diamond glistening under the soft glow of the fitting room light.

"A ring that says you're mine."

I go to protest, but then Emory's hand starts to grip the silky fabric of the dress. My leg is fully exposed, and we're both drawn to it. My pulse thrums, and my heart races.

What is he doing?

His hot whisper sends heat in between my legs. "The only desperation I see is how desperate you are for me to touch you again."

Deny it.

"You're only supposed to touch me when people are around." My voice is breathy. "That's what the contract says."

"There are plenty of customers roaming around. Not to mention, the saleslady who has walked past multiple times."

Emory's hand grazes the bare skin of my leg, and the room spins. My eyes shut, and my legs grow unsteady. I lean against his chest, ignoring the little voice in the back of my head that's telling me to escape the trap.

"*Emory.*" His name is more of a whine than a whisper. "Last night was a mistake, and you know it."

"I'll stop if you want me to." He grips my thigh, running a finger to the inside of my knee and up again. "But I think this is the only way to get you to understand that you're fucking irresistible, Scottie, despite how mouthy you are when it comes to me."

"So you're touching me because you want me to believe you?" My hips betray me and tilt forward in an attempt to pull his hand up higher.

Scottie, focus.

"What if I were to tell you I'm only touching you because everyone outside this dressing room needs convincing that we're a happily married couple that can't keep our hands to ourselves?"

I open my eyes, and when I see the desire etched into his steely features, I give in.

"Then I say you better keep it up because, after all, this is my job, right?"

Forty

EMORY

I DON'T CARE what she calls it.

With her looking at me like I can hang the moon, I'd do just about anything she asked of me.

"You wouldn't want to get fired," I say, creeping my fingers up her thigh. Scottie relaxes even more against my chest. I stare at her lips and have the urge to kiss the shit out of her.

I would be willing to do all sorts of things to stick my tongue in her mouth for another taste.

This wasn't what I was planning to do when I followed her in here, but there is no way I'm leaving this dressing room with her not having the confidence she deserves while in that dress.

If I asked her outright, she'd deny it.

But her little pelvic movements and sky-high pulse give her away. She's beyond turned on, and to hell with the fact that she doesn't want to cross the line again. If I have to use the excuse that the customers in this dress shop are paying close attention to us, then so be it.

My parents are at my house, waiting—something Scottie

309

doesn't know—but the world could be ending, and I wouldn't be able to pull myself away until the job was done.

A job.

That's what this is.

"Tell me what you want." My nose skims her neck, and I breathe her in like she's my lifeline.

She smells so sweet, and I suddenly feel calm for the first time today.

The smell of fresh ice is usually my comfort, but lately, I'm starting to worry that it's her.

"Uh..." the word is more of a breath coming from her lips.

My hand disappears between her legs, hidden by the silk of the dress I'm buying for her one way or another. Heat pools there, and as much as I want to drag this out, there's been one too many sets of footsteps outside the dressing room. With my luck, I'll get arrested for public indecency.

"Right here?" I slip my fingers under her wet panties.

She looks like an angel, but the noise she just made came right from the devil. I clench my eyes because watching her in the mirror is going to make me lose sight of where we are.

"I could ravish you right here." I press my mouth to her neck, and her pulse pounds against my lips. Before I can stop myself, I nip her delicate skin and suck. Scottie curves her hips to meet me halfway, and I slip another finger in, moving slowly and deliberately.

She feels so good against my fingers that I *want* to make her mine. I'll play make-believe every single day of my life if this is how good it is.

I think my fake wife just became my vice.

The heel of my palm presses against her clit, and she whimpers.

My eyes fly open. "Shh."

Euphoria paints her face, and a hot swallow works itself down my throat. Blood pumps through my veins, and I'm captivated. My perfect, angelic wife with an attitude that could rival anyone I know is completely entranced in the pleasure I'm giving her while in public.

I move my mouth to her ear. "Open your eyes and look at yourself."

Scottie's eyes slowly open, and I swear to god, they're glowing.

Her pussy clenches on my fingers the very second she looks at my hand in between her legs.

Mmm, I wish she wouldn't have done that.

"You like watching me touch you, don't you?" I ask.

Her cheeks flare with heat when she starts to move against my hand. I press on a spot that makes her suck in air and wait for the finale.

"Don't worry, I like watching too." My teeth sink into her earlobe, and I give it a good tug. "You're beautiful when you're at my mercy." She gasps, and her entire body shakes. Her pussy traps my fingers, and instead of watching her come, I turn her face to mine and swallow her whimpers.

The kiss is deep and so fucking hot I can hardly stand.

I silence every one of her quiet moans, not taking a single one for granted.

Her orgasm is over, but I go in for more because I can't help myself. She's addicting and has been on my mind far too much since last night. Maybe if I get my fill of her, I'll be able to focus on tomorrow's game.

"Is everything okay in there?"

Scottie breaks our kiss with wide eyes and flushed cheeks.

I drop my gaze to my fingers still inside her and look down in the mirror at the saleslady's heels right outside the curtain.

"Yes." I sound completely unfazed, but I am the opposite. "I think we've found the one," I add, dragging my fingers out from between Scottie's legs. They're soaked, and I love seeing every last drop, especially as I brush them against the bottom layer of fabric of her dress.

Scottie, still red-faced and bright-eyed, gapes.

I smirk while unzipping her dress. "Guess we really have to buy it now, huh?"

She looks at me like I'm crazy, and I'm almost certain that I am.

While holding her dress to her body, she shakes her head at me. There's a twinkle in her eye that wasn't there before. "All of that just to force my hand into letting you buy the dress?"

Bending down to swipe up her bra, I hold it out for her before she rips it away. "That's just an added bonus."

After Scottie quickly gets dressed, all while avoiding eye contact with me, she unclips her hair and tries to fix it in the mirror. I watch her every movement, unable to tear my eyes away, but then I see something she's going to *hate*.

"Want to know what else is an added bonus?"

Besides her orgasming all over my hand, of course.

She's hesitant. "What?"

My fingers get lost in her hair as I push the strands behind her shoulder. I push on her chin gently and nod to the hickey I gave her. "That."

Her hand flies to the little red bruise, and her mouth falls open. "Oh my god."

"Don't worry," I tease. "It'll just prove to the media that I can't keep my hands off you." I pause. "And my parents."

Scottie is glaring at me now. "What?"

With my back to her, I say, "Oh, did I forget to mention that?" I glance over my shoulder because I have a feeling she'll try to throw something at me in a second. "My parents are waiting for us at the house."

Forty-One

SCOTTIE

"I COULD HAVE BEEN ARRESTED!" I seethe quietly while following Emory out the door. I avoid eye contact with everyone in the dress shop because I'm mortified.

But am I?

I bare my teeth to my subconscious. *Shut up.*

Emory pulls his sunglasses onto his face and hoists up the dress bag so it doesn't touch the ground when we find ourselves on the busy street. This is the first time he and I have been in public together that doesn't revolve around hockey, and I'm noticing more and more looks from random strangers.

He laughs under his breath at my irritation. "Jail isn't so bad. Take it from someone who's been there."

His comment is a slap to the face. I know he's kidding, but it hits me in a way that it wouldn't hit most. I jolt backward with the thought of William and remember why I'm in this predicament in the first place.

Emory steps forward and grabs onto my upper arm, shaking me out of my thoughts. When he lifts his glasses up, he bounces his eyes back and forth between mine. "I was just kidding," he says. "Why are you pale all of a sudden?"

A rush of anxiety moves through my stomach over the fact that, in less than a year, Emory and I will be nothing but a memory, and I'll be in and out of the lawyer's office again, spending every last dime he gave me on even more legal fees.

"Hey." Emory's face comes into view, and I don't think I've ever seen him look worried before now. He didn't even look this concerned when I cornered him with a photo-shopped picture of us that could have destroyed his career even further. "I wouldn't have let anyone put you in handcuffs."

For some reason, I actually believe him.

His gentle smile turns devious after another second of staring at me.

"If anyone is putting you in handcuffs, it's me."

Then he winks, and I have the urge to laugh, but instead, I playfully roll my eyes and place my hand out. "Give me my keys."

"No," he argues, putting his arm around my shoulders to walk down the street. Knowing we're in public, I slowly wrap my arm around his waist, and we walk a little ways down the sidewalk before he explains why he won't give me my keys. "What are my parents going to think when we show up to the house in separate cars?"

"That we *must* be in a contract marriage, obviously. There is no way that we could have been out doing something without one another, right?" I'm full of sarcasm, and he snorts.

"You're all jokes now, but just wait until we're at my house and in front of my parents."

I pause when we get to his car. "What does that mean?"

Emory unlocks it and opens my door. I want to make a joke about how gentlemanly he's being, but when he lifts his sunglasses up and pierces me with those blue eyes, my stomach tumbles. "It means you better get your game face on. I don't want my parents to know that we're in a fake marriage."

"Why not? Surely they wouldn't go to the media." It's an assumption, of course, because I know better than anyone that we don't get to choose our parents. I have no idea what kind of people they are.

I slip into the passenger seat and gaze up at him, waiting for his answer. His arm rests on top of his car, and he shakes his head. "Of course they wouldn't..."

He glances away, and there's a tug on my heartstrings. I sit on my hands because I want to reach out and comfort him, which is...very confusing.

"They worry too much," he finally says. "With my sister's diabetes diagnosis and then my recent stumble with the media... I just don't want them to be bothered by this. They won't approve." He shakes his head quickly. "They won't approve of a fake marriage, I mean. I'm not referring to you."

My features soften. This may be the first *real* thing Emory has ever told me about himself. It feels like I've won the lottery when he rounds the hood and climbs inside the car. He's quiet, and I wonder if he's angry that he let me see a layer of himself that no one else has.

When we're on the freeway and the silence has gone back to a comfortable quiet, I make the decision to say something I no longer want to keep to myself—not now, anyway.

"Your sister was wrong." I feel his stare, but I continue to look at the blurring yellow line of the highway.

"About what?"

"She said you weren't caring or affectionate." I swallow my pride before glancing at him. "But I think you are. Even if you choose to hide it behind that grumpy face of yours."

"READY?" Emory's hand falls into mine, and we walk up the front steps of the porch. His calluses rub against my soft palm when I bend down to pet Shutter. To my surprise, he doesn't make a rude comment about how my dumpster cat is a true menace to society.

"Should we introduce him as their first grandchild?" I ask, acting completely serious.

Emory scoffs, but I see the humor lingering when he pulls me upright.

"You're ridiculous," he whispers.

I half-shrug. "You married me."

Our eyes catch for a brief second before he reaches up and frees my hair from my clip. My blonde locks fall around my face, landing over my shoulders. "Hiding your mark?" There's a bite to my tone. "I can't believe you gave me a—"

"Surprise!"

Emory turns and, thankfully, doesn't hide his reaction of *not* being surprised.

I'm struck speechless when I realize that his mom is what fairy tales are made of. I'm immediately wrapped in a warm embrace, and she smells like sugar and flour. She pulls back after a few seconds, and her hands move to my shoulders. "You're even prettier in person."

A soft smile moves to my lips because she's so *genuine*. Even Shutter, who doesn't like anyone but me, rubs his black, silky fur along her legs.

Emory grumbles. "I think that cat has it in for men."

At that exact moment, Emory's dad, who is nearly as tall as him, bends down and gives Shutter a pet on the back. Shutter purrs, and I smash my lips together.

He pops up and grins at his son. "Nope, he just doesn't like you."

I laugh out loud, and Emory turns at the sound coming

318

from me. My hand immediately covers my mouth. He squints his eyes playfully.

"You're lucky I love her," he says to Shutter, "or else you'd have to find a new stoop to live on."

I play it off well, reminding myself that this is all fake.

But the glow inside my chest feels awfully real, as if I could reach inside and touch its warmth.

"Ford told you, didn't he?" Emory's mom asks, placing her hands on her hips. She clicks her tongue and turns to head back inside. Her husband follows after her, grinning kindly at me. Emory catches my smile before I can wipe it off, and I see his mouth curve too.

I question whether he's smiling for show or smiling because he's proud of how we just acted in front of his parents, or if he's actually...happy.

It doesn't really matter, though, because either way, we have to play the game.

Forty-Two

EMORY

"THIS IS NEW." I grab the wet dish from Scottie's soapy hands to dry it.

She tucks a light strand of hair behind her ear and peers up at me. Her nose wrinkles. "What is?"

The corner of my mouth lifts, and I lean in close so my parents can't hear. "Seeing you in the kitchen."

Scottie grimaces at me and begins washing the next dish with a little more aggression than before. "If you want a wife who makes you a home-cooked meal every night and cleans the kitchen afterward, I guess you should have put that in the contract." Her voice is low, but I can hear her perfectly fine.

Without putting much thought into it, I take some of the bubbles from the sink and sweep them over her cheek. "I like my wife the way she is."

Surprise flickers over her features like a lightbulb. She has no idea what to do with my incessant flirting. I've been doing it all evening with my parents as our audience.

Each time Scottie tries to sass me in private, I shut it down quickly with some act of teasing followed by a subtle touch against her skin or a wink. It takes her a moment to recover each time, and I love it.

"So, Scottie..." My dad taps his fingers against the counter while finishing his dessert.

It was no surprise to me that my mom made Scottie and me a home-cooked meal followed by dessert, but Scottie was thoroughly confused when she saw what my mom had managed to do in just a matter of hours.

"Have your parents met Emory? Or are you hiding him from your family, like he was with you?"

I jerk my attention to Scottie, waiting to hear her response. There has been no talk of her family, and I'm sure that's purposeful. When a plate slips out of her hand and into the sink, I reach inside the warm water and give her palm a squeeze.

"I'm never gonna live it down, am I?" I call over my shoulder. "And I wasn't hiding her. Scottie just doesn't like attention, so we were keeping our relationship and marriage under wraps until we felt it was right. If you haven't noticed, I've gained some attention from the press."

Scottie's shoulders visibly relax, and she breathes out a tiny breath. She turns slightly with our hands still joined in the water. When she smiles sweetly at my dad, I zero in on the hickey I'd gave her earlier in the day.

Shit.

I reach out with my other hand and pull her hair forward. The tender act will surprise my parents to the point that they won't question *why* I did it. Scottie knows, though.

"I sure hope my son asked your father for your hand in marriage." My dad sends me a look, like he'd be disappointed if I didn't.

Newsflash: I didn't.

"Actually..." Scottie drains the water from the sink and

busies herself while answering my dad. "My father passed away when I was very young."

I should have known that.

"Oh, sweetie. I'm so sorry." My mom sends her a soft look before smacking my dad on the arm.

A sweet burst of laughter leaves Scottie. "It's okay. If I don't talk about him every once in a while, then I'm afraid he'll be forgotten." She shrugs in a sad way, and I don't like it. "He would have liked Emory, though."

Pride swells, and I can't pretend that isn't completely fucked up.

Her pretty eyes linger on my face for a couple of seconds before she moves back to my parents. I start to busy myself with drying dishes and act uninterested, but I'm hanging onto her every word.

"My father was a huge hockey fan. He is the reason I got into hockey, actually. He'd get us season tickets, and we'd go to all the Blue Devils games together. I actually still have his shirt with the old team logo on it."

How did I not know that? I feel like such a dick.

"So he'd be over the moon if he knew I was married to their goalie." She and my parents laugh while I'm left standing there with a knot in my stomach.

"And what about your mother? Has she met Emory?"

Scottie immediately stiffens. It isn't noticeable to my parents, but I feel the way she closes off right away. I'm not sure when it happened, but I somehow just know what she's feeling now.

"Okay, that's enough, you two." I turn around and give my parents a look. "I've got a game tomorrow, so my wife and I are going to bed."

Scottie's head nearly falls off her shoulders.

If her eyes were weapons, I'd be dead.

I can almost hear her silent rebuttal.

My father stands and claps his hands together. "Right, right! Get to bed. I'm here to watch you win, not lose." The way my mom purses her lips at my dad is something I've seen a million times before.

"Everything's the same as you left it in the guest room. Unwashed bedding and all." I chuckle quietly.

My mom places her hands on her hips again. "Emory Olson! I taught you better than that."

I shrug. "You're the only one who sleeps in there. Why wash the bedding after one night of sleep?"

The heat coming from Scottie burns me. I'm prepared for the reprimand as I drag her away, saying a quick goodnight to my parents. They promise to see us in the morning and tell Scottie they can't wait for her to sit with them at the game.

She's so good at acting like my wife that I know they suspect nothing out of sorts.

It isn't until we're halfway up the stairs that I feel the wrath flowing from her tight little body.

"You are such an asshole!" She attempts to hit me in the stomach, but I take the opportunity to quickly scoop her up in my arms and drape her over my shoulder.

Her gasp hits me in the back, and I laugh to myself, climbing the rest of the stairs. The moment I place her down on her feet, she scowls and darts down the hallway like a child.

"What the hell are you doing?" I quietly laugh, going after her.

She pushes the door at the end of the hall open and turns around with her arms crossed. "You had a guest bed this entire time?" She's fuming, and I have to purposefully keep myself from laughing at her expense.

"Yeah, so?"

"I've been sleeping on the couch!" she hisses.

My lip hitches, and she glares before pushing me off to the side to stomp down the hall. I follow her swaying hips all the way into my room. When I turn and shut the door, I hear my bathroom lock click.

"Really?" I say through the door. "You gonna stay in there all night and be angry?" I chuckle under my breath. She is impossible but so goddamn amusing.

"I can't believe you had a guest bed but forced me to sleep on the couch!"

I grip the doorknob and give it a twist. It's locked, but it didn't stop me from trying. I talk through the door. "I didn't force you to do anything. I basically begged you to sleep in the bed with me. Your belongings are already in the closet. Why not just sleep in here too?"

"Well, I can't do that!" she snaps back.

"And why is that?" I tease, knowing very well why. "Is it because you don't trust yourself in bed with me?"

Silence.

I wait a few more minutes, and when it's apparent that Scottie is being her usual stubborn self, I sink down to the floor and rest my back against the door. The shower turns on, and I *hate* that the door is locked. Reaching up, I give the doorknob another twist just for funsies.

"You're so stubborn," I say, not sure if she can even hear me.

"Well, you married me!" she shouts back.

My chest rumbles with a laugh. I don't think I've ever laughed as much as I do with her around. I stay planted against the door the entire time she showers, hating that all I can picture is her naked in there with water rolling over the curves of her perfect body.

I swear, she takes an extra-long shower, and by the time the water is off, I've forgotten all about our little verbal grapple. I've calmed my dick down long enough to relax on the floor. I pull my legs up and rest my forearms over my knees. "You did good in front of my parents," I say, knowing damn well she's listening just as intently as I am.

"I know."

My lip turns up at the corner.

"Can you hurry up? I have a game tomorrow."

At that exact moment, Scottie whips the door open, and I fly backward.

She peers down at me with a pleased look on her face, and the competitor in me acts fast. I grab her ankles and slide myself farther inside the bathroom, until I'm right between her legs. "What a nice sight," I muse, looking up her towel. She is absolutely perfect in every way, and her pussy is no exception. My mouth waters when she squeals.

"Emory Olson!" Scottie jumps away, and I'm left laughing on the floor with a half-hard cock.

"Scottie Olson!" I echo.

I quickly climb to my feet. "You'll never win when it comes to me, Biscotti."

I have the biggest urge to grab her towel and strip her bare when she stomps past me, but I refrain. Instead, I give her privacy and shut myself behind the bathroom door.

The fact that I have a game tomorrow has crossed my mind several times, and if I don't get my shit together, I might be just as unfocused as I was in practice today.

After quickly rinsing off and brushing my teeth, I step out into my bedroom, expecting to see her in my bed, but she isn't there. Neither are the extra pillows.

Walking a little farther into my room, I pause when I see two adorable feet lying on the floor. I peer over the side of my bed. "Are you serious? You're that stubborn?"

Scottie, dressed in nothing but one of my T-shirts—just to spite me—looks up at me with damp hair and a clean face. She's entirely too beautiful without a speck of makeup on.

I wonder if she knows that.

She pulls the extra blanket up to her chin. "I obviously cannot be trusted with you." She looks away disappointedly, like she's at her wits end with herself. "You're right."

Irritation skips up my spine. I sigh before bending at the knee. I scoop her up and let the blanket fall to the floor. "Emory, I'm serious!" She pushes at my grip, so I throw her onto the bed.

A tiny yelp escapes her, and I shoot her a serious glare. "You are not sleeping on the floor."

Scottie's jaw clenches.

"I won't touch you." I hate what I just promised. "But my wife is not sleeping on the fucking floor."

My tone seems to resonate with her. She remains quiet, but I know she wants to say something.

After swiping a pillow off the floor, I hand it to her. She takes it with a hesitant grip but eventually settles onto the very edge of the bed. If she so much as turns in the middle of the night, she'll fall off, but at least she's on the bed.

After I flip the light off, I climb onto my side without saying a word to her.

I typically go to sleep early on game nights, but I'm wired with her being so close. The constant touching, quick glances, and subtle moments that we've shared in front of my parents are catching up to me.

Not to mention, the dressing room.

The fucking dressing room.

"Are you sleeping?" Her whisper does nothing but make me excited.

"No."

"Okay."

A rush of air leaves me. "Why? Were you gonna sneak out of the bed or something?"

Her soft laugh fills me up to the brim. "No. I just…"

Again, I'm hanging on her every fucking word.

"I just wanted to say thank you."

Her shy tone hits me in all the wrong places. "For?"

"The dress."

I'm surprised, considering she was so against me buying it. But after learning about her father and watching her panic when asked about her mother, I'm beginning to learn that Scottie isn't used to someone taking care of her, or better yet, buying her expensive things.

I clear my throat. "You're welcome."

I want to reach out and grab her in the worst way, but I promised I wouldn't touch her, so instead, I remain unmoving.

We both lie there in silence for what seems like hours.

Thankfully, she's the first to break.

"Are you sleeping now?" she asks in a soft tone.

I can't help but chuckle. "No."

"I can't sleep," she admits.

"I can help with that," I say, completely joking.

"*Emory.*" My name sounds like a scold, and I smile to myself.

"Get your mind out of the gutter. Wasn't the orgasm I gave you earlier enough?"

She exhales loudly, and I wish I was closer to feel her breath on my face.

"I'm kidding, Biscotti." I reach over and poke the side of her torso to lighten the mood. I keep my hands on top of the covers because even though she thinks *she* can't be trusted...it's really me. I'm the one who can't be trusted. "What do you typically do when you can't sleep?" I ask.

I almost choke on the question.

If she says she gets herself off, I'll have to lock myself in the bathroom.

"You're going to laugh," she says with a quiet voice.

A hum vibrates out of my mouth. "Try me."

"I watch hockey."

My brow furrows. "You watch hockey to relax?"

"I know it's weird, but–"

"It's not weird." It's fucking adorable.

Reaching over to my nightstand, I grab the remote, and the room glows with the light from the flatscreen. I find a hockey game and turn to look at her.

Blue lights flicker against her high cheekbones as she sits up a little taller in bed. Her shoulders relax, and there's a tiny smile on her lips.

I forcefully swallow.

God, she's...*perfect*.

Warmth fills my stomach the longer I stare at her. My heart starts to beat a little quicker, and I try to think of a time that I've ever felt this way.

There isn't a person, or even a situation, that comes close.

I never want to leave this bed with her in it.

Her eyes widen when the Hawks score.

She's engrossed in the game, and I'm engrossed in her.

Which is a huge fucking predicament.

Forty-Three

SCOTTIE

"LOOK AT THEM," I chide.

Gloves are off, helmets are thrown to the side, bare fists are clenched tightly.

Emory adjusts himself on the bed, but I keep my sights locked on the TV. "Just another day in the rink. Probably a lot of chirpin' on the ice. It irks us."

I sigh, feeling myself get sleepier the longer I stare at the screen. "There haven't been many fights this season for you guys, though."

"That's because the team isn't on the same page yet."

I turn slightly to catch a quick glimpse of Emory. He's leaning with his back on the headboard, and he's shirtless. His abs ripple with each breath he takes while he watches the fight unfold on the screen.

All pro hockey players are obsessed with the game, and Emory is no exception. He's been watching the screen like he's studying for a test, and if his furrowed brow and laser focus are any indication, he'll pass with flying colors.

I look back to the TV quickly so he doesn't catch me staring at him. "What do you mean? You guys have been playing better with each game. The defensemen have gotten so much stronger too. Malaki does really well along the wall. I noticed during the last game that his passing is more accurate. Honestly, I'd say he's becoming one of the best skaters in all three zones."

I stop mid-sentence when I feel Emory staring at me. We make eye contact, and there's the smallest smile playing on his lips.

My face warms. "What?"

"It's kind of cute that you know so much about hockey."

I purse my lips and scoot farther under the covers. He thinks I'm annoyed that he called me cute, but the small compliment makes the butterflies swarm so fast that I have to put my hand over my stomach.

Emory continues to talk about the game. "When the team does something like that"—I look back to the screen and see that most of the hockey players are fighting now—"it means they have each other's backs. They're working as a team and have a bond that goes further than making good plays." Emory runs a hand down his scruffy face. "It's kind of what I'm trying to get the Blue Devils to become. When you trust each other, you play better."

I say nothing because I'm afraid of what'll come out of my mouth. It would do neither of us any good if I were to say what I'm really thinking, because truthfully, I think Emory Olson is one of the best hockey players in the league.

He's calculated when he's in between the poles of the net. On multiple occasions, I've seen him pull his teammates together and give them a pep talk too.

Emory doesn't only look out for himself on the ice.

He looks out for his team.

"Can I ask you something?"

His chin dips with a nod.

"What happened the night you were arrested?"

I don't know why I ask the question or why it matters. But there's something about the quiet of his room with soft sounds of the hockey game on TV that makes me comfortable.

Emory grabs the back of his neck and gives it a quick squeeze. Just when I think he isn't going to answer me, he starts to talk.

"I did get into an altercation that night," his tone lowers, like he's disappointed. "But I wasn't the one who initiated it or even really had any connection to it other than just being in the wrong place at the wrong time."

I continue to stare at the side of his face when he takes a pause. His temple is flickering back and forth, and if I didn't ban myself from touching him, I'd probably reach out and grab onto his hand to calm the anguish.

"Nelson started to shit-talk. He's mouthy on the ice and even worse off it. One thing led to another, and he started a fight. I was trying to separate the two when it became a brawl. Next thing I knew, there was a broken beer bottle up to my throat, and I acted fast. In the midst of it, I somehow caused most of the damage, even though I was just trying to stay alive. My teammates bailed, too afraid it'd ruin their image and get them kicked off the team. Coach Berkley had zero tolerance for that shit."

Emory turns to me, and the blue of his eyes is so bright it's hard not to fall into them. He looks away after a second, and I know it's to hide what he's really feeling. "I guess they were right to stay quiet."

Anger fuels my response. "No. They were wrong to let you take the blame. Only cowards do that." He has no idea how infuriated I truly am. The same thing happened to William, except he doesn't quite get it.

Emory's lip curves upward, and he sort of smiles at me. When he turns back to the TV, he quietly mutters, "I think everything happens for a reason. If I didn't get into that fight, then I would have missed out on other things."

I want to ask him what other things he would have missed out on, but I don't because I know there is absolutely no way he's referring to marrying me, even if, deep down, there's a very quiet part of me that wishes he was.

I'm clearly going insane.

Silence passes between us while we both quietly watch the rest of the game. My eyes start to get droopy toward the end of the third period, and Emory is fully relaxed on his side of the bed. I sneak a few glances at him here and there, and each time, he watches the screen with intense concentration, nodding occasionally when Maier blocks the puck.

As soon as my eyelids drift shut, I hear the TV turn off.

I tense. Emory must feel me jerk, because he's quick to turn it back on.

"Did you need it to sleep?" he asks quietly. His sleepy face softens, and I can't help but lose my train of thought.

I shake my head and pull the covers up higher.

"You sure?"

I want to tell him to stop being so nice to me. I need him to go back to being like an annoying roommate who enjoys irritating me instead of acting so sweet—like when he grabbed my hand in the kitchen when his parents asked me about my family.

When he turns the TV off again, the room is filled with silence. It's a calm silence, though. Comforting in a way...until he climbs underneath the covers, and I can feel his warmth from across the bed. Each one of his breaths sounds louder than the one before, and I'm positively insane for thinking such a thing.

Suddenly, everything feels heightened, and I'm lying in my fake husband's bed, trying to think about all the ways he's aggravated me since starting our little marriage game so I don't think of other things.

"Hey."

Excitement erupts from my chest when his smooth voice fills the room.

"Yeah?" *I sound eager. God.*

"Can I ask you something now?"

I smile to myself. "Technically, you get one question a day, remember?"

He makes a noise that sounds an awful lot like a sarcastic sigh. "Why'd you close off when my parents asked about your mom?"

My body breaks out in a sweat.

He noticed?

"You don't have to answer."

"Oh, so I get a choice?" I whisper-tease.

"This time? Yeah." Emory's tone is smooth and steady, which *must* be the reason I'm considering telling him about her. There can't be any reason other than that.

"I'll tell you." *Shit, what?*

"You will? I surely thought you'd put up a fight."

I'm just as surprised as he is.

I turn away from him, as if putting my back to him will lessen the dread I'll feel when speaking of her out loud.

I start with the basics. "She's alive."

Emory stays quiet, and I tell myself he isn't even in the room—not that I could ever believe that. I feel his presence like I feel my own heartbeat.

"But the woman I once knew is no longer a woman I recognize." My throat starts to feel tight and itchy. "I don't like to talk about her, and it's easier to just tell people she's dead, but it feels wrong to do that. Like it gives her an easy way out."

There were times when I wished she was dead, and I'm not

proud of that, but abandonment causes you to become bitter at times.

"If she isn't dead, where is she?" Emory moves under the covers, and for a split second, I wonder if he's going to get closer to me.

But he doesn't, so I keep going.

"Right now?" I ask. "Probably on the corner of 1st and Mcallister."

He repeats what I said, dragging the words out with a familiarity that I highly doubt is true.

"How often do you go there to hand out coats and food? Do you go to check on her?"

I pause.

Ugh.

I flop onto my back and look over to his side of the bed. My eyes have adjusted to the dark room, and I stare at his strong profile.

"You never did tell me how you knew about that."

He turns, and I know he's looking at me.

"I followed you one night—before I asked you to marry me."

My face burns with mortification. Seeing her in person makes me feel so incredibly vulnerable, and I loathe that he witnessed that.

"I needed to know more about you."

"To see if you wanted to marry me?" I ask.

"No," he answers with confidence. "I just..." I hear him turn away, and suddenly I'm watching his chest rise and fall in the dark. "I just wanted to know more."

My teeth sink into my lip before I go back to staring at the ceiling. I haven't been back there since that night. It's a part of my life that I want to keep private, especially from the media. It wouldn't do anything but make people ask questions, and that would lead to more speculation, and before I knew it, everyone would be questioning our marriage.

Emory knows now, though.

But he doesn't know about William, and that's something I'd rather keep under lock and key. Otherwise, I'm afraid he'll tell me exactly what everyone else has told me—that trying to get him out of prison on an appeal is a lost cause.

Several minutes of silence pass between us, but just when I think he's asleep, his quiet, smooth voice fills the void. "I'm sorry, Biscotti."

He sounds so genuine.

So believable.

"For what?" I ask with a blip of irritation to my tone. He's being compassionate again, and I don't know what to do with it. "You had nothing to do with her choosing the path she's on."

"And what path is that? Why is she homeless? Is that why you need money?"

"No," I rush out. "I stopped giving her money a long time ago."

Turning away, my stomach fills with dread. I hate talking about her because it brings up unwanted thoughts and feelings that I'd rather bury.

"She's sick."

"Sick?"

He doesn't get it, and I can't expect him to.

"She's a drug addict." The four words fly out of my mouth and into the open room so quickly I'm not even sure he heard me.

"Oh."

He's surprised, which is also understandable.

Not many people consider their loved ones to be sick when they're addicted to drugs. There are many things that drug addicts are referred to and being sick isn't one of them. But it hits differently when you're the one affected by it.

"If I don't think about it as an illness, then I'll hate her, and I just don't have it in me to hate her anymore." My heart starts to beat a little faster the more I open up. "I used to," I clarify. "But I guess that's just a part of growing up. I don't agree with her decisions or behavior, but I understand that she's sick."

Emory doesn't hesitate for even a second. "I'm beginning to realize that you grew up a lot faster than you should have. It's no wonder you're infuriatingly independent."

I wonder what he'd think if I told him that I've been taking care of my mentally ill brother too.

"Infuriatingly?" I try to crack a joke, but I'm pretty sure he can hear the desolate tone in my voice. "Rude."

His deep chuckle fills the room again before he turns to his side.

Just when I think he's going to sleep, after I just spilled one of my deepest, darkest secrets, the room is illuminated in a bluish glow again. Hockey fills the screen, and when I peek at him, he's looking directly at me.

"We can watch it for a little longer, yeah?" he asks.

I turn away to hide the gloss in my eyes that's been there since the second he asked about her.

I nod and settle further into the bed, basking in the little bit of comfort he's giving me.

Forty-Four

EMORY

I'M HOT, yet I feel no covers on top of me.

I squint at the dim glow filtering through the window. I shut my eyes again, feeling entirely too comfortable. My fingers stretch before I place them back down on something silky smooth. My neck cracks as I lean toward the right, and when I inhale, I'm wide awake.

God damn, she smells good.

My hand is on her thigh, and that thigh is resting on top of my leg.

Ever so slowly, I peer down at her head on my shoulder. Her soft breaths caress my bare skin, and I've never felt so content in my entire life.

There is something about her touch that calms my world, and the urge to pull her in closer is getting worse as each day passes by.

I wish I could snap a picture so she could see how content she looks wrapped around me in our bed.

My bed.

Not my, *our.*

Tension pulls on all my strings, and I low-key panic at the

annoying thoughts that keep hitting me at all the wrong times. *What the fuck is going on?*

Scottie shifts in her sleep, hiking her leg up higher on top of mine. I practically swallow my tongue when the inside of her thigh brushes against my dick.

I promised her I wouldn't touch her, but this is obviously her doing. I'm in the exact spot I was in when I fell asleep hours ago, after I admittedly watched her like a fucking creep with the hockey game well over and the glow of the TV swiping across her features.

My head wouldn't stop spinning.

I kept chasing all the negative things I thought about her weeks ago, wishing I could make them ring true, but they just don't.

She may be mouthy and defiant with a streak of independence flowing through her that often comes off as patronizing, but I can't deny that she's a good person down to her soul. She's sweet when she becomes vulnerable. She's kind to the homeless community, donates clothes and food, checks in on her drug addict mother who she should hate, rescues asshole cats, watches Rhodes's daughter without any hesitation, and Jack told me about how Scottie rocked his daughter to sleep during one of the games because his wife needed a break.

Scottie is much too kind to be stuck in an arranged marriage with me, and it's irritating that I still don't know why she needs the money.

I won't pressure her to tell me, though.

I pressed too much last night. I regretted it the second I saw her pretty eyes fill with unshed tears.

Scottie adjusts in her sleep again, and my hand tightens. My dick is sensitive to the touch, so in an attempt to keep my word for the first time since meeting her, I try to slide my palm away. But then...she makes a noise.

My jaw slacks.

She doesn't want to cross any more lines.

I have to respect that.

I'll admit, I've purposefully egged her on and touched her in all the right spots because I like to mess with her, and I crave to see her body react, but something feels different now.

I made a promise to her, and although I wouldn't say I'm a saint, I'm not going to break it.

Not now.

She moves again, and I can't breathe.

Right when I try to take my hand off her leg for the second time, her soft palm lands on top and traps me.

"Scottie," I say her name in a low voice.

I may have all the right intentions, but my body does not.

My dick is harder than ever, and her skin is warm to the touch. She makes a breathy noise as she pushes my hand up her leg, and it's the hardest test I've ever had to take.

"Scottie." *Wake up.*

"Hmm?" she half moans in her sleep.

I wonder if she's wet.

I bet her body is reacting to my hand without her head even knowing it.

What I wouldn't give to find out.

She scoots closer, and I shut my eyes.

"Stop testing me," I snap, unable to keep it together any longer.

Her chest begins to rise quicker, and I grind my teeth. I'm ready to throw her off me, but then a soft gasp leaves her. Our eyes snag, and with her soft lips parted and doe-like eyes, I am a goner.

"If you don't want to be touched, I need you to get out of our bed."

Fuck, I said it again.

"You mean your bed?" Her voice is raspy, and adorable. *Fuck me.*

I narrow my eyes. "No. I meant exactly what I said."

Don't go.

Scottie's sleepy gaze bounces back and forth between mine, and I swear I see the smallest smile threatening to appear on her lips. I trick myself into believing that she likes the sound of it being our bed, instead of just mine.

Suddenly, I'm thinking of plans to get my parents to stay for another night so she doesn't move back downstairs or into the guest room when her shaky sigh fills the tight space between us.

"Do I need to give you a countdown?" I ask.

I'm not sure if she thinks I'm kidding, but if she doesn't get the hell out of this bed, I'm going to stick my tongue down her throat and make sure she doesn't sleep anywhere other than beside me from now on.

The innocent, sleepy-faced Scottie changes right before my eyes. Her leg moves, and her attention immediately falls to my lap. I hear the way her mouth opens with surprise, and I expect her to get out of the bed as soon as she feels how hard I am, but as always, she keeps me on my toes and surprises me.

"Three." I grip her thigh and turn my head farther toward her.

Her chest rises and falls, and each breath she takes pulls me in closer.

"Two." Testing the waters, I drag my palm up her bare thigh. *I can't stop touching her.*

Goosebumps fly to her flesh, and I curse under my breath.

When our eyes catch again, I lay it out straight. "If you don't want me to cross lines, stop drawing them, because you're tempting me, and I'm a man who saves all his restraint for the ice."

"You have a game tonight," she says, like I forgot.

Which I did.

Because when she's in my line of sight, all I fucking think about is her.

"All the more reason for me to reserve my self-control." I stare at her mouth, and mine waters. "So either get out of our bed or get over here and act like my wife."

"Your bed," she corrects again, moving her leg against me.

I breathe out a raspy breath and glare at the ceiling. "*Our.*" When I turn back toward her, I zero in on her sparkling white teeth digging into her plump bottom lip, and all restraints break. *"One."*

Scottie's eyes grow bigger, but if she wants to escape now, she's going to have to beg for it.

I flip on top of her with agile speed. The leg that was playing games with me falls to the side, and I'm suddenly pressing into her with my pelvis. She gasps and thrusts her braless chest into my face. Warmth spreads to every muscle in my body.

"Correct me if I'm wrong," I whisper while taking her hands and pinning them above her head. Blonde locks of hair lay around her, and I swear she looks like an angel. "I gave you plenty of time to remove yourself from this bed." Her nostrils flare, but she nods curtly. With her wrists trapped, I drag my other hand down her curves, memorizing every last one even more than I already have.

I pull the cotton of her oversized tee up and expose the silky pair of panties she's wearing.

I bring my mouth to her ear and inhale her scent. "I warned you too. Right?"

"Right." The word is breathy.

I press into her a little harder with my hips, and her head flies backward on the pillow.

"I don't know if you're testing me on purpose, but I wasn't kidding when I said I was saving my self-control for the game."

My groin tingles.

The only self-control I'll be practicing tonight during the game is not picturing her in nothing but my fucking jersey.

"I was testing myself," she admits.

I pull back to peer down at her.

I want to fuck her so bad it hurts.

"Testing yourself?"

Her teeth sink into her lip again, and I wish she would stop fucking doing that. I reach up out of instinct and free it. Her eyelashes flutter. "I failed."

I skim my hand up the side of her belly until I land at the very bottom of her breast. She's *addicting*. The way her breathing picks up pace when I touch her slowly and how her eyes fill with want, even if she tries her hardest to hide it.

"You're a woman." I rub my finger over her nipple, and when it hardens, I burn. "And you have needs. Why not let me take care of you?"

Take care of her?

When have I ever fucking said that to a woman?

But that's exactly what I want to do. I want to make her come over and over again until that pretty, perfect shade of pink paints her cheeks, and my name is nothing more than a wistful breath on her lips.

We could lose the game this evening, and I'd still feel like a winner knowing that I get to come home to this. *To her.*

My thoughts are spiraling.

My touches are lingering.

My mouth begs to be on hers.

"Because we're not real," she finally says. "This isn't real."

I press myself into her again, and she gasps. The only thing that is keeping me from making her mine is the thin silk of her panties and my sweats. I catch her chin with my hand when she tips her head back with pleasure. I zero in on her mouth and make it my job to show her that what's happening in this current moment is as real as it gets.

"This is every bit of real, baby."

I press my mouth to hers, and suddenly, everything feels *right.*

She's as eager as I am. Her legs fall open when our lips touch, and she gives me the silent go ahead to explore every inch of her mouth. Our tongues intertwine, and our kiss grows deeper. The softest, sexiest whimper moves within our kissing, and I can't keep my hands to myself.

I keep kissing her, only stopping to take a quick breath, and pull her panties down her legs. Her hands fall to my biceps, and I flex beneath her grip because just the touch of her against me sends me into a fucking frenzy.

"This..." I groan, sticking a finger inside her, "is real."

She curves her body, and I lift her shirt. Her breasts are perfect. I blow on one nipple, and when it puckers, I give it a quick flick of my tongue.

"Emory."

"Yes, wife?" I'm breathless.

She tightens against my finger. *Fuck me.*

"You were telling the truth. You do like it when I call you *wife.*"

Her body moves against my hand, and I'm in awe, watching her completely let loose in front of me. It's mesmerizing. Making her mine feels an awful lot like I've won the Stanley Cup.

"You're beautiful like this." I say it without even registering how intimate it sounds. Scottie's cheeks flush an even darker shade of pink, and I bend down to kiss her again and again until she can't hold on any longer.

My hand falls to her mouth when she cries out, because although the only thing I can think about is how I want to live in this moment forever, I remember my parents are down the hall.

"Fucking beautiful," I mutter, watching her eyelashes flutter.

The blue of her eyes is electrified, and I swear when she drops her attention to my mouth, they grow wild.

"You wanted me to act like your wife, right?" she whispers, still moving against my hand to ride out her high.

There's a slight edge to her voice that is sexy as fuck. A quick flick of my chin is all I give her. I'm frozen when she reaches down in between us and slowly pulls my hand out from between her legs. My finger is covered by her, and I'm obsessed with it.

Crazed, even.

"Well, go ahead, then," she whispers, lying there for the taking. "Treat me like your wife."

Forty-Five

SCOTTIE

I'M GOING to regret this.

I know it.

When this is all said and done and we've made it to the end of our contract, I'm going to miss the way he makes me feel. I'm going to miss the fire in his touch when he grazes a hand down my arm. And I'm especially going to miss the eagerness in his eyes when he's taking care of me.

Not just in this way.

But in other ways too.

"You want me to treat you like my wife?" Emory's brow line deepens, and his jaw tightens. "You sure about that?" he asks.

Of course not.

I'm likely to regret this the second he's not on top of me with that look of obsessive desire in his eye, but God, what I wouldn't give to know what it feels like to be his wife in the real sense of the word.

Call it curiosity.

Or self-sabotage.

Either way, I want to know what it feels like to give in to Emory Olson.

"I want to know what it feels like to be a wife." I lick my lips.

Emory's hot grin sends my stomach tumbling. I trip over my thoughts when he sits up and gazes down at me like I'm all he sees. His calloused hand trails down my bare arm, and he sends me a look that steals my breath. "You want to know what it feels like to be *my* wife, you mean."

I try to swallow, but everything locks up. I nod, even though there's a super-vulnerable part of me that keeps tying my nerves together.

"Then get on your knees and let me show you what you do to me."

The hunger I feel to please him is something I have *never* felt before.

I have never had a man talk to me like this, and if they tried, I would have given them the finger.

But there's a delicious pull in my stomach, and I think I surprise us both when I sit up slowly, swing my legs over the bed, and plant myself on the floor.

Emory inhales from up above.

His hand falls to my chin. "You keep fucking surprising me." I open my mouth slightly when his thumb rubs over my bottom lip. My tongue jolts out, all on its own, and he curses under his breath before staring at the ceiling.

Tired of waiting for him, I slip my fingers under the waistband of his boxers and free his cock. His hand lands on my head, and he backs away before shooting me a dirty look. I raise an eyebrow, like I have something to prove, and grip him hard.

He hisses, and I grow excited.

Seeing Emory—as rugged as a man that he is—try to hold back is addicting.

I want to make him buckle at the knees like he does to me, even if he's more willing to admit it than I am.

"Your wife is at your service," I muse from below, wrapping my hand around his hard length.

His fingers tangle in my hair, and he glares at me. "Don't say things like that to me, Biscotti."

I can't help it, I smile. I run my hand down his length and pull back, peering up at him. "Or what?"

With a look of pure passion on his face, he tugs on my hair, and my head goes backward. "Open."

I drop my jaw, and as soon as he's in my mouth, heat pours from in between my legs. Emory moves in and out of my mouth, and when I peer up at him from my knees, he's staring at me like he's in a haze. I've never seen anything hotter than him losing control.

Watching him jerk himself off in the shower was one thing.

Feeling him fill my mouth paired with the tugging of my hair is on an entirely new level.

"You on your knees for me is the highlight of our marriage. *Fucking hell*." His hips move faster and deeper, and I take every bit of what he's giving me. "Quit looking at me like that."

I don't know what he's talking about, but with the way he can barely get any words out, I think he likes the way I'm looking at him.

"You..." He pulls out for a second, and my lips feel wet and swollen. "You look so innocent, but you're so into this, aren't you?"

I nod.

Emory's jaw is as sharp as a knife. A faint growl leaves his throat when he tugs on my chin. I open my mouth again, and when he's inside, I taste the little bit of saltiness on the tip of his cock.

"I hope you know you're mine after this," he mumbles. "I know everyone else already thinks you're mine with that ring on your finger, but I need *you* to know it." He presses his cock against the back of my throat one more time, and that's when I open wider and let him empty each of his desirable thoughts he has about me down my throat until he finishes and pulls out.

I take the back of my hand and wipe my glistening lips, but my arm falls swiftly when Emory grabs me by the bicep and pulls me to my feet. My back presses backward with his palm being the only thing resting between me and the wall.

"Tell me," he demands.

His eyes drive into mine, and I blink several times.

My body curves toward him when he tugs me closer and hooks one of my legs around his waist.

I can't breathe with the feel of him pressing against me.

How easy it would be for him to just slip inside and *really* make me his.

"Tell you what?" I ask, slightly confused at how hoarse my voice is.

"That you're mine." Emory's eyes bounce back and forth between mine, and I'm stuck between admitting it and being too afraid to say it out loud.

Because we both know I'm not.

We both turn toward the noise coming from the hallway.

Oh my god. His parents.

I gasp, and he's insane, because my surprise actually makes him smile.

"Oh my god. Your parents are here. What if they heard us?"

"My parents...who are also your in-laws..." he adds with a hint of humor.

Does he think I forgot that we're married? After all of *that.*

"Don't sweat it," he coaxes, running his hands through my hair. "Of course I'd be in here shoving my cock down your throat. You're my wife." He winks at me and goes to step away but not before I smack him lightly in the chest. He catches my hand, and I tumble into his hard body.

"We do need to get downstairs. I put an order in for biscotti to be delivered this morning when I knew they were coming to visit."

Surprise makes me lose my train of thought, and my tense shoulders relax. He lets go of my hand, and I rush to beat him to the bathroom to make myself look presentable instead of like I just got fucked in the mouth by their son.

Through the closed door, I hear Emory say, "Our conversation isn't over, by the way."

With the little bit of distance between us, I shake my head and go to argue, but I already hear his bedroom door opening and his footsteps moving down the hall.

The conversation is absolutely over.

Because what happens when he discovers all the baggage that comes with having me around?

Forty-Six

EMORY

"WHAT'S GOTTEN INTO YOU?" Malaki flings a puck at me during warm-ups, and I get fancy with it. I catch the biscuit and do a spin on the ice like I'm seven years old instead of twenty-six.

It's more like *what I've gotten into* instead of something getting into me, but sharing anything about this morning with anyone feels like I'm betraying Scottie's trust in some way.

I've never really been private before when it came to hooking up with someone. Locker-room talk is as old as time, but this is different. I don't want anyone to know how obsessed I am with my wife, because when it's all said and done, who's to say they won't try to wine and dine her into their bed?

I fire another puck down the ice, and Kane whips around, skating toward me. "Did that puck do something to you? Jesus."

Nope. Just the thought of anyone touching my perfect wife did.

"Oh, got the whole fam watchin' today, eh?" Malaki points with his stick to my parents and Scottie sitting in

357

between them with her hair in a high ponytail, showing off her bright eyes and laser focus on the ice.

"Not the whole family." Kane smirks beneath his mask. "His sister and best friend aren't here."

"Don't even start." I sound bored because the whole Olson's-best-friend-fucked-his-sister bit is overused. It doesn't bother me anymore, even if Ford disagrees.

The Falcons enter the rink, and we turn our attention to their position on the ice. They start flinging pucks and stare at us from across the ice with a look of intimidation.

"You guys ready for River?" I eye their top winger, who used to play for the Blue Devils. He got traded around the same time I did, and although he is skilled on the ice, his attitude and behavior do not outweigh it, according to what my teammates said during practice yesterday.

As the goalie, stuck between the pipes, I don't have a lot of evidence to back up my claims other than word of mouth, so who knows if it's true. I know better than anyone that the truth can be skewed.

Warm-ups are coming to an end, and the crowd is beginning to get settled with their beers. My teammates are loose and focused, and when I look over at Scottie, I know I will be too.

Except, she isn't there. I jerk my attention elsewhere and almost skate over to my parents to ask where she went, as if she isn't allowed to even use the restroom without my permission.

Fuck, chill out.

I bounce my gaze all over the stadium one more time, looking for a blonde-haired beauty with my name on her back. I glance at the box seats where the rest of the wives are, but I see no one. That's when Rhodes skates out onto the ice with his shoulders tense and his face angrier than usual. He does a lap before heading to the bench, which just so happens to be close to where my parents are sitting.

That's when I see her.

She's standing behind the sin bin, and Rhodes is angrily talking to her. The more he talks to her, the closer she gets. When her hand lands on his arm, jealousy chokes me. Knowing we have a couple of minutes until the game starts, I skate over with my gaze set directly on them.

The crowd roars, and I hear my name. It's not often that the goalie leaves his post, but I can't stay there without knowing what has my wife and teammate in such close quarters.

The closer I get, the more I realize how insane I am.

Why the fuck am I jealous?

My lungs scream for oxygen when I finally make it over to them. I lean against the rink side, and when Scottie turns to look at me, I can finally breathe again.

Her eyebrows were furrowed when talking to Rhodes, but the moment she sees me, her tight features smooth. I don't know if she's playing the game of being my wife or if it's genuine. Either way, I'm obsessed with it.

"What's going on, baby?"

Surprise moves over her features, but she recovers quickly.

You like that?

"Ellie is refusing to sit with the new nanny." Scottie looks back at Rhodes. "Just have her come sit with me. It's fine."

Rhodes grumbles. "Why is it so fucking hard to find a nanny to help me with her?"

Rhodes and his nanny chronicles exhaust me.

"Go get her," I say to Scottie.

I turn to Rhodes. "My wife can handle it. Get on the ice and focus."

He doesn't take orders from other teammates often, but surprisingly, after a few seconds of debating, he hops onto the ice and rushes to fling a few pucks into the net.

Before Scottie can turn and head for Ellie, I act impulsively.

"Wait."

She turns, and her pretty lips part with a breath. "Yeah?"

I switch my stick into my other hand and reach out to swoop an arm around her waist. There are a couple of 'awws' from fans in rows nearby, but they fade the second she's pressed against me.

"I like seeing you in my jersey," I whisper. "Almost as much as I like seeing that ring on your finger."

Scottie squints at me incredulously before glancing at the bystanders. She comes in closer. "Did you take acting lessons? You're acting very husband-like." She giggles through her whisper, and I suddenly can't breathe again. "I almost believed you."

She has me in the palm of her hand and literally has no fucking idea.

I don't know if I had any idea either.

My grip around her waist tightens, and I bend down farther. My mouth falls to hers, and it's enough to wake me up so I can play another good game. When I pull back, she's gazing up at me. "I wasn't acting."

I leave her with a wink and move to get into my position on the ice. I follow her movements until she disappears into the crowd to get Rhodes's daughter. When I glance at my parents, they're both looking at one another with confusion and a little bit of wonder.

I may be just as surprised as they are.

Acting like I'm in love with Scottie is becoming easier and easier, and with the way my heart beats through my chest until I see her settle in between my parents again with Rhodes's daughter sitting on her lap, I'm pretty certain the acting part is nonexistent.

Forty-Seven

SCOTTIE

"IT'S no surprise that our son would find someone as into hockey as he is."

I turn to Emory's dad and smile. "You know how he is. He loves the game."

My stomach flips, and I turn back to the ice. I'm not sure if I'm referring to hockey or *our* game, but I think he likes to play both.

Ellie jumps up with her freshly braided hair and Blue Devils bow swinging from the bottom. "Let's go, Daddy!"

Just then, Rhodes uses his shoulder, and a player flies onto the ice, losing their stick in the process. The crowd boos, and Ellie crosses her arms. She turns to us. "He's being a little bit of a bully."

I shrug. "Sometimes that's necessary in hockey."

Ellie sighs. "Well, I don't like bullies."

"Me either." I can't help but think of William and all the times I've had to knock a few guys on their ass or embarrass them in some way or another for messing with him. "Do you have a bully, Ellie?"

Suddenly, her face pales. She turns her back to me.

Emory's mom and I catch each other's attention. Her lips flatten, and I nod. I make a mental note to say something to Rhodes, but not tonight—if they can't get their shit together, they're all going to be in angry moods later.

The offense takes advantage of Rhodes being in the penalty box, and pucks continue to fly at Emory. He blocks them, but if Rhodes doesn't get back on the ice to even up the game, they're going to keep coming after our goalie, and that angers me more than it should.

One of the players swipes the puck from Malaki, and I growl under my breath. "Play like a team, guys!" I yell, remembering what Emory and I were talking about last night.

They can't hear me, and I'm not the coach.

But the game brings out something in me that I can't hide.

I blame that on my father and his passion for hockey that he obviously passed down to me.

Rhodes glances at Ellie before the penalty box door opens, and he's back on the ice. We both sigh with relief, but Rhodes goes directly to the guy he shoulder-checked before, and I swear they're exchanging words.

A puck flies past, and Emory misses it by a hair.

"It's okay!" I'm quick to add. He can't hear me, but it makes me feel better to say it aloud.

"Something is off," Emory's dad mutters. "The Devils look tense out there."

I nod.

They freeze the puck, and there's a short break in the game. I think the fans, me included, collectively take a deep breath. I'm staring at the focus on Emory's face from his post when I hear one of the Falcons say a familiar name.

"Cherry?"

I turn out of reaction.

Recognition flashes across his red face, and I quickly break our eye contact.

Shit.

Peeking at Emory's parents, they seem unfazed. I exhale.

But nothing gets past Ellie. She stares at me with confusion. "Cherry?"

I shrug. "Maybe he likes cherries?"

She thinks for a second. "I don't like them."

I pretend to be amused. "Neither do I."

Little does she know how true that statement is.

The game is slowly coming to an end with a tie of 2-2. I'm tense in all the wrong spots, and I can't take my attention from number eleven.

I know exactly who he is.

He used to play for Chicago until he was traded. I don't know the specifics of why he was traded, but I do know that when he'd come into the strip club, he was a sloppy drunk and awfully handsy.

Not that Russ cared.

But I did.

I have no idea how he recognized me since he was always drunk and I looked a lot different than I do now, but he does, and that doesn't sit well with me at all.

The more I think about it, the more my stomach tightens. I suddenly want to disappear from the stands and go to the bathroom to hide until the end of the game.

In the midst of the fans yelling, I stare at my shoes. I'm too afraid to look at the ice and see him staring at me again. My irrational thoughts take a nosedive and start spinning all kinds of outlandish things. I picture a whisper spreading through the stands, and everyone knowing that I'm a fraud. They'll know I'm not wife material and that Emory only married me as a ploy to make everyone think he's on the up and up with his reputation.

Until, of course, everyone finds out the truth.

In that case, his reputation will be shredded even further.

"Come on, son! Don't fall for it."

My head snaps up, and my eyes lock onto Emory.

I suck in a ragged breath when I see him slowly climb to his skates with his helmet half on. His steely gaze, the one that he typically reserves for the ice, is set on number eleven.

Oh no.

Just when I think Emory is going to show everyone that the rumors are true and he is just some hotheaded goalie, he pulls his mask down and gets back into position.

Thank god.

I exhale slowly, and a warmness flows through me when Emory's mom grabs onto my hand for a quick second and gives it a squeeze. I smile softly at her but turn away quickly when my eyes fill with tears.

How healing would it be to be accepted into a family like this?

As soon as she drops my hand, we all jump backward. A Falcon is smashed against the glass right in front of us, and Kane is suddenly throwing his gloves off to the side and bumping Rhodes out of the way to get a swing on number eleven. I quickly put my hands over Ellie's ears. There are too many inappropriate curse words filling the atmosphere, and when I hear the word Cherry, my stomach rolls with a wave of nausea.

Suddenly, both teams are at each other's throats. Emory makes his way over and takes off some of his gear, throwing it to the side.

Instead of throwing punches, though, he's pulling his teammates backward and sending them a chilling stare. When he gets to Kane, he pulls on his collar and sends him in the opposite direction. The ref grabs Kane and barks at him to get into the penalty box. His sick smile is full of blood, and I scoff.

These men!

I turn back to the ice and watch as Emory skates over to

River. The entire arena freezes around me. I see nothing but my husband with a calm yet intimidating look on his face. He mumbles something to him before River heads to the opposite sin bin. Emory swipes his mask off the ice and glances at me on his way back to his post. His lips turn slightly upward, and he winks at me.

The dread and worry I felt moments ago disappear within a second.

A calmness flows through me, and I can suddenly breathe again.

Even more so when I look across the ice and stare at my husband, who is beginning to fill my head with all kinds of crazy thoughts—like how I really wish this marriage was real.

Forty-Eight

EMORY

"**WHAT DO** you all have to say for yourselves?" Coach Jacobs is leaning against his office door with an unreadable expression on his face. It's hard to know what he's thinking, especially because I haven't been with this team for that long.

He's a stoic kind of coach. The kind that likes to stew on his speeches before laying into us, but in my opinion, even though we were defeated, I don't think it was a total loss.

I stand from my bench, and the entire team turns to look at me.

"I'm not going to speak on behalf of the team," I start. "But with our captain already gone, I'm going to take the initiative."

Rhodes dipped out the moment we stepped off the ice, likely knowing that it'd be a while before we were able to head home due to this moment right here. One of the reasons Rhodes is on this team is because Coach never puts limitations on him when it comes to his daughter and putting her first.

"Well, go on," Coach barks.

I look him dead in the face with confidence. "I don't think it was a total loss."

His eyebrows dip.

"For the first time since the season started"—I spin my attention around the locker room at my teammates' red faces and sweaty hair—"we acted like a team."

Someone makes a ridiculous noise, and a few copy him.

"One of the guys"—I look directly at Kane, who is seemingly fuming on the bench from the loss—"got himself into a fight, and instead of letting him take a punch to the face, you all swooped in and fought alongside him."

It's the same thing I was explaining to Scottie. When a team is truly a team, they work together. It's one of the oldest fucking bylaws in hockey. They fight, we fight. They go down, we go down. It's called being a team.

"Sure." I shrug. "It wasn't about the winning puck or the last block. It had nothing to do with the actual game, but we fucking worked together for the first time since I joined this team." I look back at Coach. "Have you ever sat and watched the teams at the top of the league and looked outside the box? They work together, on and off the ice." I point at him. "That's important."

I feel myself becoming way too involved in the team talk. My heart beats, and a passion I didn't realize I held grounds me to keep going.

"My last team fucked me over," I admit. "I took the fall for something I had nothing to do with, and not a single one of my teammates batted an eye. It landed me with one option." I glance around at all the blue on the walls. "Here."

I plop back down onto the bench and lean against my locker.

"And I'm fucking proud. I'm proud to be on a team that has each other's backs, and coming together like that on the ice means one thing." I stare at Coach Jacobs, and I'm surprised to see pride instead of anger. "We're fucking unstoppable now."

The locker room erupts in chaos. My teammates clap and howl like idiots, but it's obvious they all agree.

Coach nods at me before turning and slamming his office door.

Pride swells in my chest.

Things are falling into place, and the only person I can seem to think of is Scottie.

And that has nothing to do with the fact that River was running his mouth about her.

The anger and resentment I'd been carrying around since last spring has faded, and I hadn't even realized it until this moment.

I feel content, and that feeling drives even deeper when I slip my ring back onto my finger and turn to head home to my mouthy, beautiful wife who is teaching me more about myself than I ever knew.

————

SHUTTER EYES me lazily in his makeshift bed that Scottie made him on the porch, out of *my* old T-shirts.

The house is quiet when I open the door.

The lights are off beside the faint glow from the kitchen.

There's something in the middle of the island, and when I get closer, I see a note written in feminine handwriting.

I warmed up the leftovers from the dinner your mom made after dropping them off at the airport.

It's in the microwave.

xo

I open the microwave and smile to myself. Look at her, being all wife-like without even being forced to do it. After shutting the microwave because suddenly I'm hungry for something else, I look into the living room. I expect her to be lying there, pretending to be asleep like she usually is after a game, but the couch is empty.

I casually walk over to the stairs and head up them, bypassing my bedroom and heading straight for the guest room.

If she thinks she's going back to sleeping in a separate room from me, she's out of her fucking mind. I'm already prepared to plead with her and make promises of not touching her—that I don't want to keep—when I push open the guest door and see an empty bed with the bedding stripped.

I stare down the hall.

The thumping of my pulse quickens with each step toward my bedroom. When I step inside, I already know she's in here without even laying eyes on her.

I feel her before I see her.

My heart fucking races when I see that she's in my bed. Her quiet body is covered, and unlike last night, she isn't on the edge of the mattress.

I don't waste a single second.

I brush my teeth and strip off my shirt. I climb into bed with my chest tight and my muscles begging to touch her. She exhales softly, and although I want nothing more than to pull her in close and kiss her senseless, I don't. I stay on my side of the mattress and decide to give her the reins.

If she wants to find me in her sleep, then I'll be here waiting.

There's a hushed voice in the back of my head that I can't seem to hide from, and although it's hard for me to wrap my head around, I listen to it.

I'll wait forever for Scottie.

I told her before this whole thing started that I wouldn't lose.

I didn't realize it at the time, but that statement had a double meaning: I don't want to lose *her*, and I'm not even sure I really have her.

Forty-Nine

SCOTTIE

MY EYES FLY OPEN, and William's name is on the very tip of my tongue.

I stare at the ceiling, waiting for my eyes to adjust. I'm trembling. I can't remember what I was dreaming about, but I know it had to do with him because, while at the game, he called, and I missed it.

I've been so distracted by Emory and our marriage ploy that I haven't even called the lawyer back. I haven't thought about the future at all—unless, of course, I'm daydreaming about Emory's and my future.

It's a ridiculous thought and one that I have to stop.

Emory is lying on his back with one arm above his head and the other draped across the mattress, like he's reaching for me.

God, stop it.

I force myself to look away when my face heats. I take a deep breath.

I'm acting like a thirteen-year-old girl with her first crush.

It's ridiculous but not in the same breath. When I was

thirteen, I was too busy cleaning up my mother's messes and trying to keep our house in order so social services didn't show up and separate my brother and me.

The sweet taste of first love was something I never experienced.

When I had my first real adventure with the opposite sex, I didn't even mention that I was a virgin. I just jumped headfirst and needed it to be quick so I could get on with my responsibilities.

But with Emory, it's different.

When he looks at me, I can't think straight.

When he touches me, I lose my footing.

When he kisses me, I'm *his*.

I've never wanted to be on someone's mind like I want to be on Emory's.

I'm obsessed with the thought of him needing to touch me.

Like he can't breathe without it.

That's how he makes me feel, but it's too scary to admit out loud, so instead, I just scoot a little closer to feel his warmth through the blankets and close my eyes.

A moment later, his finger grazes my arm.

My heart skips a beat, but I act like I'm asleep. My body relaxes with every single swipe of his knuckle against my skin. Without meaning to, I move even closer. There's a needy dip in my stomach, and my lungs expand with a secret that I'm afraid I'll tell if I move even an inch.

But then his hand falls to my thigh.

Heat rushes to the spot.

Emory inhales and pulls my leg higher. I drape it across his strong thighs. Moving my knee just slightly, I get a quick brush of his desire, and it is too much to ignore. I don't have to act on it, but I most definitely can't pretend it isn't there. Every nerve ending is frayed with the chemistry swarming between us.

The silence is deafening.

The darkness blankets me like protection, and that's the only reason I allow myself to act without reservation.

My touch against his skin has obvious doubts, but his against mine feels purposeful. I'm acting with hesitancy, whereas he is acting with possession.

"Stop holding back," he whispers, grabbing the side of my face. His calloused hand scratches my cheek, and when his fingers bury themselves in my hair, I do as he says. For the first time, I initiate the kiss.

I'm immediately swept away.

I start off slow, kissing him with caution, but as soon as he pulls me on top of him, I deepen the kiss and lose myself.

My legs fall to his sides, and I press down. I'm in nothing but one of his shirts and my panties. With each subtle drag of his hands up my thighs, I kiss him harder. My tongue swipes against his, and a little moan leaves me when his fingers dig into my hips.

"That's it," he encourages, gripping me tightly as I rub against him. "We're too far gone to hold back now, Scottie."

The more I move, the harder he gets. He curses under his breath, and I tingle. My skin is on fire, so I grip the hem of the T-shirt and strip it from my body.

His hand creeps up my back, and he presses me toward his mouth. I gasp when his tongue flicks against my nipple.

"Show me that you want me as badly as I want you," he says, giving my other breast attention.

It's an addicting thought and one that has me breezing right past my worries. I grind against him, and he grabs my hips to push me down harder. The feeling sucks me in, and I find myself lifting up so he can remove my panties.

His sweats go next, and I touch him all over, running my curious hands over the ridges of his hard muscles.

"Do you?" he asks, nipping at my lip.

"Huh?" I say, breathing hard.

"Do you want me so badly you can't think straight? Because that's how I feel when it comes to you." He kisses me hard and fast, like he's afraid I'm going to deny it.

I can't.

Not like this.

"Yes," I say without any hesitation.

I want you so much that I'm terrified.

Suddenly, I'm flipped onto my back, and my legs are spread wide open. Emory hovers over me, balancing on his strong forearms.

"Let me make you mine." His plea grazes my lips. "Right here. Just like this."

I pause. There is no going back if I give him the okay.

"Please, Scottie," he begs, rubbing himself against me.

I'm done for.

"Make me yours, Olson."

"*Fuck*," he rasps.

I gasp with pleasure when he pushes himself inside.

"God, you were fucking made for me," he groans.

With every slow thrust, I build higher and higher. My hips spread wider, and I'm enthralled with the way my body loses control.

"Emory," I moan.

He peppers my neck with kisses before making his way back to my lips and swallowing my moans.

I break apart when his kisses become feverish, and his thrusts get deeper.

He takes his mouth from mine, and I don't even care that he's watching me succumb to the pleasure. The ride is too much. I'm in a lustful daze, and every part of my body sings.

"Mine," he grits before pumping into me one more time.

I almost pout when he pulls out, but then I feel his come spill out onto my belly, and my teeth sink into my bottom lip.

God, that's hot.

He flops to his back, and I smile to myself when he says, *"Wow,"* under his breath.

Because...same.

I HAVE NEVER WANTED to get home more than I do at this moment. My body is wrecked, and although we won and came back from our home loss, the team has been rowdy since climbing back onto the plane. All I want is to be at home with Scottie.

I've never looked forward to dressing up in an uncomfortable suit and spending my evening at a charity event, making small talk with businessmen and women with pockets larger than the majority of the country, but the fact that I get to have Scottie by my side in that sexy red dress has me counting down the seconds until we're landing on the runway.

As soon as the seatbelt light goes off and we're steadily flying toward Chicago, I stand from my seat and head to the back of the plane where it's quieter. Some of my teammates call me a grandpa, but I keep walking with my middle finger raised up high.

They all laugh. Even Coach Jacobs chuckles. When I get to the last row, away from the majority of them, I grab my phone and silently thank the National Hockey League's air program for putting Wi-Fi on their planes.

It's a shared jet between the teams, which is why we have to take off right after a game so someone else can use the plane, but at least we have Wi-Fi and don't have to fly commercial with fans pretending not to take candid photos of us.

> You up?

Yes. Good game, Olson.

Where are you?

I grin.

> On my way home to you.

Why does that make me so fucking excited, and why do I miss her? I was with her no less than ten hours ago. I've never missed anyone like I do her.

> Why? Miss me?

I wait like a child on Christmas morning with my phone in my hand. I'm twenty-six years old and hanging on a woman's every last word via text message.

Who am I?

I wouldn't admit it if I did.

I chuckle while typing.

> I'll take that as a yes.

Her next text surprises me.

Do you miss me?

I have no problem admitting that I miss her.

> I miss you when you're across the room from me.

It's not a lie. It's the truth, even if I've yet to say that out loud.

You do not.

It doesn't surprise me that she doesn't believe it. I swear something has happened in her life that made her insecure. What makes her think I wouldn't miss her? I miss everything about her. I bet anyone who has come into contact with her misses her presence the second she's gone. Scottie leaves her mark on everyone, even if she doesn't realize it.

> I miss everything about you. I miss your snarky comebacks that keep me on my toes. I miss the way you roll your eyes at me when you think my back is turned. I miss watching you sink your teeth into a biscotti and how your lips wrap around the rim of your coffee mug in the morning.

I hit send, and my heart beats so loudly I can't even hear the rumble of the plane's engine.

I become irrationally angry when I reread her text. I'm about to make it my sole purpose to show her how much I miss her after every away game.

Hell, maybe I'll show her how much I miss her when I'm just at practice for a few hours.

> Wait until I get home. I'll show you how much I miss you then.

I can't decide if that's a threat or not.

A line of desire zips down to my groin, and I adjust myself in my sweats. I quickly swipe out of our texts and pull up my camera app. Bouncing through all the camera angles, I finally find her in our bed with one of my T-shirts on. There's a bunch of papers and envelopes off to the side, and the TV must be on, because I see the glow of the screen flickering over her face.

I quickly swipe the video of her to the side and share the screen with my texts.

> Nice shirt.

She smiles at first, but then her smile falls, and she flicks her gaze to the camera.

> You're being a creep.

> Not unless you start to do something naughty. Maybe I'm just being protective. Making sure you're okay.

I glance at my dick. Its rigid appearance has nothing to do with it.

> I already took care of that. 😉

> And I'm perfectly safe inside the house. Shutter will protect me.

I swallow my thick spit and slouch farther in my seat so none of the guys up front can look back and see the desire on my face.

> You better not have taken care of that.

> And I'm the only one who's going to protect you.

I'll protect Shutter too, since he means so much to her.
I press on my dick to make it stop throbbing.

> I'm the only one who's going to take care of you too.

Could I be any more possessive? Fucking Christ.

The thought of anyone taking care of her sends me to the edge, though.

Which is completely unhinged.

Says who?

I drag my attention to the little video beside my texts and clench my jaw. The blankets are flung off to the side, and all the papers and envelopes that were scattered around her have disappeared. Her legs call to me, and when she pulls up the T-shirt, I nearly die.

> Stop it.

Stop what? Surely you're not telling me I can't touch my own body.

I swear to God.

She will regret this when I get home.

With her shirt pulled up high enough that I can see her panties, I start to sweat.

You know I don't like to be bossed around.

> You know what? I think you do. I bet you're so fucking wet at the thought of me watching you on the camera. Want me to tell you what to do too?

Please say yes.

I glance at the clock. Thirty minutes until we land. Fifteen-minute bus ride to my car.

So, one hour tops until I get to her.

I'm a patient man. I can wait.

Scottie doesn't text back, and I wish I could call her so fucking bad so I could hear her hot breaths, but with other ears a little too close for comfort, this will have to do.

> Slip those panties off. Let me see you.

My mouth dries when she follows my command. This woman surprises me every single day. What I wouldn't do to grab her blonde locks and pull her head back so I could kiss her.

When her panties are off to the side, I send her another text.

> Good girl.

Scottie's teeth sink into her lip, and I curse under my breath.

> Spread for me.

She hesitates. I watch her gaze fly to the camera when her bottom lip plops out from her teeth.

> Don't be shy. I'm your husband. Let me see how perfect you are.

Because she is. I wonder if she knows that. Surely whoever she's been with before me has told her so.

A tug of possession grips me by the throat, and I'm suddenly typing faster than I ever have.

> Spread wider. If I were there, I'd be pushing on the inside of your thigh before I ran my finger up to touch that throbbing little clit.

I watch with rapt attention as she drags her finger up her leg and stops right at her sweet spot. Her other hand disappears under the shirt, and I know she's playing with her nipple, just like I want to do with my teeth.

> I'd be inside of you within seconds to prove to you that I am the only one who can take care of you like this.

My core twists with need the longer I watch her. I type another text with shaky fingers.

> Don't come.

I'm selfish as fuck. I would give up my life to feel her underneath me, withering from pleasure. I want to be the only one to make her come. I want my name to be the only name on her lips when she's filled to the brim.

Scottie lazily looks up at the camera, and if I could zoom in on her face, I bet her eyes are lust-filled and hazy.

> I'll be home in thirty. Be ready.

I click my phone off.

If I stare at her any longer, I'm afraid I'll come right here, and I will be damned if I don't fuck my wife tonight and prove to her that she's *mine*.

Fifty-One

SCOTTIE

THE MORE TIME THAT PASSES, the more my legs throb.

I've tried to talk myself down from the high I'm feeling after rereading Emory's texts, but nothing is working. I've jogged up and down the stairs, splashed water on my face, and now I'm in the kitchen, gulping down water like I haven't had anything to drink in days.

My mouth is dry with the thought of denying myself the simple pleasure of watching his blue eyes take me in. They're always so serious and brooding, but lately, when we're alone, they're full of something else.

I don't know what it is.

Desire?

Craving?

Longing?

Every time he touches me, it feels like he's trying to prove something, and I can't pretend that I'm not starting to believe him.

My glass of water clanks on the counter when I hear the door open.

389

Heat rushes to my toes, and suddenly, I'm weak at the knees.

Emory mumbles something that resembles a curse to Shutter, and I silently laugh.

I quietly tiptoe to the pantry with my phone in hand. When I hear his bag drop and his footsteps grow fainter, I type a message.

> I've always been good at hide and seek.

It's true. I don't discuss *why* I was so good at hide and seek, but there were times I would hide all night long—well after my worst nightmares would stop seeking.

I stare at the ceiling when I hear his footsteps seize. I roll my lips together until I feel the buzz of my phone.

> You know I don't like to lose.

> You can't be a winner all the time.

> When it comes to you, I can.

Warmth spreads, and my stomach flutters. I nibble on my thumb with a smile hiding behind my hand. It's an unfamiliar feeling. I'm light and airy for the first time in my entire life, and I don't know how to handle it.

I just know that I don't want to let it go.

My senses sharpen when I hear his footsteps approaching. I step away from the door and press my back into the shelf lined with pasta.

> The longer you make me wait, the longer I make you wait.

I hear his knuckle rap against the counter, and my legs wobble. A burst of flirty nerves rush up my throat.

Sounds like something a loser would say.

You're asking for trouble again, wife.

Guess you'll have to punish me.

I freeze when the door to the pantry opens slowly. I see his large hand first, pushing on the wood with the tips of his fingers. In the dark of the kitchen, he's nothing but a looming shadow, but I know it's him just by the width of his shoulders.

"You like playing games, don't you, wife?"

His low tone makes me drop my phone. I'm weak-kneed and dizzy with a yearning I've never experienced before. If he asked me to strip right here, I would without any hesitation.

He walks closer, only taking a few steps until he's right in front of me. I peer at him from my shorter stance and nearly fall into his chest when he cups my waist and pulls me into the kitchen.

My tongue jolts from my mouth to lick my bottom lip, and the sound that leaves him goes right between my legs.

"You want to be punished, baby?" I've never heard the tone he's using with me right now. My breaths are choppy, and I'm practically panting. Blooms of pleasure rush to my breasts to the point that the cotton of the shirt sends hot tingles everywhere.

"Maybe," I answer.

The room spins as he turns me. I feel his mouth against my ear when he grips me tighter around the waist.

"Hands on the counter."

I don't like to be bossed around.

He knows this.

I know this.

Yet, I do exactly what he says.

My shaky hands fall to the edge of the granite. The slip of my shirt being pulled up against my skin excites me. *What are we doing?* The headstrong part of me is withering inside, but the way his hands feel on my body outweighs every single breath in my lungs, let alone every willful thought.

Emory's palm grazes my curves at the same time his teeth pull on my earlobe. My head flies backward, and I grip the counter so I don't slip. "No panties? You do want to be punished."

I gulp before letting out a shaky breath.

"Hold on tight, baby."

I gasp when he smacks my ass. I turn my head, still holding onto the counter, and catch his wild eyes. The light over the stove shines on the side of his face, and he's so hot I forget that he just spanked me.

It blinds me so fiercely that I don't even realize how much my body enjoyed it.

Emory smirks while sneaking his hand down the front of my body and in between my legs.

He groans. "Ah, fuck. You *do* like being punished."

My head falls to the crook of his neck when he feels how wet I am. I want to be embarrassed because I've never shown anyone this side of myself—not to this extent, at least. But I feel so safe with him that I'd show him all of me, even the ugly parts.

"I just like you," I admit.

I love the way he touches me, like he knows exactly what I need and wants to give it to me.

Emory's hand disappears, and he spins me around again, but this time, I'm facing him. I'm plopped on the counter in the blink of an eye, and he crowds my space as soon as he spreads my legs. He acts so swiftly and confidently. I love every single second of it.

"But I'm your husband," he whispers, dipping down to his knees. "You're supposed to love me."

If he keeps it up, I just might.

He pulls me to the very edge of the counter, and my palms fall to the cool stone to brace myself. His hot mouth disappears in between my legs, and I'm instantly on the edge of madness.

The strokes of his tongue push me to move my hips against his face, and a whimper falls off my lips the more he licks me. I can't think straight. I don't feel anything but pleasure and him, which is a very dangerous concoction.

"Emory," I breathe out his name like I'm going to faint. *What is he doing to me?*

My body twists, and so does my heart.

He pulls back and stares up at me with passion. His hot mouth is covered by me, and when our eyes connect, I feel my pulse skyrocket. "Tell your husband how much you love him, and then maybe I'll put you out of your misery."

I pause when the tiny voice in the back of my head says it without hesitation.

We're both caught up in the moment, so if I say it aloud, he'll think it's just because I'm turned on and can't deny him.

Right?

He flicks an eyebrow at me while standing, and I give in.

"Fine," I say. "I love you."

I do. I really think I do.

Emory's eye twitches, and his hand sweeps up my leg. My hair tumbles down my back when my head tips from pleasure. He moves against my clit, and it sends me spiraling.

"Tell me you're mine, Scottie." I feel his gruff voice against my skin when he leans in closer to my ear. He's so possessive of me, and it seems so *real.*

"I'm yours, Emory."

"Tell me your name." His finger enters me, and he pushes on the spot that makes me feel like I'm flying.

"Biscotti," I say, trying to win back some of the control.

393

"Don't play with me." His palm scrapes against my clit. "Tell me your name."

I tighten all over. "Sc-Scottie..." *Jesus.*

My hips move against his hand, and I don't care that this crosses every single line I've drawn between us. I don't care that he's seeing me in this vulnerable state and that he's asking me to say things I wouldn't say otherwise.

"Scottie what?" He's as impatient as I am. If I weren't mistaken, I'd think he likes to watch me fall apart from his touch just as much as I like to show him.

"Scottie Ols–Olson."

"That's my girl," he coaxes, adding another finger inside me.

I break apart in his grip like shattering glass.

He swallows my moans and licks up every single whimper that falls from my lips.

I'm barely coming down from my high when Emory pulls his hand out from between my legs and places me on my feet. He turns me around, and my world spins.

"Mine," he grits.

I spread my shaking legs, eager for more.

A gust of air cools me as he pulls his pants down. He positions himself from behind and grips onto my hips like they're his lifeline before pushing inside.

"Fuck, Scottie."

My hands spread on the counter, and I push against him to get a better angle. The deeper he goes, the more I succumb.

"You feel fucking incredible."

I whimper each time he hits a certain spot. His hand falls to mine to steady us, and when our fingers intertwine, my knees buckle.

"I've got you," he whispers, taking me deeper with his other hand wrapped around my waist. "Let go for me again. I'll catch you every time."

My body trembles, and my legs shake. He grips me tighter, and I fall over the edge again with his name falling from my lips.

"Tell me you're mine again," he groans, pumping into me faster and faster.

"I'm yours," I moan, tightening around his cock.

"Fuck, you've got a hold on me, baby."

In the middle of a whimper, Emory's fingers dig into my hips, and he pulls out of me. A gush of warm liquid hits me in the lower back, and the sound he makes is the hottest noise I have ever heard.

We stand there for so long his cum drips over the curve of my ass and falls to the kitchen floor. His forehead rests against my sweaty skin until both of our raspy breaths are calm enough to move again.

The shuffling of fabric catches my attention, and when I peek behind my shoulder, Emory is shirtless. He bundles his shirt up and wipes the mess between my legs and back before turning me around slowly. He weaves his fingers through my tangled hair and stares down into my eyes.

My head is messy.

It becomes even messier when he presses his mouth to mine and leaves me breathless with a kiss that ends with me having an unforgettable feeling.

Fifty-Two

EMORY

I KNOT my bow tie in the mirror for the third time, and yet it's still too early to leave the house. I've been counting down the hours until the charity event but only because that's when I get to see Scottie again.

She left in that hot rod of a car of hers hours ago to go to Vivian's with her dress in tow and a pretty blush spread across her cheeks from the leftovers of what we were doing right before.

I can't get enough of her.

I don't know what it means, and I don't want to question it.

All I know is that somehow, between the moment she cornered me in the arena bathroom and now, she's become my favorite thing in the world.

I stare at the jumbled covers on our bed, loving that it's all out of sorts because I had her in it hours ago. I smirk with the thought of how pointless it is for me to be making it again when I know damn well I'm going to strip her out of that dress I bought for her as soon as we're home, but I move to do it anyway.

Swiping my hand down to snag a pillow off the floor, something crinkles beneath my shoe. I bend, as much as my dress pants allow, and slide the piece of paper out with my shoe until it comes into sight.

Standing upright, I grip the envelope and scan it quickly. I furrow my forehead as I reread the letterhead.

Deacon Law Firm.

It's tempting. It really is.

A month ago, I would've torn into it without caring how that made Scottie feel.

But now?

I have second thoughts. It's a betrayal of her privacy.

I place the envelope on top of the dresser and leave it in plain sight. If Scottie knows I've seen it and still doesn't offer up some type of explanation, then I'll question her.

After all, I'm her husband. We're supposed to share things with each other, right?

I pause and look down at my ring finger.

That's a double standard coming from me.

If we're supposed to share things with each other, then I should probably stop being such a pussy and tell her how I really feel about her.

I sigh and swipe my keys from the dresser, heading to the event way too early. But standing here and arguing with myself over whether or not to tell my wife that I no longer want our marriage to be a ruse seems counterproductive.

———

"OLSON." Coach Jacobs nods at me while he swirls amber-colored liquid in his glass cup.

"Coach," I say, nodding back at him.

We're all dressed to perfection, him in a navy-blue suit, me in a black one. Some of the guys are dressed in other colors.

Malaki is in a dusty-pink suit, which at first I thought looked ridiculous, but somehow, with his confidence, he pulls it off.

"I want to say something to you," Coach lowers his voice, which is a change from the grumble I typically hear within the locker room. He gestures over to an empty cocktail table, and I follow after him.

I stare out into the crowd, waiting for Scottie and the rest of the women to walk in like they own the place. I'm jittery without her by my side, which is unusual for me.

"I want to thank you."

I turn to Coach and shoot him an incredulous look. "For?"

He takes a sip of his whiskey. "You've been an asset to this team. I wasn't sure when we signed you if it was the right move. The board went back and forth over the decision." He places his cup down. "Especially after trading some... agitators."

I snort when River's face pops into my head. "That's a nice way of putting it."

"With your background, I was hesitant because you seemed to be one too."

I flex my jaw. "I'm not."

"Glad you proved me wrong." He turns away, and I stare at the side of his face. Coach Jacobs is young for a hockey coach. Most are in their fifties, but he's barely in his mid-forties, and I can't help but notice that he isn't sporting a ring like I am.

Being a married man makes you think differently.

"By the way..." He stares out into the growing crowd. "You didn't need a fake marriage to fix your reputation. You've done that on your own with your leadership on the ice."

He turns to look at me, and I narrow my gaze.

"I'm not that dense, Olson. You guys think I know nothing about you other than your stats, but that's not true. I do a full background check on all the men before I let you walk into my domain. I also know that she was employed at the Cat House."

My heart beats right out of my chest, and I can't decide if it's anger, possession, or protectiveness that I'm feeling. With my blood pressure rising, I think it may be all three.

I have the sudden urge to prove to him that my marriage with Scottie is real, even though in the back of my head I know it isn't.

Not from the start, at least.

Now, I can't help but feel like it is.

He chuckles. "No surprise."

"What?" My voice edges on the brim of anger, and although he's my coach, I'll put him right the fuck in his place if I need to when it comes to her.

He turns away. "No surprise you've fallen in love with your fake wife."

Silence.

I say nothing.

I don't deny it.

I just stay quiet.

"I knew her father." Coach knocks his knuckles on the table before swiping his glass. "He was a good man. Knew his hockey, that's for sure." He clears his throat. "She resembles him."

I feel the jealousy simmering, which is fucking absurd. Just because he knew my wife's father doesn't mean he knows more about her than I do. However, this pushes me to find out every last thing about Scottie. I want to know *everything* there is. Her childhood, her favorite memories, her worst memories, her goals, her fears. All of it.

"Better go get her," he says, stepping away. "She's gaining a lot of attention in that dress." His deep chuckle catches my attention. "Her father would drag her out of here so fast if he were here."

I turn, and my stomach drops to the floor.

I have tunnel vision, and the only thing I see is her.

God damn.

She's mine.

The room seems to revolve around her, and the closer I get, the more my pulse races. Her hand is wrapped around my heart, and she's squeezing with every flutter of her eyelashes.

I'm thankful she didn't overdo it because to be honest, Scottie doesn't need makeup to be beautiful. She's gorgeous in the quietest ways—soft features without a single flaw, baby-blue eyes that suck you in after one glance, and the shade of her lips is already calling to every man in the room.

Her sweet laugh catches my attention through the chatter of the room after Georgia whispers something to her. Matthew swoops in behind his fiancée and dips her backward for a quick kiss. Scottie's eyes light up, and she smiles.

I move in.

Her light gasp fills the gap between us, and surprise flickers over her face.

"Hey, baby," I say softly.

She blinks several times and inhales. Her ribs expand in my grip. "Hi." She exhales, and it's the sweetest scent I've ever smelled.

Without giving it much thought, I drag my hand up to her face and grip her cheek. My mouth falls to hers, and I smile to myself when she gives in right away. Her body relaxes, and her lips part. She lets me claim her in front of everyone, like she can't fathom denying me.

After I pull away and the room comes back into view, I peer down at her.

"You look beautiful."

My stomach fills with nerves, but they're unfamiliar.

They're not the same ones I get before I take the ice. These are fragile, like they're capable of doing much more than giving me a lasting feeling of anger or disappointment from playing a shitty game. These ones can destroy me.

"Wow," she whispers into my ear. "That was awfully believable. Are you trying to prove something to someone?"

"It better be believable. It was real."

She playfully rolls her eyes, and I grip her tighter around the waist. "And yeah, I am trying to prove something."

Little does she know, I'm trying to prove something to her.

Fifty-Three

SCOTTIE

HE'S GOING to shatter my heart.

For the first time in my life, it feels full. I feel complete and safe. I can't think of a time where I've ever felt like this, even with William near.

It's like I have the world in my hands when, in reality, I don't.

In fact, the only thing I have in my hand is my fake husband's with a ring on his finger that isn't permanent.

Emory whispers into my ear, "Do you want a drink?"

I shake my head. The last time I drank, I spiraled. I'm not doing that again.

"What about a biscotti?"

My mouth twitches. "They don't have biscotti here."

"Yes, they do." A sly grin falls to his mouth. "And she tastes extra sweet."

"*Emory*," I whisper-warn.

He shrugs, and for some reason, I'm chock-full of butter-flies. My feet shuffle against the glossy floor, and I smile at the familiar faces I see until we're standing beside Rhodes with his tense shoulders and broody stance.

"Where's my girl?" Malaki asks him when we step into the conversation.

Rhodes grunts. "At home with a new nanny."

"Another new nanny?"

Rhodes glares at Malaki. "If you say one word about fucking the nanny, I'll knock you clean on your ass."

Malaki appears to be appalled at the statement. "I would never."

"Yeah, you would," Emory adds.

I giggle, and Emory grins down at me.

Malaki scoffs before grabbing my hand and placing a kiss on it. "You look stunning, Scottie."

I smile. "Thank you."

Emory pulls my hand away and clasps it with his. "That's Mrs. Olson to you."

"Oh, stop it," I chide, squeezing his hand.

Everyone laughs, and even Rhodes snickers under his breath.

Emory doesn't budge, though, and I wonder what has gotten into him. He's laying it on thick tonight. In fact, he hasn't stopped touching me since I walked into the event, which I appreciate because, to a girl like me, this is intimidating.

I feel like I stick out like a sore thumb, as if I have *white trash* stamped on my forehead, or there's a scent following me, telling all the wealthy people in this building that I'm not from this world and that I don't even belong.

The dress feels too expensive wrapped against my body, and Emory looks much too attractive to be mine.

"What are you thinking?" Emory whispers down into my ear, ignoring the conversation between Malaki, Kane, and Rhodes. Though, Rhodes is hardly speaking.

I swallow a lie and tell the truth. "Honestly?" I peek at

him, and zero in on the little crevice between his eyebrows. "I'm thinking about how I don't belong in this world."

Something resembling anger flashes across his face. "How so?"

"Emory. Come on," I whisper, raising an eyebrow before nodding at the mingling crowd. "Look at them, and then look at me."

Even when I was getting ready with the girls, I couldn't help but feel out of sorts. They're used to this life and had no issues slipping into their elegant dresses, even more lavish than mine. The men are all well-groomed with their bow ties and amber liquor in crystal glasses. It's a wonderful event, raising money for childhood cancer, but let's face it, I don't belong. In fact, I'm a charity case myself, and Emory is the fucking donator.

"Oh, I am," he states. "In fact, I can't look anywhere else."

Emory pulls on my hand, and I follow after him, smiling at Hattie and Angela as they sip on fancy cocktails.

"Where are we going?"

Emory picks up the pace, nodding at a few of his teammates here and there. When we disappear into a quiet hall lined with elegant wallpaper, he gently pushes me against the wall and tips my chin backward.

"I don't want to hear you say that ever again."

"Say what?" I ask, scoffing. "The truth?"

"The truth?" Emory's eyebrows furrow, and he bounces his attention all over my face. "Scottie, you are probably the only person at this event that actually belongs."

I roll my eyes, feeling suddenly self-conscious yet angry at the same time. "Emory, I'm a fucking charity case. I do *not* belong here."

Both his hands cradle my cheeks. He speaks so low I can hardly hear him. "You are the most righteous person I have ever met." I try to look away, but he squeezes my face gently. "I want you to look at me while I praise you, because it's what you need." He pauses. "Especially from your husband."

"But you're not—"

His eyes flare for a split second. "I'm not doing a very good job as a husband if you think anything but highly of yourself."

My heart beats hard.

It's hard to think straight when Emory is this close.

He makes everything he says so believable that I find myself staying quiet and listening.

"You're kind, giving, and empathetic. You appear unbothered by things that I know bother you—like when it's chilly outside and I catch you taking an extra blanket to Shutter and wrapping him up like a burrito as he purrs." My cheeks feel warm, but I still keep my eyes on Emory's. "You take care of the team's kids when no one asks you to, and you're happy to do it." Emory chuckles deeply, like he's in disbelief. "You're so goddamn selfless that you *married* me for money, and I would bet my life that you don't need the money for yourself."

I gulp, but I don't deny it.

"You have a heart of gold."

My chin wobbles.

"You've been abandoned as a child and left to fend for yourself, yet you don't have an ounce of hate for your mother."

My eyes gloss over, and this time, I do look away.

Emory's thumbs rub gently against my cheekbones, pulling my focus back to his eyes. "And just so we're clear, no one is around right now. This isn't for show, Scottie. I mean every single word."

My hands begin to shake when Emory grabs my hips. Our eyes catch, and he looks right at my mouth. "When I touch you..." His words fade as he drags his hands lower, cupping me around the ass. "Whether it's in front of a crowd or inside our home..."

Our home.

God, I love the sound of that.

"It's because I want to."

Emory slowly pulls my leg out from the high slit of my dress and wraps it around him. I curve my body to get closer. Heat covers my flesh with the feel of his palm slipping closer. He's teasing me, and I'm not even sure he means to. "Thirty more minutes, and we're leaving."

He stares at me intently before slowly swiping the outside of my lace thong. "And then I'm going to strip you out of this dress and make sure you believe every last word I just said to you."

Can't wait.

My eyes shut when he pulls the lacy material to the side and feels how wet I am.

"You want me to touch you now?" he murmurs, kissing the side of my neck.

I'm desperate, and it's pathetic. I don't even mean to nod, but I do, and I pair it with a, "Mm-hm."

He clicks his tongue. "What kind of husband would I be if I denied my wife?"

His finger sinks inside, and I pant. Every time he calls me *his wife*, my heart tumbles.

"Such a good girl," he mutters, pulling on my earlobe with his teeth. He fingers me deeper, and I move against his hand faster, showing him how good of a girl I can be for him.

I grip onto his shoulders for stability. My knees shake, and I whimper. "I like being a good girl for you," I admit shyly.

I don't know what has come over me, but with the look of pure possession on his face, I know he liked hearing it.

"I'm not waiting until we get home."

"Wha—"

Emory drops my leg and pulls me with him toward the

bathroom. He's a man on a mission, and who am I to stop him?

"The men's bathroom?" I ask, panicking.

He opens the door, and there's an older gentleman inside. He takes one look at us and smirks before leaving us alone.

As soon as the door shuts and Emory locks it, he turns with his blue eyes darker than normal and his jaw flexing with need. "You like to be my good girl?"

I nod timidly and lean against the sink.

"Good," he states, draping his suit jacket on the locked door handle.

My heart does a triple flip when he rolls his white dress shirt sleeves up his forearms. His veins pop, and I swear to god, he gets ten times hotter.

"Then you're going to be my good little wife and let me fuck you in this bathroom."

Fifty-Four

EMORY

I'M FUCKING my wife in the men's bathroom, and I'm treating her like she's a slut, but fuck, I think she likes it.

She's soaking wet, and my dick slides right in, giving us both the relief we're desperate for. I take her from behind and push her down so she's flat against the counter. I pump in and out, obsessed with how good it feels. I kept her thong on because I was too eager, but now I want to see all of her. I rip it off, pulling on the strands of lace until they fall on top of my dress shoes.

"Look at you," I say, pulling us upright.

She's flushed all over, and her cheeks are bright with pleasure.

"Look at you letting me take you in a bathroom like you're some dirty little slut." Her cunt tightens, and I pump in harder. *God damn.*

"*Emory.*" She says my name like it's her lifeline, and I love it.

I clench my jaw to keep myself from coming. "You're only a slut for me, though..."

A moan leaves her, and I shut my eyes. *God, she likes when I talk dirty to her.* "Say it."

"I'm only a slut for you." She's so obedient when I have her like this. It's the best balance.

As soon as she says it, she explodes. She squeezes my cock, and her tight body moves against me as a wave of pleasure rocks her.

"Fuck." I make a noise I don't think I have ever made before. I quickly pull out and move her to the side, shooting my come into the sink.

We're both panting and gripping whatever we can to keep us upright for so long that there's a knock on the door.

Scottie sucks in air and quickly fixes her dress against her body. I scoop up her panties and stuff them in my pocket before staring at her.

I'm in love with her.

I'm totally fucking in love with her.

I slip my hand into hers when there's another knock. I give her a wink. "Relax, baby."

It's me. I'm the one that needs to fucking relax.

"Relax?" she rushes. "Emory! I just let you fuck me in this bathroom, and there's probably a long line of men out there who are going to think I'm a slut."

I grab my suit jacket, and with my hand on the doorknob, I glance at her worried face. "The only thing they're going to be thinking is how lucky I am to be your husband." Her furrowed brows relax slightly. "You may be a slut for me but never for them."

She blushes.

Goal achieved.

When I open the door, I'm not surprised to only see one man standing there. Men don't go to the bathroom in groups like women do.

I raise my eyebrows at Scottie. *See?*

But she isn't looking at me.

She's looking at him.

And I really don't like the look on her face.

I turn to the man and give him a once-over.

He's wearing a nice suit, and considering I know just about everyone affiliated with the league, he's likely to be one of the donors.

"Excuse us," I say with an uptick in my voice.

I pull Scottie to the other side of me because I'm selfish and don't want his eyes on her, especially with the look of familiarity occurring between the two of them.

His chuckle skates down my spine, and I pause with my back to him. Scottie tugs on my hand, but I ignore the pull. I look over my shoulder, and he's got this sly smile on his face that needs to be wiped the hell off.

"Are the rumors true?" he asks.

"The rumor of our marriage?" I'm sure he isn't referring to that, but I make sure he knows that it is. "Yep."

"Nah. The one about her tasting like cherries."

Scottie growls softly under her breath before stepping forward. "Wouldn't you like to know? The answer is still *no*."

I tug my bold, smart-mouthed wife behind me with a little bit of pride swelling in my chest. She doesn't need me to fight her battles, but I'll gladly do so anyway.

"You must hang out at the Cat House."

He looks proud, but I step forward to squash that right away.

"Emory," Scottie warns.

I turn and wink at her over my shoulder. *Relax.*

"You want to know what she tastes like?" The man is eyeing me with suspicion. I'm a swing away, which means I could knock him out if I tried, but I don't because I'm a grown-ass man, and there is nothing more demeaning than learning that the hottest woman at this event isn't yours. "She tastes like me."

Shock moves over his face, and I smile with confidence. "It'd be best if you remembered that."

I turn around and look directly at Scottie's hidden smile. My hand falls to hers before I say over my shoulder, "Oh, and if you ever talk to my wife, it better be with fucking respect."

Scottie and I enter the event and act like nothing ever happened. Whenever we share a look that lasts longer than a second, I grin, and she blushes. I keep snagging her attention when she's standing with the wives, just to watch the pink spread across her cheeks. I pat my pocket the next time she looks at me, and she rolls her eyes with a twinkle in them.

When an older woman approaches the wives and starts to talk to them, I go back to standing in silence with Rhodes.

"That's some pretty impeccable acting, Olson."

I pop one of the appetizers in my mouth and ignore Rhodes's knowing glint.

"You tell her you're in love with her yet?" he asks.

I shrug. There's no need to explain it to him. A man as quiet and as stoic as him? He sees everything. "Not entirely."

He sighs. "I thought you were smarter than that."

I lean back onto the cocktail table and watch him leave before turning back to Scottie. My hands grow sweaty with the thought of telling her that I love her, because I've never told anyone I loved them, other than my family.

It's not a phrase I use often, and it's definitely not a phrase I use without thought.

But maybe I should.

The three words have been on the tip of my tongue more than once, and I've had to dismiss them every time.

I push off from the table when Scottie starts to head over to me. Most of the team has left by now, and with Coach

Jacobs heading out the door after Rhodes, it's our cue to go too.

"You ready?" I ask eagerly.

Scottie blinks a few times and glances at the woman she was talking to moments before. "Um..."

"What's wrong? Did she say something about you tasting like cherries too? Because I'll knock her down a notch too, if need be."

A burst of laughter leaves her, and it's genuine.

I grin. "You think I'm kidding?"

"You're being awfully possessive," she teases. "Of course I don't need you to knock that woman down a few notches." She can't hide her smile, and I can't stop staring at it. "You may need to knock me down a few notches, though."

"Why?" I wrap my arm around her waist and pull her curled hair off to the side as we make our way to the exit. "The quick fuck wasn't enough?"

She chokes on a gasp. I poke her side to make her laugh again.

I'm flirting with her, and I don't even mean to.

"She...wants me to take photos for her company."

I stop us right outside the event door. "Wait, what?"

Scottie nibbles on her lip, and I zero in on it. "Yeah, she said she saw our wedding photos." She shrugs. "I posted a few more the other day because I just...really like them. I'm proud of them."

Me too.

"Anyway, she owns a high-end boutique downtown, and she asked if I could take photos of some models in the dresses for her website and a few magazines."

"Scottie." Pride swallows me whole. "That's..."

"Crazy. Right?" She throws her hands up in the air. "I am not some fancy photographer. My camera battery is such shit

417

that it barely lasts twenty minutes. I don't have the right equipment, and I'm..."

I finish the thought for her. "Fucking talented."

Scottie stops babbling and stares at me with skepticism.

"Did you say yes?"

She chews on her lip again, and I quickly reach up to free it so she'll snap out of it.

"Well, yeah." She's talking so fast I can hardly understand her. "But I have to call her and tell her I can't do it. I am not a professional photographer. I can't—"

"Why can't you?" I grab onto her arms, and she presses her mouth shut.

She bounces her worried blue eyes between mine. "Because..." She glances elsewhere. "It's not practical. It takes years to build a reputable clientele and to create a thick portfolio. It's not financially stable for someone like me with responsibilities and..." She trails off, and I don't understand.

"And what?" I ask.

I watch her shut down immediately. She shakes her head and begins to walk toward the door. If she thinks I'm letting this go, she doesn't know me as well as I thought. It's time she and I got everything out in the open. She's my wife, and I want to know everything about her—even her fears.

I trail after her. "You do know we live together, right? Just because you walk away doesn't mean the conversation ends."

My teasing tone fades when I catch up to her. Her entire body tenses, and she takes a step backward. I watch the color on her face fade. "Scottie." Her eyes drop to the sidewalk, and I do the same. Anger burns my skin with a clench of my jaw.

"Let go of my wife," I demand, flexing my fist.

Scottie's nostrils flare, and I hear her heaving breaths. She pulls on her hand, and the homeless man digs his dirty fingers into her wrist.

The only reason I haven't plummeted him backward is

because I don't want to scare Scottie. Remembering what Scottie told me about her mom, I suspect there's something buried here that I'm not exactly privy to.

"I'm going to ask you one more time to let go of my wife before I physically remove your hand."

The homeless man grumbles under his breath. He finally lets go of Scottie, and she stumbles backward. I see Kane staring from the event doors, and he's over to us before I can signal to him. He catches Scottie around the waist. She's shaking like a leaf, and I could throw up at the sight. I turn around to threaten the man but stop when I see him muttering to a woman who is lying on her side on top of a cardboard box right behind him.

The realization of who she is crashes into me.

Shit.

I turn around and see that Kane has moved in front of Scottie. Malaki begins to walk over, and he takes one look at the situation before stepping in line with Kane. I don't give her mother a second look as I head right for my wife.

I step in between her and Kane and weave my fingers through her hair so she'll look at me. The hazy gloss cuts me deep. "Let's go home, baby."

Her bottom lip trembles, but Scottie is resilient. I watch as she silently reprimands herself before she places her hand in mine and lets me lead her to my car.

Neither of us say anything when the engine starts up.

I place my hand on her thigh as she stares out the window, silently letting her know that I'm here if she needs me.

Except, I'm not entirely sure that she'll ever really need me.

And if she does, I don't think she'll admit it.

———

I'M in and out of an unrestful sleep, waking up every hour on the dot.

A yawn flows from my mouth as I reach over for her, making sure she's okay.

Scottie hasn't said a word, other than a clipped, *'I'm fine.'* After we showered, she climbed into bed with me, and I could hear her troubled thoughts like they were my own.

I didn't press or force her to talk to me.

I wrapped my arm around her waist and listened for her breathing to calm before I fell asleep too.

"Hey," I rasp. "You okay?"

Something soft brushes against my arm, and I pull my eyes open.

What the hell?

It takes me a second to adjust to the dark room. I stare at her side of the bed, but instead of Scottie, I see two glowing eyes gazing back at me.

I immediately sit up.

"Shutter?"

To my surprise, he lets out a loud meow. The dumpster cat walks over to me and nudges my hand before nipping me gently on the thumb.

He jumps off the bed and prances over to the open bedroom door.

I look around the room. "Scottie?"

Shutter meows again, and he's staring at me from the threshold.

My heart slips when he comes back onto the blanket and glares at me from the foot of my bed.

He meows again, and this time, it's louder.

I fling the covers off my legs, and Shutter rushes to beat me to the door.

"Scottie?" I repeat, glancing around my room one more time.

Shutter meows and zooms past my legs, racing me to the stairs.

I follow after him with unease backing my every step.

Where is she, and why is Shutter inside?

The house is blanketed with darkness, and there's a nip in the air that I know is from outside.

I stare at the open front door, and a fear like I've never felt wraps around my throat and chokes me.

"Scottie?" My tone is stern.

Shutter brushes against me and nips my ankle. I pull my leg back and glare at him. As soon as he sees me looking at him, he prances to the kitchen and stands in front of the pantry door. He claws at it a few times before I walk over and slowly pull it open.

Shock makes me drop to my knees when I see her. I pull her into my lap and quickly unclench her fingers from the tight grip on the knife. It slips to the floor with a clank.

"Baby, what are you doing?" I try to keep my tone normal.

Her entire body trembles in my grip, and when our eyes meet, I'm not sure she even recognizes me, which scares the fuck out of me.

Fifty—Five

SCOTTIE

I CAN'T BREATHE.

My hand hurts, and the room turns on its side.

"Scottie."

My heart beats too fast. I push my palm into the center of my chest to make it stop, but it won't.

"*Shit.* Baby."

Why won't the fucking room stop spinning? I'm present, but I'm not. The pain in my hand grounds me to reality, but the deep ache of fear clouds everything until I'm in a spiral.

But then, it stops.

Suddenly, air fills my lungs, and the thoughts evaporate.

Even the sting of pain running up my arm disappears.

His lips are calming, and the taste of him against my tongue is like a remedy. When the room rights itself, I stare up into Emory's worried eyes, too afraid to look away, yet embarrassed enough to want to.

"Who is William?" he whispers, wiping my wet cheeks.

"Wh...what?" My body grows with heat. I'm sweaty but also chilled to the bone.

"Shit." Emory pulls my hand close to his face and inspects it. "Your hand."

He sweeps me off my feet, and the confusion follows me until he places me on the kitchen counter beside the sink. His grip never leaves me. Even as he reaches for the dish towel and wets it under the stream of water, he keeps his hand on my leg.

"Come here," he mutters softly, pulling my hand closer. One by one, he loosens my fingers and reveals my sliced palm. I jerk at the touch of the cool towel. A hiss slips between my teeth from the sting, but it disappears when Emory winds his hand up my neck until his fingers are buried in my hair.

"Who is William? Did he come into the house?"

"What?" I shake my head at the absurd thought. "No."

"The door was open," he argues, bouncing his eyes back and forth between mine. There's a worry line in between them, and I hate that I'm the reason it's there.

I'm mortified and embarrassed. It's been years since I've done this. I can hardly look Emory in the eye because he probably thinks I'm certifiable.

My bottom lip trembles for the second time in less than twenty-four hours. "I am so sorry." I swallow the tight lump in my throat. "No one is in the house."

I lean forward slightly and look at my feet to see if they're covered in dirt.

Thank God, they aren't.

"Scottie, the door is open. Are you sure no one came inside?"

I nod, fully confident that I was the one who opened the door. "I'm so sorry. I had a nightmare..." A tear slips down the side of my cheek, and I turn away to hide it.

It was because I saw her.

Stop crying.

"Don't do that." Emory speaks so softly I hardly hear him.

I clear my throat after swallowing the tight lump in my throat. "Don't do what?"

I'm doing my best to act unfazed, but I know it's a pathetic attempt.

"Don't shut me out. Let me be here for you."

My chin wobbles as I contemplate running out the front door and never looking back, but I'm a realist, and I know I wouldn't even make it out of the kitchen without Emory pulling me backward.

"I was trying to give you space earlier." He grips my chin and brings me to look at him. "But you don't need space." He pauses. "You need me."

The first thing that rushes to mind is how I don't need anyone.

But the longer I stare into his calm eyes and the more his thumb brushes against my chin, the more I feel myself teetering.

It has nothing to do with trust.

I trusted him the moment I cornered him in the bathroom and tried to exploit him.

It's about me being afraid to need someone, as much as I don't want to admit that.

Emory pulls my face closer to his, and our foreheads rest against one another. "For better or for worse, Scottie. I took vows. Give me a chance to keep them."

I pull away and stare into his eyes. I don't worry about not crying, because it takes too much effort, and if I'm going to do this, I'm going to need all the strength I have left.

"Before I tell you everything, I need you to promise me something," my voice croaks.

"Anything."

It's surreal to see such a strong, willful man become so soft and genuine. It's hard to believe that he wants to be like that with me.

"I don't want you to try to fix it." His eyebrows furrow, but I keep going before he interrupts me. "Promise me that nothing will change. You and I have a deal, Emory. After a year is up and the contract ends, that's when you pay me. Nothing changes."

Otherwise, it's too easy. No matter who Emory is to me, this is not his responsibility. We started this on simple terms, and I won't go back on them because he feels sorry for me.

He looks like he wants to argue, but instead, he nods. "Alright."

Shutter jumps onto the counter, and I expect Emory to shoo him outside, but he doesn't pay him any mind, not even when he climbs onto my lap and rubs his face against the back of my injured hand.

"William is my brother," I start with the most important thing. "And he's in prison."

Emory's tense shoulders loosen, and I furrow my eyebrows. "Why do you look...relieved?"

He sighs quietly. "With the way you said his name, I knew he meant something to you. I was afraid it was an ex."

The smallest smile falls to my lips, but it only lasts a second.

Emory pulls the towel away before pressing it back down. He scoops me up into his arms and walks us over to the door. He shuts it with his foot, and as he's walking us toward the stairs, I watch Shutter follow on quiet paws.

"You know Shutter is still in here, right?"

"Yes." Emory places us both on the bed but keeps me on his lap. "He can stay."

I'm shocked. I glance at him as he watches Shutter lie in a comfy spot at the foot of the bed. "He can?"

"The dumpster cat came all the way upstairs and woke me up. Then he led me to you." Emory pulls me in tighter. "So yeah, baby.

426

He stays. Now tell me why your brother is in prison and why you're hiding a stack of lawyer letters under our bed. Tell me what has you so twisted in your sleep that you felt you needed a knife."

"You found those?"

He nods against my back. "I didn't open them, but yeah. I saw the letterhead."

A shaky breath slips from my mouth, and Emory places a soft kiss on my shoulder. "Take your time," he reassures me. "I'm not going anywhere."

He shifts us on the bed, and it causes Shutter to look back at us. He hisses at Emory.

"Apparently, neither is he," Emory notes.

The touch of a smile grazes my lips, and I relax into his sturdy chest. "It started when my dad died."

I feel Emory's grip tighten against me.

"My mom was always the chaotic one of my parents. She liked to party and go out with her friends, which left my dad at home with me a lot."

"Were you close with him?"

I nod.

"After he died and my mom was left to take care of me, I think she became resentful. One thing led to another, and she wound up pregnant with William—father unknown. I didn't realize it at the time because I was too young, but she didn't take care of her body like she should have."

Emory's hand skims my leg back and forth in the most comforting way. "What do you mean?"

"She drank while pregnant. Probably did some drugs." I shrug. "William is technically undiagnosed, but after years of raising him and researching, I'm certain he has lasting effects." I choose not to divulge the entire medical definition to Emory because we'd be here all night discussing my brother's cognitive impairments. Instead, I go the easy route. "Long story

427

short, he doesn't make the best decisions. He's easily influenced, impulsive, and he doesn't grasp social cues. It was a struggle all throughout his adolescence, and as soon as he turned eighteen, he caught himself in a mess."

I take a deep breath.

"He was caught breaking and entering. They tagged arson onto his sentence too." Frustration skims up my spine. "He wasn't even the one to do it. He was blamed, and he took the fall for it because, again, he's easily influenced and just... doesn't understand."

Emory remains quiet for a few minutes, and I start to feel anxious.

It isn't until his hand rests against my side and he gives it a quick squeeze that I relax again.

"So you're trying to help get him out. That's the reason for the lawyer's letters and why you need money." It isn't a question, so I don't answer. "You've been taking care of him all his life, haven't you?"

My lip slips beneath my teeth, and I nod.

"Is that what your nightmare was about? Protecting William? Is that why you had a knife?"

I shut my eyes in hopes that it'll give me the confidence to answer him.

"Yes." I swallow a gulp. "I didn't grow up in the best home, and after seeing my mom, it brought up some unwanted memories."

Emory pulls me into his chest and kisses the top of my head. I hold in my tears, but emotion chokes me up regardless. "You're safe with me, Biscotti."

I know.

───

IT'S BEEN four days since I confided in Emory, and each day, I feel a little bit lighter. Every morning that he's still lying beside me with a lazy smile on his face is another morning that he doesn't serve me with divorce papers from realizing how much baggage I have.

I wasn't sure what to expect after I told him about William's condition and the situation that landed him in prison. For the woman who is supposed to help his reputation, I have a pretty fucked-up background that goes against everything the media has said of me thus far.

Neither Emory nor I thought we'd get *this* much attention, but after I posted our wedding photos and his *Scottie Biscotti* interview went viral, we've been idolized. The Chicago Blue Devils are projected to be in the fight for the Stanley Cup, and that comes with even more media coverage.

If it leaks that I'm an ex-stripper from the Cat House who Emory met one day and was married to the next, paired with my mother's background and the fact that my brother is in prison, well...let's just say not all publicity is good publicity.

Shutter purrs from somewhere that feels like the top of my head. I peek one eye open, and his tail flicks me in the face.

"Really?" I groan. "Good morning to you too."

I turn toward Emory, but instead of seeing him lying there, a box is in his place.

Sitting up in my groggy state, I slowly reach out and pull it onto my lap. I laugh softly when I see tiny teeth marks on the side from Shutter. "Did you think this was for you?" I ask, giving him a look.

He sighs and turns his head, like he's upset that it isn't.

After pulling the top of the box open, I freeze.

There's a piece of torn notebook paper with Emory's messy handwriting.

This battery should last longer than twenty minutes.

Good luck today.

My eyes gloss over.

He got me a new camera?

Without even thinking, I grab my phone and call him.

"Morning, Biscotti."

He's out of breath from conditioning, yet he still answered.

"Are you serious?" I ask.

My phone makes a noise, and I roll my eyes when I see he's trying to switch it to FaceTime. I quickly run my fingers through my hair and blink a few times so he can't see my teary eyes. As soon as his face fills the screen, my stomach fills with butterflies.

"Dead serious," he says.

"Emory. This is too much."

But I love it.

He takes the back of his hand and wipes his face after chugging water. Sweat drips over his cheek, and it's insanely hot. "Considering what I want to do? It isn't."

He's referring to paying the legal fees off right now instead of following through on our terms. But I made him promise, and he isn't one to break promises.

I give him a look, and the only thing it does is deepen his grin. It drives me wild, and suddenly, I find myself smiling too.

"Look at that," he coaxes. "My wife is smiling in our bed with nothing but that thin T-shirt on."

Heat coils in my stomach, and my teeth sink into my bottom lip.

"Stay right there." Emory moves through the weight

room, and I watch in silence as he enters the quiet locker room, away from his teammates. "I'm coming home."

I laugh. "Stop it."

He pauses. "You stop it."

"Stop what?" I ask, laughing again.

Emory's flirtiness fades. My heart beats harder when he opens his mouth, but then he closes it before opening it one more time. "Stop making me fall in love with you."

I drop the phone.

It slips right out of my hand and onto the bed.

I look down at it and repeat what he just said to me inside my head.

Did he?

Emory is still staring at me when I pull the phone upright again. In complete denial, I take a breath and quietly ask, "Who's with you?"

"Not a soul," he says, leaning back onto his locker.

"Show me," I challenge, unsure if I believe him.

The camera pans around the empty locker room, and my mouth runs dry. When his face comes back into view, he raises an eyebrow at me. "I didn't say it for anyone but you, Scottie."

"You're not falling in love with me," I say.

He nods. "You're right."

I pinch my thigh to distract myself from the complete and utter disappointment I feel. But then he smiles. "I'm already there."

My mouth parts, and something warm buries itself inside my chest.

"Olson! Get back to your reps!"

Emory's attention shifts, and he flicks his chin at his coach before looking back at me. "I'll see you later. Good luck today, and that camera is a gift. There are no take-backs."

Emory stands and begins to move through the locker room.

"Wait!" I shout.

Emory's eyebrows shoot to his damp hair.

"I love you too." The four words flow out of my mouth effortlessly, but I'm not surprised.

I've known that I've loved him for far longer than I'm willing to admit.

And with the look he gives me, I think he's known too.

Fifty–Six

EMORY

"SCOTTIE DIDN'T COME?" I brush my mom's hand away as she attempts to push a strand of my damp hair out of my face. "I was hoping she would."

Me too.

"She couldn't." I'm eager to brag about Scottie, even if it's just to my parents. "She had to work."

"Work? I didn't realize she had a job. Though, we didn't really get to chat much about that yet. You've been so secretive about her, and your father made her uncomfortable already, so I didn't want to press."

My dad stops talking with Rhodes to interject. "I didn't make her uncomfortable."

Rhodes only came over to let me know that the bus was leaving in ten to head back to the airport, but he got caught in the Jay-and-MaryAnn trap, and now he's knee-deep in a conversation with my dad about home improvement.

"You did too," my mom argues. She turns back to me, and it's clear she wants to know more about Scottie.

"Scottie is a photographer. An amazing one."

Shortly after she was asked to photograph for the clothing

435

shop, Vivian asked her to take Nola's photos, and Georgia is begging her to take her and Matt's engagement photos plus cover their wedding. Since Scottie absolutely refuses to let me help with her brother's legal fees, I've been encouraging her to take every opportunity given, even if she doesn't feel like a "professional"—her words, not mine.

My dad pipes in again. "A photographer? Maybe she can photoshop us into your wedding photos since you didn't think to invite the family."

For fuck's sake.

"We will have another wedding with all of our friends and family. How's that, Dad?"

He thinks I'm being a sarcastic ass, but the thought of having a real wedding with Scottie walking down the aisle is too inviting of an idea. We will need a honeymoon too—wherever she wants to go.

Knowing Scottie, it'll be somewhere simple.

Which is fine with me.

"We gotta go," Rhodes interjects. He gives a clipped goodbye to my parents and rushes off.

"That one isn't much of a talker, huh?" My dad notes, staring after my captain.

"No." I shake my head. "But you should meet his daughter. She's the complete opposite."

My mom moves in for a hug, and I wrap my arms around her comforting frame. When she pulls back, she has a little glint to her eye. "Do you think you and Scottie will have kids?"

She'll definitely carry my baby one day.

The thought stuns me.

I have never felt more sure about something in my entire life.

Thinking about Scottie carrying my child in her stomach? That's a high I didn't know I could reach. I hadn't even thought about children. Before Scottie, I hadn't even thought about marriage.

"Oh, will you stop it? You did the same thing to Taytum and Ford the other day, and you freaked them out too."

My mom slaps my dad's chest lightly. "Correction. I freaked Tay out. Not Ford. He was elated by the idea."

I think to myself while my parents argue over Taytum and Ford. I now understand what my best friend was feeling when he decided to pursue my sister behind my back. He told me he couldn't help it, and now it all makes sense.

After hugging my dad, I say goodbye to my parents and tell my mom I'll call her when I figure out a good time for them to come visit again. The only reason they came to the game this evening was because it was only a few hours from home. Otherwise, they catch me on TV and call it a night.

Once I'm settled on the bus, I pull open my phone and text Scottie.

> Do you want kids one day?

It feels like hours before she texts back, but it's only been a minute, if that.

> That's what you text me after you just played an absolutely amazing game? Is that what you were thinking about when blocking those pucks?

> I'm always thinking about you. Now answer my question.

> I'm trying to decide which answer will freak you out less.

> The truth. Always the truth.

A text bubble pops up while she types, and I block the

conversations of my teammates out as I wait nervously. If Scottie doesn't want children, then that's okay. Understandable, even. She's been taking care of her brother for most of her life, drowning in stress, and there's a lot of trauma lingering from her own mother. Scottie would be the most amazing mom in the world. I've quietly watched her with Ellie and Nola, and I'd love nothing more than to watch her with our child. But again, if she doesn't want a child of her own, then that's okay. I'm still flabbergasted that she confided in me, but there's a sense of pride there too. I want to be there for her, and I'm so fucking proud that she purposefully let herself become vulnerable in front of me.

> I do want a child one day. Only one.

My tight stomach loosens, and I blow out a heavy breath. I didn't realize how nervous I was while waiting for her to respond to me. That was worse than asking her if she'd be my fake wife.

> Do you want children?

> With you? Yes. I'd love nothing more than to see you carry my baby.

> Stop making me blush. Plus, who said I'm going to let you get me pregnant, Olson?

> Don't play games with me.

She texts back with a laughing face, but I don't respond until we're settled on the plane and waiting for takeoff. Now that I have her waiting at home for me, these plane rides seem to take longer and longer.

> Why only one?

I panic after I hit send and type another message.

> I'm fine with whatever you want. I'm just curious. And seriously, stop playing games. If you're going to have anyone's baby, it's mine.

A heavy dose of possession comes over me. I am so fucking greedy when it comes to Scottie. I don't even want another man to look at her.

> It makes me feel guilty to admit this, but I only want one because if anything were to happen to me, I don't want the responsibility of parenthood to fall onto my firstborn like it did with me and William. I've been taking care of him for as long as I can remember, and now that I'm an adult, I know that it really wasn't fair.

My chest aches. I reread her message a few times before attempting to rectify her guilt and fear.

> It wasn't fair. You're right. But William is so god damn lucky to have you, and I don't ever want you to worry about something like that when it comes to the future. You may not have the family you wished for growing up, but you do now. You have me, Scottie. In fact, you have me wrapped around your pretty little finger so tightly all I can think about is getting home to you anytime we're apart.

I let out another puff of air when another strong set of emotions hits me.

> Go to sleep. I'll be home in the morning. I love you.

439

I love you too. Be safe. Xo

I settle into my seat and smile. Who would have thought that a simple marriage of convenience with a feisty woman who tried to exploit me in the arena bathroom would turn into *this?*

———

MY SHOULDER ACHES after blocking the puck from Kane. That man has a fucking swing on him.

"Fuck, bro," I say when he skates past. "That one stung."

He snorts. "I can make it sting worse if you want."

I scoff. "Maybe if you weren't hungover, you could."

He sends me a scowl, and I laugh under my breath. He's a beaut, and everyone in the league agrees. We're lucky to have him on our team, but he has some maturing to do.

Maybe he should find a wife too.

"Olson." I turn to look at Coach Jacobs at the bench but still manage to block the next puck Kane sends in my direction.

I drop it to the ice and smile sickeningly at him. "Weak," I say before skating to the side.

Coach Jacobs nods for me to follow him, so I hand off my stick and accompany him to the locker room. When we're tucked in his office, my heart starts to beat a little faster.

"Is there an emergency?"

Coach doesn't interrupt practice often, and I instantly think that something is wrong. I'm having flashbacks from college whenever I'd get a call about Taytum and her diabetes.

"No." He sits at his desk. "Not really."

"Not sure I like the sound of that."

He holds his finger up and presses a button on his phone. "Alright, Joseph. I have him in here."

440

Joseph? As in my agent?

I sit up taller and start stripping some of my gear. Sweat drips down my back, and I stare directly at Coach. "Are you trading me?"

He laughs out loud. "Absolutely not."

"Then what am I doing in here with my agent on the line instead of practicing?"

"Emory." Joseph clears his throat, and my eyes drop to the phone. "We have a slight problem. We're going to need to do some damage control."

What the fuck does that mean?

"Probably a press conference?" Coach asks, directing his question to Joseph.

"For what?" I ask.

Surely someone hasn't come forward and said I tried to fuck them again. I'm married, for fuck's sake.

"For this..." Coach says, turning his computer monitor around.

There are numerous photos of Scottie.

Or should I say, *Cherry.*

My heart beats right out of my chest.

I start to shake in my seat.

The bones in my hands crack.

"Get that shit taken down right now," I grit.

Joseph scoffs. "The photo of your fake wife is the least of our concerns."

I pull my glare from the phone and look at Coach. *Did he fucking tell him?*

He shakes his head, knowing what I'm going to ask. Instead of answering, he points to the third article title.

Olson's Social Media Fluke - A Staged Marriage to a Stripper

I'm more concerned about Scottie than I am anything else at this moment. They're referring to her as a stripper, like that's all there is to her. I grow nauseated with the more titles I read.

A Disturbing Revelation about Star Goalie, Emory Olson's, Wife

Mrs. Olson or Just Another Puck Bunny?

Scottie Monroe and Her Ties to Prison

"Fucking hell." I slap my hand on the desk and shout into the phone. "Get it all taken down now, Joseph! They're making her out to be something she isn't."

"It's better than them making you out to be the bad guy," he says.

He's fucking fired.

I stand and head for my locker. I hear Coach follow after me, and in the middle of changing and grabbing my phone, he puts his hand on my shoulder and gives it a tight squeeze.

"This is the only time I'll accept you walking out on practice. You got that?"

I nod and snag my keys. On the way to my car, I swipe away all my messages and notifications because of the leak. My only focus is Scottie.

I dial her number from my car, praying to God she hasn't seen the news.

She doesn't answer, and the pit in my stomach could swallow me whole.

Fifty-Seven

SCOTTIE

I LEFT my phone on the counter and purposefully kept my back to the living room camera so Emory wouldn't see the utter devastation on my face when he finds out I'm gone and looks at the footage.

Play stupid games, win stupid prizes.

It's the only thing I can think as I sit in my parked car and stare at the homeless camp I know my mother frequents.

I find it truly pathetic that the first place I go when I'm in a pit of despair is here, but sometimes I like to pretend that the woman who birthed me and told me fairy tales before bed while my dad leaned against the door is still in there somewhere.

My heart aches with every beat.

I wipe my face again as another tear escapes. Shutter looks up from my lap when the droplet lands on his sleek fur, but he goes back to resting a moment later.

Glancing at the clock, I know Emory is home from practice by now.

I'm positive he's heard. He's likely read all the articles and is trying to fix things or, knowing him, trying to figure out

445

who found out about us...*about me*...and revealed it to the press.

A jealous woman?

Maybe another hockey player with a vengeance for the Blue Devils and their recent success?

It doesn't really matter.

There's too much evidence and too many conspiracy theories roaming the internet like a plague to deny it all.

I put my car in drive after placing Shutter on the blanket in the front seat. I have one thought in my head, and it's how I'm going to beat Emory to the punch.

The media may think we're a fluke, and we did begin that way, but things have changed.

What hasn't changed is that I signed up to do a job, and I am *not* a quitter.

Emory Olson married me so I would fix his image, and that's exactly what I'm going to do.

As soon as I pull up to the Cat House, Shutter meows.

"Don't worry." I smile softly at him. "I'm not leaving you here."

He climbs out of the car after me and stays right beside the tire as I head for the door. Only a few cars are in the parking lot, and I've gotta make this quick because Emory's determination runs deep, and he'll come looking for me.

I open the door and head for the back, hoping to avoid my ex-boss.

When I step into the dressing room, Chastity is applying her eyelashes. With one half attached, she turns and envelops me in a warm hug.

"I knew you'd show up here," she whispers, pulling us apart to look me up and down. "You okay?"

"You've heard? But you don't even watch hockey."

My face heats. God, does the whole world know?

She shrugs, and I can't stop staring at her eyelash hanging

on by a thread. I take the glue from her and tip her chin to fix it.

"It has to do with the Cat House. Russ was making a whole production over it."

"Great," I mumble. "Is he pissed? I should go before he sees me."

I hand the glue back to Chastity, and she laughs. "Are you kidding? He's elated. He said, and I quote, '*Someone get Cherry back here! She needs a raise.*'"

I feel an insane amount of dread at the thought.

"In that case, bye."

Chastity laughs again and pushes lightly on my shoulder. "What do you need, babe? I know you're not actually thinking of coming back to work here." She glances at my finger, and my stomach falls.

"Your phone," I say. "For five minutes, max."

"You've got it." She rushes over on bare feet and pulls out her phone.

"I'll be right back."

Before I leave her, she grabs onto my hand. "Hey, I'm serious. Are you okay?"

No.

I've never been this *not okay* in my life, and that's truly saying something, considering.

"I'm fine." The lie rolls right off my tongue.

My heart beats harder with each step I take to the back room.

When I shut the door and log in to Emory's social media, I clear my head and get to work.

———

BETTY SNORES. Loudly.

With her deep snoring and Shutter chasing cockroaches all night long, I haven't slept in days.

Without a phone, I haven't checked the internet. I have no idea how long it took for Emory to see what I posted or if it went viral like everything else relating to us.

I've been living the last several days on autopilot. When I showed up at Betty's, it was because I had nowhere else to go. I snuck through without Gerald seeing me, and since then, he hasn't noticed the girl and her cat living in his crabby ol' tenant's apartment—not even when I tag along to work with Betty to help her clean houses.

All I can seem to think of while wiping windows and mopping floors is Emory. But each time he pops into my head, I run from him, only to think of my brother a moment later. I wonder if he's called me or left any messages.

Everything feels messy and chaotic—even as I lie on the scratchy couch and watch Shutter play peek-a-boo with a bug.

Betty snores again, and it doesn't even faze me as I reach for the remote. A tinge of fear rolls around my head when the TV comes to life. I'm half-afraid to see my face on the screen as breaking news, but my life doesn't mean much to the real world.

It only means something to Russ, for the popularity it's bringing to his strip club, and the hockey gurus. Emory's parents' faces flash in my head, and I quickly shut them out too.

I shut everything out until I'm left with nothing.

I'm numb.

It's a skill I learned very early on in my life.

If something hurts you, stay away from it.

And thinking of the last few months, and what could have been, is a knife in my back.

My finger presses on the remote over and over again as I lie mindlessly on the couch, too afraid to let myself think.

I don't know which way is up or down.

I'm not sure what the future brings or how I'm going to pay those legal fees I promised William I'd take care of.

There's some money in my account from what Emory pays me monthly and from taking the photos for Serena Sinclair, but until she outsources them to magazines, it's all I have. Considering the hockey wives now know I'm a fraud, I can probably toss them off my clientele list.

I laugh sarcastically.

What a fucking mess.

My finger freezes when hockey fills the screen. A tight knot forms in my throat when I see the blue and black jerseys on the ice.

Turn the channel, Scottie.

With Emory, I felt like I had it all.

I had the world in my hands.

We had a plan. I could see a future that wasn't so...scary.

But now, everything is gone. I know I did the right thing by coming forward and telling the social media sharks that it was all my idea and that I blackmailed their star goalie. Emory Olson is a good man, and he doesn't deserve to be viewed as anything but.

We started out playing such an innocent game, but I lost, and it's a loss that's hard to accept.

Fifty-Eight
EMORY

I WALK into the locker room with my heart on my sleeve.

I can't make eye contact with much of anyone, and if I do, it comes off as a glare. It's not purposeful, and they don't take offense.

Most of my gear is on, and I seem ready for the game, but I'm not. My phone is in my hand, and I swipe away the texts from my parents and their constant concern and check to see if I have any random messages. I keep hoping Scottie will reach out to me somehow, since I deleted the social media account that she used to her advantage, but she hasn't.

It hurt like hell when I finally figured out the password: *Emorysbiscotti.*

That wasn't a fucking punch in the gut or anything.

After tossing my phone to the side, I get up from the bench and storm onto the ice without making much small talk with my team.

Warm-ups are mostly over, and this is the first game I've played since the news of Scottie and I broke, which means I'm being watched very closely.

Hockey fans love the game.

They love it even more when emotions are attached. We're sold out tonight, and it would be dense of me to think it has nothing to do with the recent revelations about my personal life.

They're hoping for a fight.

Everyone is predicting the hotshot goalie will lose his shit because of the *trauma* he's been through. They think she blackmailed me and forced my hand, because that's what she admitted online.

Which, yeah. She attempted to do just that.

But what she didn't finish telling them was that she backed out because her heart is much too big for this world.

She can't avoid me forever, though.

We're legally married, for fuck's sake.

She better come out of hiding soon, because she doesn't know the lengths I will go for her.

A small group of players start to circle the ice, and I can already tell they're wanting to start their shit and get into my head. *They better not say a fucking word.*

I grip my stick and focus.

Rhodes, who already has a huge presence on the ice with his attitude, drives it a little deeper with his glare set on our opponent and his deep voice vibrating around the arena. "Back the fuck off," he barks to them.

Kane skates past and mumbles something to Rhodes, and then they both take off, leaving the yellow jerseys with a silent threat.

We play hard and fast.

Malaki is up for MVP of the year, and he's slicing and dicing on the icy floor like his life depends on it. But our guys are tired, and we're tied 1-1.

Kane has been in the penalty box three times, and Matthew twice, which isn't the norm for him. But when we play a team this good, there's bound to be some mistakes.

Scottie pops into my head.

So many mistakes were made.

I should have told her that I love her much sooner than I did. Or expressed just how much I love her.

Maybe then, she would have stayed, and we could have figured this out together.

Instead, she fled and tried to fix it on her own because that's what she's used to.

Being alone.

I focus on the black puck whizzing directly for the top left corner of the net. I block it with my shoulder, but the relief is gone when I'm flung backward, cracking my helmet off the ice.

Fucking shit.

"You motherfuckers!" Kane shouts, jumping on top of several other players with me at the bottom of the pile.

Jesus fucking Christ.

The refs and teammates intervene and try to pull everyone off of each other. Fists are flying, and I'm stuck lying underneath them. Number seven smiles slyly at me.

"I'd let that girl blackmail me too."

I know he's trying to get me riled up.

The old Emory would throw his gloves off to the side, and the smug fuck would be on his ass with a broken jaw in seconds.

But I'm not ruining the work Scottie just put in to make me seem like I'm a good man.

She makes me want to be the guy she painted me out to be in the media. I want to show her how good of a husband I can be, without the threat of our stupid marriage contract hanging over our heads.

Fuck.

I have to fix it.

Nothing seems to matter to me, unless I have her.

"Kane!" I shout. "He's baiting you."

"He's baiting you!" he shouts back, flinging the ref's hand off his pad.

"And I'm not takin' it. Get your fucking head in the game."

I should take my own advice, but there's another game that my head is in, and right after we win this one, I'm going to go win that one too.

———

"OLSON." Coach Jacobs seems irritated. "They want you for the press conference tonight."

I knew they'd want me, so I'm not surprised.

"You can refuse it. You'll be fined, but I don't think anyone will blame you."

I'm still in my uniform, minus my helmet. I walk past Coach and pat some of my teammates on the back because we won, and it's all because they worked together as a team.

Kane clicked back into action after I scolded him, and although there were a few other remarks here and there, and some penalties, we were able to come out with a win.

"You sure you want to do this?" Rhodes acts truly concerned for once.

I nod, and he raises an eyebrow.

"I've gotta see this," he says, trying to hide a smirk.

"I'm surprised you're not running off to get Ellie. I feel sort of special that you're waiting around to watch me take a press conference."

He turns away and shrugs. "She's with the nanny."

"The same one or another new one?"

"Same."

"That's a record. How long has this one lasted? A week?" I ask.

"Shut up," he snaps, opening the door. "Don't cuss anyone out if they ask you about Scottie."

"If?" I glance over my shoulder. "You mean when."

If no one brings her up, I'll do it for them.

Silence fills the room when I enter. The only thing I hear are a few clicks of cameras, which only remind me of Scottie.

I take a seat, and strangely enough, I feel calm.

Calmer than I've ever felt in front of a camera—unless, of course, Scottie was the one behind it.

I nod to one reporter in the front because she looks like she'd be the one to bring up the recent drama. She speaks loud and confident, but to my surprise, she only asks about the game. I answer her question fluently and point to another woman, but the moment she opens her mouth and squeaks, I know she isn't the one. After answering her, I scan the crowd and land on a man. He looks like he has enough balls to ask me the question everyone thinks I don't want to answer.

"Now that we've gotten your side of the game, do you care to give us your side of the recent allegations over your marriage?"

Bingo.

I lean back in my seat and smirk.

"I thought you'd never ask."

There's a low buzz of chuckles and whispers. I glance at Rhodes, and he shakes his head. I shrug and turn back to the reporter.

"It's true," I start. "Scottie Monroe did try to blackmail me." I lean forward. "I want you all to underline the word *try.*" After I'm satisfied that they've all done what I've asked, I rap my fingers on the table. "She didn't blackmail me. She's much too righteous for something like that. But it got me thinking."

I pray to God Scottie is watching.

And if she isn't, I'm just going to have to go find her.

I'll go to the prison and wait until she visits her brother if need be.

"It was my idea."

There are a few gasps, and my agent is probably throwing his TV across the room by now.

"I had a contract written up. She would marry me to help fix my image—since so many of you reporters wanted to spread rumors that I was just an angry, cagey goalie who put some guy in the hospital, and run with the gossip of women saying I did things that were never true—and I'd pay her when the job was done."

"So, she *is* a gold digger?" one of the men asks.

I flick my eyes to him, and he immediately shuts his mouth. "You talk like that again about my wife, and you're going to need a new profession."

A new set of teeth too.

"Scottie married me for money, yes, but to respect her privacy, I am not going to tell you what that money was going toward. But the last thing this woman should ever be called is a gold digger."

All they'd have to do is see the car she drives to know that.

If they knew the heart she hid from everyone so well, they wouldn't be saying that either.

"I'm here to set the story straight. My marriage started off as a ploy. I was attempting to fix my reputation and to silence the constant rumors, but it wasn't her idea. If the league wants to ban me for extortion, then that's their right. But I can't play another second of hockey with everyone thinking that Scottie *Olson* is anything but a selfless, self-sacrificing, kind, yet sometimes spirited, and compassionate woman that I'm in love with."

I stand and leave, with my heart bleeding right through my hockey uniform.

———

THE ARENA HAS CLEARED OUT, and the parking lot is mostly empty. The cleaning crew hesitantly asked me to leave after they attempted to clean the locker room around me and my gear, so I finally gathered everything and left without saying a word.

I silenced my phone because I already know that my post-game interview is everywhere, and most people I know have seen it.

The only one that needs to see it is Scottie, though, and I have no way of finding out if she did.

Not until she emerges from wherever she's hiding.

I've checked everywhere I could think of several days ago.

There aren't many places she can go to, yet I can't find her.

A thick gust of chilly air whips around me as I head for my car. I click the key fob a few times to light up the area and pause when I see something on top of my car.

What the fuck is that?

The closer I get, the more I can make out.

Two glowing eyes stare at me, and my first reaction is to scold the cat for being on top of my car, but that's when I see the blue collar I wrestled onto Shutter the day before Scottie left.

"You let him get on top of my car?" I ask, hoping like hell I hear her voice answer me back.

Please.

I hear her scuffed-up Converse step on the loose gravel. When she appears from the other side of my car, the breath leaves my body.

Thank God.

"He insisted," she says quietly, like she's afraid to talk.

All I want to do is reach out and grab onto her, but I play it safe. I walk closer to the driver's side door and reach my

457

hand out to pet Shutter. He stands on top of the hood in between Scottie and me and, surprisingly, lets me pet him.

"Are we going to have a custody battle over Shutter?" I joke, trying to break the tension.

She crosses her arms over that tattered Blue Devils shirt that I now know was her father's. "Why did you do that?"

I shrug off my hoodie and slide it across the hood of my car. She stares at it for a second before moving it away from Shutter and pulling it over her slender frame.

"Why did I do what? Tell the truth?"

"That wasn't the deal," she whispers. "We had terms."

"Fuck the terms," I say, matter-of-fact.

She huffs quietly. "Then what was the point?"

"The point?" *Fuck this.* I round the front of my car, and it stuns her. She attempts to step away but stops when I move into her space. I put one arm around her waist and grip her face with the other. "You," I snap. "Us." I shake my head and stare into her eyes. "That's the point."

She opens her mouth to argue.

"No." I tighten my grip on her, and she peers up at me with so much hidden hope that I almost choke. "Do you remember when I told you I take care of the people I love?"

She nods slowly.

"I love *you*, Scottie."

Her chin wobbles, and I fucking hate to see her cry. I've never hated anything more in my life.

"Nothing else matters unless I have you. Not the game. Not the team. Not my fucking reputation." I shrug. "My agent could call me right now to tell me that the league is suspending me indefinitely for admitting that I exploited some poor innocent woman, and I wouldn't care."

"Yes, you would."

"If it proved to you that you're the most important thing in my life? No, I wouldn't."

She looks away before swinging her eyes back to mine. "I have nothing to offer you," she admits.

"All I need is you," I say.

A breathy sigh slips from her lips, and I fall for her all over again.

It's just the two of us, standing in an empty parking lot, exactly like it was when we started this entire thing.

"For better, for worse," I whisper, moving closer to her mouth. "For richer, for poorer." A tear slips down her cheek. "In sickness and in health." I brush the tear away.

She moves closer to me. "To love and to cherish."

I pull her mouth to mine and whisper against her lips. "Until death do us part, baby."

Scottie reaches up on her tiptoes to seal our kiss, and my knees go weak. *Thank God.*

When we break apart, my voice is more of a rasp. "Let's go home."

I stare at her pretty mouth when a tiny smile appears. She peeks around me. "Did you hear that, Shutter? Let's go *home*."

Fifty-Nine

SCOTTIE

HE WANTS to take all my burdens away, but the best I can do is introduce him to my brother.

"Take it or leave it, Olson." I raise my eyebrow from the passenger seat with the barbed-wire fence looming behind him through the window.

"Why won't you let me take care of you?" he asks.

I flatten my lips and almost get lost in his dreamy eyes before snapping out of it and giving him my reasons—*again*. "You do take care of me." *Every single time you look at me.* "It is not your responsibility to take care of William, though."

Days after the news leaked and Emory ushered Shutter and me back home, we had a long talk.

And by long talk, I mean I sat Emory down, slapped his hand five hundred times while he tried to distract me by touching me all over, and filled him in on my plans for the future. I thought it showed great growth, considering I am *infuriatingly* independent according to him, but he still fought me tooth and nail.

I explained that I no longer wanted him to pay me the $100,000, which naturally, he argued with right away. He went as far as pulling out the contract and threatened to get his lawyer involved.

So, we compromised.

He pays the remainder of what I owe the lawyer to get me caught up on the past dues, and I will cover the new legal fees to appeal William's case from whatever I make from taking photos. Despite all the drama that was stirred up when the news leaked, it took a dramatic turn after Emory made his statement during the post-game conference.

He was labeled as a romantic, and I was labeled as the league's sweetheart.

It didn't take long for inquiries to pile in for me to offer up my photography skills either.

I'm booked for the next several months. Weddings, engagements, family photos, you name it.

Hattie and the rest of the wives forced me to sit with them at the next game too. I thought they'd want to keep their distance from me, considering everything, but they proved me wrong.

Georgia begged me to still take her wedding photos, and by the end of the first period, I had Nola cradled in her Blue Devils blanket while Vivian cheered our team on with her face pressed against the glass.

Things aren't perfect.

But I'm happy.

"But—" Emory attempts to argue with me again about the legal fees, but I put a stop to it by leaning over the center console and planting my lips on his. My hand just so happens to fall to his lap near the place that I know will make his thoughts scatter for a second.

"Not fair," he says against my lips. His hand falls to my ass, and he gives it a good squeeze before going back in for another hot kiss.

I moan accidentally. He breaks us apart, and his eyes flare with something wildly enticing.

"Oops," I say.

"Get out of the car before I end up behind bars for publicly fucking my wife in broad daylight."

There they are. My favorite words: *my wife.*

"Don't look at me like that, Biscotti." Emory smirks, and my stomach does a flip. "Or else the first time I meet your brother, I'm going to be hiding a boner."

I make a face and glance at the prison behind him. "Probably not the best place to have one of those, huh?"

Emory chuckles. "Come on, baby. Let's go."

He climbs out of the car, expecting me to follow, but I don't.

I watch as he rounds the hood to my side, and when he opens my door, he only has to take one look at my face before understanding what I'm feeling.

He squats down and reaches his hand toward mine.

One squeeze and I look at him. "You nervous?"

I clench my teeth and nod. "I just don't like to see him like this. In here."

Emory gives my hand another squeeze. "Do you want to leave?"

I shake my head and chew on the inside of my cheek.

His thumb starts to rub against my skin in the most comforting way. "I'm here, okay? I'm with you, and you can lean on me when things become...too much."

My stomach is still in knots, but a few untie just from the unwavering devotion in his eye. I'm glad he's here with me, and for the first time in my life, I'm not alone. I don't have to do this by myself.

Emory straightens the wedding ring on my finger and waits until I look at him again. "Come on, Biscotti." He grins. "I'm ready to meet my brother-in-law."

I smile hesitantly and climb out of the car. Our hands intertwine as we head toward the prison gate as *husband and wife.*

Epilogue

EMORY

MY BACKYARD LOOKS nothing like it did this morning.

Warm, glowing lights are strung from the trees, and there's a makeshift dance floor in the middle of the yard that I know for a fact Ford will be on in a matter of minutes.

It's a balmy spring evening with a nice breeze, but the suit I'm wearing is still suffocating. I know the feeling will disappear the moment Scottie walks out of the French doors, though, because that's how it is when I lay eyes on her.

She's all I see and think about.

"What do you think?" Taytum slides up beside me and gestures to the decorations.

I reach my arm around my sister. "Scottie will love it."

"I take full responsibility." She smiles.

Her best friend, Claire, pops up from her husband's chest. "Hey! I helped."

Theo pulls her back toward him with a grin on his face.

I'm surrounded by friends and family, teammates, and probably the most important person—William.

He leans against a tree with his hands in his pockets, seemingly looking anxious while staring at the French doors.

I get it.

I feel anxious when Scottie isn't near too.

It didn't take long to get him out of prison, considering the evidence putting him there was completely skewed. Unfortunately, according to the new attorney that selflessly stepped forward after catching wind of the media, William was an easy target, and the investigators on his case ran with it even though there were holes in the story leading to his conviction.

What they thought was an easy confession turned out to be a nightmare shortly after an appeal was made.

Scottie fought like hell to get William the help he needed after he was released. With the help of the fans who were fully invested in our lives after the drama, William had a social worker lined up, and he's on his way to being a successful member of society despite his diagnosis.

He even has his own place with a few other people who are also under the care of the social worker.

"Where is Ford?" I ask my sister. He's been the most welcoming to William.

Because, well, that's just Ford.

Taytum looks like she's up to something.

I glance at our dad, who is talking to Coach Jacobs. My mom is off playing with Ellie while

Rhodes stands awkwardly beside his nanny, who he's pretending not to be obsessed with.

Most of the team is obsessed with her, actually, making jokes every other practice about how they want to ask her out, only for Rhodes to threaten to throw them through a locker a moment later.

The French doors open, and we all turn to look. My heart beats out of my chest, and a hush of silence moves through the backyard.

"For fuck's sake," I mutter, seeing that it *isn't* my wife.

Taytum can't keep it together. A laugh begins to slip from her lips, and before I know it, most of the backyard has erupted in laughter.

"Biscotti, anyone?" Ford wafts his arms out in front of him, showing off the absolute ridiculous costume he's wearing.

"Where the hell did he even manage to find a biscotti costume?"

Taytum turns to me and smiles.

"Was this your idea?" I ask. "Real funny."

She shakes her head and smiles. "Our little Scottie Biscotti has jokes."

Of course. I shake my head. I know exactly why Scottie set this up.

My girl doesn't like attention, and by sending Ford out first—in a biscotti costume, no less—she thinks everyone will be distracted, and they won't notice her.

How wrong she is, though.

When I turn and see her, my world tilts.

My beautiful, compassionate, mouthy wife slowly enters the backyard with her white Converse peeking out from her floor-length, simple, silk dress. It's cut low in the front, and with her hair up in a loose bun, I can't help but stutter over my thoughts.

I walk to her, and everyone else disappears, even Ford in his biscotti costume.

"God damn," I mutter, wrapping an arm around her waist. She peeks up at me with her shy eyes, and I watch the pink spread across her cheeks. "You're beautiful."

"Stop it," she whispers, trying to hide a smile.

"Can I cancel the party? Everyone already knows we're married. I'd rather take you back upstairs."

"No way. Do you know how hard it was to get Ford in that costume?"

I chuckle. "Nice touch. Thought we'd all be so distracted by him that we wouldn't see you, huh?"

She nibbles on her glossy lip. "You know me too well."

"And I love every part."

Her smile warms me. I intertwine our fingers and face the crowd. I raise our joined hands, and Ford shouts from the dance floor, speaking into the microphone, "Let's give it up for Mr. and Mrs. Emory Olson, everybody!"

An applause hits our ears, and I gently pull my wife toward my parents, who are waiting to give us a hug. I watch as William pushes off the tree and heads for us. I move to stand off to the side, but he catches me by surprise and holds out his hand to me.

"Thank you, Emory," he says, shaking my hand. "For everything."

I nod once and watch as he hugs his sister. My chest is tight, and my heart does this weird movement that only ever happens when I know Scottie is happy. Like it can't beat properly if she is anything but.

Scottie pulls back and smiles at William. Her eyes twinkle, and there's a shiny gloss filling them the longer she stares into his eyes.

But then, there's a little hand tugging on Scottie's dress, and she glances at Ellie, whose nanny is off to the side, watching the entire interaction. Scottie bends down and gets on her level. Ellie whispers in her ear, and suddenly, I want to be privy to their conversation.

After they stand, she and Ellie walk over to me, and I raise my eyebrows. "Telling secrets, are we?"

Ellie holds something out for me to take with a hopeful look in her eye. I bend to inspect it further.

"What's this?" I ask, watching her dangle a bracelet with blue and black beads in front of my face.

"I made you a bracelet."

"Me?" I ask, unable to hide my shock.

She nods. "Well, I made Scottie one, but then I realized that you needed one too. It's a wedding gift."

With a father as grumpy as hers, I have no idea how she can be so damn sweet.

Scottie holds out her delicate wrist, and I drop my head with a chuckle. The word *Biscotti* is surrounded by gold and blue beads. I have a feeling that has something to do with Rhodes and his silent way of joking.

I hold my own wrist out, and Ellie slides a bracelet onto it. *Biscotti Lover.*

"Nice touch." I wink at Ellie, and she giggles.

I swoop her up, and a gleeful giggle leaves her mouth. "Wanna go show Scottie how to dance?"

Ellie nods her head with excitement.

I catch Scottie's pretty grin, and we all head to the dance floor to celebrate being Mr. and Mrs. Olson, once and for all.

The End

Afterword

Ready for another Blue Devil? Head to **sjsylvis.com** for information on the next book in the series!

Three Summers

Yours Truly, Cammie

Chasing Ivy

Falling for Fallon

Truth

About the Author

S.J. Sylvis is an Amazon top 50 and USA Today bestselling author who is best known for her new adult sport romances. She currently resides in Arizona with her husband, two small children, dog and cat! She is obsessed with coffee, becomes easily attached to fictional characters, and spends most of her evenings buried in a book!

Stay up to date at: sjsylvis.com

Acknowledgments

As always, I like to thank my husband first because without him, I wouldn't know what it's like to be loved (as cheesy as that sounds). So, thank you to my favorite guy and partner in crime. I love you and couldn't ask for a better dad for our babies!

To my TU girls – Emma, Bri, and Bella. Thank you for always making me laugh, or laughing at my expense right along with me (mini hand, anyone?!), AND for making this job a little less isolating! Forever thankful that we met and clicked right away! Love you so much!

Mary (my pa), Jenn (my editor), Emma (my proofer + a million other things), Sarah (my proofer), Ashlee (my cover designer) and my VPR girls (so many jobs that I can't name them all, lol)—THANK YOU so much for all that you do for me. There are times where I am so swamped, I can't even think straight and not only do you take some things off my plate but you are happy to do so.

To my pink ladies—pinkies up! I love you forever!

Last but not least, thank you to my ARC team, content team, author friends, and readers! I feel so blessed to be in the position that I am in today, writing book boyfriends that make us swoon and female main characters that we can relate to, and I owe it to you! Without your support, reviews, messages, content, etc., I wouldn't be able to do this! So, thank you so much!! I am forever grateful and counting my lucky stars that I have you!

xo

Made in United States
Cleveland, OH
21 March 2025

15365000R00288